Talk Data to Me

Talk Data to Me

Rose McGee

First published in paperback in Great Britain in 2025 by Corvus,
an imprint of Atlantic Books Ltd

Copyright © Rose McGee, 2025

The moral right of Rose McGee to be identified as the author of this work has been asserted by her in accordance with the Copyright, Designs and Patents Act of 1988.

All rights reserved. No part of this publication may be reproduced, stored in a retrieval system, or transmitted in any form or by any means, electronic, mechanical, photocopying, recording, or otherwise, without the prior permission of both the copyright owner and the above publisher of this book.

No part of this book may be used in any manner in the learning, training or development of generative artificial intelligence technologies (including but not limited to machine learning models and large language models (LLMs)), whether by data scraping, data mining or use in any way to create or form a part of data sets or in any other way.

This novel is entirely a work of fiction. The names, characters and incidents portrayed in it are the work of the author's imagination. Any resemblance to actual persons, living or dead, events or localities, is entirely coincidental.

10 9 8 7 6 5 4 3 2 1

A CIP catalogue record for this book is available from the British Library.

Paperback ISBN: 978 1 80546 292 7
E-book ISBN: 978 1 80546 294 1

Printed and bound by CPI (UK) Ltd, Croydon CR0 4YY

Corvus
An imprint of Atlantic Books Ltd
Ormond House
26–27 Boswell Street
London
WC1N 3JZ

www.atlantic-books.co.uk

Product safety EU representative: Authorised Rep Compliance Ltd., Ground Floor, 71 Lower Baggot Street, Dublin, D02 P593, Ireland. www.arccompliance.com

For C.P. Haynes. You'd be delighted and scandalized.

THREE YEARS EARLIER

Erin Monaghan

The bicycle pedal scraped under her sneaker, its rasp punctuating her hard breathing—ragged with excitement, with nerves, and with the effort of cycling up Sand Hill Road. Erin's heartbeat steadied while she braced her body weight against the bar, waiting for a traffic light to direct her toward Innovation Drive and the Silicon Valley Linear Accelerator National Laboratory campus.

SVLAC: where quarks were identified, where cutting-edge research on the black hole information paradox was conducted, where new truths about humanity's place among the stars stood ready to be revealed—

—and where Dr. Erin Monaghan would discover them.

She probably should've taken a taxi for her first day on campus, so she wouldn't meet her new colleagues in her sneakers and with helmet hair, but Dr. Nadine Fong had recruited her straight from Stanford's astrophysics lab for her doctoral work on gravitational waves, not her appearance. Anyhow, she'd be making contacts today that would affect her prospects in the physics field, and she didn't want to dress in a way that might give the wrong impression and make her coworkers view her as a woman first and a scientist second. The traffic light turned green and she pedaled through the intersection, then up a last incline toward SVLAC's research grounds.

"Identification, please." A guard waved her to the window of a security gatehouse. She retrieved an employment letter from Dr. Fong on her phone, which authorized her to enter the campus today without a security badge. Messages chiming in from the Monaghan family chat almost hid the document, while the guard checked the name on the letter against her driver's license. Nodding at the outpouring of well wishes, he motioned her forward a minute later. "Head left to the Science and Public Support building for your orientation."

"Thanks." She tucked her phone away, dodging bird droppings on the pavement and a few caterpillars dangling from the trees overhead as she walked her bicycle to a set of nearby racks. Yes, sneakers and a helmet had been the right choice. She locked up her rear tire, and the click of turning metal rotated the next several years of her life into position: department research on government-funded projects, but also her own individual inquiries into the space-time ripples created by colliding black holes. She'd study gravitational waves on the lab's precisely tuned Laser Interferometer Gravitational-Wave Observatory—called LIGO for short—and probe the extreme edges of human understanding about the most violent and energetic processes in the universe.

So many unknowns, mysteries that only science fiction authors had dared to explore in the past—all this would now be her work. It didn't seem real. But she could count the months of research, analysis, writing, and aggressive networking that had won her this recruitment to SVLAC's Relativistic Mechanics group. Now she'd collect data alongside the leading minds in physics, including her department head and several other scientists whose work she'd admired for years.

Her nervous excitement spiking higher than ever, she ran a hand through her ponytail, wiped the sweat off her nose under her glasses, and was ready to greet Nadine Fong when her supervisor came rolling around the Science and Public Support building on a scooter. Dr. Fong nodded at her, skidded to a halt, and raised an air horn.

The noise was brief, but deafening.

Erin blinked in confusion until Dr. Fong's voice cut through the echoes in her ears.

"Welcome to SVLAC, Dr. Monaghan. Sorry for the fanfare, but"—she pointed over Erin's shoulder, where a flock of wild turkeys straggled away from the building—"the cafeteria's upstairs, and they come pecking for scraps. We try to scare them off so they don't leave feces on the pavement. Looks like you sidestepped the worst of it. Those sneakers were a good choice."

Dr. Fong was wearing sneakers, too.

She found herself grinning now when she answered, "I'm excited to be here, Dr. Fong."

"Call me Nadine. May I call you Erin? Good." Propelling her scooter at a walking pace, Nadine gestured for Erin to follow her along a thoroughfare called Ring Road, then toward a squat cinder-block structure housing SVLAC's Modern Physics department. She waved to a yawning woman shuffling back toward the parking lot with a danish and a coffee cup clutched in hand, identifying her as Dr. Martina Perez—"She's coming off a night shift at one of the experimental halls"—before badging into the main entrance, continuing, "You'll run through an administrative onboarding today, then meet the team for lunch and a tour of the campus. It's a generic schedule for all new staff, though, so tell me if there's anything in particular that you want to see."

Erin couldn't rearrange her giddy smile into a more professional expression as she entered the building. "I assume we'll be touring our branch of LIGO, but will we also see the experimental hutches? The results from SVLAC's prototype holometer could be groundbreaking, especially for Dr. Ethan Meyer's work—"

"—on quantum mechanics?" Nadine paused while pointing out the office coffee station.

"Quantum mechanics offers a conflicting view of reality to our field, but Dr. Meyer's research on practical quantum measurement is still incredibly elegant. Even if he theorizes that mathematical space-time is small, discrete, and probabilistic, instead of a large, smooth, deterministic continuum. I have some questions that I'd like to ask him about what the recent theories on quantum gravity could mean for modern physics."

Nadine's pregnant pause morphed into raised eyebrows. "You've done your homework, haven't you?"

"Yes."

"Of course." She directed Erin down a hallway toward the central office bullpen, passing a closed door with an emphatic Do Not Disturb sign taped to its front. "Well, Dr. Meyer is finalizing a measurement report and also revising a paper with Dr. Kramer—*Nature Physics*—so he's unlikely to be available for a while, especially since he's off to Switzerland for two months after the resubmission tomorrow. Both men are perfectionists. I'm actually surprised that they even received a revise-and-resubmit from the journal. Or that Dr. Kramer would deign to do—"

The next moment happened more quickly than a synapse firing.

The Do Not Disturb door swung open with enough force to drag sparks of friction from the industrial carpet. Arms stacked high with spiral-bound documents and what might've been an airline travel itinerary, a man stepped out into the hall, tripped over a loose extension cord, and plowed into Erin.

"*Ah!*"

Paperwork mushroomed into the air, reports landing heavily on her sneakers. Despite the joint impacts of the man's shoulder and the documents, however, she managed to steady herself on a bullpen divider.

She didn't fall.

But when she caught his startled gaze, she *felt* herself fall. Vertigo looped abruptly around her ankles and her stomach, flipping her over so that a burning nebula of color hit her cheeks, because: *dark hair, finger-raked and needing a trim, stubbled cheeks, irises swirled with gray and blue, flecked in silver around blooming pupils, his fleece vest charged with static, data analyses spilling from his hands—*

—and the title of his reports: "The Use of Interferometer Technology to Isolate Quantum Units in SVLAC's Experimental Holometer."

This was Dr. Ethan Meyer.

The Dr. Ethan Meyer.

Damn.

"*Um.* Sorry, do you need help with…?" She hoped she'd said something like that, at least. Something useful. She bent down and reached for a white paper.

"No, it's fine. I…" His voice was low, rough with tiredness or too much coffee. Close, too. Dr. Meyer knelt to take the report from her and stacked it with the other documents.

She reached for his travel itinerary.

But so did he, and static from his vest or the carpet jolted between them, quick as the surprised glance they shared again, eyes widening now with shock or curiosity—

"The revised data exports for *Nature Physics* are ready, Meyer. Correct?"

His attention flashed past her at that, down the hall toward another voice addressing him with a question that apparently wasn't a question at all. He blinked and instantly straightened from his hunch. His hand retracted into a fist when he answered, suddenly louder and clearer, "Yes. I finished them yesterday. They're—"

"In my inbox?"

"Yes, and—"

"Right. Good morning, Dr. Kramer. Excuse us, Dr. Meyer." Nodding at her colleagues, Nadine urged Erin up and away from a conversation that seemed ready to happen directly through her, sidestepping the papers and Ethan Meyer on his knees. She steered her instead toward a desk in the bullpen, where a Human Resources representative flagged them down. "They have their resubmission form to complete, and you have some onboarding paperwork. I'll formally introduce you to the rest of the Modern Physics staff later."

"Erin Monaghan?" The woman at her new workstation pointed Erin into a chair and indicated a series of virtual forms on the desktop monitor. "Sign and initial where indicated. Finance will want to record your onboarding hours and it's the last day of the pay period, so please submit the documents as soon as possible."

"I'll be back at noon for lunch and the tour," and Nadine left her to it.

Was Dr. Meyer still collecting his reports?

She couldn't see over the top of her monitor and divider…

No: *focus*.

She swung her chair back to the desk. She could parse academic grandstanding and also outpace her second brother in speed-reading; boilerplate legalese shouldn't prove too much of a time or content challenge. She crossed her legs on her seat and settled down to develop her carpal tunnel syndrome.

Conflict of interest form—initialed.

Release of liability for workplace injury due to wildlife encounter form, which mandated the distribution of a protective air horn to each staff member—initialed.

Employee handbook.

At over two hundred pages, she was still deep in the handbook's anti-harassment section when the woman from Human Resources returned to squint at the forms that she hadn't reviewed yet. "Ms. Monaghan—"

Dr. Monaghan.

"—it's eleven fifty-five. Initial the rest of these now and I'll send you copies to read through later."

Not inspecting every inch of the fine print ran counter to her years of scientific training, and even more time spent as a gullible younger sister. But the Human Resources representative didn't move away from her desk, and Nadine would be back soon for their team lunch. She forced a smile and made her mark on the employee handbook. Then, galvanized into action under the woman's continuing stare, trying not to wonder if *he* would be at the cafe, she repeated a quick *E.M.* on the remaining documents, her initials whirring away into the ether as the seconds ticked down until noon.

"Done. Thank you." The representative walked off, past Nadine returning to collect her employee.

"You survived? That's always the worst part. But administration is a necessary evil." Nadine shook her head at the retreating woman. "Now, lunch. The cafeteria in the Science and Public Support building makes a good curry on Mondays, if you can handle the spice—and you must be hungry after that digital sprint."

"Curry sounds delicious." It did feel like she'd been running trial time laps.

"We'll take the scooters over and meet the team on the balcony, then. It overlooks the campus and the turkeys, so you'll get an aerial preview of our tour track. We'll visit the interferometer control room first, obviously, and then the klystron gallery at the linear accelerator…"

Erin followed Nadine from her desk while the last onboarding form flashed a notice of its successful submission. She would read the documents she'd signed when Human Resources sent them back again.

It would be fine.

TWO MONTHS LATER

Ethan Meyer

Having sat cramped in a middle seat for eleven hours with his knees bumping the tray table, his window-side neighbor standing up to pace the aisle every thirty minutes and his aisle-side neighbor muttering over a slide deck, Ethan had willed himself to snatch a few minutes of sleep during his return flight from Switzerland.

Mind over matter. Mind over matter.

He couldn't afford to lose productive time in the office for something like jet lag, which should be well within his control.

Mind over matter.

He'd touched down in San Francisco's pervasive summer fog late on Sunday night and arrived at SVLAC this morning before seven o'clock, eyes gritty, tongue thick, head tender, and ready to tackle Dr. John Kramer's backlog of research and administrative needs. Not to mention, the follow-ups from his stint overseas. He'd already forwarded a list of new contacts to his supervisor. Now the process of outlining why Dr. Kramer's finicky, experimental holometer was the physics field's best chance at identifying quantum units of space loomed. The European Organization for Nuclear Research's Large Hadron Collider hadn't been powerful enough to generate the energy required to isolate those infinitesimal and hypothetical units, and maybe a machine with ten tera electron volts could do it, but the LHC at CERN was already the world's most potent particle accelerator at just under seven tera electron volts. There might be a viable paper in contrasting its energy failure with the potential success of the holometer, however. *Thank God* Dr. Kramer had promoted him out of the bullpen and into an actual office last year. The months he'd spent untangling his supervisor's data after Dr. Kramer's spreadsheets went haywire from a virus-filled download had been worth every minute for the quiet he could now command with a closed door.

It didn't matter that he'd had to tack his nameplate over the door's existing designation as "Supply Closet." Even if he'd had to move out several industrial shelving units to fit a chair and a convertible standing desk inside, it was still a closing, locking space. It was still his own office.

If he'd still been seated in the bullpen, though, would he have seen *her* again?

Strawberry blonde ponytail tilting past her flushed cheek and over her shoulder with a cascade of sweet, fresh scent, kneeling to organize his reports, dark eyes behind tortoiseshell glasses catching on his before swiveling to his research, lighting with interest—

But she hadn't been wearing an SVLAC badge.

She might not be on the Modern Physics staff at all.

Or maybe she was just new?

Ping.

An incoming message chimed into his inbox before he could waver in his resolve not to crack open his door for a scan of the bullpen desks.

Dr. John Kramer (*Urgent*): *Nature Physics Article*

A muscle spasmed along his neck at the simple, innocuous subject line.

Frowning and wondering how long he'd be suffering cramps from his transatlantic flight, he opened the email. Its only content was a link to a *Nature Physics* paper proposing their methodology for measuring quantums of space—the paper that he and Dr. Kramer had submitted after a brutal revision process, just prior to his term at CERN. He knew every word of its ideas about measuring the universe's smallest unbreakable unit of distance. He'd written them all, under Dr. Kramer's first-author directorship.

He expanded the document and scanned through.

What the hell?

The paper was missing several critical revisions.

Those critical revisions—*Ethan's* revisions—had been made late in the editing process, after he'd reconstructed a data set in Dr. Kramer's section. Another virus must've disrupted several of his supervisor's inputs, he'd assumed, given the mess he'd uncovered upon closer inspection during the revision work. Dr. Kramer had been occupied with negotiations for a high-profile collaboration with Lawrence Livermore National Laboratory, so he'd initialed the revise-and-resubmit form certifying that the necessary changes had been made, then instructed Ethan to manage them. Like many geniuses, Dr. Kramer was temperamental and secretive, but he'd trusted Ethan with revisions to *his own work*.

He'd been exhausted and ecstatic when he'd finally submitted the revise-and-resubmit form. Maybe he'd even be moved into an office with a window, he'd rhapsodized through his sleep deprivation.

Except that his revisions weren't in the published paper.

No. No, fuck, no—

His fingers flexed over the keyboard in a futile effort to erase or at least mitigate the damage. But there was no time for that—

for anything—because the door to his office swung open now, so hard that its mounted stop vibrated against the wall. Dr. John Kramer caught the rebounding panels on his palm, which quaked and stilled. Then he looked at Ethan.

"What happened, Meyer?"

"I…"

"This paper was published less than an hour ago." Dr. Kramer took a step toward Ethan's desk, voice neutral even while a vein ticked in his temple beyond a line of receding but immaculate iron gray hair. "Six o'clock Pacific time is nine o'clock Eastern. It would've been the first email in every subscriber's Monday inbox."

"Yes—" His own voice cracked.

So did Dr. Kramer's neutrality. "Do you know how many calls I've already fielded, asking what *idiocy* has been published under my name?"

His stomach dropped, hard and fast.

"Explain this."

"I… I sent the corrected version—" It didn't matter what he had or hadn't done, however, because the flawed *Nature Physics* paper was incontrovertible proof right now that he'd failed under his supervisor's trust. *That* was the fact that mattered to Dr. Kramer. He swallowed the rest of his explanation with a jerky nod.

Explain this, Dr. Kramer had said.

He could. He had to.

He located the paper in his desktop filing system—*correct, all revisions present*—then ran a query through his email for a confirmation of receipt for the revise-and-resubmit form from *Nature Physics*.

The search was void.

He should've received confirmation on the date of his resubmission. But that had also been the day he'd left for CERN. He'd opened more than thirty actionable emails on that date alone: airport gate changes, first day itineraries, invitations to and solicitations for presentations, a map of the Large Hadron Collider with directions to his adjacent control room, and dozens of others. In the chaos, he hadn't noticed the missing message from *Nature Physics*. He hadn't checked his spam folder for it. That meant that he'd committed a scientific cardinal sin. He'd only examined the data he had, rather than considering what data might be missing.

"Well?" Dr. Kramer rapped his knuckles on the desk.

"*Uh.*" His gut tightened into a knot now as he opened his spam folder. He willed its list of messages to be irrelevant, useless, exculpatory. But the data didn't lie: an automatic bounce reply for his revise-and-resubmit form from *Nature Physics* shone back at him, bold and unread. His index finger twitched, and the message opened.

> *Duplicate revision forms for papers submitted to* Nature Physics *will be rejected. Contact the journal through the general help center to provide further updates or corrections.*

What?

He'd submitted his edits on the date of his departure for Switzerland. He knew he had. The link in his revision form attached to the bounce reply showed the corrected paper.

But when he returned to his spam folder, there was an earlier automated message. Sent the day before his own corrections, the reply confirmed receipt of Dr. John R. Kramer and Dr. Ethan Meyer's revise-and-resubmit form. The paper linked in that form was a half-edited version, a draft from before he'd inserted Dr. Kramer's reconstructed data. Certifying the updates, Dr. Kramer's initials were present on the form from his preemptive signing during the Lawrence Livermore negotiations.

So were Ethan's.

E.M.

And the most critical of his updates were missing.

"I don't know what... I never would've submitted it like this."

"But it *was* submitted, wasn't it? Now it's published, Meyer. Published under *my name*. Fix it."

"I don't know if I—"

"*Fix. It.*"

"I will."

"Good." Dr. Kramer turned on his heel. "Tell me when it's done. I have damage control to do."

The last time he'd committed a mistake under his supervisor's name, he'd spent the subsequent two weeks running a punishingly detailed analysis on Dr. Kramer's latest ideas about what lens materials were optimal for splitting lasers in the holometer. That error had been a miscalculation presented during one of SVLAC's department-wide monthly research updates. An internal inaccuracy. But this? He'd just forfeited a solid portion of his own research hours for the next several months.

It was a learning opportunity. He knew he'd be grateful for it, once his anxiety subsided. Dr. Kramer was a brilliant scientist, and Ethan had benefited hugely from his mentorship, had even received opportunities to contribute to Dr. Kramer's publications, but Dr. Kramer suffered no fools—he was right not to—and clearly, he'd either been a fool in his hurry to leave for CERN, tripping over extension cords, fumbling through his reports with a stranger, or...

No.

No, he'd submitted the corrected paper, and done it once.

His initials were on the form for the error-riddled version of his supervisor's submission, yes. But he wouldn't have signed off on it in that condition. *Ever.* So the conclusion remained: someone else had initialed the *E.M.*

He dialed the line for SVLAC's IT department. "This is Dr. Meyer. I need a digital trace on a signature for a form sent through SVLAC's email system. I've forwarded the document."

"Received. Please hold, Dr. Meyer."

He waited. One minute, two, and he reached for his daily sudoku calendar. His pen drafted in the numbers without pause, clean and easy, a precise grid of nines, then scrawled beyond the margins as two minutes became five. Seven. Nebulae formed and swirled, the ink pristine against the page but the lines edgy, restless—

"Thank you for holding, Dr. Meyer. The form you've provided was initialed by Dr. Erin Monaghan."

"Monaghan?"

"Yes. Dr. Nadine Fong's latest recruit to the Relativistic Mechanics group."

He muttered his thanks and replaced the receiver.

Dr. Erin Monaghan.

He tabbed back into his inbox and queried her name. His search returned a few general departmental threads, but also a message directly from her. That email displayed a staff identification photo in the sender line.

Dr. Erin Monaghan wore tortoiseshell glasses.

Her.

She'd sent him an introduction. He opened her message too quickly, reading even faster. An explanation for why she'd signed his form? *No*. Her salutation was pleasant, however, while her recap of their run-in was honest and wry, and her comments about his work were complimentary… her *many* comments. She must've read every paper he'd ever published, including his graduate dissertation on hypothetical quantum measurement at Berkeley. Her inquiries about the ramifications of recent quantum gravity theories on modern physics were articulate and insightful.

But his frown deepened.

Because she hadn't apologized for—or even acknowledged—what she'd done, and again: she was very, *very* familiar with his research. It didn't matter that static had struck through every inch of his body from a brush of her hand. By signing his *Nature Physics* revision document, she'd stymied his progress for at least several months while he dealt with the fallout from the field, the journal, and Dr. Kramer. And her work on the interactions of matter within the space-time model was in diametric opposition to his.

His failure was to her benefit.

The data was clear.

This was sabotage.

PRESENT DAY

1

She'd beaten her own best time running the Stanford Dish trail this morning.

Erin's legs quivered with exhaustion and sweat dribbled into her eyes as she grabbed her bicycle and pedaled back to Menlo Park. But she grinned up at the sky, its color just beginning to morph from gray to pink, to the smoggy blue and gold of a May sunrise over the East Bay mountains. She needed a shower, and also a celebration—she'd beaten not just her own record, but her brother Adrian's, too.

Carrying her bicycle up her apartment's exterior flight of stairs, mindful not to catch creepers of trailing bougainvillea in the spokes, she locked her rear tire to the railing, nodded at one of her roommates leaving for work while she shucked off her running shoes on the mat, then padded into the bathroom. The apartment on Live Oak Avenue was a three-bed, one-bath layout, which wasn't ideal for three women and various partners who dropped by for the night, but the location was good, close to a weekend farmers' market, public transportation, and Kepler's Books, and they managed.

On a government salary, living alone wasn't usually viable in Silicon Valley.

She dropped her sports bra and running shorts, slipped on a pair of rubber shower sandals—which she'd learned were a necessity second only to good headphones in a shared living situation—

and stepped under a sluice of hot water. After luxuriating in the heat for a minute, she switched the temperature to tepid out of consideration for her other roommate, who would need to use it next. She was toweling her hair dry in her bedroom a few minutes later, while scanning through the influx of Monday emails flooding both her SVLAC and personal addresses, when a message chirped into her private inbox: *Your Submission to Galactica Magazine.*

Dear Aaron Forster,

We are delighted to inform you that your short story, "Pandora Rising," has been accepted for publication. You will receive a complimentary copy of the next issue of Galactica Magazine, *where your work will be printed. Our editors enjoyed your story and would be pleased to receive additional submissions in the future.*

She'd done it.

She, Erin Monaghan—or "Aaron Forster," for anonymity—was going to be a published author!

She'd submitted "Pandora Rising" to the Bay Area science fiction magazine almost three months ago, and had largely given up hope of hearing back from the editors by this point.

But now?

Her fingers danced over her phone, closing out her personal email and opening the Monaghan family chat. But before she could bombard her parents and brothers with multiple exclamation points, a notification from her SVLAC inbox zipped onto the screen under her thumb.

Journal of Supermassive Astronomy and Astrophysics: *Submission Results*

The peer review committee from one of the most prestigious, if admittedly niche, journals publishing work on large-scale astronomical objects and phenomena had completed its evaluation of her sole-author research paper—and on the same day that the editors from *Galactica Magazine* had also made their decision.

Oh, God.

Pressing her tongue against a slight gap between her front teeth and crossing her fingers and toes for luck—she would've crossed her eyes, too, if it wouldn't have impacted her ability to read the committee's decision—she swallowed, exhaled through her excitement at *Galactica*'s acceptance, and opened her second set of results.

> *Dear Dr. Erin Monaghan,*
>
> *Thank you for submitting "Investigating the Impact of Tidal Disruption Events on the Axis Rotation of Galaxies Proximal to Black Holes" to the* Journal of Supermassive Astronomy and Astrophysics. *Following a process of peer review, your manuscript has been recommended to the journal's editors for publication in its current form. No revisions are required prior to the appearance of the paper in the journal's September issue.*
>
> *We remind you at this time of the journal's copyright and open-access policies, and request your signed author agreement by June 1st.*
>
> *Regards,*
>
> *Dr. Ronald Sams, Editor-in-Chief*

Her paper was the result of years of experimental lab time and data analysis, assessing and describing the behavior of galaxies when nearby stars were consumed by black holes. It was the first sole-author piece she'd submitted for publication, and it had been accepted without even requiring revisions!

That wasn't unheard of. But it was rare.

Almost breathless now with too much good news, she clicked back into the Monaghan family chat.

> **Erin**
> So, it's a big day for me.
> Galactica accepted Pandora Rising…
>
> **Erin**
> …and the Journal of Supermassive Astronomy and Astrophysics accepted my research paper! Next up: take down quantum theory and definitively prove the superiority of relativistic mechanics.

Typing notifications immediately bubbled across her screen; early morning on the West Coast was post-caffeine time for her family in Michigan and New York.

> **Mom**
> I'm so proud of you, sweetheart. I can never quite get my head around these competing theories, but it sounds very impressive.
>
> **Wes**
> That's your scientific paper with an unpronounceable title about tides, right? You didn't consult my professional expertise before you wrote it. I'm hurt.

She snorted, smiling, bouncing on the balls of her feet.

Erin
Only because you would've tried to shoehorn in a joke about starfish.

Wes
It would've been hilarious.

Erin
Scientists famously have no sense of humor.

Wes
I guess you've just proved your point. And scientists also have no ability to simplify their research for the layperson. Mom, here's the plain-language version of what our Dr. Monaghan has been spouting off about for the last ten years. Relativistic mechanics plays well with gravity, planets, and galaxies. Quantum mechanics deals with matter on an atomic scale. But the logic of relativistic mechanics falls apart if it's reduced down to the quantum size of things, and if you try to apply quantum mechanics on a cosmic level, that fails, too. Plus, everything goes sideways for both of them when their different explanations about the behavior of matter collide around Erin's black holes. They're separate theories of reality with separate formulations. It's all still physics, though.

Mom
That's helpful, darling. Thank you.

Erin

Don't listen to him, Mom. The relativistic versus quantum mechanics debate is much more complex and interesting than that.

Wes

But stripping away your fancy jargon, does my breakdown make sense?

Erin

No!

Erin

...sort of.

Erin

Fine. Yes.

Adrian

Great. But can we leave any leftover litigation between you two to Dad? It's always going to be too early for this topic.

Erin

Fine!

Adrian

Now, back to your story. If you didn't negotiate a contract of at least five figures, we'll need to talk. (Seriously, though: science and all, I'm happy for you, Frizzy.)

Erin

I'm happy for me, too. Because I also beat your Dish time this morning.

Adrian
WHAT?!

Wes
Is this story going to the sci-fi magazine that wanted you to add tentacles?

Erin
Not yucking your yum, but I turned that option down. You're the one with experience, anyway. Not everyone has gone sea diving to photograph octopuses. Why don't you write it?

Dad
What about tentacles?

Wes
Never mind, Dad.

Erin
Ignore him.

Dad
Well, good job, kiddo.

Erin
Thanks. I need to head to the lab, but I'll be on our call later.

Adrian
Good. I've got some questions about the route you took on the Dish.

Erin
I'm sure you do. Bye, slowpoke!

> **Adrian**
> I have QUESTIONS.

The conversation pivoted away to Robert Monaghan's progress on the model train track he'd begun to construct through the back garden of their house in Grand Arbor. Laughing over Adrian's competitive outrage, she turned to her messages with Martina Perez while she shimmied into a pair of jeans and combed her damp hair into a ponytail.

> **Erin**
> I have exciting news! (How was your shift?)
>
> **Martina**
> Did you find an error in Ethan Meyer's latest data set? (Ugh. A couple of grad students kept trying to enter an accelerator hutch while the machinery was active. I had to babysit and adjust beam quality at the same time. So tired. Heading home now.)
>
> **Erin**
> As if he'd ever let me see his raw data. Jerk. No—it's even better than that. (Get some sleep!)

She whirled up a protein smoothie in the kitchen, then hurriedly brushed her teeth before another roommate stumbled into the bathroom for a shower, texting one-handed and spraying toothpaste in her glee.

> **Martina**
> What could possibly be better than spotting

flaws in his quantum research? Unless you got to spot it publicly?

Erin
Two things. Having a sole-author paper published in the Journal of Supermassive Astronomy and Astrophysics, and having a short story published anywhere. Now… drumroll, please… Galactica Magazine said yes—and so did the journal!

Martina
What?! Oh my God! Both at once? That's great, Erin! Much better than finding a data flaw.

Erin
They'd all be about equal. But yes, I'm so excited!

Martina
I want full details this evening.

Erin
Definitely.

With that, she shouldered her jacket and backpack, ferried her bicycle back down the stairs, and sped off for SVLAC alongside a cavalcade of commuter cars rumbling up Sand Hill Road. She waved to a guard at the campus gatehouse, flashing her employee identification badge and another smile, and grinned wider still when she passed through the parking lot outside the Modern Physics building.

Ethan's car wasn't there.

She'd beaten him to the office on the last Monday of the month, which meant that she'd get to schedule her next five weeks of lab time in the experimental halls before him. Numerous graveyard shifts with the machinery during her early tenure at SVLAC had taught her the importance of punctuality on scheduling day, and the even greater importance of getting her hours scheduled first.

Of course, it was his sleight of hand several years ago—her work calendar had inexplicably switched its a.m. and p.m. listings, so that a normal lab time selection of twelve noon on her calendar view became midnight on the scheduling sheet—that had brought her into contact with Martina Perez during one of the night shifts; as an operator in the experimental halls, Martina worked a brutal rotating combination of three fourteen-hour days on and four days off per week. But the fact that Ethan had inadvertently introduced her to her best friend was cold comfort.

To think, she'd once anticipated sharing theories with him! Had been so flustered when she'd collided with him...

Well, Ethan Meyer was late to SVLAC, she'd beaten her own Dish run time, her work would be published in both *Galactica Magazine* and the *Journal of Supermassive Astronomy and Astrophysics*, and it was a beautiful, beautiful morning.

Waving a greeting to her fellow early birds as she passed the Modern Physics coffee station and kitchenette, she sat down at her desk, tugged her utility jacket off over her light taupe sweater—SVLAC's air conditioning was vicious—forwarded her paper acceptance email to Nadine with a few lines of gratitude for her supervisor's support, double-checked her research plans to gauge whether she should book one weekly slot or two on LIGO, then opened the scheduling calendar.

Calendar: *SVLAC East and West Experimental Halls Lab Hours*

Before she could select her date and time, the grid flickered under her cursor and closed. SVLAC's IT equipment was old and sometimes cranky. She sighed and opened the calendar again. It froze. Then it disappeared from her monitor altogether. She tried a third time with crossed fingers. It refused to open at all.

"Damn."

Muttering under her breath, eyeing the clock, she scanned her unread emails for an explanation from the IT department about the program's failure, ready to write a very precise, very displeased message if no information was forthcoming, and—*oh*.

To the SVLAC research community:

The Silicon Valley Linear Accelerator National Laboratory was the recipient of a malware attack this morning. The attack failed. However, SVLAC's systems will be restarted out of an abundance of caution, with new security measures installed during the process.

The reboot will take place at 6 a.m. Pacific on Monday.

Email and internal messaging systems will be prioritized for restoration and are projected to be live by 6:45 a.m. Pacific, but the scheduling calendar for SVLAC's experimental halls will be unavailable from 6 a.m. Pacific through 6 p.m. Pacific (approx.). Please submit any lab time requests prior to the system reset at 6 a.m. Pacific.

Regards,
IT at SVLAC

The IT department had sent this critical information at two o'clock in the morning. The rush of other Monday emails had pushed the message out of view in her inbox... and it was already after eight thirty.

Erin bolted up from her desk.

She hurried back past the coffee station, out the building's main entrance—Ethan Meyer's hatchback was in the parking lot now, alongside a shuttle bus ferrying SVLAC's new cohort of interns to the campus—and over to an adjacent cluster of IT buildings, which housed the technicians, their servers, and SVLAC's technical library.

"Good morning." She brandished her badge past the scanner for entry and attention as she stepped into the technicians' domain. "I need to be added to the lab calendar. I didn't see your email about the malware attack and system reboot until just now. If you could slot me in manually for the LIGO control room, that would be helpful."

"You only read the email about the system shutdown... now?" A technician seated at the support desk glanced up at her badge-waving. He paused a Linux tutorial window open over a scroll of running reboot code with a meticulous click before extracting first one earbud, then the other. He wound up the headphone cords in a circle on his desk. "And you want to be manually added to the scheduling calendar?"

"Yes."

"Our email was clear about completing your time requests prior to six o'clock."

"I know that. But it was sent at two o'clock, and I just saw it—"

The technician shrugged. "Should lack of planning on your part constitute an emergency on mine?"

Who in their right mind would check for IT emails at two o'clock on a Monday morning?

But the seconds were ticking by, so despite her frustration, she smiled, leaned forward over the support desk, and said, "The malware attack was an emergency for you. Scheduling my lab time isn't. I realize that. But it's urgent for me, so I'm asking: could you please add me to the schedule?"

She waited, continuing to smile.

It felt like hours before eventually—*eventually!*—the technician sighed. He scrubbed a hand over his cheek, elbow knocking his headphone cords askew. "Sure. Yeah… look, it was a long night. I'm not in a great mood, and this Linux tutorial is complicated as hell. Sorry. What's your name?"

"Dr. Erin Monaghan."

"All right. Now, from the backup…" he closed his tutorial and pulled up the pre-reboot legacy schedule, "…it seems like I can fit you into the Matter in Extreme Conditions control room for LIGO on Tuesdays from twelve midnight to twelve noon."

"There's nothing from twelve noon to midnight?"

"No." He tilted his monitor toward her. "The instruments will be tuned to the Quantum group's holometer during that block."

Of course.

Half of the East and West Experimental Halls' control rooms were routinely out of order with software or instrumentation breakages that a government-funded lab had no money to fix. So cables patched the readings from various experimental hutches and distant machinery—like SVLAC's branch of LIGO—into a few overburdened control centers.

And LIGO shared a control room with Ethan Meyer's holometer.

"How about any other day?"

"This is the only slot left."

"But I should count myself lucky to get a full twelve hours at this point, right?"

Her smile was bitter as she thanked the technician and returned to the Modern Physics building. *Of course*, Ethan had the better time. Now she'd have to see him not just in the office, but in the experimental halls, too! Once, she would've been thrilled. But that was before she'd known the truth. Now? *A nightmare.* She smacked her keycard into the entry scanner and bulldozed back toward her desk, passing the coffee station again—

—where Dr. Ethan Meyer stood leaning against the counter, waiting for the appliance to finish brewing his drink. He brushed his slightly too-long hair past the pencil tucked behind his ear as he examined a selection of oat, almond, and soy milks, and his gestures were unrushed while he retrieved a steaming coffee mug from the machine and added a splash of creamer. His stir stick made an irritating *click*, *click*, *click* against the ceramic. When he glanced up to toss it away, straightening to his full height and turning from the counter in her direction, she scowled at him.

Ethan's eyebrows lifted in parallel with his coffee mug. Through a coil of steam, he took an evaluative sip, scanning her flushed, angry face and fisted hands. A dot of oat milk clung to the stubble beside his mouth. He nodded, gaze hooded and lazy. "Monaghan."

One press of a scheduling button, one word, and he'd ruined what should've been a happy, happy day!

She snatched a mug from a nearby shelf and thumped it into the coffee machine. Erin jabbed a few buttons at random. She crossed her arms while the appliance sputtered and spewed.

"What were you doing awake at two o'clock this morning?"

Espresso shots fired into Erin Monaghan's mug.

What were you doing awake at two o'clock this morning?

Even articulating her surname with the required sarcasm had been a struggle in his exhaustion, but now her voice and the artillery of the coffee machine wrenched Ethan into alertness.

Bunsen had eaten something disgusting in the park yesterday, so he'd been awake until almost five o'clock cleaning up the golden retriever's vomit. Yes, he'd slept less in the past, on some insomniac nights… but he'd usually been lying down for at least a few hours. Hell would freeze over before he'd share that information with Erin, however, who glowered up at him with a curled lip and dark, flashing eyes—though not very far up because, even in sneakers, she was barely three inches shorter than his six foot two—as if she'd like to shove him into SVLAC's Matter in Extreme Conditions hutch, power on its faulty X-ray, and roentgenize him. Steam from the milk frother streaked her glasses while her glare narrowed at his silence.

He took another insouciant sip of lackluster coffee, just to frustrate her—and then his brain caught up with the implications of her attack. Right, the calendar shutdown. Being awake for IT's scheduling email had been the one saving grace from last night.

That, and the fact that his rental's floors were hardwood, not carpet.

"You got on this month's lab time schedule. What were you doing awake at two o'clock?"

Why not let her think that he was so dedicated to his research that he remained conscious and watching for work emails at two in the morning? It had happened before. Ethan shrugged under her accusatory stare.

"It's probably fine if you're lackadaisical about scheduling your hours, Monaghan. Relativistic mechanics is a relic. All other modern theories include quantum effects. So it's not very important for you to publish any new research. You don't need fresh data."

Erin snatched her mug from the machine. "You have no idea what my research or publishing situation is. The *Journal of Supermassive Astronomy and Astrophysics* just accepted my sole-author paper on tidal disruption events—"

"Sole author? Good for you. But that publication has a readership of—what? A hundred people? Not much reach in the field, and not much opportunity for citation. Not like *Nature Physics* or *Reviews of Modern Physics*. And you still have…" he paused, "six papers to my seven."

"I'd much rather have just one sole-author paper published in any journal, if the alternative is being Dr. Kramer's lackey and second author. No matter how many publications that position got me!"

He took another sip. "A publication is a publication. Numbers don't lie. You're behind."

"You've had access to the lab machinery for more months than I have—and anyhow, LIGO's database takes time to update with all the readings coming from Washington and Louisiana, so my exports take longer to render than your holometer's isolated data sets—"

"Excuses? I didn't expect that," and he watched, satisfied, as the annoyed color on her cheeks seeped lower to stain her throat.

"I'm not making—" She took a swig of her own brew, and

choked.

"You put in four shots of espresso," he told her, smirking at her contorted face. "I thought you might've been trying to boost your productivity, to make up for lost time in the experimental halls, but now it's clear that—"

"—that unlike you, since it seems you're just going to harass people at the coffee machine all morning, I have a sole-author paper accepted for publication—and things to do," and then she strode away, pausing only to empty her noxious concoction into the sink.

Laughter rose up in his chest. But before he could call out after her with one last parting shot—something clever, he didn't know what—Dr. Tomasz Szymanski entered the kitchenette with yesterday's mug in hand.

"Dr. Meyer," and a nod.

"Dr. Szymanski. Late night?" Still smiling, he gestured at his colleague's mug, which bore telltale rings of dried coffee.

"I have not yet gone to bed, and I have just now returned to my desk. I have been in the West Experimental Hall since yesterday morning. It is the last day of my data collection cycle. I have been busy. As have you, I see." Szymanski nodded after Erin's retreating figure. "She is angry again, yes?"

"Isn't she always?"

Pushing back his sandy hair with a shrug, Szymanski rinsed his mug and placed a fresh one into the coffee machine. "What is the trouble today?"

"The scheduling calendar for lab time is down. She probably didn't get a slot. Or if she did, not one that she wanted."

"*Hmm.*" Szymanski selected his creamer. His tone was very bland when he inquired, "Dr. Meyer, you did not break the calendar for her?"

Coffee sloshed over Ethan's mug onto his thumb. "What?"

"You did not break the calendar for her?"

"No! I'd never intentionally inconvenience a colleague that way."

"Any colleague but…"—Szymanski dusted cinnamon over his drink—"…Dr. Erin Monaghan?"

He'd phrased it as a question. It wasn't. Fastidious Szymanski wouldn't make such a claim without data to back it up. Ready data, and plenty of it. Three years of evidence was incontrovertible proof, Ethan had to admit. But then, he'd never denied the facts. It wasn't as if he was the only guilty party in the situation, either.

Erin Monaghan had caused so much damage by signing her tricksy initials—

God, when he'd been at CERN, he'd actually anticipated seeing her again.

He hadn't known who she was, though. What she was like. What she'd done.

Idiot.

It had taken him months of sleepless nights to alleviate Dr. Kramer's displeasure over the *Nature Physics* fiasco. He'd explained the revision error to the journal's reviewers, of course; they'd identified problems in the paper's data upon its initial submission, although with a name like Dr. Kramer's listed as the first author and his sign-off on the revisions, they likely hadn't reviewed the edits as closely the second time around. That was a procedural failure on their end. It was no use blaming the reviewers, however, because Dr. Kramer blamed Ethan.

That would've been bad enough—*very, very bad*—but there had also been the accompanying fallout of damage to Dr. Kramer's professional standing from the publication, which had cost him his collaboration with Lawrence Livermore National

Laboratory. After his testy exchanges with the *Nature Physics* reviewers, Ethan had put his own holometer lab time on hold and spent six months running calculations on a variety of Dr. Kramer's other quantum hypotheses in an effort to regain even a modicum of his department head's confidence. The formulas still haunted him.

In his frustration and fury during those first horrible days after the paper's release—it had been retracted, but the harm had already been done—he'd reacted to Erin Monaghan's sabotage with his own machinations around time zones and the lab time schedule. A quick switch between a.m. and p.m. on her calendar when she was away from her desk had been so easy.

Only later, after he'd slogged through the backlog of emails accumulated during his stint at CERN, had he located a note from Human Resources, alerting him about a document signing mix-up in Erin Monaghan's onboarding process two months before.

> *We apologize for the glitch, and trust that the situation has not caused you inconvenience.*

Erin Monaghan had received his revise-and-resubmit form for *Nature Physics* from Human Resources, and she'd signed it. Maybe she hadn't actively intended to obstruct his work at that point, but she also clearly hadn't read the document's contents, evidence of a sloppy process from the beginning—and now?

The mix-up *had* caused him inconvenience.

It still was.

Because the p.m.-to-a.m. calendar switch-up might've seen the situation conclude on frosty but final terms, except that Erin had discovered and retaliated to his sabotage in kind. A few weeks later, she'd mistakenly received his holometer data from the West Experimental Hall, due to that unfortunate similarity in their initial-based SVLAC emails. Rather than just forwarding the information to him, she'd run a binary program on a single file to switch its zeros and ones before she'd passed on the full set of spreadsheets. He'd identified her vandalism and resolved it prior to the data erasure that occurred monthly in SVLAC's outdated digital storage system to accommodate all new exported files, but then he'd spent several days checking his other spreadsheets for damage… which turned out to be nonexistent. She'd made him waste his time. And that had led to an ever-escalating war over the past three years. Lab time, funding, visibility with SVLAC's directors—they jockeyed for everything, all means fair and all tactics employed—

"Any colleague but Dr. Monaghan," Szymanski repeated, recalling him from his unpleasant retrospection. He retrieved his coffee and left Ethan to his frown. "Good morning, Dr. Meyer."

It hadn't been a good morning before—except for when he'd set Erin back on the wrong foot and seen her choke on her espresso—and it certainly wasn't now. Ethan stalked off to his office. Instead of talking with Szymanski, he should've been starting an application for the annual Eischer-Langhoff Grant in Physics—prestigious, competitive, lucrative, notoriously difficult—to fund his and Dr. Kramer's next year of research. Volatile markets and an economic downturn had vaporized several sources of SVLAC's anticipated funding, and the lab's operational funds from the Department of Energy were stingy at best, not enough to fund fixes for the out-of-order control rooms and lab hutches, let alone his experimental work.

Working for a National Lab offered a high degree of research freedom, but not as much funding as he would've had in private industry, as his parents never failed to remind him.

A noisy typing *clack*, *clack*, *clack* sounded from the bullpen while he unlocked his office.

"Sole-author Erin" was likely applying for the Eischer-Langhoff grant right now, too.

He swung his door closed and bypassed his ordinary morning rounds of sudoku and sketching, locating the link to the grant application in his email instead, bending to follow the message as his standing desk spasmed into an unprompted descent. He grabbed his roller chair without looking, slung his fleece vest over the back, and took his seat while the desk locked in its new height. Then he reached for his noise-canceling headphones. He'd start on the grant today and have a working copy by the end of the week.

Before he could tune his hearing to white noise or begin entering justifications into the grant's "Need Statement" field, however, a new message appeared in his inbox: *Your Submission to Galactica Magazine*.

Dear Bannister,

We are delighted to inform you that your pen and ink illustration, "Hunger," has been accepted for publication. You will receive a complimentary copy of the next issue of Galactica Magazine, *where your work will be printed. Our editors enjoyed your art and hope that you will consider participating in* Galactica's *anniversary artist–writer collaboration later this year.*

A smile broke through his frown—until he sobered at the chatter of his rival loudly, emphatically, tauntingly discussing her research paper's acceptance with Nadine Fong, debating the possible leverage that it gave her funding pitch in the Eischer-Langhoff application. She seemed to be speaking directly outside his office, in defiance of his closed door.

But at least Erin Monaghan couldn't ruin this for him.

2

"How's your work on the grant coming, now that you can cite your pending paper as evidence for the funding req—*ugh*, she's kicking." Nadine eased down into a chair, one hand splayed against her spine and the other cupping the swell of her belly. She grimaced at Erin across her desk. "Sorry. Staying until the end of the quarter's funding cycle seemed like a solid choice when I was still early in this pregnancy, but now…"

"Can I get you anything?"

"No. Just take my congratulations on your paper, then update me on our latest binary pulsar data and your grant progress before I have to run for the bathroom."

"I'll make it quick." Erin enlarged a summary table and turned her laptop toward her supervisor. "Our current group research is on two compact neutron stars orbiting each other in a star system. One of them is a pulsar, which emits a tight beam of radio waves. Here's the exciting part: our newest batch of data shows that we can replicate the exact frequency of the pulsar's waves in the lab. Instead of needing to locate and measure other neutron stars in the wild, we can model different levels of gravitational force coming off them and test our theories about their radio waves functioning as an interstellar energy source—all in-house."

"That's excellent news. Good work."

"The credit goes to the department. I made these tables, but since I've been busy with LIGO, it was Dr. Rossi and Dr.

O'Connor-Young who ran the labs. You've attracted top talent, Nadine."

"I headhunted you. *Sole author*," with a nod. "That's made all the difference. I promise you'll have support on LIGO soon, too. When there's funding for more staff, anyway. But the existing group will be in good hands while I'm out."

Thank God Ethan wasn't under Nadine's departmental jurisdiction. He never would've submitted to Erin's leadership, however temporary. Those snide comments about her research history, his easy dismissal of her paper's acceptance by a publication that he considered too esoteric to be a threat, his laughter when she'd taken her gulp of espresso shots—

Opening her work on the Eischer-Langhoff grant, she jammed a finger against the laptop's trackpad. Her knuckle cracked. "Now, the grant."

"How's the application this year? Horrible like always?"

"No, it's fine. Or it will be, since I can cite the experimental methods in my paper to justify my funding needs."

If only she could be so certain of besting her rival.

She reviewed her progress—the form wasn't due for more than a month, and she was ahead of schedule—and noted the areas where she'd reference her own work on methods and cost breakdowns, then waved Nadine off to the bathroom. Rubbing her finger, she returned to her desk and ran through a data collection plan for her obnoxious Tuesday lab time with the interferometer. At least Martina was scheduled to be the operating technician for her shift. And given the hour, maybe there wouldn't be as much signal interference from the Bay Area's ubiquitous traffic to scrub from her exports.

But her knuckle hurt, and she couldn't call up much excitement at this silver lining.

The lab time scheduling fiasco had been bad, but running into Ethan had been much worse. Today, of all days!

That publication has a readership of—what? A hundred people?

Ethan Meyer wasn't human. He couldn't be. With his insanely productive publication history and his evidently equally insane sleep habits?

He was an automaton, all inputs and outputs.

So many outputs.

It seemed impossible that she'd once hallucinated him as human and even attractive, that he'd once left her breathless.

Before—*everything*.

She glowered at a neglected air plant hanging from the wall of her cubicle. It was shedding fronds into a mug filled with pencils and emblazoned with the slogan "It Ain't Easy Being Write." Her brothers had given it to her after a heated Monaghan family trivia tournament, which she'd lost at the age of twelve after being asked to name the winner of the 1953 Hugo Award: Alfred Bester. She'd kept it on display all these years in defiance…

Well, she could dismiss Ethan to the ranks of artificial intelligence easily enough, but the truth was that she'd only submitted "Pandora Rising" to *Galactica Magazine* after one too many taunts about her continued failure to match his publication record. She hadn't known at the time that her paper on tidal disruption events would be accepted, and even now that it was: *You still have six papers to my seven. Galactica* wasn't *Nature Physics* or the *Journal of Supermassive Astronomy and Astrophysics*. But a science fiction magazine was adjacent to their field, and having "Pandora Rising" in print would settle their score—if only in her mind, because it wasn't as if she could ever tout her triumph around him. His ridicule for any output as subjective as fiction would be unendurable. He probably never read anything except scientific journals.

He drank his coffee with oat milk, however. Which was odd. *She* liked oat milk. For him, a plain black brew—or diesel—would've been more fitting.

Hours later, she could still taste the bite of this morning's espresso shots.

His fault.

There was only one thing to do about that. She swiped past her phone's photoshopped graphic of the Monaghans at a Michigan theme park and opened her text thread with Martina.

> **Erin**
> I ran into him in the kitchenette today. He actually chastised me for not being online at 2 a.m. to schedule my lab time, after IT had a security meltdown and rebooted the calendar system!

No typing bubbles appeared with sympathy.

> **Erin**
> But, of course, he was awake. I don't think he's human. Just an advanced research robot prototype that Dr. Kramer's developed.

She drummed her fingers on her screen, opening a calculator, the latest panel of XKCD comics, a list of trending STEMinist Online posts, *Galactica Magazine*'s front page, and her search history for astronaut ice cream. Martina's thread remained stubbornly static.

Erin
(Ethan Meyer, obviously.)

But equally obviously, Martina would be asleep now after her night shift. She wouldn't see Erin's griping for hours.

Erin
Sorry to bug you after your shift. Talk later.

When she pulled up her presentation for the Modern Physics group's monthly research all-hands meeting, though, she continued to fidget. The irritating sound in her ears was her own teeth grinding. She shifted position. She stared at the slides. She attempted a few rows of digital sudoku, and failed. She scrolled through her reference spreadsheets. The data on creating laboratory models for pulsars was visual white noise.

She checked her phone.

Nothing from sleeping Martina.

She changed position again.

The door to Ethan's office opened, then closed. She knew its scrape against the carpet. She glared at the data exports on her monitor, refusing to look up as her rival's footsteps receded down the hall.

Another coffee? She resisted the urge to peer over her cubicle.

Nadine's office was also just across the way. But she wouldn't complain to her supervisor about petty interpersonal problems with a colleague. Nadine was leaving the management of their department to Erin during her maternity leave, which meant wrangling both projects and people, and if she couldn't handle herself with a single annoying coworker, who wasn't even in her research group—

Adrian and Wes would never ignore an urgent message from her, unless Adrian was in the middle of pitching his sustainable urban planning proposals to investors, or if Wes was underwater in search of marine iguanas off the coast of Ecuador. They'd answer her complaints with immediate suggestions for either juvenile or outright dangerous pranks. SVLAC's air horns would likely be mentioned, as would plastic rattlesnakes, real turkey droppings, or even the rewiring of turn signal directions in Ethan's car. That, or promises to break his arms. They'd never given her an easy victory during childhood baseball games or board game tournaments—winning had been all the sweeter for that—but both could and would fly out to California without hesitation if they thought she needed them.

She didn't.

A kindergarten bully had once pushed her off the swing set. He'd lost two front teeth that day. Only one of those had been her brothers' work.

As for her parents?

In a volunteer aide's apron covered with finger paint, mucus, or glued bits of pasta and beads, Lori Monaghan's Monday afternoons were busy shepherding Grand Arbor's first graders on their weekly field trip to the library; apparently, it had taken the energy of twenty-five six-year-olds to replace Erin, Adrian, and Wes after they'd left home. She'd always make time for her daughter, of course, but then she'd offer the same simple, sensible advice that she gave her students: *treat others as you'd like to be treated, and they'll return the favor*. Sensible, yes, and useless in Erin's situation. Her father would just nod at his wife's wisdom, smiling over his glasses before returning to his model train project. Retired from a soulless job in corporate law, he now spent his days figuring out timetables for maneuvering around the backyard sprinklers…

Timetables: *time*.

The Modern Physics all-hands kicked off in an hour.

She hadn't finished adding the new data to her slides. Good data. Interesting data. It warranted a paper and several conference talks. She was proud of it, and proud of her department's contributions to the field—even if she wasn't proud of her run-in with Ethan this morning.

She began to type.

Nadine would have a polished presentation ready for their all-hands. A concise one, too, since today's agenda also included time for an announcement from SVLAC's director, Dr. Elias Schulz. Hopefully, it concerned some miraculous resurgence in research funding, because whatever she'd told Nadine, the Eischer-Langhoff application really was nasty, sole-author paper citations or no.

Ethan parked an SVLAC scooter outside the Science and Public Support building, glad to set both feet on solid ground, despite having to sidestep a minefield of turkey shit. His trip along Ring Road had been precarious. He was still off kilter from his two conversations in the kitchenette this morning.

Could Erin have somehow slipped an espresso shot into his coffee? The jangling of his nerves suggested a *maybe*. Blaming her was so easy. A habit, like sudoku and caffeine.

Hitching his shoulders against the weight of a messenger bag dragging on his arm, he badged through the doors. Fluorescent lights flickered overhead; he'd arrived early at Maiman Auditorium, and the meeting rooms and small public exhibits of interactive touch tables and klystron models on the ground floor were quiet except for the scuff of his shoes. This peaceful place was better than his office, with its proximity to the noisy Modern Physics bullpen. He exhaled his relief, shoulders settling.

Then another badge swiped and beeped for entry.

It was hers. He knew it.

Her footsteps hesitated on the threshold. She'd seen him. But she didn't retreat back to the parking lot. She didn't speak. Fine, let her lurk by the klystron model. Passing one hand quickly over a wash of heat on his neck, he extracted his laptop from his bag and hunched toward its screen. He had data to check. *Dr. Kramer's* data to check.

For the fourth time, he clicked through his department's slides, reviewing their numbers and speaker notes. His supervisor wouldn't tolerate another error from him, not after the *Nature Physics* situation. If he got himself fired and blacklisted by one of the premier scientists in the quantum field, every future opportunity for research, funding, or recognition that he could've received by association with Dr. Kramer's name would vanish.

That, and more.

Ignoring Erin's percussive typing on her own computer, ignoring the squeak of her sneakers shifting on the floor, he added a few transition phrases to his speaker notes.

He'd meant to run his final check on the presentation last night, until Bunsen had started heaving up whatever he'd eaten in the park on Sunday, and maybe he could've finished his review this morning, but then he'd run into Erin's wrath and Tomasz Szymanski's commentary before he'd even reached his desk.

So, here he was.

Soon enough, other badges began to swipe in at the building's main entrance. The hall outside Maiman Auditorium filled with his colleagues, all carrying laptops and glancing longingly toward the cafeteria upstairs. A buzz of conversation eddied through the corridor as they congregated near the auditorium, their reluctance to enter the stuffy, windowless room and their speculations about Dr. Elias Schulz's announcement making them circle in indecisive fractals on the threshold.

"These meetings always take so much longer than they need to."

"I'm already starving. The cafeteria's serving curry again today. Can you smell it?"

"Any takers for a bet on whether there'll be some left by the time we get out of here?"

"No point. Not when Dr. Schulz is making a speech."

"We'll be here until five," with a groan.

"Yes. Plus, there's also…"

"*Uh-huh.*"

A bubble of unspoken communication expanded between a group of particle physicists chattering near Ethan's station against the wall. He felt it, a prickle on his spine.

They were watching him.

He elbowed his way into the auditorium.

He nodded at Szymanski when his coworker joined him at the room's tiered rows of tables but continued to add punctuation to his speaker notes. No other colleagues taking their seats for the all-hands were still working on their slides. Well, no other colleagues had lost Dr. Kramer a collaborative opportunity with Lawrence Livermore, either—

"You're finished with the presentation? Good." Dr. Kramer set his briefcase on the table beside Ethan's laptop. He leaned into the adjacent microphone and depressed the speaker button without waiting for either an administrative speech to open the meeting or a confirmation from Ethan.

Dr. Kramer knew he'd deliver.

"I have a one o'clock call with Fermilab. Quantum will present first." He took Ethan's laptop down to the podium—*just don't let the hardware crash*—and gestured for IT to connect the presentation cables. Immaculate slides flickered into focus on a descending projector screen behind the stage. "Quantum Mechanics is currently running another cycle of data collection on SVLAC's prototype holometer, following upgrades last month to the quality of the laser beam."

A cross-section of the holometer's design appeared on his click. "The instrument's dual mirrors bounce a laser, which a half-reflective surface splits into two perpendicular beams, along a pair of thirty-meter tunnels. The beams are calibrated to register the exact locations of the mirrors. If space can be measured in defined quantum units, the mirrors will move slightly during the laser bounces—on a technical level, space itself is moving, rather than the mirrors—to create a constant, random variation in their positions. When the beams are recombined after bouncing between the mirrors, I hypothesize that the twin lasers will be consistently out of sync by a statistically significant percentage. This discrepancy will reveal the scale of units of space.

"Preliminary results will be available by the end of the year, and collaborative and individual papers in progress shortly afterward, likely in partnership with Dr. Greg Logan, Fermilab, and the University of Chicago. Meyer will assist with analyzing any subsequent practical applications from the quantum measurement. Beyond work on the holometer, the department is also conducting experiments to stabilize LED performance in medical equipment under extreme temperatures, with Szymanski leading the project."

A pause. Then, "Questions?"

Ethan had drafted answers to the inquiries that he'd anticipated might come from his slides. But Dr. Kramer gave a pointed glance at his Patek Philippe wristwatch, and no microphones crackled in challenge.

"Good." Dr. Kramer removed the presentation cables from Ethan's laptop. The projector screen shone white and blank as he left the stage.

It was done.

He inhaled deeply while pressing his palms against the table. The prints were slick and damp. So were his underarms. Although Dr. Kramer gave a short nod when he handed back the computer—a positive data point, isolated but unambiguous—Ethan only exhaled that breath again after his supervisor's focus moved away to a colleague's Optics presentation. He lost the first half of the group's research review in his relief. Then Nadine Fong shuffled up to the stage.

Erin Monaghan sat at attention in the front row of the auditorium while her department head presented the group's data on a new binary pulsar model and the recent impact on space-time that the interactions of distant astrophysical bodies had made, via undulating gravitational waves. Her glasses reflected shards of color gleaming from the projector screen as she nodded along to the diagrams, her ponytail swishing lightly between her shoulder blades. Her lips moved, timed to the animation transitions. She'd designed this presentation.

Fong's maternity leave was scheduled to start soon, wasn't it?

Erin was primed to manage the Relativistic Mechanics group in her supervisor's absence.

"…which we can confirm with telescope images from Kitt Peak National Observatory. Questions?" Smiling, Fong concluded her talk and scanned the room for raised hands.

Dr. Kramer's index finger tapped the table.

Another isolated data point, but Ethan also knew the meaning of this one.

He forced himself to concentrate and turned on his microphone. Though he had no specific objection to Fong's presentation prepared, Dr. Kramer now expected him to challenge their rival department over the validity of its research aims, or its latest data, or its methods—*something*. Anything to prove the superiority of the Quantum Mechanics group and his work. Ethan's work, too. He had to speak. "Dr. Fong, I have a question."

"Go ahead, Dr. Meyer."

"Your department's research presupposes that you can identify when space-time ripples originate from the movement of black holes or stars, rather than from any other localized source."

"That's correct."

"There must be a large amount of noise in the data. The Relativistic Mechanics group's machinery measures micro-vibrations, and SVLAC's interferometer is in the middle of Silicon Valley traffic and the airspace from NASA Ames."

"Yes. Differentiating signals from noise is Dr. Monaghan's wheelhouse." Fong motioned for him to continue—then grimaced. Her hand fluttered to her stomach, and a harsh exhale rattled across her microphone. "*Ugh*. Excuse me. Erin, could you—"

"Of course."

His rival made way for her supervisor to rejoin their grouping, then wheeled her chair around to face Ethan's quantum colleagues seated several tiers higher in the auditorium. Leaning sideways onto an elbow, she spoke into her tabletop microphone rather than moving to the podium, sarcastically earnest when she asked, "What can I help you to understand about my work, Meyer?"

"How do you prove that you're analyzing signals, rather than noise?"

"Right." A cynical smile angled her mouth. His hurried question was clearly too trivial to merit her upright attention; she shrugged and tilted farther onto her forearm. Her sweater slouched with her. Its neckline slid off her collarbones to reveal the narrow strap of a camisole. "I understand your confusion. This can be difficult for non-specialists to understand. And also for people who don't make their data publicly available."

"I'm not confused, Monaghan. I'm asking—"

"Yes, thank you for your interest. I separate the Laser Interferometer Gravitational-Wave Observatory's signals from local noise by transforming the positive and negative deviances of my data into frequencies. Prior data points in the public research pool from LIGO's branches in southeastern Washington State and Livingston, Louisiana—which are already confirmed as originating from astrophysical movements—indicate the Hertz frequencies that I should expect to see from colliding black holes and their destruction of nearby stars. Once I've run a Fourier transform on my data to configure its deviances as frequencies, any valid signals are clear from the noise." She adjusted her glasses, eyebrows raised, daring him to continue when she'd closed the subject.

But he hadn't finished.

Dr. Kramer was watching.

And she'd given him an opening.

"You're using data that you haven't generated yourself. How do you verify its accuracy? If the data at LIGO's other sites is incorrect, your own analysis will be faulty."

"My analyses are perfect."

"Is the *data* in your analyses perfect? Not just SVLAC's measurements, but the database where you're pulling your controls?"

"Well, I don't check my colleagues' research like we're still in graduate school," and now she straightened. Her second shrug was more of a jerk. "But when possible, I verify my own signal observations with telescope data. Maybe you've heard of multi-messenger astronomy?"

"So you rely on fallible visuals."

"Visuals from specialized telescopic astrophotography cameras."

"Which are maintained by someone else. Manned by someone else. Generating images taken by someone else. You're relying on this, and public data."

"Fine, yes. But are we discussing science right now? Or philosophy? Because your questions aren't really about my methodology. Are they? This is about whether I trust my colleagues in the field—"

"Science isn't based on trust."

"—and about whether I believe that anyone else is using brain cells while they work!" Color pinched over her cheekbones.

"Science is based on facts," he retorted, calm and logical under Dr. Kramer's eyes. It didn't matter that his ears were warm. "Justifications for sloppy, unempirical processes like *trust* become justifications for sloppy research. Dirty results."

"Except that my research and results are obviously acceptable, because my sole-author paper on tidal disruption events is—"

"—based on inputs that you haven't independently verified. I'd consider a retraction before it goes to print. Publishing fraudulent data, Monaghan? That's career suicide, even for—"

"Excuse me. *What?*" Her amplified words and the screeching pivot of her chair reverberated across the auditorium. Erin stood, sweater falling down the exposed curve of her shoulder when she abandoned her microphone to face him head on. "*Fraud? What are you—*"

"*Um!* That's all the time we have for departmental updates today!" An administrative assistant at the podium gave an awkward wave, attempting to redirect the room's focus from Erin, breathing hard under the slanted projector beam with a glittering nimbus of pixels and dust in her hair. "Thank you, Dr. Kramer, Dr. Van Buskirk, and Dr. Fong. We'll close today with an announcement from Dr. Schulz. Dr. Schulz, if you'd come to the stage?"

As Erin sank slowly back into her seat, static from the assistant's adjustment of the microphone almost muffled the noise of a pair of hands clapping somewhere in the auditorium.

Almost.

Clap. Clap. Clap.

Heat crept from Ethan's ears into his neck. Chafing at the discomfort, he turned away from Dr. Kramer's encore nod and Szymanski's watchful frown—to Erin again, who was pulling her sweater back into place, cramming her laptop into her backpack with her head bowed, ponytail falling over her shoulder. She swept it away in irritation. She was biting her lip.

Had she also heard the clapping?

And his accusation: *fraudulent data*.

She'd definitely heard that...

"Well done, Meyer." *Dr. Kramer.*

"*Uh*—thank you."

Erin wrenched at the zipper on her bag. Her jaw twitched. Her eyes were downcast.

Rubbing harder at his nape, Ethan was grateful for Schulz's arrival at the podium and even for the next hellish microphone shriek, which signaled the director's readiness to speak.

"Thank you, Marcie. Now: I'm pleased to announce that both the Secretary of Energy for the United States and the Department of Energy's Office of Science will be visiting SVLAC this quarter. Secretary McCandless will tour our departments and our research facilities and attend a presentation by Dr. Helena Quarles on SVLAC's contributions to American science education. I don't need to tell you that this is an honor for the lab—and an important event."

He didn't. At his mention of a government visit, anticipatory murmuring swelled through Maiman Auditorium. The Department of Energy's on-site presence afforded opportunities to angle for additional research funding by speaking directly with federal officials, unimpeded by the usual paper bureaucracy.

Funds were tight this year and competition for the Secretary's attention would be fierce.

Erin was already in consultation with Nadine Fong, her gaze up again, quickly refocused, and presumably discussing the best way to present their research proposals to the government representatives. Plotting revenge, too. Though he couldn't hear her words through the crowd, Ethan knew this about her.

But there was only so much capital to go around, and his field needed those funds. Dr. Kramer needed those funds.

He needed those funds.

"Security will perform a building sweep on Thursday, and Secretary McCandless will arrive on Friday. Staff must display identification badges at all times—"

He couldn't let her win.

3

He had to beat Erin Monaghan to the Secretary of Energy's attention—and to the Eischer-Langhoff grant. After a hurried lunch, Ethan stared at the application, flexed his fingers over his keyboard, demanded brilliance from himself, then stalled, wondering whether Erin had already submitted her form. What if the reviewers were nodding over her narrative and her data right now, swayed by the promise of her sole-author publication? What if the hypothetical genius of her proposal impressed them so much that they stopped considering any other submissions?

What if—

He grimaced and rubbed his temples. The earlier microphone screeches from the auditorium continued to ricochet in his ears.

Clap. Clap. Clap.

He snatched up a pen and began to sketch around the margins of his sudoku calendar.

If Erin won the grant, had Fong earmarked a portion of the funds for her own research? Possibly. But possibly not, given her pending maternity leave. Which meant that, if his rival was successful, she'd receive the full amount. She could devote her time to pure science for the duration of the funding cycle, instead of slogging through the administrative bullshit of writing additional applications…

He *had* to secure funding for his research.

And for Dr. Kramer's projects, of course.

If he failed—

His pen skidded off the sudoku grid and a pulse of anxiety drove his fingers back to the keyboard, where he began to explain the importance of his and Dr. Kramer's work in dense, stilted paragraphs. When a familiar set of footsteps strode down the hall, however, he paused his typing to tape a Do Not Disturb sign to his door.

He added his headphones and the lull of white noise soon after.

Outside his office, Erin's aggressively lively conversation with Nadine Fong and Dr. Marco Rossi about authorship, funding, and the Secretary of Energy's visit faded to a murmur. *I, me, mine, we, us, ours…* If she was discussing sources for additional research dollars, she probably hadn't submitted the Eischer-Langhoff grant yet. He exhaled, and nodded to himself in the quiet.

Realistically—*theoretically*—it was possible that another physicist from a different National Lab could receive the award. But… *no*. He knew his competition.

Ethan returned to the application.

He paused again an hour later when his desk elevated to standing height, its rise punctuating the end of his first draft. The grant proposal still required several intensive edit sessions before it went to his supervisor for feedback—but Bunsen would also have feedback in the form of gnawed shoes and shredded pillows if he didn't return home soon for their evening run. He powered down his computer and headed to his car, calculating how many socks he'd forfeit while sitting in the northbound congestion toward Redwood City. Living in Menlo Park or Palo Alto would be more convenient for his commute to SVLAC, but who could afford privacy there?

He exited the traffic jam onto Farm Hill Boulevard, where the vehicle demographic changed from Teslas to trucks hauling flats of construction stone or piping, and the cattle-dotted hills around Junipero Serra Freeway became light industrial buildings. Passing Stulsaft Park, he pulled into his designated parking space near a cluster of older condominiums. The units weren't in a good neighborhood, were outfitted with unembellished builder's grade fixtures, and likely had asbestos in their shingles, but the prices for one-bedroom rentals were affordable. The chirp of his hatchback's lock roused a crescendo of frenzied howls from his unit as he checked the soles of his shoes for turkey shit.

Well, he had *some* privacy.

"Hey, buddy."

Bunsen launched himself at Ethan, wiggling with anticipation and covering him in slobber until he shucked off his sneakers on the interior mud mat. Then the dog dove for the shoes, sniffing hard.

"I didn't get it all off, did I? Maybe we need a mat outside, too."

Karen Meyer would be pleased. She hated what he'd done with the place.

Or what he hadn't.

He scratched Bunsen's ears with a sour smile, then hung up his vest beside the retriever's leash, dropped his bag on the second-hand Craigslist couch that he'd somehow managed to cram into his car on pickup several years ago, scanned the floors for vomit—*nothing fresh*—and changed from his jeans into running clothes. Bunsen abandoned his shoes to seize Ethan's discarded work socks, carrying them like a prize while he tore around the living room, eager for exercise beyond the confines of the condo's back patio.

His mother hated that patio even more than she hated his lack of a welcome mat.

She'd planted succulents in the dirt behind his unit one afternoon, and Bunsen had dug them up. He hadn't let the retriever kill her plants to annoy her—not explicitly. He was just busy, and giving his dig-happy dog access to the patio while he was at SVLAC was easier than hiring a walker.

"But your condo is so—starter home. You need better furniture and art. You need friends, too. Real friends, not the dog. You could share a much nicer place in Palo Alto, and invite your brother's colleagues on the Peninsula over for dinner once you're settled. You just need to make the effort."

When he wasn't vomiting on the floor, Bunsen was better company than any of Chase Meyer Jr.'s friends.

And maybe even when he was.

"Come on. Frisbee and a run through Stulsaft Park?" He jammed in his earbuds.

Bunsen's tail thwacked against the couch, the wall, and his knees.

"Give me the sock, first."

The retriever paused in an agony of choice between the sock and the leash.

"There might be squirrels in the park."

Bunsen dropped the sock and leaped for the door, towing Ethan outside and down the street. He kept pace with the galloping dog, the pounding of his strides against the sidewalk timed to the chords of Green Day. They raced traffic to the nearest crosswalk and sped across the boulevard to the edge of the park, where Bunsen halted to sniff at a bollard. He left his scent, staring at Ethan without shame as he tottered on three legs, then loped toward the illicit snack hunting ground under a swing set.

"What did you even find here yesterday? You'll eat coyote scat with no problem, but vomit up—what, a Lunchable?" He tugged the retriever away, setting off along Stulsaft Park's central hiking trail. "We'll go for an hour, but I have to work when we get back. Get everything out of your system."

Holding their pace, they jogged past barbecue pits with picnic tables and branching trails before heading for the off-leash paths and open grassy fields south of the creek. Five minutes on the trail became fifteen, then twenty. Ethan's breath came harder, tiredness dragging at his legs, his face and shirt wet with effort, and Bunsen's tongue lolled. But it was good, this single-minded focus of *stride*, *stride*, *stride*, the steady motion like a metronome under his ribs, moving with physical purpose and a blank mind while the rock band wailed in his ears, approaching the field now, Bunsen beginning to pull despite his panting, eager to chase the local black squirrels and frisbees.

The phone strapped to his arm vibrated.

Incoming Call: *Chase Meyer Jr.*

"*Damn.*"

Wiping sweat from his eyes and mouth, he slowed to a walk. The phone continued to chime over his music while he unclipped Bunsen's leash. He ordered the dog to sit, to wait, then threw the retriever's frisbee in a flat, smooth spin across the field. "*Release!*"

Bunsen exploded from his sit and streaked after the disc.

Incoming Call: *Chase Meyer Jr.*

He answered on the fourth ring. "Chase."

"Congratulations are due."

"*Uh*." He hadn't said anything about "Hunger" to his brother, had he? Or about humiliating Erin Monaghan in the auditorium today. "Why?"

"She said yes."

"Who?"

"Don't tell me you forgot her name. *Bella*."

Right: *Bella*.

Isabel Wright, Canadian beauty, Chase's girlfriend… and, apparently, now his fiancée after eleven months of dating? He *had* forgotten her name. Then again, he'd never actually met her. Chase had introduced Bella to the Meyer family during a ski week last year in Steamboat Springs; Ethan hadn't been there. He'd had a data set under review for his and Dr. Kramer's research, and the Meyers had assumed—correctly, if he was being fair—that he wouldn't leave his numbers half-cleaned to go with them to Colorado over the holidays.

They'd made plans without him.

After Chase mentioned the trip during a family dinner, Ethan had received what was clearly an afterthought invitation to sleep on the pull-out couch of their rental cabin. They'd booked a unit with two bedrooms. They'd all known that he wouldn't come.

But…

—Bunsen returned his frisbee, and he flung it hard across the field again—

…the fact that they'd just assumed?

It had stung.

He'd been savagely productive on Dr. Kramer's project during that week, though. His supervisor's subsequent—and after the *Nature Physics* debacle, rare—approbation had been more than enough to counter his bruised ego. Dr. Kramer, who only acknowledged excellence, had been pleased with his output.

He'd been pleased today, too.

Well done, Meyer.

Had implying the use of fraudulent research in Erin's paper crossed a line, though? She'd admitted to employing chunks of public data for her work on the large-scale interactions of astrophysical matter, yes… but in front of Elias Schulz?

Again, however: *Well done, Meyer.*

That was what mattered. Not her naked shoulder, not her lowered eyes—and not Steamboat Springs with its damn pull-out couch—

"Ethan? You there? Did you hear what I—"

He chucked the frisbee a third time, a bit breathless. "Yeah. *Uh*—Bella. That's… congratulations."

"Thanks. The wedding's next June. Probably at the St. Francis Yacht Club, since she's a beach babe. But should we already conclude you won't be bringing a plus one?"

Asking that, like he was sympathetic.

Like he cared that Ethan might have trouble finding dates—when really, he'd just stopped trying. Why bother, when every time he'd asked a girl to a dance or a family function, she'd ended up with Chase by the end of the night? Chase Meyer Jr. was a neurologist—a real doctor like their father, his namesake and colleague at UCSF Medical Center—who didn't have to get by on a government research scientist's salary in the Bay Area. Chase wasn't shy about touting his medical degree from Baylor or his bank account, to Ethan or to any girl that Ethan had ever liked enough to bring home.

Baylor College of Medicine was Chase Meyer Sr.'s alma mater, too.

Yes, he'd stopped trying.

Bunsen's next frisbee flew off into the undergrowth.

"...Ethan?"

"I had to get Bunsen out of the bushes. Sorry."

"So, that plus one. Maybe we should hold a spot, just in case. I could probably swing it with Bella. Since you're my brother. And you never know. I'll be off the market. Maybe you'll have better luck."

"I don't believe in luck. I believe in work."

"Then why not bring Dr. K?" Imitating their mother's voice, Chase said, "*We've heard so much about him—*"

"Shut up."

"Anyhow. That's what's new for me. What's going on with you these days?"

Galactica Magazine's acceptance.

Clapping in the auditorium.

Erin Monaghan.

But Chase wasn't really asking.

He wiped the frisbee on his shirt and clipped on Bunsen's leash. "Running. Work. Sudoku."

"Jesus, you always were a loner."

Loner wasn't what Chase meant, and they both knew it.

He could demand accolades for his research successes and his pending publication of "Hunger," of course. But he wouldn't.

He knew better.

With the historical data documenting Chase's reactions to his science fair wins and his acceptance to UC Berkeley's graduate physics program?

No.

"Ethan? Still with me?"

"Bunsen's trying to eat something disgusting. I have to go."

Sitting obediently at his side, Bunsen gave him a reproachful look.

"All right. But don't forget: family dinner next week. Mom will get testy if you miss it a fifth time."

"Bye, Chase. Congratulations again."

He jogged back along the trail toward Farm Hill Boulevard with Bunsen heeling and nosing against his thigh in concern. His eyes stung. Frowning, he mopped the sweat away as they crossed the street toward their condo. When the golden retriever paused to relieve himself on a neighbor's wilted, weedy shrubbery, however, ignoring several signs in the grass that ordered the reader's dog to *Be Respectful!*, he couldn't help smiling just a little.

"I won't tell them," he promised Bunsen, nodding at the condo. He didn't even know his neighbors' names.

He hadn't told Chase about "Hunger."

He unlocked his door, walking into the quiet, austere space.

But then, he also hadn't told anyone else.

The apartment kitchen was piled high with pans, the counters streaked with grease, grubby dishcloths draped over the bar on the oven door. A powerful odor of garlic mixed with fish sauce hung in the air. Beside a whiteboard of rotating chore assignments on the refrigerator, a cheery yellow magnet tacked up a note: *Sorry for the mess! Will clean everything later.*

Kai or Ashley must've made an early dinner before heading out for the night.

Two sets of silverware and two plates were stacked in the sink, not quite making it into the dishwasher. Maybe one of them had invited a friend over?

Though, after Ashley's previous company had been acquired last year by an organization that offered fewer benefits and numerous layoffs, she'd taken a job as a lab tech at Thermo Fisher Scientific, near where Kai worked in full-stack development at Google. They sometimes carpooled for their commute; Thermo Fisher and Kai's office building were both down in Sunnyvale. Maybe they had dinner sometimes, too. Were Kai and Ashley out together now?

SVLAC was north of Menlo Park, in the opposite direction from the Googleplex and Thermo Fisher. Erin couldn't have commuted with them, even if she'd wanted to. And when had she last been home for dinner at a normal time?

It had been a while.

But being busy was no excuse to skip the Monaghan family's regular Monday night call. Leaving the sink and the counters alone, she warmed up a hodgepodge of leftover vegetarian chili and greens from her weekend meal prep, propped her phone on a table crammed behind the living room couch, and video-called the chat.

One by one, Monaghans appeared on the screen, her brothers already talking over each other in a continuation of some earlier conversation that she'd missed.

"—so I explained that I could fly out to Austin on Friday to discuss a proposal for the new university campus infrastructure, but that I had investor pitches booked solid in New York for the rest of the week—"

"Did I tell you about the time I flew in the cargo hold of that seaplane in the Cayman Islands, so I could keep an eye on my equipment—"

"Only twice. Or maybe it was three times—"

"Sweetheart!" Lori Monaghan interrupted her sons with a smile for Erin, who lifted her spoon in acknowledgment. "What's for dinner on your special day?"

"I made your veggie chili on Sunday." She tilted her bowl into view.

"Good chili," from her father, sitting beside his wife at their kitchen table.

"I'll put on a crock-pot tomorrow before school." Lori patted her husband's arm, then turned back to her screen. "But leftovers aren't a proper celebration meal, Erin."

"You should spice it up," from Wes with a wink, his eyelashes bleached by Ecuadorian sunshine.

She pointed her spoon at him. "I'm not putting jalapeños in it. That's sacrilege, and I can't believe you—"

"We only added the peppers to your bowl," Adrian noted. "We didn't sabotage the whole batch. Besides, you ate it, didn't you?"

"It's been fifteen years, and I still have numb patches on my tongue, you jerk!" Their unapologetic laughter drowned her out. Somewhere in the background of their parents' house, Cassie—the Monaghans' aging Australian Shepherd—began to bark. Raising her voice, she continued, "I ate the chili because I wasn't going to let you win. Then I got you back later. With the Icy Hot."

Adrian winced. "I couldn't feel my ass for a week. You were a menace."

"Still is," Wes added.

Shouting at Ethan Meyer in the light of a project beam—data fraud—her sweater slipping off, everyone watching—

"She's a published author, too," Lori redirected them before their conversation and Erin's attention went completely off the rails. "She should celebrate with more than chili."

Right. *Focus.*

"I'm *almost* published, Mom. 'Pandora Rising' will be in *Galactica*'s next issue, and my paper's queued for a September printing. Assuming no one sabotages it. Then I'll celebrate. But I've got a late shift on LIGO tonight, and there's a grant that I need to work on. Adrian, if you think Texans can be hard sells on investing in xeriscaped urban infrastructure, you should try getting research funding out of the Department of Energy. If it's not something politically expedient, like work on semiconductors, things that create industrial jobs, something for a campaign platform? Forget it. So, if I can't get my funds from a private grant—"

"When's the application due?"

"Next month."

"Then you have time." Adrian shrugged and sobered. "You can go out tonight. You'll get these particular funds, or find some other way. You always do."

"But—"

Ping.

A message from Martina zipped onto her screen above the Monaghan video squares.

> **Martina**
> (Awake now!) Sounds like you've had a DAY.
> Meet at Left Bank to discuss? 6:15 p.m.?

Her fingers hovered over the notification. "It seems like Martina agrees with you. She wants to meet at Left Bank."

"Martinis with Martina?"

"You know I hate olives."

Ethan Meyer wouldn't be out at a brasserie tonight. He was probably hunched over the Eischer-Langhoff application right now. That, or gloating about his digs from the all-hands. Not to mention, she needed a clear head for her research shift…

"Erin," Lori recalled her. "Just be happy for yourself tonight, like we're happy for you."

"Go see your friend, kiddo," from her reclusive father.

"All right, but just for one glass of wine." And, despite the pressure of the grant, her midnight lab hours, and her irritation from the workday, her stomach bubbled with joy again. Ethan Meyer's attempts at torpedoing her research and challenging the validity of her methods notwithstanding, she *did* always find a way to reach her goal. She'd wanted to see "Pandora Rising" published and wanted sole authorship of a paper, so she'd put in the time, put in the effort with a thesaurus and data analytics tools, and now—

Her father smiled at her. "Good. Go."

"No, wait!" Adrian waved on her screen. "You have to tell me what route you took around the Dish this morning."

"I'd like nothing more than to detail my runtime win for you," she smirked, "but Dad just told me to go to Left Bank with Martina."

"You can't avoid me forever—"

"Give Cassie an ear scratch for me, Mom. Bye!"

Leaving Adrian to fume and Wes to laugh him down, she closed the Monaghans' video call. Then, since her watch showed a half-hour before she was due to meet Martina, she launched a familiar web forum on her screen.

STEMinist Online: *Diversity, Equity, Inclusion, and Smashing the Patriarchy*

Log in?

SnarkyQuark64 joined the conversation.

A scan through the top posts offered a slant on news from *National Geographic*, *Popular Mechanics*, *Scientific American*, *Time Magazine*, and *The Economist*. But instead of breathless profiles of visionary billionaires, alarmist calls for regulation in the financial technology sector, or discussions of the latest Silicon Valley job perks, STEMinist Online provided commentary on the origins of billionaire brilliance—

> JustAKeysm@sh0K: *There's a consulting firm under an NDA that comes up with most of his new product ideas. And he's got a short fuse. You're probably okay to ride with him in an elevator, though. He's not handsy.*

—and the quiet firing of an analyst at a tech startup, who'd spoken about the professional penalties that parents faced for taking advantage of the organization's advertised flexible hours:

> Doc_Spoc1701: *I asked for flex time so I could leave early on Fridays to pick up my daughter from daycare, since all the men were out on the golf course by 2 p.m., but HR told me that the trips were actually strategy meetings. Suddenly, I was on a performance improvement plan…*

Twenty-four hours a day around the globe, the network whispered truth to power, challenging and occasionally confirming whatever glossy headline was fueling the media cycle. It dragged back the curtain and showed the emperor naked. STEMinist Online was all the news that wasn't fit to print.

It was invaluable.

It was also a place to scream into the void, whether in frustration or in triumph.

Leaving the trending headlines for another day, Erin toggled through the site's menu to a section called "Accomplishments."

SnarkyQuark64: *Just got a paper accepted in the Journal of Supermassive Astronomy and Astrophysics. First time as a sole author! I didn't even have to pull the first-initial, last-name trick to get past the submission software, either. Can confirm: their review procedures are equitable. I'll document the process under Journal Reviews—Positive tomorrow.*

Instant validation from the forum's anonymous user handles unfurled beneath her post. She watched the comments and exclamation points bubble, hugging her elbows and grinning. The influx of positivity paused only when a lone user vented her frustration that she'd submitted a paper to *Reports on Progress in Mathematics* and had it denied by a peer review committee, while a resubmission of that same paper under her male supervisor's name resulted in immediate acceptance, but the forum moderators quickly moved the poster and her ire to the "Journal Reviews—Negative" page. The congratulations continued.

The minute hand on her watch did, too, ticking along toward six fifteen.

So she pocketed her phone. She ran a comb through her ponytail, refreshed the hints of iris and juniper perfume behind her ears, dusted loose powder across the freckles and persistent pinkness on her nose, switched out her sweater for a camel-toned suede motorcycle jacket over her jeans (no one who'd lived in the San Francisco Bay Area for more than a month went out during the evening without layers, even in May), then headed off along Crane Street toward Santa Cruz Avenue.

Martinis with Martina.

Examining a poster outside the French Film Club, Martina quickly pivoted to embrace Erin when she arrived. In the embroidered flats she wore, Martina's curly brunette bob barely reached Erin's chin. Her grip was fierce with excitement and weekly Pilates classes, however, and her voice turned heads at the bar when she urged them in through Left Bank's double doors, exulting, "Congratulations! I knew you could do it, you genius—two acceptances on the same day!—and now everyone else knows, too. We'll take a corner booth if you've got one, Rye."

Left Bank's maître d' nodded, unfazed by her enthusiasm. "Honey, for you? After you got those city assholes and their faux legal shit about a corporate transfer of real estate ownership out of here? Any table you want, any time," and he gestured toward a curved leather booth in the cozy, shadowed rear of the brasserie, where Norah Jones crooned from a speaker overhead and a waiter appeared to take their order for Chenin Blanc and truffle fries.

"*So.*" Martina leaned forward over the table, her smile bright. "Tell me everything. About your research paper. About your story. All of it."

Erin luxuriated in resurgent happiness for a few moments. "Well, my paper's been recommended for publication in September. And my short story will be in next month's issue of the sci-fi magazine. The editors apparently really enjoyed it—"

"Of course." Martina nodded her thanks to the waiter for the swift arrival of their fries and wine. "It's brilliant. Both are, actually."

"—and *Galactica*'s open to future submissions from me. Or from Aaron Forster."

"Would you ever publish your creative writing under your own name?"

"Someday, maybe. But for science fiction, being 'Aaron' is easier than being 'Erin'. That's true with the physics journals, too. Though hopefully that won't always be the case for either industry."

Martina bit a fry in half. "Having a secret identity must be fun."

"Not completely secret, since you and my family know about it."

"But to the public, you're someone else. You can write anything without real-world repercussions. Say anything."

"Such as?" She swirled her own fry in a fragrant puddle of truffle oil.

"I don't know. Maybe whatever you'd say—or do?—to Ethan Meyer if your colleagues weren't around."

"*Ugh*. Don't tempt me." She took a fortifying sip of Chenin Blanc. "Not only did he castigate me for sleeping through IT's two o'clock email, but the time slot I finally managed to get on the schedule is right before his, so we're bound to run into each other. At least you'll be on duty with me. You'll have to give a countdown so I can get out of the control room before he arrives."

Martina hummed in sympathy and crooked a finger for her to continue her rant.

After swallowing another mouthful of fries and alcohol, she talked her friend through her awful morning, culminating in Ethan's questions about her gravitational wave data sets. Well, *ostensibly* about her data sets, but she knew—

She went for another gulp of white wine. Her glass was empty. She blinked at it, then refocused.

"And then—Martina. *And then*. Someone in Maiman Auditorium started clapping. Someone *actually started clapping*, as if our argument were a... a professional baseball game with a score to count."

"Really?"

"It started off as a standard debate about research methodology. But he went nuclear with implications about fraudulent numbers in LIGO's database! I might've gotten in his face a bit after that, and then: *the clapping*. I don't know if he also heard it, but if he did..." She reached for a lonely truffle fry, swiping up a last trail of oil.

"I wouldn't have clapped."

"I know *you* wouldn't."

"No." Martina's lips tilted into mischief around the rim of her own glass. "I would've been too busy with my popcorn."

4

Data pings from the wall monitors.

Static pings along her spine.

Her breath hitches as the shocks corkscrew down through her stomach, hot and fast, a vicious and delicious helix. She grips an operator desk with white knuckles and angles her body for leverage, gasping again when she's slammed forward across the surface in retaliation, weight and heat intensifying behind her, over her, inside her—but then fresh static sparks up her back, and it's accompanied by fleece skimming her skin with contradictory softness.

"Easy, Monaghan."

Though when has she ever been easy?

So she bucks against the softness and that command in challenge, against the fingers digging into her hips while an open palm strokes between her shoulder blades, demanding a choice, a commitment to either pain or pleasure, because she won't wait for him to decide—

—and she can't, not with the spirals in her belly tightening, drawing taut now, her vision brightening with stars and breathless impact, blurring—

But the data pinging on the monitors isn't blurring.

It should be fading with the deafening rush of pleasure that's just an inch—a breath—a pulse away, except it isn't, it's sharpening instead, distracting, and—

Beep. Beep-beep. Beep. Beep-beep.

"Ah!"

She thrashed awake, tangled in damp sheets, a pillow crushed between her thighs, heart pounding, disoriented, *aching*. Her chirping phone read a quarter after eleven. Erin switched on her bedside lamp and silenced the alarm with trembling fingers, groaning at the light, at the coil of frustrated emptiness in her core.

What the hell?

She smacked the pillow back into shape while her hands and breathing steadied, while she reminded herself of her location. She couldn't have been napping for more than a few minutes, could she? But instead of resting itself for her research block in the control room, her brain had decided to do…

Whatever *that* had been.

An after-effect of the alcohol at Left Bank?

Possibly, but she'd gotten home by eight o'clock after only one glass of wine, since Martina was due at SVLAC for her brutal shift soon after their meetup, while she herself would be cycling to the campus not much later. She couldn't still be tipsy. She shuffled out of bed on legs that wobbled only a little, across the dark living room, and into the bathroom to splash some cold water on her face.

Easy, Monaghan.

The next splash verged on a slap. Only one person called her "Monaghan" in that mocking—though not usually so breathless—voice.

"*No.* Wake up," she told her reflection.

Maybe this was just the product of a disrupted sleep schedule. Weird dreams and hallucinations. A nightmare about fleece and data and—*him*.

Or could her conversation with Martina have triggered it?

She wondered, brushing her teeth until her gums stung, then pulling back her hair into a tight French braid. Even though she wouldn't be responsible for manually manipulating machinery during her lab hours, loose hair in the experimental halls was never a good idea. In the bathroom's unflattering light, her eyes were puffy, her skin blotched.

Not that it mattered.

She padded back to her bedroom, shook wrinkles from the jeans and graphic Sally Ride t-shirt that she'd set out earlier—the dress code in the halls was even more casual than SVLAC's usual mode—and got ready.

11:31 p.m.

Then, with a salute to her posters, which featured prominent women in science and literature, acknowledging that all of them had certainly braved worse hours (though probably not such bizarre dreams), she grabbed her steel-toed work boots and headed for the kitchen.

At Left Bank, they'd discussed Martina's latest daylight community activism efforts on behalf of Menlo Park's small businesses; decades-old family operations now came under threat from commercial developers and heavyweight lawyers in San Francisco with increasing frequency. They'd also discussed Ethan Meyer some more. She'd known that their vendetta was an open secret at SVLAC. Neither of them had tried to conceal it. Especially not yesterday. However, she'd assumed that Human Resources had intentionally left them to their own devices, believing that the excellent research that they each produced in consequence of their rivalry was the reason that neither had been burdened with mediation sessions.

Now, though?

As she shoved a few energy bars and a milky cold brew coffee into her backpack, a new thought surfaced: maybe… just maybe… their research results weren't the reason that Human Resources hadn't reprimanded them.

Clapping.

Popcorn.

Was their rivalry *entertaining* to their colleagues?

Why?

She shrugged into her jacket at the door with a frown and stomped into her boots, then shouldered her bicycle down the stairs in the flickering glow of Live Oak Avenue's street lamps. She pushed off from the pavement, tires wheezing against the cool roadway. Every stroke of her pedals repeated the question.

Why? Why? Why?

But it didn't matter. She'd dealt with worse than Ethan's hostility in graduate school: an assistant professor attempting to publish elements of her pre-LIGO work on the behavior of gravity as his own, or colleagues in her research group conveniently forgetting to list her among the authors on a collaborative paper that described comet orbits in the Oort cloud. As the sole woman, she'd seen the warning signs and hit back proactively and hard before any threats against her could solidify from risks to outcomes. She'd had to.

And now, a physicist at a National Lab, slated to manage her department while her supervisor was on leave—and a woman in STEM?

She *couldn't* back down.

Couldn't be easy.

Bumping over a scattering of gravel too fast, skidding through her turn, pivoting hard away from that thought, she swung onto Middle Avenue, sped along Olive Street, and up Oak Avenue to its intersection with Sand Hill Road. She wiped a film of sweat from her chin and unzipped her jacket at the stoplight, glad to glare at the red glow ahead, to focus on a simpler adversary than her own brain.

God, it was dark.

Maybe she'd include something in her next story about the crushing physical and psychological weight of getting up without light? Regardless of the hour, though, she couldn't afford to be late for her start in the West Experimental Hall. Ethan wouldn't grant her even a moment of grace if she ran over her allotted research block.

He never would've urged her to be *easy* about anything.

Just a hallucination.

The traffic light switched to green. She pedaled through the intersection, past SVLAC's security booth, and along Ring Road to the experimental halls. Her watch—an analog beauty from Wes with two timekeeping faces, so that she could always track the time where he was, no matter how far away—showed its California hands pointing to eleven fifty-five.

Locking her bicycle by the west door, she swiped her keycard over a scanner and made her way inside the cold, functional building to LIGO's makeshift control room, a vestibule outside the Matter in Extreme Conditions hutch. MEC housed machinery for experiments requiring the presence of—what else?—extreme conditions. The behavior of black holes was nothing if not extreme.

The hutch itself was out of order, however, its bright yellow laser enclosure waiting on a materials upgrade. With the X-ray laser powered down, the computers in MEC's control room were as viable as any others in the West Experimental Hall for running the software required to remotely manipulate the lab's interferometer.

"Morning." She greeted the area engineer, Dr. Viktor Hasselblad, and the hutch operator, Martina—cheerful despite the ungodly time and her indulgences at Left Bank. "Ready to eavesdrop on some neutron stars?"

"I never would've guessed how much overlap there'd be between my job and the work of a reporter for a Hollywood tabloid." Martina scooted back her chair from her operator computer and Erin entered her credentials into the running LIGO software, concentrating on her keystrokes, not on how she was bent over the desk. "*Stars, they're just like us*. Weird and incomprehensible."

"Currently, at least." She stepped away. "But if I could somehow solve the quantum gravity problem—"

"You'd graduate from beat reporter to CEO of the *New York Times*."

"That, or publish as many sole- and first-author papers as I wanted in *Nature Physics* or *Physical Review*."

"Right," with a wink.

Access Granted

Half a mile west near the lab's klystron gallery, an L-shaped Michelson interferometer hummed to life. Mirrors placed at the ends of its forty-kilometer arms and near the beam splitter in each arm prepared to reflect light, creating an interference pattern that LIGO's photodetector measured and converted into electrical signals for analysis. On Martina's activation, forty-watt lasers entered the instrument, bouncing between each arm's mirrors almost three hundred times before merging—*interfering*—with the laser beam from the parallel arm, the machinery exploiting the physical properties of light and space to detect the compression and dilation of gravitational waves rippling across the planet.

"The interference fringes are sharpening." Any lingering distraction neutralized, now; she couldn't help holding her breath while the lasers ping-ponged down LIGO's arms, while the beams split and reunited, any measurable interference between them signaling the existence of a gravitational wave—and depending on the signal, even its origin. Stars colliding? Black holes swallowing galaxies? Less than a mile away from the control room, instruments were tracking movements in the fusion of the three dimensions of space and the single dimension of time: space-time.

She'd once imagined that her work at SVLAC would advance the frontiers of science, enhancing humanity's understanding of and relationship to the universe. Her radical optimism had submerged occasionally beneath the petty annoyances of paperwork and office politics. But that irritation vanished whenever she stepped into an experimental control room, whenever she saw data appearing on the monitors, knowing that it meant weeks of cleaning and modeling, months of analysis—and newfound knowledge about the interactions and behaviors of distant astrophysical bodies. No matter how many times she ran a collection cycle, her breath still shortened in her chest. Goosebumps still rippled over her skin like LIGO's waves.

"…and now, we let LIGO eavesdrop, and just hope there's a star-studded argument." Sitting back from her controls, Martina yawned and raked her fingers through her hair. "Do you think Blue Bottle is serving coffee yet?"

"Probably not. But I brought a cold brew, if you want some."

"*God*, yes."

"No food or drink in my control rooms," the area engineer reminded them. Then he held out a travel mug in preparation for stepping away to check on his other hutches in the West Experimental Hall. "Just a splash."

Smiling, Erin divided her coffee three ways. She drank with the engineers in the camaraderie specific to very late nights and very early mornings, the bright lights and flashing monitors alienating them from any sense of time. There was a dissociative giddiness to those hours, potent with caffeine, sleep deprivation, and from her thrill at the march of data over the screens.

It wasn't really necessary for her to remain in the control room for LIGO to take its measurements. Lab policy only required that she enter her access credentials to activate the interferometer each time it ran a data collection cycle, her time slot was atrocious, she couldn't begin analyzing LIGO's electrical signals until they were exported to her computer, and if the instrument's lasers or mirrors went haywire, there wouldn't be much that she could do to physically fix them.

But how could she stay away?

After an hour or ten, she set down her empty bottle and went to study the monitors more closely. "Any variations between the laser beams are too small to see with the naked eye—but still. Just imagine the pressure on the fabric of space-time necessary to generate even the tiniest real data blip!"

"Enough pressure to make a diamond, definitely." Martina joined her at the screens. "Maybe that's a commercial angle for your research: no more blood diamonds. All you need is a black hole."

"Easier than growing them in a lab, obviously."

"Obviously. Your next grant application—or another sole-author paper?—will be dazzling. Data is a girl's best friend."

Erin rolled her eyes at Hasselblad as he returned to their control room after another round of checks. "If we're doing bad song lyrics: did you know that when the white dwarf star BPM 37093 cooled, its center crystallized into one of the largest diamonds in the universe? It's nicknamed 'Lucy'. Lucy in the sky with diamonds."

Martina burst into laughter. "I want to hate it. But I can't. Now you have to use that reference somewhere in a paper or an all-hands presentation."

"I heard that yesterday's all-hands was an interesting one," Hasselblad added. He fiddled with his phone, and the electronic opening bars from "Lucy in the Sky with Diamonds" began to play. "Everything's better with a Beatles reference, though. My kids love 'Yellow Submarine'. Drives me crazy sometimes, but I always end up singing along—"

Beep. Beep-beep. Beep. Beep-beep.

"Wait... *damn*, that's not a submarine." Erin hurriedly fished through her backpack. The alarm on her phone was pinging again, announcing lunchtime.

Noon.

Her hours were gone, both the sun and the turkeys were up outside, Ethan would be here soon for his lab stint, and stories about yesterday's meeting had clearly circulated through SVLAC.

Easy, Monaghan...

"*Damn!*"

Ethan pulled his hatchback off Ring Road and parked in a paved lot outside the experimental buildings. Edging between a shipping container and a forklift, he badged into the West Experimental Hall, opening the door wide enough to bump against a bicycle stationed by the entry.

Erin Monaghan's wheels.

His watch read a full minute after twelve o'clock. He'd caught her infringing on his hours and violating the lab calendar. Exasperation mingled with satisfaction as he made his way through the hall's vestibule, then into the central corridor with its branching arteries of control rooms and hutches. He scanned himself past the MEC door—and yes, Erin was there inside, bundling a jacket into her backpack, a wall of monitors still displaying the interference fringes from her latest LIGO cycle beneath wreaths of bundled cables. The area engineer was consulting a research schedule on a tablet and pulling up a list of requirements for the room's next scientist: him. Dr. Martina Perez was inputting laser specifications into her controls under her colleague's terse direction.

A tinny Beatles song played from someone's phone.

"You said you'd warn me…" Erin mumbled something quick and heated under her breath to Perez, dragging a braid out from under the strap of her backpack.

He let the door slam shut behind him.

She startled at the noise, and grimaced. He folded his arms over his vest, static snapping from a few stray Bunsen hairs; a flush stained her cheeks, overbearing the chill of her frown to creep down her neck and under the collar of her graphic t-shirt. But then she adjusted her glasses with a stiff, defiant motion and raised her chin. Fluorescent illumination flared off her lenses while John Lennon crooned about kaleidoscope eyes.

He crossed his arms tighter.

Because who the hell had scored such a slow tempo for the song? It was like listening to molasses, to the passage of light-years between Maiman Auditorium's *clap, clap, clap…*

Data fraud.

When he swallowed with a dry mouth, his ears gave a painful *pop* of punctuation.

Mercifully, Erin averted her gaze to zip her bag.

"You're over your time, Monaghan." Glad that his voice didn't crack, even more grateful to redirect his own attention, he tapped his watch. "Not—not that I'm surprised, though. You can barely manage the timelines for journal submissions. Why would you be punctual in a control room? Or anywhere else, since—"

But she didn't cut him off with the interjections he'd expected, and his caustic, aborted commentary died away with the Beatles' tune, the engineers staring at him, Erin staring at the floor now—*again*—with her lips pursed until she finally said, stiff and polite, "Thank you for your assistance, Drs. Hasselblad and Perez. I'll see you next Tuesday. When will LIGO's data exports be ready?"

"They need to synchronize with the Washington and Louisiana databases, so forty-eight hours, give or take."

"That's fine. I apologize for running over time."

She wasn't apologizing to him.

But: "For someone who studies space-time, your own sense of—"

He was repeating himself. He knew it. He couldn't stop.

And still, she didn't look at him. She was rude, she was late, and she was—*leaving*.

When she strode back out into the hall, however, her backpack knocked hard into his ribs. Then she bit out two brief words of acknowledgment. "Dr. Meyer."

Dr. Chase Meyer Jr.: medical doctor, BMW driver, engaged.

Dr. Ethan Meyer: none of the above, and every family dinner or call reminded him of that, but here at SVLAC, he was someone with value, someone with—

—no answer today for her brusque words and backpack.

The door to the control room clicked shut behind her, cutting off any other retort to her dig that he might've made—when had she ever called him *Dr. Meyer*? only his surname—and jolting his focus back to the engineers watching him over their computers and instrument panels. His fingers curled into his palms under their continued scrutiny. Dr. Hasselblad had the grace to return to his scheduling tablet, but Perez raised an eyebrow.

"Dr. Meyer, are you all right?"

"I…" Maybe Erin's backpack had hit him harder than he'd thought. Rocking forward off the heels of his metal-capped boots, he reminded himself to breathe. "I'm fine. Are the lasers ready?"

"Almost." Perez turned back to her controls. "I need to confirm the position of the holometer's optical instruments. There was an earthquake with a one point six magnitude on the San Andreas Fault over the weekend, and since the machinery isn't in an isolation chamber like the particle accelerator and LIGO, its mirrors might have shifted. I'm checking the instrument readings."

While a micro-scale earthquake would've registered on Erin's protected interferometer as noise to scrub from her data, it wouldn't have delayed her collection cycles, not like he was delayed now. If Dr. Kramer agreed, maybe some of the Eischer-Langhoff funding could be used to build a protective housing for their machinery, extending its tunnels while also upgrading the prototype from its off-the-shelf parts and its exposed location on a disused loading dock behind the lab's industrial maintenance buildings. He wouldn't have to deal with this wait time again.

"The half-reflective mirror shifted by eight degrees in the quake. I've remotely adjusted it back. Are you ready for the laser to activate, or do you want to check my positioning?"

He did.

It wasn't that he didn't trust Martina Perez's expertise. But trust had no place in science. So he stayed on location in the control room to oversee the holometer's cycles, double-checking settings or acceptable margins of error (*none*), investigating potential problems with the instrument prior to them reaching Dr. Kramer's desk, and ideally resolving them before his supervisor knew they'd occurred. Dr. Kramer relied on Ethan to generate accurate data, which he employed in formulating new quantum hypotheses; the only way to ensure that accuracy was to monitor the holometer and its readings live.

Ethan himself had begun to question the basic assumption of Einsteinian physics—that space was continuous and infinitely divisible—in graduate school. What if space was actually microscopically chunky? If it was, how could those chunks be measured? A pixel was the smallest unit of image on any modern device, while a photon was the smallest light unit. Why couldn't there be an equivalently tiny unit of distance?

A quantum of space.

The idea was bizarre at first glance, plausibly the product of too much late-night philosophizing over cheap boxed wine in a dorm. But Dr. Kramer concurred that it had merit. Besides, if light was both a unit and a wave, why shouldn't space be similar? If he could measure space at its base unit, if he could prove Dr. Kramer's hypothesis about the existence of quantum units correct in experimental conditions—

"Activating the laser," Perez said.

He approached the control room monitors. At the end of long lengths of cable that stretched from the experimental halls to the machinery's physical location, focused light entered his device. The holometer split the laser, which bounced along its tunnels between mirrors and registered their precise locations, tracking any changes in their placement that resulted from the wanderings of space. Millions of readings per second leaped onto the screens.

If space could be broken into individual units, the data would show a constant, random, and microscopic variation in the mirrors' positions. When the two laser beams recombined after bouncing off the incrementally moving reflectors, they would be out of sync. Dr. Kramer hypothesized that a replicable, standardized amount of asynchrony would reveal the scale of a quantum unit—up to a million times smaller than a hydrogen atom…

Behind him, the engineers conferred in low voices about beam quality, bounce frequency, diamonds, and—*popcorn?*

"…wasn't as salty as usual."

"I wonder if she…"

He ignored the itch of hair rising up his neck and the arrival of the next shift's area engineer and operator. The chatter and staff changes didn't matter. He edged around a cluster of cables to the farthest monitor. An invisible hand seemed to trace out glowing lines and numbers on the screen, the patterns abstract, jagged, and almost too complex for a human eye to recognize as art.

His breathing steadied. He watched the data flicker, and scroll, and scroll, and scroll. It was beautiful.

5

Monday. Tuesday. Wednesday. Sunday.

One week, then another.

The days passed in a whirl of hours spent revising his grant application, working with Dr. Kramer to showcase the Quantum group's research for the Department of Energy during the Secretary's visit, cleaning and analyzing the data from his lab time—and when he carved out a minute, centering himself through a round of sudoku or a sketch.

Despite his exhaustion, he was very careful with his ink. His hands remained clean, with no pigment stains to explain to his supervisor.

He was equally careful to avoid the twice-weekly calls from his parents.

Every Wednesday evening, his phone shrilled to rouse Bunsen from a nap and send the retriever racing to the entryway, barking at a nonexistent doorbell. It rang again on Sundays whenever he failed to make an appearance at the Meyers' family meal—a requirement for model families.

Fortunately, his parents rarely left messages.

He called them back, but always when he could be certain of his father and Chase being at the hospital, or when his mother would be leading tours through one of the East Bay Garden Society's estates.

You've reached Dr. Chase Meyer Sr. Leave a message.

You've reached Dr. Chase Meyer Jr. Leave a message.

Hello, you've reached Karen Meyer's voicemail. If you're inquiring about the East Bay Garden Society's June fundraiser, please leave a message and I'll return your call shortly. If you're inquiring about scheduling a tour, please call the society's office at—

On other nights, however, his condo was silent and peaceful. Only the occasional muffled thump of a door closing in an adjacent unit or the sough of water in the pipes disturbed him. He knew his neighbors' schedules by their doors and their noisy plumbing; the tenants to his right were still watering the landscaped portion of their patio, despite the drought. They likely knew his schedule in the same way. But that was the extent of their acquaintance. Intimate and distant. His mother would've made herself known to every household in the Farm Hill Boulevard complex within a few days, but he'd lived here ever since he'd graduated from Berkeley and moved across the bay to the Peninsula, and he couldn't remember the name of even one neighbor. That was preferable for privacy in such close quarters. His, and theirs.

But Erin Monaghan's new, persistent silence was *not* peaceful. Twelve o'clock on Tuesdays came without the inconvenience of waiting for her to complete a data collection cycle or running into her as she left the research building. He sometimes spotted her bicycle parked at the door to the West Experimental Hall—locked up with a complicated combination cable, but ripe for switching its brake configurations, if he'd had the tools—but she was never near the control room when he arrived.

No coffee rings on the operator desks.

No Beatles songs.

Where was she?

What was she playing at?

Scheming for the Secretary of Energy's visit, making strides on the Eischer-Langhoff application, solidifying her department takeover, bolting down her lunch in the cafeteria—when she wasn't eating a sandwich at her desk, glasses smudged from impatient fingers pushing the frames back up her nose, shoulders hunched in focus toward her monitor—before rushing back to Modern Physics on a scooter.

On Thursday, Ethan got to the parking rack first. There was one scooter left.

Erin came striding out the door from the Science and Public Support building, aiming directly for it. He took hold of its handlebars at her approach. A familiar flush rose across her cheeks as she registered his presence. She caught her breath and hesitated for a moment, scanning the pavement around them—empty of turkeys, rattlesnakes, and alternative scooters—but then continued on in the direction of Ethan and the racks, hands fisted, scowling.

His stomach flipped in a victorious somersault. "Going somewhere in a hurry, Monaghan?"

"Yes." Her teeth snapped.

"You *were*. It seems like I got the last scooter."

"Good for you."

"Did you want it?"

"Obviously."

He leaned back against the rack, fiddling with the handlebars. "So, we have a problem."

"Really." Another flash of her teeth. Not a question. Then, unexpectedly, disconcertingly, she smiled. "No. *You* have a problem—"

—and she lunged forward to wrench the scooter out of his grip. His stomach flipped again, the loss of its ballast tilting him off the rack. Erin's smile tilted, too. She sneered at his empty hands while she pivoted her purloined handlebars toward Ring Road, planting one sneaker on the scooter's running board.

"Enjoy your walk back to Modern Physics."

Somehow, he got a foot in front of her wheel. "You can't just—"

"Don't tell me what I can or can't do!"

She pushed off against the pavement and left him by the racks with a rubber skid mark across the top of his shoe. She hadn't eased back on her acceleration or swerved to avoid him—had he expected her to?—and he'd barely avoided a crushed ankle by tripping out of her way. Cursing under his breath, he watched her glide down the road. Only when she passed the Blue Bottle coffee stand and swung out of sight did he bend to probe his toes.

The damage to his sneaker was no worse than if Bunsen had chewed on it.

He walked back to the Modern Physics building and deflated Erin's bicycle tires.

That evening, he gave the shoe to Bunsen.

At least the dog didn't get sick from his gift or from anything in Stulsaft Park during their post-work run. He was grateful for the sake of the golden retriever's gut, for the security deposit on his condo, and for his own schedule. Already stretching into dinnertime—a convenient excuse to miss the Meyers' Sunday gatherings—his workday crept later over the next two weeks, first to ten o'clock, then eleven, before edging past midnight. But he wouldn't have slept, anyhow. Not until both his grant and his funding pitch to the Secretary of Energy were perfect.

Bunsen sprawled across his feet and Ted Chiang's collection of science fiction short stories were good company in the silence. Whenever Tomasz Szymanski's icon went live on SVLAC's instant messaging system between eleven o'clock at night and three o'clock in the morning, however, he frequently found himself with questions about his colleague's LED research. They were tangential to his own quantum measurement work at best, but still:

> **Dr. Ethan Meyer**
> Could LED infrared radiation potentially illuminate space and matter at micro-scales, if enough energy was applied?
>
> **Dr. Tomasz Szymanski**
> You are working at this time?

It was almost two thirty. Bunsen had given up hope of coercing Ethan into the bedroom, but had managed to get him from his desk to the couch and into a pair of flannel pajama pants. The dog twitched in his sleep on the cushions now, kicking Ethan in the kidneys.

> **Dr. Ethan Meyer**
> You're working, too.
>
> **Dr. Tomasz Szymanski**
> Yes. But it is the middle of the morning in Poland.

Maybe Szymanski was talking with his family abroad while he cleaned his data. Maybe that was why he never seemed to mind graveyard shifts at the lab. Maybe it was easier to have parents and siblings halfway around the world, separated by a nine-hour time difference? His fingers hovered over his keyboard in a question, but then his colleague continued.

> **Dr. Tomasz Szymanski**
> No. Electroluminescence would not provide the brightness necessary for your work, and not for the duration or energy levels that you require. The life of an LED is short at high currents and temperatures. It is not practical for your voltaic needs.

That's what their late-night messages were: practical and short.

If the brevity of Szymanski's words and Ethan's similarly terse responses were occasionally grating—well, he was just low on sleep. Any communication would've irritated him, even if he initiated it. Which he usually did.

But he didn't ask Szymanski about his family in Central Europe, or if he had a spouse or children. He didn't ask if Szymanski had read Ted Chiang's *Exhalation* collection. He said nothing about Bunsen's recent near-miss with a skunk in Stulsaft Park, either. Nothing personal.

Why introduce change to a stable system?

Several weeks later, he also said nothing when he received a singleton's save-the-date for Chase Meyer Jr.'s wedding to Isabel Wright.

They made an attractive pair in their engagement picture, Chase handsome, broad, and smiling with a white grin even wider than his shoulders, Isabel all angles and icy blonde luminosity. The font and graphics on the card reflected Karen Meyer's taste.

A frequent patron of Carmel's art scene and a contributor to the de Young Museum's annual *Bouquets to Art* installation, Ethan's mother had an eye for design, but still had never taken any interest in his early forays into drawing; their refrigerator had been decorated with curated vacation magnets and posed family photographs, not the stick figures and brightly colored finger-paintings that other parents seemed to prize. His admiration for her undeniably elegant work on Chase's save-the-date card was also undeniably bitter.

He tacked up the notice in his kitchen beside an appointment reminder from his dentist. At least he'd be numb for the root canal.

Friday brought a more welcome piece of mail. A copy of *Galactica Magazine* was waiting for him when he returned to Redwood City after another afternoon spent on the Eischer-Langhoff application in his office. Having dropped his bag, fleece, and shoes at the door, prodded his ancient air conditioner to life, and greeted Bunsen, he unfurled the issue. Behind the magazine's glossy cover art of a human and an alien figure grasping hands and tentacles while admiring a firework display of planets and bolides in the night sky, his piece was in print.

He shuffled into the living room while thumbing through *Galactica*'s pages. Art… poems… a wall of short story text… and then, there it was: an explosion of ink, more sound than image in its visceral vibrancy. He could hear it in the quiet: "Hunger."

He dropped down onto his Craigslist couch, smiling, and appraised his own abstract, geometric ink rendering of a black hole swallowing a sun. The strokes of his pen were broad at the margins and narrowed toward the center of a ravenous darkness, creating an optical illusion of gravity so that the viewer plummeted over the black hole's event horizon with the star. It was unsettling and beautiful.

He, Ethan Meyer, had made this. He tore out his sheet and tacked it over Chase's card on the refrigerator.

Then he leafed back to the beginning of the magazine, making his way through the other artwork—hypothetical blueprints of an Eridian spacecraft from Andy Weir's *Project Hail Mary*, a calligraphic rendering of Neil Armstrong's bungled quote on the moon—and then on to the poetry and short stories, nodding his appreciation for the better narratives, until:

Pandora Rising, by Aaron Forster

> *First came wonder.*
> *How could it be otherwise?*
> *Tumbling through a sea of stars, space and time passing as currents, unmoored and breathless, weightless, they watched while sky became earth and earth became sky. The way was vast and uncertain, but they were neither afraid nor lonely aboard the* Pandora Rising *on her final voyage, for they had the curiosity of all scientists, and around them were marvels beyond imagination: dwarf stars and meteors, the scattered fragments of stardust from the primordial Nothing and All.*
> *On Earth-That-Was, they had often looked up and pondered:*
> *When I raise my eyes from this bleak wasteland, when I seek answers from the emptiness above, who sees me in my supplication? Who hears my call?*
> *They had this question to satisfy, and they had each other.*
> *Their trajectory took them beyond the glimmering sprawl of the Milky Way, to the very edge of Alpha Centauri's binary stars,*

past nameless astral supergiants burning brighter even than their Sun-That-Was, and onward still. Their years stretched long. The wonders of the universe stretched so much farther.

He stopped nodding. He stopped breathing.

He joined the crew of the *Pandora Rising*, following the ship past expanding galaxies and to the rippling edge of lightless space where its instruments swung into madness. He shadowed the astronauts through their approach to a black hole, and he waited with them when they could do nothing but observe the coming of their own end. The author sucked him deeply into the fears and fate of these hopeful, desperate people with a lyrical brutality and a gravity so fierce that he couldn't look up from the text.

But the last page of the story was missing.

At its climactic moment, he flipped forward—but not to the end of "Pandora Rising." The next page in *Galactica Magazine* was an inane poetic tribute to the astronauts who'd died in the Space Shuttle Challenger disaster.

Where was the rest of the story? He turned to the table of contents. "Pandora Rising" spanned five pages across the magazine's centerfold, and should have adjoined his own piece in the print layout—

—but he'd already extracted "Hunger" from the issue.

He raced to the kitchen, ripped his drawing off its magnet on the refrigerator, and: *yes*. The missing page from "Pandora Rising" was here, right here, paired beside his art.

He began to read again.

A thick block of text shone from Erin's monitor: reams of verified data, justification, hope, journal citations (*publication pending:*

September), and a request for four million research dollars from the Eischer-Langhoff Grant in Physics. She'd made her case for each cent and done all she could to enliven the logic of her numerical arguments, outlining the benefits that advancing the field's knowledge of black hole behavior would provide to humanity—if only SVLAC's LIGO branch ran for more than twelve hours per week, and wasn't routinely missing astrophysical events in the lab's quest to save on energy costs.

More accurate depictions of event horizons in science fiction, for one.

Implications for the future of space travel, for another.

The dry, terse application was as compelling as it could be. It might be enough… and her watch read five o'clock on Friday afternoon.

Click, and the grant was submitted.

Home run—hopefully.

She stretched backward away from her computer, rolling the kinks from her neck, anticipating the freedom of her weekend. Maybe she'd finish Weir's *Project Hail Mary*, then pick up N.K. Jemisin's *The Broken Earth* trilogy from Kepler's Books. She'd probably get in some sudoku practice, she reasoned, as she hopped a loose cable in the hall, waved goodbye to the interns waiting for their shuttle in the parking lot, and retrieved her bicycle. Its tires were at a normal pressure, taut in the heat and sealed without punctures; both her portable pump and a canister of repair slime remained in her backpack. She pedaled past a rack of abandoned scooters outside the Science and Public Support building and back to Menlo Park, thinking.

Maybe she'd start brainstorming her next short story. Her copy of *Galactica Magazine* was due any day, and with

"Pandora Rising" finally joining the ylem of the universe, it was time. She'd been considering something about circadian rhythms and astronaut ice cream, hadn't she? No more shoehorning a narrative into her data. Just language and imagination.

Except that lately, Ethan Meyer had given her writer's block.

Some sort of block, anyhow.

Newly aware of her colleagues' stares whenever they jostled for lab time, for SVLAC's scooters, or for the last serving of cafeteria curry, she'd done her best to avoid him in the office and in the experimental halls over the past few weeks. When she couldn't help running into him publicly, however, she kept her elbows away from his stupid vest and bit back her usual retorts about data methodologies. She wouldn't risk being labeled by her coworkers as *emotional* or *reactive*, as unable to handle the stresses of her field. These were gendered labels, ones that she'd been dodging for years. Very sticky labels.

Almost as sticky as the neural residue of... *that*... dream.

So she kept her distance to keep her sanity, too.

Damn him.

At least she found *Galactica Magazine* in her mailbox that evening. Tucking it under her arm, she hefted her bicycle up the apartment stairs. Her phone vibrated while she dropped her sneakers on the mat.

> **Wes**
> I've lost track of the days out here on the Quest V. But something tells me it's a special one...

She tapped into the Monaghan chat, which was pinging enthusiastically.

Mom

Congratulations, sweetheart!

Erin

Thanks, Mom.

Adrian

All words present and accounted for?

Erin

I just got home and grabbed the magazine. And I want to see Wes's latest marine iguana photos and hear about your infrastructure deal in Austin—but right now, I'm going to read my story.

Then, leaving her family to Galápagos wildlife and Texas negotiations, she swapped her plain gray sweater and jeans for loungewear—glad to wiggle out of her bra, since its underwire had sprung loose earlier in the week and was jabbing her ribs—and settled down on the couch under a fan. She smoothed the fluttering pages of her magazine. Her hands were suddenly shaky. She'd read "Pandora Rising" many, many times, but that had always been in the privacy of her room, within the privacy of her own head.

Now, though?

Now, other people would read her fable about a skeleton crew of astronauts as they took their final voyage away from a ravaged Earth. When the *Pandora Rising*'s propulsion mechanisms failed and she fell past the event horizon of a black hole—accurately described as a lightless, featureless space, rather than Star Trek's visible, energetic implosion—her team despaired. However, upon asking themselves what it was that they'd leave behind in death, they discovered that their losses weren't so terrible. They'd already given up their Earth-That-Was, made desolate by a changing climate and human destruction. They'd just intended to drift to the edges of their understanding and consciousness… though they'd hoped for one last miracle in the expanse, of course.

They'd found that miracle in their black hole.

It wasn't the miracle of salvation, but of curiosity in the face of the unknown. Their fall was a careening dance toward mystery, toward something that, out of all humanity, only they would experience. They found their peace and their excitement even while they vanished, because without the dull downward drag of earthly gravity, the *Pandora Rising* wasn't falling into the black hole at all. She could just as easily be ascending toward it; if gravity was still a law of mutual attraction in space, it was also free from any planet's upward or downward binary. They fell, or they rose, and they would see what no other eyes had seen. They would bear witness to each other's awe.

> *There is tremendous power in a black hole, in darkness and in fear.*
> *But there is no match for the power of human curiosity.*
> *Their wonder was the last thing to leave them.*

The words surged to meet her, thrilling and somehow new again, and when she turned over the last page, smiling and breathless with a wonder of her own—

A pen and ink illustration of a black hole.

Immediate, irresistible—it drew and held her focus. The geometric darkness had ensnared a sun, sucking it close to swallow the light, and its pull compelled her forward, too, tilting her into its nothingness, daring her to brave the secrets beyond its event horizon. The lines of the piece were angular. The demarcation between light and shadow was so stark as to be almost painful. The compulsion to let herself be devoured by this mesmerizing menace was overpowering.

"Hunger."

It wasn't an illustration for "Pandora Rising." But it might as well have been. And though the piece had no relationship to her research paper on the consumption of stars by black holes, *still...*

So she stared, tracing the sun's final orbit until she fetched up against a miniscule word in the bottom right corner of the page, half-hidden under the staples in *Galactica*'s spine.

Bannister.

The artist.

She flipped to the contributor credits at the end of the magazine.

Bannister: "Hunger" (medium—pen and ink). Contact at www.bannisterart.com.

Nothing else.

Her listing as Aaron Forster was similarly brief.

Maybe Bannister was a pseudonym, too?

Fumbling for her phone and ignoring the flood of Monaghan messages continuing to chirp in the chat, she located Bannister's website. It was as spartan as the artist's credit, with just two screens: abstract prints for sale and a contact page. No headshot, no full name. But it listed a phone number and an email address for purchase inquiries.

Erin watched her hands move.

She muted the Monaghan thread.

She tapped Bannister's number into a new message.

> **Erin**
> Hi, I saw your illustration in Galactica Magazine. (I have a short story published in the same issue: Pandora Rising.) You've captured in a single visual what I've spent months trying to articulate with words. It's extraordinary. I'm honored to share page space with Hunger.

Her thumb was steady now and didn't hesitate to press *Send*.

Ping.

Before she could second-guess the wisdom of messaging a random person through a number she'd found on the internet, a typing notification bubbled up on her screen.

> **Bannister**
> A picture is worth a thousand words. But Pandora Rising could inspire a thousand pictures.

The artist had read and liked her story! And that would've been enough to please her, so much more than enough—but then another ellipsis appeared under their message.

> **Bannister**
> Hi Aaron, it's good to meet you.

6

A notification appeared at the top of Ethan's thread with the unknown number.

Aaron Forster (Maybe)—Create New Contact?

He ignored the prompt for the moment and opened a search tab.

A query for the *Galactica* writer's name in JSTOR and a few other digital libraries returned no academic papers or books attributed to Aaron Forster. Public accounts on social media sites were uninformative. No useful results populated from a more general web scan. Yes, an Aaron Forester had fought in World War II, but the odds of that centenarian and the author of "Pandora Rising" being the same person were slim. No criminal records were listed for the name, either. In fact, the only result anywhere online for Aaron Forster came from *Galactica Magazine*'s June contributor credits.

Maybe Forster was just private with his digital life.

Or maybe he also wrote under a pseudonym?

Ethan had chosen "Bannister" during a required undergraduate humanities course at Berkeley: History of American Art, 1700–1900. The pastoral livestock scenes weren't to his taste. He'd preferred the psychological work of later artists like Sigmund Abeles and the sharp, monochromatic photographs of Ansel

Adams. But the class had introduced him to Edward Mitchell Bannister, an oil painter of the American Barbizon school who shared his E.M. initials.

Bannister had seemed a convenient choice for an alias, obtuse enough for anonymity and also self-referential…

Create New Contact?

Yes.

Forster's number began with a 650, he noticed now. It was an area code specific to the San Mateo and Santa Clara counties, divisions along the peninsula that ran south from San Francisco to the urban sprawl of San Jose. Maybe Forster was based in the Bay Area, or had attended college here? However, given how frequently people moved in and out of Silicon Valley, a 650 code was no guarantee that the writer still lived in the region.

Not that it mattered—Aaron Forster was a stranger.

But his message thread was also the only conversation not related to SVLAC or from the Meyer family on Ethan's phone, and it was past eleven o'clock on a Friday. Even if Redwood City's pedestrian street of restaurants and movie theaters in the town center was still active, its industrial sector had powered down for the night. His neighbors were quiet, doors closed and water off. Bunsen was snoring across his feet in front of the couch, drooling on his socks and twitching with dreams of frisbees. He had to admit that he'd reached his limit for working on the Eischer-Langhoff application, too. He'd never been a great writer, but he'd articulated his funding requirements coherently and his data was perfect. An exhale and a click sent his twice-revised draft to Dr. Kramer for review.

He closed his computer and picked up his phone again.

A typing notification had appeared on the screen.

Wherever and whoever Aaron Forster was, he was awake and writing to Bannister about his art—and not just to make a print order from his website, either. Not that he'd had many. Several earlier magazines had rejected his work, praising his technical skills while claiming that his visuals made viewers uncomfortable. Only *Galactica* had been niche or desperate enough to publish "Hunger." But this exchange wasn't a transaction, or a rejection, or a last resort acceptance. Forster had felt so strongly—strongly, and positively—about "Hunger" that he'd reached out to Ethan directly. Forster, the mastermind behind "Pandora Rising," who wrote both imaginatively and surprisingly accurately about astrophysics.

He'd read enough science fiction to know when a writer was bullshitting through explanations about time travel or quantum tunneling. Most did. He couldn't even blame them for web-searching their way to plausible expertise. Physics was beautifully, brutally difficult.

Forster, though?

Forster knew his subject matter well enough to write simply. He understood his science—and Ethan's art.

Ping.

Forster
Have you read any Ted Chiang? Your art reminds me of how he dissects mind and matter in Exhalation. Also, the symmetry from Story of Your Life.

Chiang's story collection was bookmarked on his nightstand.

Of course, Forster read science fiction. That he'd name-dropped Ted Chiang wasn't odd either, since Chiang was a prominent writer in the genre, and had won multiple Nebula, Hugo, and Locus Awards. His novella *Arrival* had even inspired a major Hollywood film. So the coincidence of Forster mentioning Chiang just when Ethan was reading *Exhalation: Stories* was easily explained by extant data.

But logic couldn't quell the excitement simmering in his stomach.

> **Ethan**
> Yes. I'm reading his 2019 collection.

Edging his feet out from under Bunsen's jowls, he retrieved Chiang's book, thumbing past its minimalist black cover while another typing notification popped onto his screen.

> **Forster**
> That collection has my favorite of his stories.
> Where are you in the lineup?

He checked his bookmark.

> **Ethan**
> I just finished What's Expected of Us.

> **Forster**
> The one with the Predictor device?

> **Ethan**
> Yes. Where humanity learns that free will is a myth.

Forster

That was bleak. I liked The Truth of Fact, the Truth of Feeling much better.

Pages flicked under his fingers. He skipped past "The Lifecycle of Software Objects" and "Dacey's Patent Automatic Nanny," and another message from the writer appeared as he repositioned his bookmark to stake out the story. He usually read articles and book series in order, building sequential timelines of logic for a reveal of the authors' data conclusions or puzzle box answers. There was a neatness to understanding and then executing one complete task before moving ahead to the next.

But tonight?

Forster

Let me know how you like it.

Erin

Let me know how you like it.

Propped against her headboard, pillows squashed behind her back, her bare feet tucked under the blankets—even in June, California's heat dissipated after sunset when Karl the San Francisco fog drifted down the Peninsula—and with *Galactica Magazine* spread across her lap, Ted Chiang's dog-eared short story collection flopped open to "The Truth of Fact, the Truth of Feeling," Erin watched for Bannister's response. But as the seconds passed without a notification from the artist on her screen, the nervous jigging of her legs brought her knees up to her chest.

She hadn't politely asked Bannister if they'd share their thoughts with her.

She'd demanded it.

She'd demanded that the artist continue a late-night conversation with a stranger—demanded it of a person whose work spoke to her with wondrous ferocity. They were likely someone who had hundreds of other rapt fans eager for their notice, as well, because who could look at their work and not feel that world-tilting compulsion toward awe?

On a Friday, too.

Maybe Bannister was at a gallery show tonight. Somewhere with flashing cameras, chilled champagne, and canapes. An after-hours event for connoisseurs at Soho Mod Art? Adrian had taken her during a visit to Manhattan. He'd talked about solar cooling for the gallery's skylights with the proprietor while she'd wandered along the walls, staring for too long at a white canvas and trying to determine whether it was patching a hole in the structural plaster, or whether it was supposed to be conceptual art in its own right. She had no eye for modern design...

Whether Bannister was at a gallery show or working in a studio, however, she was probably an interruption to their night. Biting her lip, she reached for her phone to turn it over, hiding the screen from her temptation to watch it for the scroll of a typing ellipsis, and—

Ping.

Bannister
(New Photo Message)

Fortitude went out the window.

She clicked into the image: the first page from "The Truth of Fact, the Truth of Feeling." Chiang's familiar collection splayed open around a bookmark beside a utilitarian digital clock and a glass of water on a nightstand. A taut gray bedspread and a single pillow were just visible in the background.

Digital clock.
No lipstick on the glass.
Gray bedding.
One pillow.
A book of science fiction stories.

The data—fallible, but statistically likely—suggested that Bannister was a man.

Another message chirped onto her screen. Her repeated rush to read it was embarrassingly Pavlovian.

Bannister
I will.

She resisted the urge to respond. The artist—*he*—would continue their conversation if he wanted to. Which would hopefully be the instant that he'd finished "The Truth of Fact, the Truth of Feeling." It shouldn't be too long, if he started the story now. He clearly wasn't in a painter's studio or at a New York gallery show, so maybe he would.

His clock had read 11:25 p.m. He was on Pacific time.

West Coast time.

Not that it mattered.

She toggled back to the Monaghan chat. The thread had continued to fill without her, despite the hour; her childhood dinners and road trips had always been noisy, and distance and adulthood hadn't dampened the Monaghans' ability to argue, laugh, and participate in ten conversations at once. Now she scrolled up to track the subject of their current discussion. Her family was reviewing Wes's extensive Galápagos photo roll: lumbering tortoises, marine iguanas, blue-footed boobies perched on rocks crusted with algae and salt spray, short-eared owls, and Darwin's famous finches.

She sometimes scared away urban racoons from the garbage cans outside her apartment.

> **Wes**
> I got this shot of a penguin colony off Fernandina Island earlier today.
>
> **Adrian**
> How the hell do penguins survive living in the tropics? Aren't the Galápagos Islands humid?
>
> **Wes**
> I'd be suffering if I didn't spend most of my time in the water, yeah. But the Humboldt and Cromwell sea currents keep things cooler for them offshore.
>
> **Mom**
> Are you wearing enough sunscreen?
>
> **Adrian**
> Look at his nose in that glamor shot he took of himself with the tortoise. He's obviously not.

Wes's typing notification flickered while he equally obviously tried to avert their mother's tirade on the importance of sun protection.

Erin jumped into the fray.

Erin
Glad to see that someone else is going to get the aloe vera talk. I still have grease behind my ears from that trip we took to see the University of Miami's marine biology program when Wes was choosing colleges.

Wes
Not helping, Frizzy!

She was, actually; Lori switched the topic back to her writing.

Mom
Have you read your story in the magazine yet, sweetheart?

Erin
Yes! Now I want to publish another one. But first, I need to finalize a concept… and write it.

Dad
What about trains in space?

Mom
Like that Magic School Bus episode where Ms. Frizzle and the class get lost in zero gravity, but with trains?

Dad
It could work.

Wes
Especially since, for the Halloween that Adrian and I were Ian Malcolm and Alan Grant from Jurassic Park, Mom made you a Frizzle costume.

Adrian
You refused to take it off afterward. You wore it to school for—what? Two weeks?

Mom
You looked adorable.

Erin
Better Ms. Frizzle than some pseudo-scientists participating in an ecological disaster! You'd both better hope that those pictures never come to light.

Adrian
Is that a threat?

Erin
I don't know. Is it?

Dad
But you couldn't use Ms. Frizzle in the story, kiddo. Copyright issues.

Mom
Anyway, we're immensely proud of you.

Wes
Will you be insufferable when you win a Nobel Prize?

Erin
Given how you wouldn't stop squawking about your National Geographic win last year? Absolutely.

She snickered as both of her brothers' responding ellipses zipped under her message. She smiled at her family's excitement for her success, too. It was gratifying. Really. But she doubted whether her parents and brothers had been able to read "Pandora Rising" yet—not when *Galactica* promoted itself as trendy in the way that polaroids had become: offline and proud of it, with no digital readership available and print copies provided only with a subscription. She'd appreciated that when she'd submitted her interstellar tale, certain that the line between her professional scientific life and her personal creative one would remain intact. Who could possibly link Dr. Erin Monaghan, sole author of "Investigating the Impact of Tidal Disruption Events on the Axis Rotation of Galaxies Proximal to Black Holes," with Aaron Forster and "Pandora Rising"?

While she welcomed her family's praise, the congratulations lacked a knowledgeable basis in fact. In Lori Monaghan's words, the Monaghans were proud of their daughter and sister. They weren't necessarily impressed with her writing. After a day spent wrangling first graders, her mother enjoyed cozy murder mysteries. Adrian and Wes—who'd chosen to go into photography rather than biology—had inherited their father's taste for nonfiction. None of them read enough sci-fi to objectively judge the merits of "Pandora Rising."

Which was fine, but...

She'd lost track of time with her thoughts when the apartment's front door thudded open. *Midnight.* Someone fumbled through the entryway, clumsy in the dark. Two someones: a man's deep laughter and a woman's giggling response. Ashley, by the pitch. Busy at SVLAC with the grant application, collecting data, and avoiding Ethan, she'd only seen her roommates in passing all week. Did Ashley have a new partner?

"*Shhh*—you'll wake people up!"

"But didn't Kai go home with that girl from the bar at the British Bankers Club?"

"My other roommate's probably here. Erin."

"On a Friday night?"

"Well, all she ever does is work and—*shit!*"

"What?"

"Stubbed my toe on the couch."

"Oh. Okay." A weighted pause. Then, "Come here. I'll carry you. Which door?"

A resurgence of Ashley's giggles seemed to distract the pair from stubbed toes and whatever she'd been saying about her second roommate. Erin pushed in her earbuds. She mostly didn't mind sharing an apartment with Kai and Ashley. She liked them in the abstract: women in STEM making Silicon Valley life work, defiant and smart. She didn't know them well, but that was part of what made their crowded household functional. They were friendly, and also a little distant to preserve an illusion of privacy—she'd thought. Except that her roommates commuted together, sometimes they had dinner, and apparently they also went out to bars on Fridays.

My other roommate's probably here.

A bedstead squealed.

Wincing, she upped the volume on Phoebe Bridgers' vocals. She snapped pictures of *Galactica*'s cover and the first page of

"Pandora Rising" with Aaron Forster's author credit, sending them to Martina beside a line of exclamation points—which Martina answered in kind. Then, closing their thread, she took another photo: "Hunger." But this time, the click of her camera was furtive. She left her phone on her bedside table against an urge to watch its screen, checked the security of her earbuds, increased their volume one more time while she swapped out her loungewear for pajamas, and padded to the bathroom in fuzzy socks and a Stanford sweatshirt. With Bridgers' track resonating through her head, she couldn't hear the faucet running in the sink as she brushed her teeth, washed her face, dabbed on moisturizer, eye cream, and lip balm—*no smears around Bannister's glass*—and braided her hair. Mercifully, she also couldn't hear anything from behind Ashley's door.

As a precautionary measure, though, she kept her earbuds in after she'd returned to her room, switching her music to the soothing Norah Jones melody from Left Bank while she tossed her sweatshirt over a chair, kicked off her socks, and returned to her tangle of blankets. A notebook for jotting down midnight brainwaves, a sudoku booklet, and a pile of new novels waited with her phone on the nightstand. She ignored them and snuggled down into her sheets with *Exhalation* in hand.

Maybe Bannister was reading "The Truth of Fact, the Truth of Feeling" right now.

Unprompted, Chiang's book fell open to the chapter. She slipped again into the author's examination of Remem—a futuristic technology that granted its users eidetic memory—and Chiang's meditation on whether a perfect recollection of the past was worth its cost. Could humans' inability to accurately remember their yesterday be a biological kindness? It was a compelling, technically elegant piece, a treatise on forgiveness and narcissism; she only resurfaced to check her SVLAC email and scan STEMinist Online's trending posts around one o'clock, before turning out her light.

No urgent flags in her inbox demanded attention.

No breaking news in the forums required SnarkyQuark64's commentary.

But a new message from Bannister was waiting on her phone.

> **Bannister**
> The difference that Chiang explores between practical, exact truth and emotional, functional truth in the story is interesting. It reminds me of the Black Mirror anthology series.

He was right.

> **Erin**
> The Remem tech feels dystopian, doesn't it?
>
> **Bannister**
> If you had the chance, would you use it?
>
> **Erin**
> ...maybe? Though I don't know what that says about me, if I can call it dystopian and still want to use it for work.
>
> **Bannister**
> What does it say about me, if I agree with you?
>
> **Erin**
> Do you?

Bannister
Yes.

Bannister
Speaking of dystopian fiction, have you read anything by Martha Wells?

She had.

Erin flopped back onto her pillows, smiling at the ceiling.

7

Ethan blinked awake after four hours of sleep. He was perched perilously close to the edge of the mattress, one ankle already dangling into space. A rear canine paw pressed into his back, twitching to kick him out of bed, while the golden retriever sprawled across three-quarters of the blankets, snoring in bliss and slobbering on his pillow.

"Bunsen…"

The dog huffed another luxurious snore.

"What's wrong with your own damn bed?"

That engineering miracle of fleece, memory foam, and gel pads for heat or cooling lay abandoned on the floor. Bunsen was happy to nap in his dog bunk, dragging it around the condo to an optimal position that only he could triangulate before dropping it onto Ethan's feet for a snooze. But after dark?

"Maybe I should sleep in it."

Groaning at the crick in his neck, he gave the retriever an ineffective shove as he stretched across Bunsen for his phone on the nightstand—and something cracked along his torqued spine, a pinch of discomfort followed by a sweet release.

"*U-ugh.*"

Snagging Bunsen's pillow, he propped himself up against the wall. His mother had been harping on him to get a bedstead for years, though what was the point? His mattress on its rolling metal frame was functional, and the lengths and slats of a bedstead would just be more things to break while stuffing them into his hatchback during a move. He'd been fortunate so far with his rent, but this was Silicon Valley. No one's luck lasted through its vicissitudes forever. Defiantly repositioning the pillow and raking a hand through his hair, he opened his SVLAC email and edged Bunsen's creeping legs off his lap before the dog could shove him toward the door for their Saturday morning hike.

A run in Edgewood Park was an inviolable part of their weekend routine.

So was Ethan's watch duty for overnight SVLAC messages.

Eischer-Langhoff Edits, read the subject line of a new email from Dr. Kramer.

> *Meyer:*
> *Draft received.*
> *Action items:*
> - *Expand overview of theoretical measurement research base (cite last year's paper from* International Journal of Modern Physics*)*
> - *Reorder placement of theoretical equations and practical research data*
> - *Cite Logan for new calculations requiring expansion of holometer tunnels from 30 to 40 meters for optimal results; otherwise, cite general Fermilab Quantum group*
> - *Correct data in Table 5*
>
> *See tracked changes in attachment for add'l revisions.*
> *— Kramer*

His thumb hovered over the linked document—but then Bunsen kicked again, this time striking into his kidney. He fumbled his phone. SVLAC's email closed. A list of text threads appeared instead.

Aaron Forster hadn't responded to his message about Martha Wells.

Well, he'd sent it after midnight. Maybe Forster hadn't seen it yet. As he'd rationalized yesterday, a 650 area code was no guarantee that the writer was local. Forster could be in any time zone.

His disappointment at the blank space under his text was irrational.

He didn't even know the man.

Swinging his feet to the floor now, he chucked his phone back toward the bedside table hard enough that Bunsen shied up in concern. When the retriever saw him shuffling toward the bathroom, however, he jumped down and heeled beside Ethan to the door, tail thwacking and the phone scare forgotten.

"Out," he told Bunsen before his golden shadow could follow him to the sink.

Bunsen plopped down a half-inch from the threshold. Ethan bent to splash water on his face and wet down his hair, and brown eyes were just visible at the bottom of the mirror, eyebrows pinched in a plea. A faint, high-pitched whine fluttered Bunsen's whiskers as he tracked Ethan back into the bedroom, but when Ethan reached for his socks, Bunsen's tenuous restraint snapped. He began to bark and spin around after his own tail.

"I'm almost ready. Get your leash."

Paws skidded off to the door. Metal jingling against leather, Bunsen retrieved his leash and dragged it into the kitchen, where Ethan was filling their hiking water bottles.

"It's probably good that you can't clip this on yourself. Or open the front door. Then you wouldn't need me at all." He holstered the bottles in a belt bag, attached the dog's leash, and was towed out through the entryway to his car.

His dashboard clock only read 7:14 a.m., but pulling into the parking lot off Old Stagecoach Road that led into Edgewood Park, he found the pavement already busy with locals gearing up for a day on the trails. Hikers in family clusters slathered on sunscreen, offering snacks to children and reminding them that rattlesnakes' vibrating tails weren't an invitation to pet them. Couples coaxed goldendoodles and a lone French bulldog in a stroller to drink from collapsible dishes. A group of horseback riders tacked up beside a trailer. Skirting the crowds, he parked near the perimeter of the lot. Bunsen came hurtling out the back seat the instant Ethan opened the door, and pointed toward the main trailhead.

He checked his phone. Its screen was still blank.

After inserting his earbuds and deciding on Mumford & Sons over Green Day, he pocketed the device, resolving not to look at it again until they returned to the car. Then he guided Bunsen across the asphalt around tantalizing bits of dropped fruit rind and jerky.

"Come on."

He took off at a jog onto Edgewood Trail. The first half-mile was a strenuous climb along a dirt pathway curving through an understory of native grasses and tri-leafed poison oak, but the strain was invigorating rather than unpleasant in the woodland's cool air. He and Bunsen made their way up the hill, pausing for sniffs, attempts to eat a dead squirrel, leg-lifting, and water from their bottles. At the intersection of their path with an offshoot leading toward the center of the park, he nodded to other oncoming hikers with dogs, rather than speaking over the running rhythms of "Guiding Light." It was easier to engineer interactions with them than with regular people.

"Are we taking Serpentine today?"

Bunsen wagged his tail against Ethan's knees, panting with excitement.

So they wound through the thick, tawny fields of the Serpentine Trail as the sun flared hotter across the exposed grasslands and wildflowers, the dog barking at jackrabbits and birds. They split off onto Franciscan Trail to avoid the equestrian group, before meeting up again with their original Edgewood line near the parking lot. They gulped more water by the car, damp and smiling.

When Ethan scanned his phone after driving back to the condo for a shower and breakfast, he had a new message from Forster.

> **Forster**
> Sorry for not responding sooner! I'd read the first three novellas in Wells' Murderbot Diaries series, but I apparently missed the release of Exit Strategy, Network Effect, and Fugitive Telemetry... so I downloaded and read Exit Strategy last night.

He grinned. Toweling off after a shower, he pulled on jeans, yanked a plain black t-shirt over his shaggy hair, and coaxed Bunsen to abscond with a squeaky chew toy instead of his socks as he padded into the kitchen to start his coffee, all while his phone continued to chirp.

> **Forster**
> Murderbot has plenty of downloaded tv shows to choose from while it's traveling around having

> adventures, but if you were heading off to a
> foreign planet and could only take one show
> to watch—potentially forever—what would you
> pick?

With the brew dripping into its pot on a timer, he laid strips of imitation bacon into a cast iron skillet and considered Forster's question. *Only one show?* The bacon began to sizzle. He prodded it to the edges of the pan to brown and cracked an egg into the empty space. Bread went into the toaster, its timing planned for readiness with the eggs—even the relative spontaneity of his weekend breakfasts (*Scrambled eggs or fried eggs? Wheat toast or sourdough?*) involved *some* optimization— and then he leaned against the counter with his spatula in hand, watching for bubbles at the edge of the egg whites, thinking.

> **Ethan**
> I'd want nonfiction. Not because I don't enjoy
> fiction. I do. But I'd want something with
> standalone episodes, so that I could choose a
> segment based on my mood or interest from
> anywhere in the series and still watch a complete
> program. I also like consistency, and tv show
> characterizations often aren't very consistent.

Of course, neither were people.

Even Erin, whom he'd thought he knew—but she'd stopped arguing with him after their last all-hands and now she was avoiding him—

Frowning, he flipped over his egg to seal its yolk against the surface of the pan, then tipped it onto a slice of toast, arranging his bacon alongside the open-faced sandwich.

Bunsen whimpered, and his phone chimed.

> **Forster**
> Attenborough's Planet Earth series, maybe? Those opening shots of the planet seen from space are incredible. Now that I think about it, though, they're probably digital graphics or composites. But I like to believe that it's some photographer's job to go to the ISS to get footage for work, and then float around in zero gravity for fun.
>
> **Ethan**
> The ideal working vacation.
>
> **Forster**
> Right.
>
> **Ethan**
> I was thinking of Bill Nye the Science Guy. But Attenborough's never a wrong choice.
>
> **Forster**
> I obviously aspire to live the sort of life that would require a series narrated by Sir David.

More typing notifications appeared while he ferried his breakfast and milky coffee to the table. Somehow, some fake bacon and a taste of egg ended up in Bunsen's kibble.

Forster

Just imagine: "A human writer stirs. Cautiously, they approach their computer. This device is often used for play by the young of the species, but the adult writer is serious in their pursuit. This is no game. This is a hunt. They open a document. Then they hold very still, fingers poised, waiting for an unwary flicker of inspiration to approach, before—snap! They pounce, and the first word appears. They feast. Or not. Perhaps they wait in futility all morning, until they eventually close the blank page in despair. No inspiration has come. But when asked how they spent their day, they'll always respond, regardless of the condition of the page: Oh… I was writing."

Ethan

I can hear him say it.

He cut into his sandwich, typing out another one-handed reply between bites.

Ethan

I tell myself that I won't ink my lines without drafting a pencil sketch first. I know what the finished piece should look like before I start, so I'll sometimes try. But it's always garbage. Is it like that with writing? You have to get through the bad early drafts to get to a good version? Or do your words come out right from the beginning?

Forster

Definitely not. First drafts are torture. I don't usually know what the story looks like at all—I go in blind. At least you have a visual of your drawing in mind. You're right about needing to start somewhere uncomfortable—even bad—to have something to finish well, though. With art, at least.

Ethan

The data is axiomatic. But that doesn't mean we have to like it.

Forster

And we don't!

He rinsed his plate before carrying the dregs of his coffee to his home desk, opening his laptop, lining up pencils meticulously organized by hardness—B, HB, F—across a pad of graph-ruled paper, and tucking a pen behind his ear. Sunlight glinting through the sliding door to his patio sparked off a beam tree mounted on the wall above his workstation; SVLAC's engineers occasionally bombarded sheets of plastic with defocused, low-energy electron beams traveling almost at the speed of light, then pricked the ductile material with a metal punch to break the electrons into visible tree-like arcs and create visual art. The piece was beautiful and bizarre, and Schulz had awarded it to Ethan and Dr. Kramer to commemorate their first data collection cycle on the holometer. (Dr. Kramer already had several beam trees, so Ethan had taken it.) A perfect unification of art and science, it was the only non-functional item in his space. He smiled at it, and smiled again at his phone.

> **Ethan**
> What show would you choose?

Leaving Forster to consider the question, he turned his earbuds to white noise and clicked into Dr. Kramer's edits attachment for the Eischer-Langhoff application. His supervisor's instruction to cite their paper from the *International Journal of Modern Physics* was easy enough; he got to work. He paused a while later to alleviate the stiffness in his wrists with a sudoku grid, grabbing the pen from behind his ear and inking orderly numbers onto the page. Then: *ping.*

> **Forster**
> I was initially thinking about the first three seasons of Battlestar Galactica. But since you mentioned a nonfiction option, maybe Anthony Bourdain: Parts Unknown?
>
> **Ethan**
> Is that a travel show?

He resumed his revisions on the grant application with a quick copy-and-paste to reorder Dr. Kramer's salient points, then replaced several of Dr. Greg Logan's citations with a generic mention of Fermilab to make his supervisor's name more prominent in the text. But the data in Table 5 still presented a problem.

He combed back through his spreadsheets, tapping his lower lip with the pen. The data looked accurate on review. Dr. Kramer had questioned it, however. *Correct data in Table 5.* His supervisor might be referencing an outdated version of their raw holometer exports, of course… but he'd do a second analysis later today, just to be certain.

Ping.

Forster
Yes. He explores places that are off the standard tourist track—for example, the Interzone in Morocco. It used to be a prime destination for the Beat Generation and rock bands like the Rolling Stones. Somewhere to escape western "morality" and its hold on experimental art. (I won a family trivia tournament with that fact.)

Then immediately again: *ping*.

Forster
Wouldn't it be nice if Silicon Valley could breathe life back into its original creative rebelliousness, the kind that was going to save the world? If it would stop auto-strangling itself by… I don't know, coding mobile apps that let you order laundry detergent and a dog walker with your Chinese takeout?

Forster
Focusing on what's easy and shiny and stupid, just to get a quick profit from mercenary mythological creatures…

Forster
…like unicorn investors?

"*Ha—*" Ethan burst out laughing.

Bunsen startled upright at the sudden noise. Loosening his hold on a stolen sock, he smacked his muzzle into Ethan's elbow, and the phone slipped through his fingers, a keysmash skidded across the screen—he grabbed for the device as it fell—he missed—it *thunk*ed to the floor—

—where it chirped. A nonsensical message zipped away.

"*Damn.* No, no, Bunsen, it's fine…"

Stroking the dog to soothe him, he retrieved his phone and typed out a quick response to his own gibberish.

> **Ethan**
> Sorry for the keysmash. My dog knocked over my phone when I started laughing.
>
> **Forster**
> No worries. (Honestly, the joke wasn't THAT good.) But—more importantly: you have a dog? What breed?

"Smile," he told the golden retriever, and snapped a picture.

> **Ethan**
> His name is Bunsen.
>
> **Forster**
> Look at that happy face! I'd also love to have a dog, but it's not easy—despite my detergent, walker, and takeout app—to manage in most apartments along the San Francisco Peninsula. I just admire other people's pets right now. So hi, Bunsen!

"Forster says hi."

Bunsen whined.

"What? You've already had your egg and bacon, and—*oh*. It's time for our noon walk, isn't it? What the hell happened to the morning?"

It was a rhetorical question. He knew exactly how he'd spent his morning, and what he'd learned:

Forster lived in the Bay Area.

Her straw made a gurgly sucking sound against the bottom of her glass, drawing air instead of the Greek yogurt, chia seed, and frozen raspberry smoothie that she'd whizzed up after her run along the Stanford Dish trail. Erin released the tube to inspect its malfunction.

Huh.

The glass was empty, warm in her hand. She must've finished her breakfast a while ago but hadn't noticed, too absorbed with her computer and her phone. With work, with Bannister—and with Bunsen.

She enlarged the picture on her screen. Bunsen was a handsome young dog, a coppery retriever with soulful eyes, a mischievous lopsided grin, a tongue a mile long, and egg in his whiskers. Cassie was forbidden from begging at the Monaghan table but, probably like Bunsen, she somehow always ended up sampling their meals… Smiling and shaking her head, she expanded the photo farther. Those columns of steel beside the retriever were the legs of either a table or an industrial-style desk, weren't they? That was definitely a sock between Bunsen's paws.

Cassie liked socks, too.

Dark blue socks with golden bears around the ankles never would've been allowed into the Grand Arbor house, however. Bunsen's sock—*Bannister's* sock—was printed in incriminating UC Berkeley colors, with an even more incriminating UC Berkeley logo.

Cal bear.

She switched from analyzing the sock to analyzing Bannister's phone number: a 510 area code. 510 was local to the East Bay. To the Berkeley area.

Not that it matters, she told herself again.

But a search for *Bannister + UC Berkeley* popped up on her screen. She scrolled, clicked, and scrolled again. The results were inconclusive. Several Banisters currently were or had previously been affiliated with the university. There wasn't a single Bannister.

She'd already considered the possibility that the artist used a pseudonym, hadn't she?

She shrugged away from her phone and her computer after a few fruitless minutes. The loose wire in her bra prodded her ribs. She peeled up her shirt; a red pressure point had formed on her skin from her hunch over her desk. She'd spent almost the whole morning curved toward her screens, messaging with Bannister in between stints of preliminary data modeling on her latest LIGO exports, and she anticipated a favorable outcome from next week's meeting with Nadine, in which she'd pitch her work on gravitational waves as an additional research area to showcase during the Secretary of Energy's visit to SVLAC.

Ethan Meyer was probably refining a similar pitch on his quantum work to his own supervisor this weekend, calculating and then optimizing each sacrosanct data point in isolation for success.

Robot, she dismissed him, rubbing at her ribs. But even if he wasn't a robot, he was likely still being more productive than she was. Because honestly: what portion of her morning had she spent with her data, and what part had she spent distracted by Bannister? Yet again: *Not that it matters*. She'd best her rival anyhow, despite her preoccupation with the artist. And his dog.

Bannister had that gorgeous retriever, while she—

Damn.

She hadn't watered her rosemary plant this month.

Emerging from her room for the first time since she'd made her smoothie just after seven o'clock, she mixed a teaspoon of fertilizer into a watering can, then fed the bushy, pungent herb sitting in the kitchen window above the sink. Its soil absorbed the moisture with instant and desperate gratitude, so she turned on the faucet and soaked it until water ran out into the saucer under its pot.

"Sorry, Grant."

She'd named the herb after Rosemary Grant, an evolutionary biologist at Princeton who studied Darwin's finches in the Galápagos. Wes had thought it was funny. Despite a fair amount of abuse, she hadn't killed it yet. Survival of the fittest.

Or maybe Kai or Ashley sometimes watered it?

She replaced Grant on his sill. When she stretched up to put the watering can back on top of the refrigerator, her bra wire jabbed her again.

"*Ouch!*" Grimacing in defeat, she switched into a shelf-lined tank top over a pair of old, faded jeans, shouldered the small backpack that she preferred to a purse, carried her bicycle down the stairs, wiped pollen from its seat, then pedaled off across the bridge over San Francisquito Creek toward the Stanford Shopping Center. She paused at a traffic signal to cross Sand

Hill Road, adjusting the straps slipping off her shoulders as she waited for the light to turn—she'd forgotten to reapply sunscreen after her shower, and she'd likely arrive back in Menlo Park with a stripey burn—while grousing at the inconvenience of having to spend her afternoon this way. She could've been working, or reading, or going to a Pilates class. Or messaging Bannister. But instead, she'd be squinting against the glare of artificial lights off a sleek department store floor and trying to see her own back in a dressing room mirror.

Lingerie shopping was rarely fun. It always took much longer than she planned, too. Not because she couldn't manage her time like Ethan claimed, but because of the fashion industry's idiocy around sizes. Men never seemed to appreciate how easy it was to fit their clothes! Also, they could get away with a standard workplace uniform of the same collared shirt or polo in multiple colors and one pair of jeans or slacks. For women, though? The required balance between professional polish and a style that was too much, too little, too feminine, too masculine, too bright, or too drab was designed to be impossible. It was even worse in STEM fields—and worse still with lingerie, because after all the effort to find a bra that fit, in the end, the choice was invisible.

At least for her. When had she last bought anything except plain basics that only she and the bathroom mirror would ever see?

It had been a while since she'd gone on a date.

Martina would sip Chenin Blanc and remind her that this was by choice, however.

The light turned green and she sped through a clog of weekend traffic, skirting the worst of the jam near the shopping center by peeling off into the Nordstrom parking lot across the street from the main thoroughfare. She locked her bicycle outside the store's massive brick archway and micro-cafe that led to the first floor, assailed by a disorienting blast of air conditioning and perfume as she navigated to the escalators while typing a message to her mother.

> **Erin**
> I'm at Nordstrom. Bra shopping. Help.

She edged around a group of chattering teenagers and consulted the directory. Level 2: *Women's Lingerie.*
Ping.

> **Mom**
> I'm happy to consult, sweetheart. What are you looking for?

> **Erin**
> Just the basics. The wire on my nude bra popped out this week.

> **Mom**
> Send me photos once you've found some choices.

Those choices spanned a solid quarter of Nordstrom's second level.
She scanned the racks and sighed.
Ignoring satin push-ups and a bralette constructed from star-sprinkled midnight blue lace, she gathered an armload of options in neutral tans, whites, and blacks, and set up in a dressing room.

> **Erin**
>
> Options 1–5.

She snapped pictures in the mirror, capturing herself from shoulders to hips, unposed, still in her jeans, and sent them off to her mother.

> **Mom**
>
> I like the third option. The tulle trim on the cups is pretty.
>
> **Erin**
>
> It's itchy, though. And it would show through a t-shirt.

In her next batch, despite selecting the same size as before, nothing fit. She braved a third round, and found two bras that were adequate.

> **Mom**
>
> The black one is very practical.

It was.

> **Erin**
>
> It works fine. Here's the last group.

Nothing.

> **Erin**
>
> Ugh. At least I found two.

Mom

They're nice. But why don't you experiment with something fun? You've been working so hard and you've just had your story published. What about a treat?

Erin

Well…

Mom

Try something on. See how you feel.

A new message from Bannister pinged across her screen while she debated Lori's advice. The preview text was a commentary on his walk with Bunsen. Despite her frustration with the lingerie fitting, she couldn't help the smile that reflected back at her from the mirror.

So she fetched the starry bralette.

The lace slipped over her head to settle in cool patterns across her skin. Its raised stitching would show through any shirt. Embroidered silver stars glimmered under the lights, barely obscuring the peaks of her breasts. It was completely impractical.

And very, very pretty.

The freckles dotting her arms and collarbones could've been constellations.

She angled herself before the glass, arched her back just a little, took the picture, and sent it—

—to *Most Recent Contact*.

Which wasn't her mother now.

She'd sent the photo to Bannister.

8

Ethan dropped his phone again.

But he couldn't blame Bunsen this time because the golden retriever was sloppily devouring a teeth-cleaning chew stick on the couch, and he was in the kitchen piling up a lunchtime vegetable bowl from prepared Tupperware portions of sliced cucumbers, tomatoes, and feta cheese, a glob of hummus on his knife making a slow bid for freedom toward the floor.

Plop.

Stepping over it, he cautiously reclaimed his device.

The picture was still there.

Forster's picture.

Delicate lingerie, scallops of lace and stars skimming a woman's bowed figure, fingers curled to cup the tiny freckles scattered across her stomach, the curve of her hip bones just visible above a denim waistband leading down out of the frame, a glass behind her reflecting two dimples set low in her back—

Static buzzed in his ears. His face burned.

What…

Why?

Who—

A new message blinked into the thread.

> **Forster**
> Oh my God. This was supposed to be for my mother.

Who sent photos of a woman in lingerie to his mother?

Skin glowing golden in the lights around her mirror, her freckled constellations begged to be drawn and mapped and observed with wonder. Was she Forster's partner?

...and who *was* Forster?

Someone he liked, he reminded himself through the buzzing in his head. Someone who'd made him laugh. But now? Now, Forster was also someone he envied. Horribly, irrationally—

Ping.

> **Forster**
> She likes to weigh in on options when I'm shopping.
>
> **Forster**
> I'm so sorry, I really didn't mean to send this to you.

A third typing notification bubbled and vanished. Bubbled and vanished. Bubbled. Then:

> **Forster**
> So, I guess that's that. It's probably obvious now that my name isn't Aaron.

My name isn't Aaron.

Knocked off balance again, he lurched forward against his counter. One sock went straight into the hummus. He didn't step back.

Forster was a woman.

This woman.

Her.

He vaguely registered Bunsen padding into the kitchen to lick at his sock and the floor, chew stick abandoned. The hummus was laced with peppers; the dog might vomit up a fountain of brown sludge later. But Ethan didn't stop him. He went on blinking at his phone until another typing notification from Forster appeared. It dissolved almost immediately.

She was waiting. For him. To say…

Something.

Hands and mind immobilized, he'd been gawking at his device for a solid three minutes without replying to her. To—*that picture*.

Focus.

> **Ethan**
> I understand. I work on my art under a pseudonym, too.

He didn't mention her photo. His response pushed it up and out of view in their thread. That was good, because the shadows articulating her collarbones and the divot of her navel had left a vacuum where his brain should be. She likely didn't want him to respond to it, anyhow. What would he even say? She was sharp and funny and beautiful, and he… wasn't. Chase would've used a more explicit word for him, and he also would've known how to use the right words with

Forster. Ethan's own reply was stilted, awkward. If only he could answer her with nibs and ink…

This was supposed to be for my mother. She hadn't taken the picture for a partner. It hadn't been meant for him. But she hadn't snapped it for another man, either.

She.

A new ellipsis blinked onto his phone. Forster was typing again. He watched her work out her answer. His last message hadn't been a question, so this could be the conclusion of their discussion if she didn't choose to extend it. He stared, and tried to parse meaning from her pauses, to extract data from the blank screen—because even an incorrect hypothesis was better than the fear that hitched itself to ignorance.

He wasn't ready for their conversation to end.

He'd enjoyed Forster's company before he'd known her gender, when she'd just been a stranger with a profound, intimate connection to his art. No, not *just*. Theirs was a kinship he'd never expected to share—or had even considered sharing. Not really. Let alone with anyone so innovative and insightful. Someone like… *her.*

But now?

His phone chirped.

> **Forster**
> It's better to keep our personal and professional lives separate, isn't it? Especially when they're in such diametric contrast. Using different names is an easy way to do it.

A question.

A deep inhale unfurled through his lungs and released the tension under his sternum. Dirty socks tossed into the hamper, tabasco bottle in hand, Ethan took his lunch to the living room and settled on the couch. Saturday's afternoon work block at his desk could wait another few minutes. Bunsen hopped up beside him, eyeing the hummus again.

He tapped the golden retriever's nose with the abandoned chew stick. "Definitely not. Here, clean your teeth. And your breath. I can smell those peppers in your stomach already." Then he propped up his bare feet, took a bite of spicy chickpeas, and returned to Forster's message.

If she was careful to separate her stories from her professional life, then she probably wasn't a writer by trade. *Diametric contrast*, she'd written. She lived in the Bay Area. Maybe she was a software engineer. Or a project manager. A venture capitalist. A startup CEO. Could she be at NASA Ames? But she'd already revealed more of herself today than she'd intended. That was clear. While he couldn't forget what he knew, he could at least respect the rest of her privacy. He erased the question he'd started to type. Instead:

> **Ethan**
> Agreed. Keeping art isolated from work is good hygiene.

Bunsen burped a pungent waft of hummus.

"That's disgusting," he told the dog. He scratched the retriever's shoulders with one hand, trying not to inhale while typing a second message.

> **Ethan**
> Better hygiene than Bunsen has.

> **Forster**
> How was his walk?

> **Ethan**
> Every walk is a good walk. Even the ones where he eats things decomposing under a bush.

> **Forster**
> Especially those ones?

"She's right, isn't she?" He tweaked Bunsen's ears.

> **Ethan**
> You must've had a dog before.

> **Forster**
> My family's always had herding breeds. I think that was deliberate when my brothers and I were young.

Even the concept of a dog in Karen Meyer's house was an abomination. His mother hated dishes left in the sink, too. Against every nagging instinct, he rinsed his bowl under the faucet but didn't wash it. *Mutiny.* He filled a water glass.

> **Ethan**
> Bunsen doesn't herd people, but he does collect socks.

Then, heading back to his desk, he returned his phone to white noise, opened Dr. Kramer's comments on Table 5, and began a second review of his own holometer spreadsheets, double-checking his assessment from earlier in the day. There was no binary switching of ones and zeros in the data. Erin hadn't gone rogue against him here. Despite the unlikeliness of her sabotage reoccurring—maybe not so unlikely right now, since they were sharing a control room?—he still examined his exports every time, and sometimes discovered other data corruptions that required resolution from the hutch operators. He couldn't reconcile Dr. Kramer's implied discrepancy, however. He was writing a carefully worded response to his supervisor, asking what data Dr. Kramer was referencing for the table, when Forster sent another text.

> **Forster**
> Does the blue sock in Bunsen's picture have a bear on it?
>
> **Ethan**
> Good eye. It does.

Her ellipsis appeared. To avoid staring at it, he switched back to his email.

> *Dr. Kramer:*
>
> *Thank you for providing your edits for the Eischer-Langhoff draft.*
>
> *I've made your requested updates (attached, changes tracked), with one exception: the data in Table 5. This data reflects the holometer's January through mid-June exports, which are my current sets. If data for the project has been collected more recently, then the table requires amendments. What data are you referencing in your edits?*
>
> *I apologize for the confusion.*
>
> *— E.M.*

He read the draft three times before he sent it.

The best outcome would be that he'd failed to accurately track the quantum measurement project's data collection cycles. (Maybe Dr. Kramer had begun to collect his own data again? His increasingly busy schedule and the viruses often disrupting his exports had resulted in him largely stepping back from the day-to-day running of the holometer, with Ethan generating, cleaning, analyzing, modeling, and forwarding data for review instead.) If so, he'd be angry with Ethan's questionable management of their work, but the solution would be a simple one: correct Table 5 to reference the updated sets, apologize, and never make the mistake again.

Ever.

…though what if his own data really was the most current? What if the sets referenced in Table 5 were accurate?

No.

Swallowing some water to ease the dryness in his throat, he reached for his phone, where Forster's ellipsis had resolved into a new message.

> **Forster**
> Bad eyes, good optometrist. But anyway: blue sock, yellow bear. 510 area code. Cal Berkeley?
>
> **Ethan**
> You're a writer and also a detective?
>
> **Forster**
> Sherlock and Watson in one. Am I right?
>
> **Ethan**
> Yes. My family's from the East Bay. I graduated four years back.

Forster
Undergraduate or graduate?

Ethan
Graduate.

Forster
So you also have a PhD: permanent head damage.

He spat a mouthful of water across his desk.

Ethan
If that's not already a panel in PhD Comics, it should be.

Ethan
And yes, I do. Like you?

Forster
Similarly injured, and also a PhD Comics reader. (I especially like the panel that converts scientific gibberish into real-world language. "Filter and gain settings varied with experimental conditions and objectives" to "We twiddled the knobs until it worked" is a classic.) Anyhow—for me, the damage was at Stanford, just over three years ago. But I'm not a Bay Area native. You're a rare breed.

He mopped up the puddle beside his computer with the hem of his shirt before it seeped into his keyboard or his graph paper, smiling.

Ethan
Where's home for you?

Forster
Home is where the dog is. So that's the Great Lakes region in Michigan.

Ethan
Do you miss it?

Forster
Not the weather. Though I do miss my family. The Bay Area has a higher population than my whole state, but the crowds here—at least in Silicon Valley—are mostly singleton transplants.

Forster
Like me.

Forster
And it's weird, but it doesn't seem to matter that there are always people around, always events going on, always something to do. It can be lonely.

Her trio of messages sent pings against the condo's bare walls. Bunsen twitched up from his chew stick. His panting breath and nails clicking across the hardwood were loud as he searched for the origin of the sounds. The notification of a reply from Dr. Kramer in Ethan's inbox was louder still.

The Meyers' house just across the bay in the Berkeley Hills was tastefully minimalist in gray and white. But his unit? Not minimalist after multiple years of living here: *empty*.

His log of skipped calls from Chase and his parents was full, despite how infrequently they left messages.

"We missed you on Sunday."

"Mom's having some people over for dinner."

"Join us if you're free."

He never avoided Dr. Kramer's emails or his work, or the late nights in service of both—nights when he sometimes traded messages about quantum physics with Tomasz Szymanski. They were cordial colleagues, yes. But not friends. And Bunsen?

He loved Bunsen. But still...

He picked up his phone.

> **Ethan**
> Even for people with family here, it's a lonely place.

Then, before he could rationalize his way out of it:

> **Ethan**
> I'm glad we've met each other.

Thump-thump. Thump-thump. Thump-thump.

It had taken several hours—several *mortifying* hours—after she'd shared her lingerie picture, but Erin's pulse had finally settled down to a resting rate. She'd gotten home from the Stanford Shopping Center somehow, and didn't seem to have crashed her bicycle or run any red lights on her way back to the apartment. *Seem.* She couldn't remember any of that adrenaline-fueled retreat to safety, to privacy.

Or to relative safety and privacy.

Her picture was digital and would exist *forever*.

She hunched over her phone in her bedroom, scrolling up through her messages with Bannister to find it again.

Fuck.

At least he didn't seem to think less of her for her mistake. Or her identity. He'd been very normal about everything, actually. Their continued easy banter was a relief: colleges, dogs, the realities of Bay Area life.

I'm glad we've met each other.

Other people wouldn't be so accepting.

She'd chosen a masculine-coded pseudonym for her creative writing, aiming to avoid the unconscious—or sometimes explicit—biases, prejudices, and penalties to which women were subjected in male-dominated fields. Like physics, science fiction was almost by definition a male-dominated space. But unlike with her research papers, which had to be searchable and attributable to Dr. Erin Monaghan for professional reasons, she could angle the biases in the sci-fi field to her advantage without real-world repercussions. So, referencing the author Edward Morgan Forster along with her own name and initials, she'd submitted her work as Aaron Forster, had been accepted as Aaron Forster, and had declined to provide an author photo for her contributor credit in *Galactica Magazine*. Her story would stand on its own. She wouldn't be viewed as either an interloper in spaces where she didn't belong, or worse: a pretty face to be sexualized and dismissed.

Bannister was doing neither.

I'm glad we've met each other.

She exhaled, scrolled back to the end of their thread, and sent her response.

> **Erin**
> Me too.

Then she carefully—very carefully, double-checking herself—switched over to her messages with Martina.

> **Erin**
> Do you remember how you said that I'd had a DAY after the last SVLAC all-hands? Well, I've one-upped myself this afternoon.

A texting ellipsis blinked.

> **Martina**
> Uh-oh. Spill.

> **Erin**
> …I accidentally sent a semi-nude picture to a stranger.

> **Martina**
> WHAT?!

She cringed, even as she snorted out a cough of embarrassed laughter.

> **Erin**
> I know.

> **Martina**
> Explain. Now.

She did: about Bannister's graphic in *Galactica Magazine* that could've been an illustration for her short story, her reckless outreach to him as Aaron Forster, their connection over the same sci-fi media—followed by her misdirected lingerie photo.

Wincing again, she hopped off her bed and paced along her wall of commemorative science and literary posters: Katherine Johnson calculating orbits at NASA, Chien-Shiung Wu showcasing nuclear weapons from the Manhattan Project, cosmonaut Valentina Tereshkova in her flight suit, Marie Skłodowska–Curie holding her Nobel Prizes in both physics and chemistry, Anne Inez McCaffrey winning the Hugo and Nebula Awards for fiction. All of them were fully clothed…

She was almost grateful to answer the call from Martina that chimed on her screen.

"*Right*." Her friend's voice vibrated over the speaker, and she pushed in her earbuds; Kai and Ashley seemed to be out, but their neighbors might not be. "What you're telling me is that Dr. Erin Monaghan, who refuses to let me set her up for dinner or drinks with some very nice men, who claims that she's always too busy to date because she's occupied with interferometers, Department of Energy site visits, or competing with Ethan Meyer for every advantage and prestige at SVLAC—that *this same Erin Monaghan* has spent the past twenty-four hours texting with a mysterious artist—and has even sent him a nude picture?"

"Semi-nude! Accidentally!"

"Regardless. It's a miracle that Adrian and Wes haven't already strong-armed him into a wedding to preserve your honor."

More hysterical laughter rose in her nose. She collapsed back onto the rumpled sheets hanging off her mattress. "I don't want to think about that. Because they'd do it. Or at least threaten it. I love them to pieces, but loving them—and being loved by them—is a balancing act. Right now, you're the only one who knows about Bannister."

"He's your dirty little secret."

"No—he's just—I admired his art. The rest was an accident. Besides, he didn't actually say anything about my picture, so he probably doesn't—"

Ping.

The message was from him.

> **Bannister**
> I hope this isn't awkward. But I'm enjoying our conversation. And this seems like a fair trade.

> **Bannister**
> (New Photo Message)

"*Uh…*"

"What?"

"*Um.* Bannister just sent—"

Presumably taken earlier in the summer, the picture was of Bunsen again, the retriever flopped beside a pile of high-tide kelp near a sign for San Francisco's Crissy Field East Beach, silhouetted against the red arches of the Golden Gate Bridge on a rare sunny day with his tongue lolling, clearly halfway through a sprint by the water.

He'd also clearly been sprinting with Bannister.

Bannister—his head cropped just out of the frame where he lounged beside Bunsen on the dunes, his camera angled to capture the dog instead of his own face.

Bannister—shirtless, a dappling of sunburn across his arms, the taut lines of his stomach flushed with sweat, sand dusting his calves, the telltale muscles of a runner creasing his thighs, golden under the spangled marine light—

Bannister—

"*Erin.*" Martina's voice. "Erin, what did he just send?"

"A… a photo."

"Screenshot. Now."

Click.

Martina's phone buzzed audibly as the image dropped into their thread. Her read receipt flashed under the picture. *Silence.* Had she stopped breathing while she assessed it? Assessed *him*? Erin certainly had. Her pulse was in her throat, her cheeks flaming, the worn denim of her jeans suddenly painful against her legs.

She wanted to bury her phone and never look at it again.

She wanted to stare at the screen until her eyes watered.

She wanted to…

But then:

"*Erin.* Either you've been catfished in the most insanely niche way, or you're the luckiest woman in the world."

9

The *swish* of an activating lightsaber sounded from her desk.

Looping an elastic band around her hair, Erin hopped over to her phone on alternating feet while she pulled up her socks, smiling despite the itch of her sunburned arms and the early Monday hour. After a weekend spent messaging… *flirting?*… with Bannister in between stints of preparation for the Department of Energy's visit, tracking a few trending STEMinist Online posts, finishing another Murderbot novella, and battling several sudoku grids, she'd switched out his generic text tone for the iconic combination of a thirty-five millimeter projector and a 1970s tube television from Star Wars.

> **Bannister**
> (New Photo Message)
>
> **Bannister**
> Before the running shoes come out.

She opened the picture, shouldering into both the sleeves of her utility jacket and the refrigerator to grab her breakfast Tupperware, then paused in the apartment's entry with her bicycle helmet perched on her head, the latch swinging loose under her chin, distracted and delighted.

The photo was of Bunsen. The golden retriever stretched in indolent ease over a familiar gray quilt, ears flopped forward to cover his eyes. From nose to tail, he sprawled across the entire length of the bed and the pillow, too, scavenging the heat from another body that had either already hauled itself up off the mattress or been kicked out onto the floor.

Cassie played the same game whenever she visited Michigan.

> **Erin**
> If you lie down with dogs...

Swish.

> **Bannister**
> ...you'll wake up with no room in bed.

Laughing, she latched her chin clip, zipped up her jacket, and hefted her bicycle down to the pavement.

> **Erin**
> That's probably more on the mark than the
> original quote.

Then she braced a sneaker against its pedal and typed out one more comment.

> **Erin**
> Because bed-sharing leads to plenty of things
> besides fleas.

Pocketing her phone before she could second-guess herself, she kicked off from the curb and rolled onto Live Oak Avenue. But she did check her screen again at the traffic light leading toward Sand Hill Road.

He'd responded.

Bannister
Not all bad things, either.

Giddy heat suffused her stomach. Somewhere in Silicon Valley's crush of grifters, dreamers, and gridlock, Bannister and Bunsen were up and alert to the beauty of the morning, just like she was. Had they gone jogging through a neighborhood in the Peninsula, or in the urban sprawl of the East Bay? Maybe they'd run past San Francisco's Sunset District to Fort Funston, where Bunsen could frolic off leash. Or they could've gone back to Crissy Field.

Pulse thudding, legs and lungs straining with effort and exhilaration at the summit of every sand dune, the rich glisten of sun on sweat—

Red light.

She skidded into the crosswalk at Innovation Drive, weight pitching forward against her handlebars. She caught herself before she ended up spreadeagled in the middle of the intersection, but only just.

Focus. Monday. SVLAC.

She gave an awkward wave to a driver in the next lane when the light flipped to green for her turn. At least the guard at the campus security booth was too far away to have seen her near-wipeout. Both the effort of pedaling up Sand Hill Road and the wind chill from her ride were legitimate excuses for her rapid breathing and her hot cheeks, too. She locked up her bicycle—no damage done to its frame or tires, just to her pride—and swiped into the Modern Physics building, heading to the coffee station for a stabilizing dose of caffeine.

Careful to avoid the espresso button, she prodded the machine to life, then warmed up her overnight oats and sliced apples. She stirred creamer into her cereal when it began to smoke in the kitchenette's fire hazard of a microwave, and kept an eye on the hallway while her coffee brewed. Most of her colleagues wouldn't arrive at the office for another hour.

Most.

She also watched her muted phone.

> **Erin**
> Did you know that the easiest time of day to identify a psychopath is before 9 a.m.?
>
> **Bannister**
> I didn't. Why?
>
> **Erin**
> Because people with psychopathic traits have a taste for black coffee, and you're most likely to spot that tell in the morning. So the studies say.
>
> **Bannister**
> The "they" who say.
>
> **Erin**
> Infallible sociology wisdom. Anyhow…

She left the message dangling, retrieving her mug and pouring a healthy stream of oat milk into it, swirling the liquids together in irreversible thermalization.

> **Bannister**
> Are you trying to guess how I drink my coffee?
>
> **Erin**
> Maybe. Unless you drink it black. Then—don't tell me.

She took a sip and waited…

>**Bannister**
>No. Definitely not black.

>**Bannister**
>You?

She added a second splash of oat milk.

>**Erin**
>I sometimes spike my creamer with coffee.

>**Bannister**
>Lawless.

>**Erin**
>My brothers tell me I'm a menace.

>**Bannister**
>I'd guess that you wear their warning with pride.

>**Erin**
>Absolutely right.

She crunched an apple at that, considering her next move until a new conversation arrived to yank her focus from her screen.

"Any good fishing this weekend?"

She spun around. "*Fish*—what—*oh*. Martina." She exhaled.

Her friend shambled into the kitchenette, yawning a greeting. Despite being ringed with deep lavender shadows from a Sunday night shift, Martina's eyes shone with mischief. She bumped her hip against Erin's while she slotted a mug into the coffee machine. "Or maybe I should ask: any *more* good fishing?"

"I'm vegetarian." She returned the hip check a bit harder than necessary.

"Shame. No raw… *sushi*… for you—"

"*Martina!*" Hot coffee went straight up her nose. She sputtered and grabbed a napkin. "*Ugh*—that's—that's just… no, but wait: why are you here? If you've finished your shift in the control room, shouldn't you be heading home to a date with your bed?"

Undeterred, Martina handed her another tissue. "Why am I getting an espresso shot? Aside from the joy of seeing you snort coffee at sexual innuendos? Because I *do* have a date this morning. But it's with the Menlo Park city council. They're trying to bulldoze the pocket park by our house to make room for some pricey outdoor exercise studio."

"Do you ever *really* sleep?" She dabbed her chin.

"Don't change the subject."

"I—"

"*So*. You were grinning at your phone a minute ago." Wiggling her eyebrows, Martina leaned back against the counter with her brew, displacing a bowl of wilting fruit left over from Friday afternoon. "Which means that even though you refuse to eat seafood—did you know that oysters are a powerful aphrodisiac?—you must've had a good time."

"*Um*. Well…"

"I thought so. After those pictures?"

Erin's smile widened past the boundaries of her napkin. "We're still talking about books—we might read *This Is How You Lose the Time War* together—and dogs—he has to keep his paperbacks on a high shelf so his golden retriever can't chew on them. Also, about what it's like to operate as clandestine creatives in the Bay Area. Some people here apparently claim that coding is art."

"You've said that before about data sets."

"That's because they elicit an emotional response. Who wouldn't be amazed by new information on the behavior of black holes and how we can track their movement through ripples in space-time?"

"Amazed by a plain data export? Honestly? Almost no one outside your field would spot artistry in all those numbers."

"Not helpful." She swatted at Martina with her tissue. "An emotional response—wonder, anger, awe, frustration, or anything else—is what makes art *art*. That's why it's subjective, because it's based on feeling more than logic. But art isn't *that* subjective. Python and Ruby on Rails are out."

"Maybe code does elicit an emotional response from software developers. They might disagree with you."

"*Bannister* agrees with me." She took a smug sip of coffee.

"That's what matters, isn't it?"

"Yes—and his graphics absolutely elicit an emotional response." She scrolled through the photos on her phone, past an influx of golden retrievers and books—arranged alphabetically by author and series order—lining the shelves of a house or apartment somewhere in the greater Bay Area, then back to the image of "Hunger" that she'd snapped from the magazine. Its compelling imagery—the sharp, edgy turbulence depicting the gravity of Bannister's black hole—and its authority to compel and consume its viewer were undiminished even by the low-grade resolution of her screen. It was time to share it, now. "Isn't he incredible?"

Martina hummed over her shoulder. "All right, I see the appeal. Especially for you. It has narrative power. Plus, astrophysics."

"'Hunger' is the backpiece for my story in *Galactica*'s June issue. The editors must've paired them together."

"He's certainly a skilled artist."

"…but you don't like his work?"

"I like color. The murals in Oakland. Buildings in the Mission District. Sidewalk chalk art in the parking lots behind Santa Cruz Avenue on farmers' market days." Martina shrugged down at the tapestried arabesque of threads patterning the hems of her jeans above her work boots. "But I can admire his talent. And I like him for you, because he's distracted you enough from your spreadsheets to have a cup of coffee and a conversation right here, instead of at your desk. You haven't mentioned the Eischer-Langhoff grant once today—"

"I finished it on Friday—"

"—and you're smiling."

"You sound like my mother."

"That doesn't mean I'm wrong. So, keep me updated on your mystery artist. But for now," she rinsed her mug in the sink, "I have to head off. Those planning commissioners won't heckle themselves."

"Take that microphone with all the confidence of a mediocre white man."

"Always," and Martina waved herself out of the kitchenette.

Erin returned to her photos in the quiet, still smiling. Bannister's finished piece wasn't the only item she'd saved in a digital album. He'd also sent images of more recent sketches to her on Sunday afternoon: a kaleidoscopic play of light on the lens of a telescope reflecting a planet from one end and a human eye from the other, and an abstract rendering of a mug with a spoon miraculously un-swirling a muddle of coffee and milk back to their discrete components. The edge of his left thumb was visible in the second sketch, a glimpse of the hand that articulated ideas from a brilliant, visionary mind—a mind with such gorgeous forearms.

Those *definitely* elicited an emotional response.

Also, the sleek cut of a runner's abdomen.

Why shouldn't she smile?

It didn't last, though.

Because the next person to enter the kitchenette was Ethan Meyer.

Both her mood and her smile dropped. She squared up in front of the coffee machine, chin raised with three years of habit, instinctive vitriol already rising—but then the main doors into the Modern Physics building swung open, admitting a group of colleagues who'd carpooled together down the congested freeway from San Francisco, and she bit her tongue hard with her newer and less pleasant habit of silence.

Popcorn.

Easy, Monaghan.

Except…

Today, *now*, with Bannister's messages clutched in her hand, it suddenly didn't matter what her colleagues overheard, saw, or even said about their rivalry.

Whatever they thought, they were wrong.

Her hallucination-dream? Also wrong.

And what was right?

This.

As the coffee machine belched out a cloud of steam, as Ethan stepped toward the counter in his fleece vest, as their carpooling colleagues filed down the hall, she moved defiantly to meet him while sweeping her ponytail off her neck. Straggles of helmet hair flicked into his face, across his mouth.

"*Argh—*"

"Sorry, I didn't see you there, Meyer. I was thinking about how submitting the Eischer-Langhoff grant last Friday would have pushed my email to the top of the reviewers' inboxes today. Obviously, this—plus the citations from my sole-author paper, of course—gives my odds a boost, and it'll be interesting to see how the award process plays out. More interesting than watching the doorway. But if you can optimize your programming for good time management this week, maybe you can use the same strategy. Minus the authorship part."

Then she left him, a hand frozen on his cheek, unexpectedly mute. *Good.* She nodded a greeting to her arriving colleagues and an intern poking at a copy machine in the hallway—"Morning, Dr. Rossi and Dr. O'Connor-Young. Hi Leah, how are you?"—as she strode off to her desk, triumphant, mind already spinning with ideas for the workday ahead. Plus, an older post in the STEMinist Online forums had gained traction on Sunday with new commentary about a Fermilab scientist from the early aughts (anonymized to protect the poster, not the man) who'd allegedly published his subordinate's research on the use of quantum effects for navigation by migrating birds under his own name; SnarkyQuark64 had thoughts to share.

It was a busy Monday. A good Monday.

She was gone, and her vicious ponytail with her.

If you can optimize your programming.

He scowled. He didn't still have her hair in his mouth, did he?

Maybe you can use the same strategy. Minus the authorship part.

He didn't, but his lower lip tingled, and a distracting, irritating hint of subtle sweetness continued to chafe his nose. The reason that he glowered after his rival rather than making a clever rebuttal to her dig about the grant—and he definitely would've made it clever, even something about her paper's data again—was because his jaw was clenched too hard to spit out the words.

Forster would've known what to say.

He extracted his phone, abandoning the kitchenette and shouldering past a crowd of his coworkers in the hall, exchanging a brief nod with Szymanski by the water dispenser as he retreated to the safety of his office. Just a nod. He didn't say anything about his run-in with Erin. Not this time. They were only colleagues. But…

Ping.

> **Forster**
> Have you ever tried sudoku? I just beat my best time!

He breathed.

> **Ethan**
> I have a daily calendar. I like the cleanliness of the numbers. It gives order to the start of my day. Better than caffeine for clearing brain fog.

Which was good, since his confrontation with Erin had left him with a stinging lip and no coffee.

> **Ethan**
> What's your best time?

He uncapped a pen and reached for the calendar on his desk. Instead of listing numbers for each cell that wouldn't contradict the simple, difficult rules of the game, however, he rubbed a thumb over his mouth and watched for Forster's response. It didn't take long.

> **Forster**
> 4:17. In my defense, though, I only started a few years ago. And I haven't been very consistent with my practice.

> **Ethan**
> That's a good time. Especially if you're not working on it every day.

> **Forster**
> Maybe. What's your record?

He couldn't help smiling a little.

> **Ethan**
> 3:18.

> **Forster**
> You're 59 seconds faster than I am.

Her typing ellipsis bubbled. Then:

> **Forster**
> I could catch you.

> **Ethan**
> You'd have to reduce your time by almost 30%.

> **Forster**
> You think I can't do it?

> **Ethan**
> You think you can?

Forster

I'm not going to admit it now if I have doubts! Just give me until Friday morning.

Ethan

What's happening on Friday morning?

The Department of Energy's visit was scheduled for Friday. But he didn't volunteer that information. It wasn't the sort of thing they shared, not when they each valued a hard line between their professional and creative work. They'd both said so. He wouldn't breach that limit.

Probably.

Forster

Our race. Pencils at dawn. I have a major work event, and sudoku will be my brain warm-up.

Ethan

Deal.

He'd certainly need a way to condition his own brain and stabilize his anxiety on the morning of the visit, too. Yes, he'd spent weeks assembling white papers and holometer data displays for the occasion, and he knew his numbers inside and out. Those preparations had been made with Bunsen at his feet and Ted Chiang's short stories at his elbow, though. Neither would be with him at SVLAC on Friday. But Dr. Kramer would be. Dr. Kramer, who expected nothing but excellence from him because he knew what Ethan was capable of, if only he applied himself to their research—

Ping.

Forster

You'd better get yourself a Big Game training regimen.

Again, he breathed. Despite her dare, the knots in his stomach eased.

Ethan

Making good on the Stanford–Berkeley rivalry.

Forster

Yes. Be warned: I show no mercy to my rivals.

Ethan

A menace.

Forster

To my enemies and my brothers. But I'll always go to bat for my friends. Pick your strategy wisely.

Ethan

I will.

Forster

It's probably for the best that we've never met in the real world. We'd be enemies on principle.

…*oh*.
Probably for the best.
Probably.
She'd mentioned a work event on Friday, toeing their lines of separation…
Could they meet…?

Brrrriiinng!
His desktop phone shrilled.

Incoming Call: *Dr. John Kramer*

Hurriedly closing his personal messages, he opened a spreadsheet on his monitor and reached for the phone. Fortunately, the holometer data set for Table 5 in the grant application was the random file that expanded across his screen. Not that Dr. Kramer could see it. But he stared at the numerical cells and graphs anyhow—*focus*—as he picked up the receiver, standing at attention when his desk chose that moment to vacillate between heights. "Dr.—"

"You're late. Check your inbox, Meyer."

Dr. Kramer had sent over Finance's accounting reconciliation needs for the department's quarterly expenses (including his networking dinners, golf rounds with journal editors, and a series of upcoming flights to Switzerland), along with a marked-up draft of Tomasz Szymanski's latest paper on LED performance stabilization in extreme heat, and edits for Ethan's weekend updates to the grant.

Table 5 had simply been reformatted. His supervisor had made no comment on the unaltered data.

"Finance wants the report by five o'clock."

Despite the administrative drudgery now set to eclipse any work time that he could've had around today's multi-hour in-person meeting, his shoulders settled. "They'll have it by one o'clock."

"Good."

Tracking down receipts and typing up cost memorandums took the better part of his morning. He forwarded Dr. Kramer's notes to Szymanski—almost supplementing his usual salutation with a hope that Szymanski had enjoyed his weekend, before quickly deleting the personal words and sending over their supervisor's amendments without comment—and updated the Eischer-Langhoff application again.

He wasn't distracted. He wasn't.

His phone remained quiet beneath its blur of white noise.

Clearly, Forster was also busy.

But Erin Monaghan was discussing her plans for the Department of Energy's visit with Nadine Fong in one of the corridors fringing the bullpen. The one outside his office, to be exact.

"I've improvised some graphics from my last International Conference on Physics poster to highlight our department's work. It's a simplified explanation of relativistic mechanics operating in extreme gravitational and astrophysical conditions, but we might only have a few minutes with the officials. For non-specialists, narrative is more important than data."

"That's the poster from the Burlingame conference?"

"The one where I had six hours with a designer, instead of an intern still learning Adobe Illustrator. Since the graphics are turning out to be reusable, arguing the expense with Finance was worth it."

"Back when I had energy for that sort of thing," with a groan from Fong. "But yes, simpler is better for the government. Good work. No edits, just—*ugh*, never mind, nature calls again—"

His rival's supervisor shuffled off toward the bathroom. It had to be her, because those weren't Erin's strides. *She* lingered in the hall outside his office, like the sweet, fresh scent still clinging in his sinuses, likely flushed with triumph at Fong's approval.

Or maybe not. Maybe receiving praise from the head of Relativistic Mechanics was just part of her Monday agenda. Maybe she didn't value it, because she didn't have to work for it.

Maybe Fong doled out approval like other people doled out and then discarded tennis balls at a dog park: casually, thoughtlessly, because they were cheap, plentiful, and ordinary. Dr. Kramer's approbation meant more. Ethan's supervisor didn't offer praise just because he had to piss.

Clamping his headphones over his ears, he focused back on the Finance report. Being forced to eavesdrop on Erin's conversation had cost him minutes in an already tight schedule. He'd have to skip lunch to finish the form now.

As usual, it was her fault.

His irritation continued during the afternoon's all-hands meeting, sitting among his fellow engineers and SVLAC's administrative staff with a growling stomach while a projector beam warmed the top of his head and Schulz's assistant read out a schedule for the Department of Energy's visit.

"…and then the tour will conclude with a presentation by Dr. Helena Quarles on the contributions of SVLAC to American science education. Dr. Quarles' talk will be here in Maiman Auditorium. Space is limited,"—someone in the room's front row of swivel chairs gave a quiet but distinct snort; recognizing Erin's laugh, Ethan swallowed his guffaw and frowned at his table—"but staff can reserve seats through a sign-up form sent out at the start of this meeting."

The assistant clicked forward to her next slide.

"Now, dress code: unless engaged in structural work on the accelerators, staff are to wear suits. Neutral colors and trousers are appropriate for all genders, but skirts may be worn if desired. Open-toed shoes are not acceptable. Hats that aren't baseball caps are subject to approval by—"

A collective groan rippled across the room at Marcie's specifications. This time, both Ethan and his stomach joined in. Accustomed to a seasonless uniform of jeans and work boots, a significant percentage of the audience would be making a run on the local thrift stores this week. Some might even brave the Stanford Shopping Center. He'd been forced into a pilgrimage to Jos. A. Bank several years ago in preparation for Chase's thirtieth birthday dinner at The French Laundry, so he'd be spared the rush, at least.

But.

The shopping center sold more than suits.

Lingerie, Forster's freckles under the soft golden glow of a dressing room's lights, the toned obliques of a runner or cyclist narrowing the dip of her waist—but though the picture was indelibly seared in his mind, her backdrop was anonymous. She could've been in any Bay Area mall. However, just maybe…

His groan lasted a second too long. He shifted in his chair.

"Stomach," he muttered to Szymanski's sideways look.

Down in the front row, Erin was conspiring again with Nadine Fong while Marcie finished delineating acceptable versus unacceptable fedoras and explained Friday's parking restrictions. Dust in the projector beam swirled above a medley of digital colors in her hair, pulled tight at her neck into that lethal ponytail.

To himself, he added: *focus*.

10

Tuesday's lab time and the whole of Wednesday passed in a whirlwind of graphics, data collection, and sleepless hours spent preparing for the impending federal visit. Somewhere in the helix of Dr. Kramer's demands, Ethan managed to submit the Eischer-Langhoff grant application. He celebrated by stretching his neck away from his computer and reading a single page of *This Is How You Lose the Time War* at… was it really after three o'clock in the morning?

Bunsen's runs were abbreviated jogs around the patio.

Still, he paused in the Modern Physics kitchenette on Thursday to inconvenience Erin by dumping the last of the oat milk into his mug—even if this super-quantity of creamer made his caffeine almost undrinkable. He smirked at his rival's outrage as he tossed away the carton in front of her, his mug overflowing. Coffee spilled out onto his jeans when he tried to carry it down the hall to his office. His messages with Forster kept him smiling, though.

> **Forster**
> Approaching the sudoku starting line. Twenty-two hours to go. I hope you're quick on the draw.

His pen paused mid-doodle. He snorted.

Ethan

Puns? This early?

Forster

I told you: I'm a menace.

Ethan

Remind me not to get on your bad side.

Forster

As long as I win tomorrow, I'll keep the peace.

Forster

…unlike the turkeys by my office building. They were circling some roadkill today like they were ritually resurrecting it. I bet they're planning a remastered version of Alfred Hitchcock's The Birds—but this time, they'll have zombies on their side.

He snorted again.

Ethan

The humans will have you, though.

Forster

Not if these feathered dinosaurs take me out before the battle starts. Then you'll be the only one who knows their plan, humanity's lone hope.

Ethan

A New Hope?

Forster

Yes. The conflict will be called the Starling Wars.

His laughter propelled his chair away from his desk. His head smacked into the wall. But he grinned while he rubbed at the ache.

If he executed his role during the government visit perfectly, maybe Dr. Kramer would promote him to an office with windows, where he could monitor SVLAC's own turkeys—or even just move him to a room that didn't smell faintly of cleaning chemicals from its proximity to an adjoining janitorial closet.

But no promotion would materialize if he didn't focus.

So he blotted the coffee from his jeans, wheeled himself a few inches back to his desk, and opened his inbox. At the top was his supervisor's feedback about a white paper summarizing the Quantum group's work.

> *Meyer:*
> *The graphics are accurate.*
> *Increase the font size on the paper heading.*
> *Format the document as a PDF and print it.*
> *— Kramer*

He savored his department head's approval for a moment. Maybe those windows weren't such a moonshot dream after all? Then he confirmed the number of copies required and sent his order to the Modern Physics media room. He inspected every plastic-bound report for errors as it emerged from the printer, checking for the slightest misalignment of margins or tables, but each one was right. Since Dr. Kramer's office door was closed, he slid a copy into his supervisor's mailbox. The report was a triumph, a clear articulation of both the theory and practice of quantum measurement, with reams of meticulous footnotes and complex, elegant graphics—but its excellence was simply meeting expectations for Dr. Kramer. It didn't merit a closed-door interruption. Excellence should be a normal expectation for himself, too. With Dr. Kramer as his mentor, it eventually would be.

He strode back toward his desk from the Quantum mailboxes, past an intern gingerly punching codes into a cranky copy machine by the kitchenette—which was empty. So, he could spare three minutes to brew a drinkable cup of coffee, couldn't he? As long as it was an espresso. Fifty milligrams of caffeine would speed him through the afternoon at twice his usual productivity. The *start* button depressed under his thumb, and—

Beep. Beeeep. Beeeeeeep!

An angry mechanical chirp sounded. Steam whirred from a vent behind the machine. Lights blinked on its menu screen.

Beeeeeeep! Beep.

Had Erin crossed the appliance's wires this morning? Or registered his fingerprints to activate a security alert? His ideas for sabotage ran riot—but then ordinary espresso began to drip into his mug. The lights on the device were green; he frowned. If it wasn't the coffee machine, then what…

"Do you need help?"

Her voice.

She wasn't in the kitchenette. She was in the hallway, ferrying her own armload of reports past the door without even glancing inside to see him, nonplussed and holding a normal brew. And she wasn't addressing him with a sardonic offer of assistance, either.

"Leah?"

Leah Haddad. She was one of the Modern Physics interns, wasn't she? The one he'd passed at the copier.

"*Um*… sorry, it's just… the machine—"

Beep, beep. Beeeep.

"I think I… broke it?"

"Let's see." *Thump*, and the electronic ruckus stopped. "No, not broken. It just needed a whack. There's probably a jam. Can you check the paper tray?"

Gliders rattled, then snagged.

"Unless you were using this—what even is that color? *chartreuse*?—flyer paper to make reminders for Human Resources about taping down loose cables, this wasn't you. Someone else left the jam, and you got stuck in it. Let's get that shredded sheet out."

Paper squealed as it was extracted from the machine's rollers.

"Thanks for fixing it, Dr. Monaghan. Sorry."

"Call me Erin. But don't be sorry for dealing with someone else's mess. Be annoyed that they left it for you. And remember: *we* fixed it. Let me know if the scanner gives you grief." Her sneakers moved on toward the bullpen.

We fixed it.

The copier hummed to life. A paper tray was filled. Its scanner chirped. When the automated stapler choked on its own teeth, the intern's *tap*, *tap*, *tap* got it moving again.

We.

Taking her cue from Nadine Fong, she tossed that word and its implicit praise around so casually, while Dr. Kramer—

Ethan poured his untouched mug of espresso into the sink, squashing the thought. His supervisor was a genius, not a hand-holding teacher, and his rival was wasting her time coaching an intern to use outdated office equipment when she should've been preparing for the Department of Energy's visit. A scientist with Dr. Erin Monaghan for a mentor would never learn independence or time management. Or excellence. With Dr. Kramer, he'd someday have it all.

His *someday* didn't come that week, but Friday morning arrived with him already showered after a quick run with Bunsen, shaved, and brewing his own coffee when his alarm blared its wake-up warning. He was wrung out from four days of insomnia and anxiety, but now adrenaline jangled in his nerves, triggering a surge of alertness to power him through the next twelve hours. Any come-down crash over the weekend would be worth it.

He'd deal with the fallout when it arrived.

And maybe, maybe if there was a lull in his workload after the government visit...

Maybe he'd ask Forster to join him for a drink.

But first: *today*.

He unearthed a suit in charcoal wool from the rear of his closet, knotting a tie and shrugging into the jacket before readying the sudoku sheet that they'd chosen by mutual blind agreement for their race.

Ping.

> **Forster**
> I'm ready to win. Ready for your defeat?

> **Forster**
> (I should warn you: I'm not a good loser. I'm a menace, remember?)

She was a menace to her siblings. He could've said the same of Chase. But that was where the similarities between their brothers seemed to end. Whenever Forster mentioned them, it was with a casual and playful—if occasionally irritated—fondness. They called her a menace, and she embraced the term because it so clearly wasn't derogatory. Or if it was, there was too much history and love behind the epithet for it to hurt. Despite their distance in Michigan, she was close with her family—and an abrupt pang of longing stabbed under his ribs, bitter and sweet.

She was waiting for his reply, however. He tapped back into their thread.

> **Ethan**
> My stopwatch is set.
>
> **Forster**
> And—go!

With the blank squares of a sudoku grid under his hand, he couldn't dwell on the fresh and sudden tension in his body that had nothing to do with the government's visit, couldn't dwell on the unsettling reality that beyond their texts, Forster was surrounded by real people, people she knew and loved—not just the violent, tender characters of Red and Blue from *This Is How You Lose the Time War*, like him. He couldn't brood on the fact that he was only one small cell in the graph of her life.

He was embarrassingly grateful for that, and scribbled a final 7 just as the timer ticked past his record.

> **Ethan**
> Done.
>
> **Forster**
> (New Photo Message)

The picture was a screenshot of her clock. She'd finished eight seconds behind him.

> **Forster**
> Damn. But hear me out: I was using a pencil.
> The graphite broke.

A second picture provided evidence.

> **Forster**
> I claim the right to a rematch!

Laughter curled his tongue. He breathed and relaxed back into his desk chair, reaching for his mug.

> **Ethan**
> Accepted. But no third chances. Use a pen next time.
>
> **Forster**
> That's insane. What if I make a mistake?
>
> **Ethan**
> Don't.
>
> **Forster**
> Ugh. Teach me your flawless puzzle technique.
>
> **Ethan**
> Only if you concede defeat next time.
>
> **Forster**
> Never!

Their argument went on until almost eight o'clock, when the time demanded the truce that they'd refused to call for themselves. Then Ethan brushed his teeth until his gums ached, rubbed Bunsen's ears for good luck, and creaked out the door in a pair of stiff Oxfords. But despite the leather pinching his feet as he merged into the southbound lanes of Junipero Serra Freeway, he caught his slight smile in the rearview mirror. He swiped inside the Modern Physics building, bypassing the kitchenette this time—he had other things on his mind—and turning down the hall toward his office, straightening his tie, sidestepping a line of jugs waiting to fill a nearby water dispenser—

He almost collided with Erin Monaghan.

Again.

Unlike that first morning, however, she was also wearing a suit.

Instead of Oxfords or her usual sneakers, she'd paired her gold-flecked ivory tweed jacket and trousers with formidable heels that elevated her height to match his. They were eye-to-eye. Seen so closely now—*too closely*—her tortoiseshell glasses reflected reticulated metallic rings around her pupils. (Had he never noticed that detail before? Or forgotten it? *How?*) A single strand of hair over her ear had escaped from her high, tight bun. It drifted in the office air conditioning, tickling her neck and the edge of her parted lips—*iris, juniper*. His own breath fogged her lenses.

Fuck.

But he cataloged every particular without stepping away, staring because he couldn't stop himself. She stared straight back. And apparently he'd stopped breathing while he gawked—suffocation was better than inhaling her scent again, wasn't it?—because only an oxygen deficiency could explain the heat in his face that was creeping down his chest. His pulse throbbed under his jaw, in his ears and skull. Still, he didn't move.

Erin was the first to recover, of course.

After a startled, unblinking moment, her mouth clamped shut. She narrowed her eyes. Her fingers darted to her lapels, as if itching to fold the tweed forward over her blouse. Her heels edged sideways to circumnavigate the obstacle he'd made of himself. But the water dispenser jugs blocked her way, and his damn Oxfords fixed his feet to the floor.

A flush of irritation swept over her cheeks, dipping along her throat, not stopping at the neckline of her usual graphic t-shirt or sweater but traveling beneath her collarbones now, under the buttons of her blouse and her silk camisole.

He inhaled again. He had to, dizzy, too hot—*so hot*—and—

"Here you are, Erin."

"Meyer."

Again, like that first day: *Dr. Kramer*.

His body torqued to face his department head coming down the hall. But it wasn't just Dr. Kramer approaching. Nadine Fong walked with her fellow supervisor past the bullpen, one hand supporting the belly that extended far past her open blazer and the other raised in greeting to her junior colleague. Erin took advantage of his angled shoulders to slip by, her heels stabbing the carpet as she moved to join Fong.

"Do we need any final changes to our visuals before the Secretary arrives?"

"The graphics are fine. Better than fine, which you already know. No, it's not that. Erin, did you reserve a seat for Dr. Quarles' presentation?"

"She's a Sakurai Prize recipient and former president of the American Physical Society. Of course I did. If there's time after her talk, I have questions prepared—"

"Quarles isn't speaking," Dr. Kramer cut her off.

Fong sighed. "Her outbound flight after the ICTP conference has been delayed."

The International Centre for Theoretical Physics was in Trieste.

"She's still in Italy?" Ethan's voice jumped octaves. But at least he got the words out.

"Which means that there's no keynote speaker on site for the Secretary's visit. That's a problem, Meyer."

Despite the seriousness of the situation, Erin and Fong traded a silent *"Houston."* Dr. Kramer, however, crossed his arms. He tapped his own elbow with an index finger. When Dr. John Kramer identified a problem, there was one acceptable result: it got fixed. *Fast.*

He tapped a second time.

Ethan couldn't quantum-leap Dr. Helena Quarles across the Atlantic. The odds that another physicist of her caliber was in the Bay Area today and available on six hours' notice to run a presentation for the Department of Energy were too small to measure, even for him. So the substitute speaker had to be someone from SVLAC's staff who was on campus and had time to put together a talk.

Not Elias Schulz, busy with wining, dining, and glad-handing promises of funding.

Not Nadine Fong, shifting from foot to foot, eyeing the bathroom down the hall.

Tap.

Producing a presentation to Dr. Kramer's standards would take days: speaker notes, click timings for animations, drafted answers to potential questions.

But:

Tap tap. Tap tap tap—

"I'll do it," he heard himself say. "I'll give the talk."

Silence.

Erin's mouth fell open again. Then:

"You're offering to present, Dr. Meyer?" Fong paused her fidgeting. "Are you prepared?"

"I will be," he told Dr. Kramer—then waited for an agonizing second until his supervisor's fingers settled, until he nodded.

"You have work to do, Meyer," serious and unsmiling.

"Yes," he exhaled.

But if Dr. Kramer didn't smile, Erin did. She ran her tongue along her lower lip, and there was naked, unsettling calculation in her gaze. "Good luck."

Losing her sudoku challenge to Bannister wasn't what irritated her this morning.

It was her feet.

She'd accepted the necessity of ordering a ride service today, since the formality of her clothes and hairstyle weren't conducive to cycling. But she wished that she'd foreseen the equal necessity of packing a pair of flats. The nude adhesive strips that she'd taped behind her ankles to create a buffer between her skin and the crisp, elegant leather of her heels was doing its job—Martina had mentioned that particular sartorial hack, and she'd be treating her friend to bottomless mimosas over a post-Pilates brunch on Saturday in gratitude, if she could still hobble to the restaurant—but her arches were already aching and the shoes' wicked pointed toes were squashing her bones.

How did Adrian's Manhattan dates and business associates do it?

Was there some trick with gel supports? Or maybe the women just got on with work or pleasure to take their minds off the discomfort. Which was what she needed to do.

Leaving Ethan Meyer and Kramer by the water dispenser, she waited for Nadine to complete her pilgrimage to the bathroom, then retreated into her supervisor's office.

Good luck.

It was.

"I'm sorry to hear about Dr. Quarles. But this could benefit us. Even Dr. Meyer can't be in two places at once, and if he spends the day preparing his talk, he can't pitch his research during the department tours—or one-on-one with the Secretary of Energy by *serendipitously* running into her on campus."

"But you can."

"Yes."

She flipped through a document she'd assembled about their department's work on pulsars and her own LIGO research. Beneath a series of charts tracking the alignment between predicted and observed radio wave frequencies from a neutron star, the page was packed with graphics illustrating the compression and dilation of space-time on Earth from the passage of astrophysical gravitational waves. They were graphics that even a layperson would find compelling; she'd used Bannister's art as inspiration. The Secretary of Energy's position was a political appointment, and she couldn't make assumptions about the depth of Elise McCandless's science expertise.

Bracing a hand against Nadine's desk to relieve the pressure on her feet, she went on, "Everything that Dr. Meyer communicates to the Secretary will need to happen during his presentation. Which means that I can redirect the conversation—or refute something in it—if I need to."

"Erin, you don't…" Nadine's lips pursed. But then she just shook her head and reached for the document. "What's your plan for Secretary McCandless?"

"Our research explores renewable interstellar energy sources and how the movement of astrophysical bodies impacts space-time. It's groundbreaking work. Or ground-rippling work, in my case. I can't let a slumping economy stymie that. I'll figure out a way to talk privately—or semi-privately—with her today. Even better, I'll corner someone from the Office of Science. They'll have more understanding of the subject matter and less security to navigate. Marcie explained the tour schedule, so I know where to be to meet them, and when. Once I get their attention, how can they not be fascinated?"

"While quantum physics, on the other hand, is generally incomprehensible to everyone except experts—"

"—especially with Dr. Meyer speaking. If he sticks to his normal presentation playbook, a non-specialist audience won't find him interesting at all. If they even stay awake."

"But you're a good speaker, Erin. Though if you could be a kind one, too…"

She *was* a good speaker. Usually.

She'd been headed to Nadine's office to confirm her plans for the day, but she'd run up against Ethan in the hall, just like on her onboarding day at SVLAC—and the abrupt and level meeting of their eyes—*slate and blue starred with mica*—with the warm, bitter spice of fresh aftershave prickling her nose (he'd been unshaven before; she would've remembered *this*), hair rising on her nape so that she itched to draw her jacket closed over her blouse, wishing that its closure were a zipper rather than delicate gold buttons, something quick and forceful and efficient—followed by a lurch in her stomach—

—*Easy, Monaghan*—

Damn him.

He wouldn't rattle her again. Wouldn't silence her. The shock was over now, her resistance against it—against *him*— was prepared, and this day was too important to bungle over aftershave or disturbing dreams. So:

"I *am* a good speaker," she repeated Nadine's assertion. *I will be.* Then she glanced at her watch. "And it's game time."

The Department of Energy's tour began with opening remarks and an orientation from the lab's director over coffee and pastries at the Science and Public Support building. Since maneuvering a scooter in heels was a stunt that even Wes wouldn't pull, she winced her way over from Modern Physics on foot and arrived just as a government motorcade rolled past the gatehouse. She knew better than to approach the cars, stationing herself instead at the building's main entrance with her staff badge displayed. Elias Schulz and his assistant walked past her to meet the Secretary, but she focused on the security vanguard advancing toward her location by the doors.

"Welcome to the SVLAC National Laboratory," she greeted them.

Their faces were expressionless behind the armor of sunglasses and earpieces. Ignoring her, they took up positions flanking the entryway. She moved aside without protest. She'd expected this.

"You've already swept the area and know the campus layout, but you might not know that Blue Bottle—that open-air cafe just down Ring Road?—will have better coffee than anything from the cafeteria. Just in case you get a break later."

No response.

"Also, they make danishes on Fridays."

Still nothing.

Well, she'd have other opportunities, though it would've been better to establish herself now with the Secretary's security team. Disappointed but undaunted, she was turning away, prepared to try her luck at lunch, when one of the suits behind her coughed.

"What kind of danishes?"

Erin had to suppress a satisfied smile before she answered, "Cream cheese." Then she kept walking, giving the officials a respectful berth and making no attempt to speak with the Secretary or the staff from the Office of Science.

That would come later.

She was in.

She spent the rest of the morning blocking out her department's research schedule for the upcoming quarter, assigning Marco Rossi and Sandra O'Connor-Young to oversee data collection cycles for their binary pulsar study and slotting in interns to assist with cleaning the radio wave signal exports. Leah Haddad had experience with running a Fourier transform, didn't she? Nadine had mentioned the cohort's various interests and backgrounds while introducing the group to their department. And she was smart but very diffident, so maybe she should lead the intern group's data review… The facilitation of growth opportunities aside, however, it was mindless work, just playing Tetris with time. Her focus remained on the Department of Energy's schedule.

> *9:00 a.m. – Opening remarks, orientation, and breakfast*
> *9:45 a.m. – Klystron gallery and Linac Light Source tour*
> *10:30 a.m. – Visit discovery site of desmostylian fossil*
> *11:15 a.m. – Break*
> *11:45 a.m. – Archival Survey of Space and Time (ASST) camera tour*
> *12:30 p.m. – Lunch*

Fund-hungry physicists had to eat, too.

She was at the cafeteria when the tour group arrived for lunch. One of the security guards that she'd approached earlier stood by the balcony doors. He was wiping his mouth with a napkin from Blue Bottle.

"Was the danish good?" She began to assemble a meal tray, slowed by the stack of reports under her arm and her glances at the cafeteria's entry. Secretary McCandless was approaching.

"Yes."

"Did you get the cream cheese one?"

"Yes." The Secretary crossed the lunchroom with her entourage and the security guard opened the doors onto the balcony, where a catering spread from Evvia was reserved for the federal personnel. Elise McCandless smoothed back her expensively colored hair when a gust of wind blew in from the terrace, revealing a pair of striking diamond studs in her ears.

Perfect.

"*Ooof.*" Erin wrenched a recalcitrant plastic cup from its stack with a noisy *pop*. She shrugged at the Blue Bottle guard. "You know, I'm studying gravitational waves produced from the movement of astrophysical masses—like the collision of black holes or neutron stars—by looking at their impact on space-time. It takes a monumental amount of force generated from thousands of light-years away to show even a tiny data blip on our monitoring equipment. Imagine if that same force, that pressure, originated on Earth. It'd be enough to make diamonds! I'm still not sure that the pressure could be greater than the vacuum sealing these cups together, though."

Her intentions couldn't have been more obvious if she'd been holding up a neon sign that read "Pay Attention and Money to Me!" But the Secretary paused. Her diamond studs glittered. "SVLAC's research could be used to make gemstones?"

Yes!

"No, Madam Secretary. At least..." She took an experimental step forward. The security guard didn't stop her. She was discussing fashion and had good danish recommendations. *No threat.* "Not yet. But my department's work indicates that there are other natural high pressure and high temperature zones in the universe with the potential to create diamonds from carbon, beyond those occurring under the Earth's mantle. With the right equipment and funding, we might be able to harness the forces producing those pressures and temperatures. Scientists at NASA have already found nanodiamonds in meteorites! They're too small for use in jewelry, though. And standard lab-grown gems are commercially available, of course, but just imagine: ethically produced interstellar diamonds…"

"Which department is that?"

"Relativistic Mechanics."

"Not Quantum Mechanics?" A man from the Secretary's retinue raised a question now. His badge identified him as the Director of the United States Office of Science. "The general consensus seems to be that quantum is the future of experimental physics. But clearly, there are other relevant fields."

"My group works with areas of mechanics that are compatible with special and general relativity, sir. Tangible, observable physics and," Erin tapped her documents, "tangible, observable reports on radio waves emitting from binary pulsars. If we can capture those radio waves—which should be much easier than capturing the force of colliding black holes, in all honesty—they could potentially provide unlimited and reliable power sources for astronauts in orbit."

"Really." He eyed her files. "Do you manage this group?"

"Dr. Nadine Fong heads the Relativistic Mechanics group. I'm Dr. Erin Monaghan."

He appraised her as he'd appraised her papers. Then he extended a hand. "Dr. Richard Hall."

"Welcome to SVLAC, Dr. Hall."

Before she and the Director could advance their professional courtesies further into outright networking, a mass of hungry government officials compelled the guard to take his charges out onto the balcony for lunch. She retreated without protest, abandoning her tray and her cup to grab a prepackaged salad. She hummed "Lucy in the Sky with Diamonds" while she walked back to Modern Physics. She hardly felt her blisters.

She was still grateful to take a seat in Maiman Auditorium that evening, and surreptitiously eased her chafed, swollen feet out of her heels. She had no intention of moving for a while, anyhow; Hall had invited her to join him in a row behind Secretary McCandless and her security detail. He'd listened to her formal research presentation during a lightning round of department tours, and now she had his ear for the next hour, too. Likely his interest, as well—Ethan Meyer was awkwardly clearing his throat into a microphone at the podium, a slide packed with microscopic numbers and dense text glowing behind him on the projector screen.

"Secretary McCandless and distinguished guests from the United States Office of Science, welcome. Dr. Helena Quarles was scheduled to address you tonight, but she's unfortunately been delayed in Italy. So instead—I'm Dr. Ethan Meyer, from Quantum Mechanics at SVLAC." He ran his fingers through his hair in a short, brusque gesture, as if searching for the pen or pencil that he sometimes stuck behind his ear. He'd either attempted to pat down his cowlicks with water, or else sweat was beading on his temples. His tie looked too tight. "This evening, I'll discuss the research that Dr. John Kramer's department is conducting on quantum measurement. When a half-reflective mirror splits perpendicular laser beams and bounces them along a pair of thirty-meter tunnels—the beams are calibrated to register the precise locations of the mirrors—"

His data was immaculate, like always. His analyses were sound, obviously. But his constant clarification about the early status of his work overbore its genuinely compelling results. Head cocked, Hall squinted at the print on his slides and frowned.

Under-promise, over-deliver was Adrian Monaghan's mantra. Ethan's conscientious scientific caution was doing him no favors with the politicians, however. Erin took full advantage of that.

"Relativistic mechanics functions at a much broader scale than the quantum field," she murmured to the Director. "Quantum is useful for micro-scales, but my department's scope is the rest of the galaxy."

"You mentioned black holes earlier."

"Yes. Gravity loses its predictive power around them. As does relativistic mechanics. More than the generation of diamond-level pressure zones, that's why it's important to study their behavior through the proxy of gravitational waves. If we can determine why gravity fails to reliably affect matter and why geometry becomes ill defined around black holes—if we can replace our current singularity theories with fact—then we'll have solved one of the greatest outstanding questions in physics. There also won't be a need for two contradictory theories of reality anymore, and—"

The crackle of a microphone drowned her out before she could explain the extent of the gulf between her field and Ethan's, and why they collided at the rims of black holes. Before she could argue why her field—why *she*—was on the right side of scientific history, too.

"…I'll take questions."

Ethan's credits faded to the white of a blank projector beam. Fragments of applause rippled in fits and starts through the auditorium as the audience realized that his talk was finished, some flinching awake and others putting down their phones. Despite his frown, Richard Hall was among those clapping, as was Secretary McCandless.

So Erin leaned forward. "I have a question."

"Monaghan."

Because she was watching for it, she saw his fingers clench on the edge of the podium, saw the corners of his mouth tighten.

He knew what she meant to do.

But hadn't he done the same to her? During their all-hands: *Dirty results... fraudulent data.* Turnabout was fair play. Now here he was, standing in Maiman Auditorium's very public spotlight of his own volition, ripe for a fall.

For her revenge.

This was easy.

"Your research concerns a measurement of the smallest possible unit of space. A quantum. This requires isolating that unit, doesn't it?"

"Of course."

"And space—space-time—is a wave."

"Relativistic mechanics and your own experimental research both currently assert that as fact," with a shrug, adding quickly, "However, unlike LIGO's gravitational wave measurements that require verification with multi-messenger astronomy, the holometer has no implicit noise to scrub from its signal. The accuracy of its readings is never subject to human error when running a Fourier transform, and it doesn't need external—"

"A wave is inherently in motion, isn't it?"

"Yes, but what does that have to do with—"

"For your holometer to yield meaningful results, you'd need to isolate a unit in a moving wave. Isn't the limitation of the Quantum Mechanical Model that it can't show speed and position at the same time? By the Heisenberg Uncertainty principle, you'll never know exactly where your unit is. How can you measure it if you can't locate it?"

"The Quantum Mechanical Model can't show the speed and location of an *electron* simultaneously. But that doesn't necessarily mean that the Model will fail when applied to measuring a quantum of space."

"You can't be sure, though."

"I—" Rigorous, exacting, honest Ethan Meyer wouldn't promise certainty if he couldn't validate his assertion with data. His fingers spasmed again.

"Relativistic mechanics, on the other hand, has no such practical limitations. General relativity has passed all observational tests. It's consistent with experimental data. Which *can be collected accurately*. It seems that you can't say the same."

The quiet as she sat back in triumph from her tabletop microphone was very loud. Ethan abandoned the stage a minute later after giving only the briefest of thanks for the audience's attention and consideration, face set as he shoved his laptop into his bag with unsteady hands. When it became clear that he wasn't coming back to the podium for an encore no one wanted, Schulz and his assistant had to finish the night. Hall passed Erin a business card while the audience filed out of Maiman Auditorium.

"I'd welcome additional details about your department's gravitational and radio wave research. You're working at the vanguard of physics. I'm interested to see more from you, Dr. Monaghan."

"I'll send the information on Monday."

"Good. Now, I have some people I'd like you to meet."

Mind buzzing with names, credentials, positions, funding lures, and the pulse of fading adrenaline, she wobbled back to the Modern Physics building almost an hour after Ethan's talk had ended. She'd made connections with the federal officials, had seen her rival publicly, definitively silenced in a forum much more consequential than an internal research meeting—if her gut twinged at a flash of memory articulating his lowered eyes and shaking fingers, she squashed it—and she'd even survived the day in heels. She was secure in both her research and her control as she stepped past the badge scanner. (She did kick off her shoes in the hall, though.) Because if she could manage all this, then her tongue-tied moment by the water dispenser must've been a fluke. *Right?*

She padded to the bullpen in semi-darkness. The building's central nervous system had powered down for the night and she made her way toward her desk by the dim hints of emergency exit lighting, Modern Physics' fluorescent bulbs and air conditioning off, its chairs deserted, office doors closed and locked.

All except one.

The rapid scratch of a pen, the hiss of curses, a paperweight or book flung against the wall—

Thud!

Harsh, shallow breathing in the silence.

Someone else was still here, too.

She was in his doorway before she even knew she'd moved.

Ethan Meyer was slumped at his desk. His head rested in his hands, fingers kneading his forehead and tugging at his hair. Scraps of graph paper littered the floor around him, fanning out beside an overturned calendar that he must've thrown at the door. His breath hitched and his shoulders shuddered. His eyelids were pinched closed.

She didn't mean to speak. She wouldn't have. But when her own breath caught with an unexpected twist in her chest, he jerked up, eyes opening—black, wilder than his hair.

One jagged inhale. Then—

"Please go," he said.

Simple, quiet words.

Please.

Not even a demand.

Please go. Toneless. And all at once… suddenly… she had nothing to say. So she went, and she left her triumph behind with him.

11

12:01 a.m.

Ethan's watch read a minute past midnight by the time he hauled himself up from his desk. Bunsen was waiting, and his neighbors—faceless, nameless, but not deaf—would complain if the golden retriever started howling. Oxfords crunching in the litter on his office floor, he knelt in the narrow space between his chair and the wall and began to collect the screwed-up notes and documents, disposing of shredded research reports and sudoku graphs, hands moving mechanically to restore order.

He didn't remember causing this chaos. He didn't remember where the hours after his rush from Maiman Auditorium had gone, either. But he remembered Erin Monaghan murmuring to the Director of the United States Office of Science during his talk, remembered her leer at the microphone—

—remembered Chase sauntering up to his booth at a sixth grade science fair, asking why he'd transformed cow's milk into plastic instead of using soy or almond milk, since he claimed to care so much about animal welfare, leaving his eleven-year-old self struggling to articulate the difference between vegetarianism and veganism in front of his classmates and his teacher, the merits of his project forgotten in his anxiety—

—remembered Dr. Kramer's frown as the audience visibly lost interest in his scientifically sound but halting discourse, aware of his failure as a public speaker but helpless to course-correct himself under the hot, bright glow of the projector beam, the catastrophe only worsening when his rival chimed in with her glib simplification of the laws and fields of physics—

—kept seeing her in his doorway, barefoot with her shoes dangling in her hand, her loosened hair gilded by lamplight, triumphant—

Paper tore between his fingers, slicing the web of skin beside his thumb.

"*Ah!*"

He lobbed the offending sheet away. It was a sudoku grid, one of the fifty or so that he'd failed at tonight in his fugue. If she were here, Forster would likely have something clever to say about insults and injuries. He didn't.

He'd won his challenge with her this morning, but he'd lost the day.

The data was clear on that.

His phone was also clear: no new texts from her. Maybe she was still at her office, too. *I have a major work event*, she'd written.

There were other notifications on his screen, though.

Karen Meyer had messaged to ask his suit size for Chase's wedding party.

Could he get a year-long research placement somewhere in Siberia without cell service? Or on an oil rig in Antarctica? Then at least he wouldn't have to attend that simpering celebration from hell.

Szymanski had also messaged, offering a brief commendation for the good parts of his talk.

His supervisor had sent three words.

Dr. John Kramer
My office. Monday.

...fuck.

He'd thrown off his tie as soon as he'd left the auditorium, but it somehow still managed to choke him. Bracing his palms against his desk, he forced himself to swallow through the pressure on his windpipe, to focus on the manageable sting of his papercut as it stretched wider with his flexing fingers.

Don't panic. Just breathe. In. Out. In—

By failing to counter Erin's left-handed questions at the podium, he'd lost attention, funding, and respect for not just his own research, but also for his department head's work. He'd done it publicly. Dr. Kramer was right to be furious. *Were* there any research positions for quantum physicists at the South Pole? He never should've volunteered to present tonight.

But Dr. Kramer would've been displeased if he hadn't.

Fuck!

No, Antarctica wasn't far enough—though why... why should he exile himself, when it was Erin who was to blame? He knew his data and his topic, and while he wasn't a gifted orator, he'd executed his talk creditably—if not up to Dr. Kramer's standards of excellence, it hadn't been a disaster—until she'd bulldozed in at the end. He'd contrived one good dig about human error with Fourier transforms, but then...

She'd meant to humiliate him, taking vengeance for his all-hands challenge. Escalating their feud. Making it public. He should've known. Who would believe him, though? He had no proof of her intention except his own instinctive, bone-deep knowledge of how she thought and acted. Who would listen to and validate his anger? Who would help him plan his retribution? Not Chase. Not Dr. Kramer. Not even sympathetic but diplomatic Szymanski, with his workplace visa to maintain.

Forster.

And suddenly, what he needed became so obvious. Not the fading pain in his fingers. Not Antarctica. *No*: he needed to talk to her. He needed to see her. Their messages weren't enough. He needed to know her. He needed it *now*.

Standing in his office after midnight with his stomach in knots, he fumbled for his phone, clicked into their thread, and began to type.

> **Ethan**
> I know that we've talked about the Stanford–
> Berkeley rivalry as a problem. But what if it's not?

He paused, exhaled. Then he tapped out a second question. *The* question. Reckless, like the photo he'd shared.

> **Ethan**
> Would you like to meet for coffee or a drink?

Zip.

With the message sent, he locked and pocketed his device. Watching the screen for her response would drive him insane. She'd reply when she was ready. Anyhow, he'd only sent his suggestion a minute ago. If she was out with friends, unwinding from her day in a rowdy dive bar or one of the Peninsula's craft cocktail lounges, she might not see it for hours. He might have to wait until the morning for her answer. He already knew he wouldn't sleep.

Despite his tempered expectations, however, Forster's response came just after he'd exited the northbound freeway. Reaching to read it, he was grateful for the long traffic light near Stulsaft Park when he pulled up to the crosswalk.

Forster

I'd like that. Saturday night?

The tension in his chest lightened, fractionally but discernibly. He drove through the intersection and up the hill to his condominium complex. When he pulled into his parking space and switched off the engine, his pulse was deafening in the quiet. But he could breathe normally.

12:47 a.m.

Ethan

Yes to Saturday. Talk tomorrow, and see you soon.

As he unlocked his front door, stepped out of his Oxfords, and knelt to greet his frantic, slobbering retriever, his phone pinged again.

Forster

See you today.

"...and sitting tall on your mat, hands behind your thighs, curl your tailbone under your body and take a half roll-down until those arms are straight."

Muscles trembled in her core. Her fingers dug into the backs of her legs.

"Roll back up, using your abdominals, leading with your belly button, not your head..."

She tried not to groan.

On a mat beside her, Martina's face was pink, sweat beading into the curls making damp snarls around her temples. When their instructor passed back to the front of the exercise studio through the class's supple, suffering ranks and away from their struggle with six repetitions of the half roll-down routine, she hissed out the universal words of a Pilates devotee:

"I think I'm dying."

"Join me in hell." Erin's jaw ached with effort. Heat radiated from her cheeks. "I'm already there."

She was. She'd slept no more than a few minutes at a time last night, and she'd even bruised a knee against her headboard with her turning and thrashing.

Would you like to meet for coffee or a drink?

Bannister.

But: *Please go.*

Ethan.

She'd tied herself into knots in her sheets.

Not to mention, she'd spent a whole day in heels—well, almost a whole day, except for that brief barefoot moment in the Modern Physics building after hours—*no! focus, roll down again*—which had left her toes blistered and her hamstrings so tight that she could've plucked them like piano wires. Her muscles continued to scream at her.

"Lie back and press your palms to your mat. It's circle time, guys, gals, and nonbinary pals! Extend your right leg with a flexed foot. Lift your left leg toward the ceiling. Remember to turn out that thigh. Good. Now circle your left leg toward your midline. Five reps. Here's *one*."

Circle. Circle.

Barefoot. Lamplight. Harsh breaths. Ethan. Please go.

Circle.

Breaths. Ethan. Go—

"And *five*. Release down to the mat. Right leg up."

"How can you be in hell?" Martina hissed. "You got one-on-one time with—"

"Circle toward your midline…"

"—the Director of the Office of Science, and I heard from a barista at Blue Bottle that you sent someone from the security team over for danishes—"

"Less talking, more circles!"

Their instructor punished them with the shoulder bridge, swimming, and saw exercises, leaving Martina with no breath to probe for details and Erin with none to answer her. Despite the lactic acid coiling in her body, however, she was reluctant to descend from her swan dive pose, huffing into her mat hard enough to fog her glasses but remaining balanced on her chest and stomach with her legs lifted behind her even after the instructor released them to their cool-down. Cool-down meant that class was over, which meant that she and Martina would be headed to brunch soon, which meant more questions.

Reasonable questions. Questions about the Department of Energy's visit—which Martina had missed due to a blue-moon schedule of three consecutive days off—that she didn't particularly want to discuss.

She rolled up her Pilates mat, rinsed off her sweat in the bathroom, dropped a twist-back tank top over her sports bra and leggings, then shoved her blistered feet into a pair of sandals, pulling her ponytail so tight against her scalp that her eyelids stretched. But these were bearable discomforts, like the swan dive pose. She twisted her hair elastic even tighter.

"*Ugh*. I'm never wearing heels again," she groused as she and Martina left the studio. They passed a barre class in the next building, a paint-your-own-pottery shop, and several young families with luxury strollers and designer dogs while they threaded their way onto Santa Cruz Avenue.

"Friday was that bad, even with the adhesive strips and your fabulous suit?" Martina directed them off the sidewalk and flagged down a waiter at Founder's Toast for a table. "Morning, Jess."

"Hard class?" Jess led them to their usual alfresco spot on the patio, where shrubs lined a wrought-iron railing and manicured trees offered shade from the sun. "Coffee's coming."

"Thanks."

They settled into woven chairs and Erin reached for her menu. But Martina steepled her fingers, eyeing her over a fragrant coffee pot that Jess summoned between them.

"Don't you want to look at the menu?"

"It's always the same. Everything's always good. Now, what aren't you telling me about yesterday? It's not just the shoes, is it? And it can't be the suit, because it's something I actually approve of in your closet. I picked it out for you for your first talk at the International Conference on Physics, remember?"

"How do you even—"

"You hate the swan dive pose," Martina said. "*Everyone* hates it. But you kept at it in class. So you were stalling. You're stalling now, too. You know that menu inside and out. Also, it's upside down. Why?"

"*Uh*—did you see that they've started making their egg tartine on challah?"

"Erin."

"Fine." She exhaled and set her menu aside. "The visit—it was *fine*. I made some connections."

"And?" Martina wouldn't stop.

But she could change their conversation to the one topic guaranteed to distract her friend, couldn't she?

"I'm meeting Bannister tonight."

"*What?*" Pushing their coffee out of the way, Martina planted her elbows on the table, the Department of Energy forgotten. "Tell me."

"At the Wine Room in Palo Alto. Seven o'clock."

"You're going on a date with your mystery artist!"

"I don't know if it's a date—"

"*Erin*. It's a date."

"I… yes." She could admit that. *Wanted* to admit it.

"Oh my *God. Finally.*" Martina motioned Jess over. "We're ready to order. And we're also having mimosas."

Jess jotted down their usuals without asking: egg tartine for Erin, croissant Benedict for Martina. "What's the occasion?"

"Erin has a date."

"Really? If you need an outfit, a new boutique just opened up the street, near where Ann's Coffee Shop used to be."

"What an iconic spot. That 1960s decor. I'm sad it's gone." Martina shook her head.

Jess shrugged. "But the boutique is cute. I'll be back with those drinks. Congratulations, Erin."

"It's just a date," she reminded the world at large as Jess weaved back into the restaurant through a raft of serving trays. "Not that I won't always take a mimosa after Pilates, because hydration is important and I owe you for that tip about adhesive strips with heels, but—"

"How long has it been since you've had *just a date*?"

"I've been busy."

"I know. You'll be busy this afternoon, too, because we have to find something for you to wear. With that lingerie picture you sent? He'll have expectations. We'll check out the boutique."

"I was planning to put on—"

"Jeans? Sneakers?"

"My suede moto jacket."

"Plus, jeans and sneakers."

"I'm cycling to the Wine Room, so yes. If I had one of those Santa Cruz boardwalk cruisers, I could maybe wear a dress without flashing traffic, but I don't… and I don't think I own any dresses."

"That can be fixed. The main problem is, though: you'll have helmet hair. Keep that genius brain safe, but—no, you know what?" Martina grinned. "I'll drive you to the Wine Room tonight."

"You don't have to do that." She hesitated while Jess approached with their plates.

"I won't if you don't want me to. But I'm curious about your mystery man. *Bannister*. I wouldn't get in your way, but then if this really is some niche catfishing and he's too good to be true—you saw those muscles and that dog!—I'll be there for you."

"How could it be catfishing? I was the one who reached out to him. And I know him now. I do. He's a good man. A friend, even if nothing else comes of it."

"I'm your *best* friend." Martina swirled hollandaise sauce across her Parma ham and croissant, tapping her fork for emphasis. "I'll be thrilled for you if your date turns out well. But Bannister—whose real name you don't know, I should remind you—is a stranger."

"It doesn't feel that way."

"Maybe not. Still, you haven't vetted him through any of the filters on a dating site. Which admittedly aren't always accurate—what sort of person labels themselves as a political conservative and expects to match with anyone around here? But what I'm saying is that you only know what he's told you about himself. You have no outside data. You've said that he doesn't have much of an online presence. You can't verify details independently. So, unless you tell me not to, I'll be in the background tonight. Just in case."

"Martina…" Erin punctured a poached egg onto her challah. Then she sighed. "Fine. You're right. Honestly, Wes and Adrian would probably thank you."

"Which is why I'm doing this. Not to snoop on your artist, or to drink Riesling in a swanky spot with cute shoes on." Martina raised her mimosa.

"I'm glad I can facilitate your fun."

"And my investigation of Jess's boutique."

They finished up brunch while Martina reviewed her progress lobbying Menlo Park's city council for the preservation of her local pocket green space—the Perezes had lived in the area for generations in the same modest house, and Martina, her younger sibling Desi, and their father had seen the Peninsula's eddies of gentrification and urbanization swell to a torrent—and then meandered up Santa Cruz Avenue to the boutique. A quick browse of the racks became an hour in a dressing room, Martina sampling herbal candles and assembling accessories, Erin abandoning her exercise clothes to pivot before a mirror in pretty, impractical outfits. She was careful to keep her phone out of reach. She didn't want to accidentally send another picture to Bannister. She didn't want the temptation of checking her work email, either. Not after Friday night. After…

"Try this one next." Martina passed a sleek blouse with semi-sheer paneling that slid off its hanger on one shoulder through the curtain. "*This* I could authorize with jeans."

Grateful for the distraction, glad to busy her twitching hands before she could cave and reach for her screen, she slipped the top over her head, then turned to evaluate herself. Shimmers of bronze in the dark, asymmetrical fabric highlighted her collarbones and a hint of her navel through the paneling. It really was gorgeous.

"Yes?" from Martina.

She shrugged at the mirror, smiling now. "Yes."

Despite her earlier protestations, she was relieved to spend the afternoon with her friend. With the shimmery top purchased, they fetched Martina's own colorful going-out clothes from her house. Then they returned to Live Oak Avenue for an assessment of potential jeans to pair with her blouse, decisions on what to do with her hair, and a wave at Kai and Ashley as her roommates headed out for a ride up Skyline Boulevard. Singing along to a golden oldies radio station kept her mind occupied and her nerves at bay while she showered, then sat still as Martina wove a slender braid behind her ear, brushing out the rest of her hair until it crackled with electricity and sweeping it over her shoulder.

When Wes's watch read six forty-five—she'd refused to swap it out for a bracelet, though she'd conceded to wearing simple gold studs in her ears—she was dressed in flats with tapered dark jeans, the semi-sheer top skimming her ribcage and hips under her suede motorcycle jacket, her half-down hair a tangle waiting to happen, perfume on her pulse points, and walking down to Martina's car on the street.

It was time.

"Are you feeling as good as you look?" Martina pulled her ancient coupe through the intersection onto El Camino Real. The vehicle trembled slightly with their southbound acceleration, but she ignored it to appraise Erin again.

"The physiological results of anxiety and excitement are the same."

"So you're excited."

"I'm excited."

They parked underneath Palo Alto's city hall, then crossed onto Ramona Street. The pedestrian block between Hamilton Avenue and University Avenue was lined with European-themed restaurants, a popular cafe chain, tea shops, and a pricey salon. Balconies overflowed with wisteria, and art projects or political signs leaned in the windows of upper floor apartments. Rock tracks blaring from a college bar clashed with an Italian eatery's Pavarotti mix. The tables encroaching onto the street and sidewalks were packed with crowds of Stanford students, patent tech lawyers, families with labradoodles, and couples leaning close over candle centerpieces. Waiters sped by with cocktails and artisanal pizzas. They edged through the crush, heat lamps blazing on their faces, twinkling lights shining from the trunks of trees in planter pots on the pavement, windows along the street fogged with exhaled conversations and alcohol.

Erin shed her jacket before she and Martina even reached the Wine Room. An adobe building modeled after the classical Old California style, exposed timbers upheld its roof above squashy leather chairs and a glossy bar. Open shutters spilled light and the shadows of bottles onto upright wine barrels doubling as tables outside. People sat on benches near the windows, leaning against the sills and trailing their hands into the fresh air, fingers tapping to the bass beats of barely audible music. Others chatted under a hanging sign by the door, friends and strangers mingling to enjoy the night and Saturday's freedom from spreadsheets or quarterly earnings reports. It was packed. Despite the heat radiating out onto the sidewalk, she shivered.

"Not anxiety. Anticipation," Martina reminded her. Taking Erin by the hand, she amiably pushed a path past the bouncer and into the front room, then cleared their way to a corner by one of the windows with smiles and elbows.

While her friend flagged down a waiter for a wine list, Erin settled onto her bench. Wes's watch showed two minutes to seven. She was early—*take that, Ethan!*—but just barely.

Was Bannister here, too?

She could've already run into him, their shoulders jostling in Martina's wake. The blond near the unlit fireplace, several buttons popped loose on his shirt to reveal a waxed chest shinier than the bar…; a group of software engineers in graphic hoodies crowding the doorway to the back room, tossing off a tasting flight of sparkling wine like shots…; the stubbled jaw with glasses and a swirl of ink on his forearms…

Their gazes caught. The man cocked his head. He straightened up from his casual lean against one of the couches. He set down his drink.

But Bannister didn't have tattoos.

So she looked away—and her stomach hopped into her throat when a hand tapped hers.

"It's seven o'clock. I'm going to fade back."

Martina.

"Flag me down if you need me, all right?"

She breathed. "I will."

"Now, knock him dead." Martina tweaked her blouse an inch lower, grinning at the result—but as she turned to the bar, her smile froze. Then it dropped. Paused mid-step in her dainty, spiky heels, she stared past Erin's shoulder. Her nails pinched down hard.

"*Ouch!* What's—"

"*Erin.*" Ignoring her protest, Martina swiveled her toward the window. "Look outside."

She did.

Ethan Meyer was approaching the Wine Room.

12

"For God's sake!"

Was nowhere safe from him? The MEC control room, the Modern Physics hallway and kitchenette, Maiman Auditorium, his office, her own sleeping brain—

She shook off Martina's hand and stood.

"Erin—"

"He can't just—no. He doesn't get to ruin this chance for me." She left her friend at the window and scooted along the bench, bumping knees and hardly apologizing for the wine and charcuterie spilling onto the low table behind her. She shouldered her way toward the entry, toward Ethan as he stepped over the threshold. Planting herself in his path, she dared him to notice her, dared him to meet her gaze.

He doesn't get this night. The hot flash of anger pulsing in her stomach was so much better than guilt.

"Erin…" Martina again, back at her elbow. "What are you doing?"

Erin ignored her. She kept her focus on Ethan, unblinking. She couldn't allow him to slip away from her into the crowd. Because she couldn't meet Bannister with him here. Not when he might be out of sight but eavesdropping at the bar. Despite the ear-splitting noise levels in the room, he might overhear their conversation. Overhear something personal. Compromising.

Forster, writer.

No.

So he had to leave the Wine Room. She marched up to the door. Cooler air stirred the translucent fabric of her blouse against her half-bared abdomen, her skin already flushed and now prickling with the temperature change—and with acute awareness, too: he'd abandoned both his usual fleece and yesterday's suit in favor of chinos and a sweater, the shape of the buttons on a collared shirt visible under the pull of heather-gray cashmere across his chest. He'd shaved again. The ends of his hair were damp around his ears and jaw, and even through the ripe odor of the crowd her nose tingled with the smoky, amber spice of his aftershave—

He saw her now. Ethan halted just inside the bar, his mouth curving into a scowl.

She fisted her hands. "What are you doing here?"

"What am I—?" The creases beside his lips deepened. He didn't move aside for the group of hoodies from the back room when they swayed to the door with hollers about getting buckets of fried chicken from a bubble tea shop down the street. "What are *you* doing here?"

"I was at the Wine Room first." She stepped closer. She breathed and swallowed, reaching for her anger again. Her inhale only pulled his aftershave deeper into her lungs. "So you… y-you need to go."

Please go—

No: *Forget about Friday.*

Forget what you saw.

Forget what you—

"Sound logic." His jaw tensed. He'd recovered from his surprise. "But I… I was at SVLAC first. That didn't stop you from hustling your way into Modern Physics."

Thank God. She needed him to fight, and squared her stance. But his gaze slid away—past her.

Looking for someone else? No, he didn't get to ignore her.

"Your being inconvenienced by my research is your problem." She whipped back her hair. Martina's braid stung her neck. "Not mine."

"You think that your work jeopardizes my analyses?" At least he was keeping to their script, even if he continued to avoid her eyes. "Your field's a relic. Relativistic mechanics is only a… a building block for more advanced sciences. It's not a frontier, not like quantum mechanics. But even if it were—that sole-author paper you keep flouting? The *Journal of Supermassive Astronomy and Astrophysics* has a focus that's too sectarian to make any real impact in the field. I don't care about your diamonds either, or whatever other commercial angle you've been using to—"

"Then if this isn't about my research data or my paper, is it actually about coffee creamer? Don't think I didn't notice you intentionally using the last of the oat milk when you saw me coming, even though it was enough for three or four people. You never put that much creamer in your drinks—"

He'd taken another stride into the room, maybe—hopefully—preparing a response to her comeback. But now, he stopped. "What?"

Don't you dare look confused.

"Coffee! You're mad because—"

"No, why would I get mad about…" He shook his head. "Who cares about the coffee?"

"You, apparently. Since you claim not to care about—"

"I don't—"

"Really? Well—"

Their argument was complete nonsense. The angles of their anger were wrong. But she couldn't stop. If she didn't keep their altercation spinning, keep its current of vitriolic magnetism rushing, she'd—

"What I care about is what you're doing here. Palo Alto's not your city."

"It's—it's not yours either, and you need to—"

"Dr. Meyer!"

"Wha—?"

Ethan stumbled back a step. So did she, pushed toward her window bench as sixty-four inches of Pilates and stilettos shoved between them: Martina, who mouthed a question and a warning—*Bannister?*—at Erin before turning to her other colleague.

"I didn't know that you came to the Wine Room, Dr. Meyer. From Redwood City, with Saturday night traffic on El Camino Real?"

"*Uh.*" Visibly flummoxed by both the abrupt shift in topic and its participants, he blinked down at Martina's bright, disarming smile. "Dr. Perez?"

"Their seasonal wine list must be excellent if you've driven all the way here. Since the wildfires haven't hit Napa or Sonoma badly this summer, the pours should stay good for the next several years, don't you think? No smoke-wine." She pressed a trendy clipboard-style menu into his hands. "Look, this place rotates their offerings every week."

"They do?"

"Yes. Enjoy!" Then she snagged Erin's elbow and hauled her away. She parted the crush around the bar in an uncompromising march to the bathroom.

"Martina—"

"Thank me later." Martina pulled her to a row of sinks and parked her in front of the mirror.

"I—"

"You can either argue with Ethan Meyer, or you can meet Bannister. Which do you want?"

"I—I was trying to get him to leave."

"Yes? Well, you can't make him."

"Can't I?" She eyed her water-spotted image darkly. Her nose was pink and her cheeks were very red.

"What you *can* do," Martina ignored her, shifting aside for a woman tottering toward the faucets and retrieving a brush from her purse, which she pointed at Erin's reflection, "is to calm yourself down, clean yourself up, and meet Bannister. *And ignore Ethan Meyer.*"

"*Ouch!*" She flinched when Martina ran the bristles through her hair. Though maybe the pain was good. *Distracting.* "That's easy for you to say. He isn't rude to you whenever you see him."

"Open." Martina refreshed the lipstick Erin had smudged off. "No, he isn't. Just awkward. Blot."

Erin pressed a tissue between her lips. "Why is he only rude to *me*?"

"That's a rhetorical question, right?"

"He's been a complete asshole, almost since my first day in Modern Physics!" She dragged the strap of her blouse back into place, scowling at her flush in the mirror, then knocked on the nearest faucet and ran a stream of cold water over her wrists.

"Well—"

"No, no—*sweetie.*" The other woman in the bathroom grabbed her arm. Her eyes were unfocused, tipsy but very earnest while she blinked at Erin's glasses. "Sweetie, *listen.* You don't need his toxicity in your life. If he's rude—if he takes you for granted?

Drop him. Find a man who appreciates you. He doesn't deserve you. I mean, just look at you! Legs for miles, complete Diana Prince. You can do *so so so so so* much better!"

"*Uh...* no, he's not... we're definitely not—"

"*Definitely.*" But as Martina confirmed this and detached the woman's hands, her gaze stayed with Erin. It was a long, long look.

Erin was the one to break it.

"So it shouldn't make any difference if he's out there, should it?" Martina went on after a moment. "You're at the Wine Room to meet your mystery artist. To get kissed. Maybe more. Ethan's just going to sit in a corner with a glass of wine, because what else would he do? If you're worried about him overhearing something—"

"Or seeing something." She stared at the water trickling over her forearms, wondering why it wasn't rising off her overheated skin as steam.

"—just think: what are the real chances of that, in this crowd?"

"*Ooh.* Unless you want to rub your new man in his face!" the tipsy woman chimed in, nodding and smearing her mascara worse than before. "Park your pretty ass right in front of him and get dirty with your guy. Or any guy. That one with the tattoos is *fine*—"

"Is he here?"

"Yeah, he's at a table near the windows—"

"Not him," Martina waved their companion away. To Erin, "*Bannister.*"

She fished out her phone. 7:08 p.m. No new messages from him alerted her that he'd arrived at the Wine Room. In fact, he hadn't sent any texts at all. She tapped back into their thread, checking the time and content of his last communication: several hours ago, confirming their meeting. She'd responded enthusiastically. But since then?

Silence.

At least he hadn't messaged to ask if she was the crazy woman blocking the door into the bar while arguing about physics and oat milk. He could've seen her do it, though—and a fresh surge of frustration coursed through her. Why did Ethan Meyer have to be here, of all the possible Bay Area bars and nights of the week? After Friday—*ugh!* Biting her lip, she swiped her thumb over her screen to lock her phone. But she fumbled and the device skidded through her wet fingers.

Down into the sink.

Directly under the running faucet.

"*Fuck!*"

She grabbed for it, frantically shaking water from the screen—which flickered and died.

"No, no, no…" She blotted the glass with handfuls of paper towels, but the screen remained black. Efforts to turn her phone off and on resulted in a blur of staticky pixels. "Martina, do you have anything in your purse—"

"Like a whole bag of rice?" Martina tossed away more tissues and blocked their drunk companion's unhelpful attempts to resuscitate the device herself. "Sorry, no."

Soaked like this, it could be hours before her phone was functional again.

"*Damn!*"

"Hey." Martina sighed and caught Erin's cheeks in her hands. "It's not a great situation. But wasn't the idea to get the two of you off your screens and meeting in person? Maybe this is a sign."

"A *sign*."

"Yes. Your phone's dead, but you're here. So come on. Let's get you some wine."

"And... what? Just hope we run into each other?"

"What other options do you have?"

Martina was right.

"Ready?"

"No." But she followed her friend back out to the bar.

Even encountering Chase at the Wine Room would've been better than this.

Erin Monaghan, here?

Of all the times they could've collided, of all the places she could've ambushed him—outside the Modern Physics building, or in the experimental halls, or in his own damn office—it had to be here, *now*, following hard on the heels of his disastrous Friday and just when he was scheduled to meet Forster.

What are you doing here?

What are you *doing here?*

You need to go.

He'd refused. What would Forster think if he switched their meetup location now? He wouldn't do that to her, and he wouldn't give Erin the satisfaction of yielding. Besides, Forster might've already driven an hour along the Peninsula from Santa Clara or San Jose in Saturday traffic, then braved the hazards of parking in Palo Alto, all to meet him. So yes, he'd refused, rehashing their old arguments, because the alternative was to back away, to let his stammering agitation silence him, and at least there was some control in denying Erin what she wanted.

But what if Forster had seen their confrontation? She might've come to her senses and left before identifying herself, slipping out a window from the bathroom or through a service door behind the bar. They hadn't agreed on a signal like characters from a 1990s romantic comedy, something like a rose or a book, so how could he know if he'd already passed her in the crowd? He wouldn't have blamed Forster if she'd run.

He could blame Erin, though.

He would.

Blame was safe. Blame was good.

Because even if he and Forster were to meet now with tentative waves that gave way to laughter as they settled with their drinks into a nook somewhere near the candles illuminating the fireplace, trading stories as if they'd known each other for years, knees bumping, arms brushing, the distance between their smiles closing… even if everything he'd dared to hope for tonight happened, how could he focus on her? How could he give her the attention she deserved when Erin was here?

Erin: *gilded in lamplight, barefoot.*

Erin: *never pulling punches.*

Erin, who if she ever met Chase Meyer Jr.—

His mouth puckered. He'd never make it past the crowds to the bathroom, so instead he elbowed his way up to the bar and pointed at a random selection from the wine list that Martina Perez had given him.

With a smooth nod and an even smoother pour through an aerator, the bartender slid a glass in his direction. "This winery—Calathus—has produced some of the best reds in its region lately. Excellent choice."

Maybe it was. It didn't matter. It was Chase who understood vintages. Ethan had spent a childhood vacation in Tuscany cooped up in a hotel room after a meal of bad airplane shrimp ravioli while his family went wine tasting and made pasta with

Italian grandmothers. His brother had returned at the end of one day's expedition to announce that if Ethan had waited to eat his—*Chase's*—own ravioli, maybe he wouldn't have gotten sick. Maybe he would've imbibed some culture and appreciation for the local grapes. Chase had touted those Tuscan adventures for years, taking dozens of dates home to demonstrate his pasta-making prowess. Or something.

Tossing back a mouthful of inky Malbec that tasted only of tannin, he edged to a corner whose open windows faced out onto Ramona Street. Maybe a few minutes away from the crush while he downed his glass of depressant chemicals would steady him. Holding the stemware occupied his fidgeting fingers, too.

He should've brought his sketchpad to the bar. That would've been better than a rose or even Ted Chiang's story collection. But if Forster noticed it, so might Erin. She'd see the evidence against him, proof of his secret second life. She'd see it like she'd seen him on Friday night when she'd witnessed him at his worst: wild and *weak*.

She'd know—

Where was she?

He took another slug of Malbec and scanned the room. She wasn't by the street door, wasn't outside at one of the upright wine barrel tables, wasn't perched on a couch near the fireplace—*thank God*. But if he couldn't locate her, then she had the advantage of surprise, could catch him unawares again, the recessed golden bulbs overhead skimming her collarbones and the tiny divot of her navel—

He choked on his next sip.

And he watched for Forster. Waited for her. After a fourth gulp of tannin, he thumbed back into their messages.

> **Forster**
> See you at 7 p.m.! I'm excited to meet you.

She'd sent that text earlier this afternoon. He'd heard nothing from her since.

It was past seven o'clock, now. 7:13 p.m. But a fifteen-minute delay in Bay Area traffic wasn't anything unusual. If she didn't text while she handled heavy machinery on a freeway, even better. Maybe she was stalled trying to find street parking. He should've told her to head for the City Hall garage. Maybe she was still circling the block.

> **Ethan**
> The garage under Palo Alto's city hall always has open parking spots, if you need one.

The text zipped into their thread. "Delivered" didn't immediately appear beneath its blue bubble, however. Sometimes it took a minute... if she was driving in a tunnel, somewhere without service. But there was nothing when the clock on his screen read 7:16 p.m., either.

Her phone was off.

Which was fine, and he'd put away his device once she arrived, too—*maybe*: what if Dr. Kramer emailed him?—but powering it down before they'd found each other at the bar? That didn't make sense. She'd have a reasonable explanation, though. He knew it. They'd laugh about the confusion together. *Soon*.

But *soon* became seven thirty. Then seven forty-three. Then eight o'clock. He fended off attempts from a couple on a first date to annex his spot. He craned his neck around a boisterous group of coworkers celebrating end-of-quarter bonuses to watch the door.

8:01 p.m.

No messages came from Forster's number, or from anyone else. The next cohort to try for his bench was a cluster of women in strappy heels. One of them almost sat on him.

"*Oops!* Sorry, didn't see you!"

He grunted. He didn't look up from his phone. He didn't move.

"Sir," from the bartender a quarter-hour later, "if you've finished, would you mind…"

He stayed where he was. "Another Malbec."

He'd downed half of his second glass by eight fifteen.

His fingers were clumsy on his keyboard.

> **Ethan**
> Seems like your phone's off, but if it isn't, I'm here near the entry.
>
> **Ethan**
> If tonight doesn't work anymore, we can reschedule.
>
> **Ethan**
> Just want to know if you're all right.

He waited.

8:22 p.m.

Still nothing. No delivery, no response.

Well, he could ask every woman in the Wine Room if she wrote science fiction under the pseudonym Forster, couldn't he? No, not without Bunsen as his wingman. Or he could stand up on his bench and shout her name. Then Erin Monaghan would certainly notice—*something*. Or he could keep waiting.

8:34 p.m.

A third Malbec arrived from the bartender. He poured it out the window into a potted plant.

8:40 p.m.

9:00 p.m.

He waited more than two hours before pushing his way through the rowdy, thickening crowd to the exit. Only when he emerged onto the sidewalk did he catch sight of the far side of the Wine Room.

Erin was there.

Seated under the opposite windows with a depleted bottle of Chardonnay and a hummus platter, head bent in conversation with her friend, she didn't notice him outside.

But he saw her: a *chiaroscuro* figure in the warm, noisy glow. He saw the damp flush on her cheeks.

She'd been crying.

Which evened their score again, after Friday's fiasco in front of the Department of Energy officials—and then that even worse moment in his office. Didn't it? Maybe the Malbec's depressive chemicals were lingering in his bloodstream, however, because as he watched Erin wipe her cheeks with a napkin before reaching for the sediment at the bottom of her bottle, Dr. Kramer's voice in his head was quiet, and the pitch through his stomach wasn't triumph. She looked… tired.

Yes, that was a safe analysis.

Tired.

As for the knot clenching under his ribs while he drove back to Redwood City—it didn't feel like it, but that had to be tiredness, too.

13

Her phone spent a full thirteen hours and eight minutes in a bag of rice before its screen flickered back to life on Sunday afternoon.

Battery at 0%

Erin exhaled and smiled at the warning. "*Thank God.*"

Closing her laptop on the day's STEMinist Online header posts, tossing aside *This Is How You Lose the Time War*, she took her device to the kitchen and shook it over the sink, then rushed back to her desk to charge it, just missing Kai as her roommate exited the bathroom while toweling off her cropped turquoise undercut.

"Erin, you okay?"

"Oh—yeah, fine."

"Ashley and I are getting a late brunch at Cafe Borrone, if you want to come."

"Sure, but maybe another time?"

She waved her phone in explanation as her bedroom door shut behind her. Then she plugged in her charging cable. While Kai called out her readiness to Ashley, she watched the battery bar turn to a buffering green. Of course, it would take at least an hour for her device to reach a full charge, the cafe near Kepler's Books did a delicious banana pancake stack, and it might've been nice to catch up with her roommates for a bit… But eating before running the hills on the Stanford Dish trail was a recipe for nausea. Plus—*her phone*. She watched the charging icon, tapping her nails against the screen, against her cheek, against her jittering leg, waiting for it to edge back to functionality.

"You're sure you don't want to come, Erin?" with a knock from Ashley.

"No, I'm set. Thanks, though."

Her roommates left for brunch, and she went on staring at her device. The instant the phone registered sufficient power to turn itself on, she unlocked the screen, checked that no emergencies had been reported in the Monaghan family chat, opened her message thread with Bannister—and made a noise like shower sandals skidding on wet tile, something between a groan and a shriek.

"*Argh!*"

He'd sent his first message just after she'd dropped her phone into the bathroom sink. The next texts had come more than an hour after they'd planned to meet at the bar.

Damn.

Last night's alcohol headache rose again, blood vessels pulsing in her skull like the bass beats from the Wine Room. A waterlogged phone, frustrated and tipsy tears over a bottle of Chardonnay, and Ethan Meyer, stiff and awkward in aftershave-scented cashmere?

Disaster.

She swallowed, breathed, and clicked into the reply field.

> **Erin**
> Hi, Bannister. I'm so sorry about not responding to your messages last night, and sorry that

> we didn't find each other in the Wine Room.
> I dropped my phone into the sink in the bathroom, and it died.

She didn't mention why she'd been so uncoordinated, or why she'd been in the bathroom at the exact time when they were supposed to meet. She didn't mention her run-in with Ethan, or why she would've been bad company for anyone—even Bannister—after her confrontation with her rival at the door. What use would that be? The odds of artistic Bannister knowing robotic Dr. Ethan Meyer were miniscule. Sharing his name would explain nothing. She hadn't left their encounter feeling particularly proud of herself, either.

Pulse, went her headache.

She closed her eyes and typed blindly.

> **Erin**
> Could we reschedule and try again?

To avoid watching the screen for his reply, she gulped down an ibuprofen, yanked on a pair of running shorts, bundled her hair into a ponytail, taped up her blistered toes, then fought her way through the head opening of a racerback tank top when a lightsaber's *swish* sounded from her phone.

> **Bannister**
> It's fine. I'm glad you're all right.

She sagged in relief, and swiveled the reversed shirt around her neck to insert her arms.

Bannister
Rescheduling is good. The bar was so loud last night that it wouldn't have been an easy place to talk, anyway.

Erin
It was! I think one of the groups there might've been a bachelorette party.

Then again, attempting to prove she'd been on site, that she wasn't making excuses for standing him up:

Erin
Did you try any of the wines? My white went nicely with the house snack platter.

Bannister
I had a Malbec. It tasted like tannin.

He'd been one of the twenty or thirty men drinking red. That didn't narrow down the possibilities for identifying him by much: any one of the people with whom she'd bumped shoulders or knees that night—people who'd seen her with her mascara dripping and her gestures sloppy. Who might've seen her confrontation with Ethan. He could've been anyone, and seen anything. So she didn't ask Bannister what he'd worn on Saturday, or where he'd waited for her. If she broached those questions, he could volley them back to her. And the truth was, she didn't want him to have seen her there. But she'd manage their second meeting differently. She'd make very sure that Ethan wasn't present, too.

Erin

Tannin? Gross. Now I'm trying to remember why I thought the Wine Room was a good idea.

Bannister

We'll pick somewhere else next time.

She slathered sunscreen across her shoulders, grateful for his easy assumption that *of course*, there'd be a next time. She laced up her athletic shoes by the door.

Erin

Brainstorm after my run?

Bannister

Deal.

The traffic lights at Sand Hill Road and Junipero Serra Boulevard were both green. She locked her bicycle by the Stanford Dish gate, cued up a playlist while she swapped her helmet for a baseball cap and stretched a heels-and-Pilates ache from her hamstrings, then set off up the first paved hill. With Stars' "Take Me to the Riot" in her ears, the incline melted under her feet. She waved her way past groups of panting hikers sheltering for water under the shade of a spreading oak woodland fringing the trail and drove herself hard on the flats near the Dish's radio antennae where the device jutted against the blazing blue sky behind a row of cattle guards, before heading down the far slope, circumventing a thermoregulating rattlesnake, then powering up another incline to merge with the initial hill, sweating out her headache.

Where did Bannister and Bunsen run?

She'd imagined them in San Francisco because of their Crissy Field photo, though that beach was a destination for dog owners all around the Bay Area. They could be in any of the North Bay, East Bay, South Bay, or Peninsula counties. So: *where?* She wondered while she cleaned her hair out of the apartment's shower drain following her post-run rinse, but when she settled down with a smoothie and elevated feet in the living room, she found Bannister's list of suggestions for their meeting rematch waiting for her. There'd be plenty of time to suss out the specifics of his routes later.

Because he didn't seem angry. At all. Last night's blunder had been an honest mistake, and he didn't hold it against her. He wasn't that sort of person, and she smiled as she scrolled through his ideas, which included Haberdasher and Salt & Straw.

> **Erin**
> What's the weirdest seasonal S&S flavor you've tried?
>
> **Bannister**
> Last summer's cinnamon and vegan honey fried chicken.
>
> **Erin**
> What did Bunsen think about that?
>
> **Bannister**
> I had to shut him out on the patio until I was finished. But then I let him lick the spoon.

She huffed into her straw.

Erin

Very noble of you. But fair warning for next time: no one gets my spoon. Part of growing up with my brothers was fighting to the death for rights to eat the leftover cake batter or cookie dough in our mom's mixing bowl. Spoons are precious.

Bannister

I'll keep that in mind. I might not be able to resist trying to swipe it, though.

Erin

Evil!

Erin

Maybe that could be the conflict in my next short story. A shortage of astronaut ice cream.

They bantered back and forth about freeze-dried dairy deficits in space, and as she scribbled notes in her writing journal, a silly idea with serious ramifications took shape: divorced from their circadian rhythms, maybe a mission's crew marked time by the content of their meals, a stabilizing influence that ruptured when one astronaut went rogue and began eating ice cream for breakfast. Philosophical questions about the preservation of social norms around food and community at the edge of the wild expanse of space were followed by a natural corollary: the preservation of humanity itself. Seeing "Pandora Rising" in print had been intoxicating. She wanted more.

Not to mention ice cream, too.

She set aside her notebook to look up a seasonal flavor list for the nearest Salt & Straw location, then scrolled through the latest additions to STEMinist Online's post about the Fermilab scientist. A user named DataDominatrix, who identified herself as having worked at SVLAC a handful of years ago, theorized that this same man might've changed labs and managed her during her tenure on the research campus, given that her work on time crystals had ended up in his first-author papers, while another woman posited that he might be the supervisor who'd appropriated her data on the hardness of random quantum circuits. Erin read with interest and a giddy rush of outrage on behalf of her fellow STEMinists—and her weekend actually closed out on an optimistic note; she had an ice cream date set for next week with Bannister and she'd sent the details of her LIGO research to Richard Hall even earlier than expected. But as for Monday at the lab…

She booted up her computer in the Modern Physics bullpen to find a new item on her calendar for the day: *D.O.E. After-Action Sync*. She had a nine o'clock meeting scheduled in the Manzanita conference room with Dr. Nadine Fong, Dr. John Kramer, and Dr. Ethan Meyer.

A sudden jitter of anxiety hit her stomach. She'd gone too far last Friday. She knew that. In attracting notice from the United States Office of Science and securing its consideration for research funding, she'd broken through yet another barrier to her success, just as she fought to do every day while navigating the lab's internal politics and shouldering her way up her field's supposedly meritocratic ladder. But her pride in the achievement was… flat. Barreling past the hurdle while also executing her revenge had left collateral damage behind. Real damage—to people. *One person.* Public damage. It was a line she shouldn't have crossed.

Nadine—and maybe Human Resources—was finally stepping in.

She grabbed a sudoku sheet. She tried to breathe. Maybe sudoku really was better than caffeine for clearing brain fog, as Bannister said—but this wasn't brain fog. This was panic. And it didn't matter if she solved her puzzle at her desk, or if she hyperventilated in the bathroom. Because when the morning ticked on to nine o'clock, she had no more time for either option.

She stood tall. Despite the exterior temperature and the heat beating in her throat, she zipped her utility jacket up to her chin. She walked into the conference room.

Meeting: *D.O.E. After-Action Sync*
Day/Time: *Monday, 9:00 a.m.–10:00 a.m.*
Location: *Manzanita Conference Room*
Required Attendees: *Dr. Nadine Fong, Dr. John Kramer, Dr. Erin Monaghan—*

—and him.

Against all odds, his Monday wasn't beginning in Dr. Kramer's office—where it also could've ended. After last week, he wouldn't have been surprised if his supervisor had called him on the carpet this morning, told him to pack up his desk, scrub the internet clean of every mention of his name in conjunction with Dr. Kramer's work, and be ready for a security escort off campus by noon. Ethan would've complied, of course. Instead, he was summoned to a meeting. Including Erin Monaghan. Which wasn't a much better alternative.

He entered the conference room to find his rival already seated at the central table, busy on her laptop. Ostensibly busy, at least. She must've heard him come in. He thumped the door closed. She didn't look up. But the glare from the overhead lights on her glasses shifted.

He took the chair farthest from her spot. She continued to study something on her computer. The building's air conditioning hummed. He tapped a capped pen against his palm. The flare on her lenses shifted again.

He waited.

Drs. Kramer and Fong joined them eventually. His supervisor dropped a briefcase onto the table, rattling the laminated wood and freezing Ethan's pen mid-tap.

Then:

"Congratulations, Meyer." Dr. Kramer's mouth was thin. He pulled out a chair and examined Ethan over his steepled fingers.

Thank you didn't seem appropriate, somehow.

He stayed silent.

Fong settled into an adjacent seat; the bulge of her belly barely fit between her chair and the table. She smiled at Erin. "Secretary McCandless and Dr. Richard Hall from the Office of Science were both impressed with the findings from SVLAC's current research in modern physics. In particular, the work from our two departments."

"McCandless read the first page of an internet search on relativistic mechanics and quantum mechanics during the weekend. Now she's an expert," was Dr. Kramer's addition. "Quantum gravity appeared in her list. The majority of the research is coming out of China and Eastern Europe, which apparently alarmed her."

"She's right that the current geopolitical situation can't be ignored. Secretary McCandless's position is a political appointment and, although it was admittedly cursory, her initiative to identify the vanguard areas of work in our fields is admirable. Dr. Hall concurs that the United States' National Labs should keep pace with the frontier, too."

"Like a new space race?" Finally, Erin closed her laptop.

"Yes. Since knowledge is power in the Information Age, the Office of Science has authorized immediate, generous funding of"—Fong named an amount that topped even the Eischer-Langhoff grant—"to SVLAC for studies on quantum gravity. The government won't put out a call for proposals. It's simply authorized the funds, with an end-of-year report on our progress and results determining whether the contract is renewed for another period. Oversight is minimal. While the process is unusual and bypasses our standard procedures for calculating the urgency of SVLAC's projects, the federal quantum gravity research study is now the highest priority for our departments."

Erin's elbow slipped off the table.

Ethan dropped his pen.

"Now, I'm starting my maternity leave later this week, and for the next ten months, Dr. Kramer will be—"

"At CERN." Dr. Kramer leaned back in his chair. "Van Buskirk will provide minimal managerial and fiscal oversight of the Quantum group for the duration of my absence."

"CERN?"

He hadn't known.

But he should've guessed. He'd been aware of his supervisor's upcoming travel plans to Switzerland. He'd reconciled the airline charges with SVLAC's Finance department, hadn't he? Dr. Kramer had recently delegated a series of departmental administrative tasks to Ethan, too, in addition to work on the holometer, and no, he'd never taken a hands-on approach to the Quantum group's operational grunt activities, not when he had much better uses for his time—but if Ethan hadn't been so preoccupied with Forster, he still would've seen the throughline in his supervisor's system inputs.

Should've. He should've known that Dr. Kramer would be gone from SVLAC for almost a year. Every neuron in his skull diverted to calculations now, because *ten months, forty-three weeks, three hundred days, seven thousand hours—*

"A collaborative fellowship with the Director-General." Dr. Kramer smiled.

"Very prestigious." Fong exchanged a look with Erin that he couldn't parse, his neural pathways continuing to fire numbers, his pen abandoned on the floor. "So, given that both of us will be out of the office soon for a protracted period: Dr. Monaghan and Dr. Meyer, you will collaboratively supervise the first year of SVLAC's quantum gravity research, and at the end of the funding cycle, you'll generate a report on your findings for the United States Office of Science."

"You will be responsible if the project fails," from Dr. Kramer.

"And credited if it succeeds."

Silence.

His brain flatlined for a brief, blissful moment—then leaped into analysis again. The responsibility was enormous. The honor of the assignment was equally large. Success didn't just mean solving one of the most pressing dilemmas in physics—reconciling the incompatible theories of general relativity and quantum mechanics into a continuous, unified theory of space-time—but a thousand follow-up opportunities as well: papers in major journals, visibility in the field and beyond—profiles in *Time Magazine*?—and a level of public recognition to which even Chase could only aspire.

But: *Erin Monaghan.*

"No," he said.

"This is not a request, Meyer."

"Dr. Kramer is right. The project is compulsory for both of you. Circumstances being what they are, and with the relativistic mechanics versus quantum mechanics showcase that you put on for the officials on Friday, this is the outcome."

Showcase?

"I expect a project charter on my desk by Friday, and weekly status reports."

"But... but that means that we'd have to start work today! My LIGO research—" Erin rose from her seat.

Ethan remained where he was. He couldn't feel his legs.

We didn't put on a showcase.

"This is a government directive. It takes precedence over any other contracts or department work and requires a moratorium on all existing projects. I'm sorry." Maybe she was, but Nadine Fong still continued with, "Anyhow, you and Dr. Meyer are already studying the fabric of space-time, even if it's from different angles. Your joint expertise with optics and lasers will be useful for the study. You might find that there's more common ground in your current research than you anticipate."

"That's doubtful—"

"Your doubt is irrelevant, Monaghan." Dr. Kramer retrieved his briefcase and stood. To Ethan, "The project charter will be on my desk by the end of the week."

"Good luck," from Fong. She followed Dr. Kramer out the door.

But luck had nothing to do with success in science. Not that it mattered. Because this—*this* wasn't an unlucky turn of events. A joint research assignment would've been unlucky last Thursday, maybe. Now, though? It was catastrophic.

It was Erin Monaghan's fault.

That single clarion thought burned away the static still rioting in his brain. Sensation returned to his legs. He pushed up from his chair to match her posture over the table. "You did this, Monaghan."

"What?"

"If—if you hadn't spent all day politicking about gravitational waves and binary—"

Her attention broke away from the door. Eyes clearing from a thousand-yard haze, she transferred her frown to him instead. "*What?* No... *no*. You—you were the one who volunteered to present in Dr. Quarles' place—"

"Someone had to."

"Not *you*." Her shoulders straightened, her ponytail whipping back. "You... you put your research in the limelight and convinced Secretary McCandless that you could deliver something actionable—"

"Dr. Kramer's work is still largely theoretical, but my data is—"

"*Actually* actionable? Good, since we're stuck together now with an impossible—"

"Project—"

"—project—and *stop interrupting me*."

A flush crept down her throat under her jacket. He'd seen the low dip of her collarbones on Saturday, knew just how the warmth would gather there. An answering bloom swelled in his chest, and—

Fuck! Focus.

He swallowed, tensing his forearms and his abdomen. "I... sorry."

She blinked.

"Quantum gravity is an impossible research project. You... you're right."

"*I'm*... right?" The silent pressure of her question and her gaze scorched his ears for an immeasurable breath—but then she rallied with her usual sarcasm. "Obviously, I'm right. Yes. But the... the issue is that it's now my responsibility to make the impossible into something possible, because your talk—"

He breathed. "*My* talk. *Quantum* gravity."

"Sure," with a snort, changing tactics. "Maybe you'll finally get a first-author paper out of this!"

Thank God. This, he could manage. This was safe territory.

"Are you volunteering to be my second author?"

"You won't get any traction without applying my expertise in relativistic mechanics, so why would I take a secretarial role?"

"*You* won't get anywhere on quantum gravity without using the principles of quantum mechanics."

"Thank you for stating the obvious."

"You want the obvious?" Turning back to her, he crossed his arms. "You would've volunteered to take a fifty percent cut to LIGO's operating budget before you would've volunteered for this project."

"I would've taken seventy-five."

"And I'd never choose to work with you, either." But when had he ever been given a choice about what he did at the lab? Dr. Kramer didn't care whether he would've chosen to clean corrupted data sets for a month straight, to sacrifice his nights and weekends to tuning the holometer, to manage budget reconciliations and second-author drudgery. He did what he had to do. Always.

The project charter will be on my desk by the end of the week. Focus.

"We... we don't want... *this*," he confirmed. "We agree. But we don't have a choice. We won't make any significant progress on the quantum gravity question if we work alone—"

"—because if I could've solved the paradox with just relativistic mechanics, I would've done it already." Erin echoed his stance, defiant. "And published my findings in *Nature Physics*. As a sole author. Just like you would've."

"Right."

"I don't like sharing glory."

He didn't bother responding to that.

"*You* don't like sharing data. Or using numbers like mine. But you'll have to. *Voluntarily*."

"None of this is voluntary."

"No. So you'd better make this year worth my while, Meyer."

What could possibly make this collaboration worth its cost? Dr. Kramer had assigned the work, though, so he'd have to find its benefit—to himself and to his supervisor.

If he didn't?

"If—*if*—we can reconcile quantum mechanics with relativistic mechanics, solve the quantum gravity problem, eliminate the need for singularity theorems, have papers published in *Reviews of Modern Physics* or *Reports on Progress in Physics*—"

"—that *might* be worth it," she cut him off. "*Might*."

Not a promising start, when Dr. Kramer would expect genius. And with Erin across the table, willful and difficult, flushed with irritation—

No.

Knees stiff, arms still crossed, since he didn't trust his hands not to shake if he extracted them from their tight balls under his elbows, barely avoiding tripping over the wheels of his chair and his discarded pen, he shouldered out of the conference room, back to his office. When he locked the door behind him, his fingers instantly curled into his palms again with tremors.

So he fumbled for a new pen and his phone, sketching one-handed while he typed.

> **Ethan**
> 10 a.m., and this is already the worst Monday.

Ping.

> **Forster**
> 10 a.m., and damn, can I ever sympathize! Who am I kneecapping for you?

Erin Monaghan, he almost answered.

But if he brought Erin into their conversation, Forster might research her name, might find her SVLAC staff photo, might recognize her from Friday night at the Wine Room—and then she'd put together the shameful pieces to identify the man with whom Erin had been arguing.

> **Ethan**
> No one. But it isn't the way I'd planned to start my week.

> **Forster**
> I still have my bat on standby for you.

> **Ethan**
> Thanks.

Then he pushed a slow exhale through his teeth, put away his inky sticky notes and his phone, and returned to his inbox. This wasn't how he'd intended to start his week, and a quantum gravity project wasn't how he'd meant to spend his next year of research time, either. *A year of Erin Monaghan.* But a government directive was just that: *a directive*. He could execute his work with her—and do it *now*—or quit. Or be fired and blacklisted from his field.

He opened a follow-up email from his supervisor.

Meyer:
Monaghan and Sec. McCandless's political idiocy salvaged your mess. But if you fuck up this opportunity for my department like you fucked up Friday's talk and the Nature Physics *article, you're done.*
— K

No pulled punches. Just bald facts, except: *Monaghan salvaged your mess.* Like hell she had. Maybe their argument had impressed Secretary McCandless, and yes, his one dig from the podium had been good, but now—this. *This* was a mess. He wasn't a complete idiot, though, so he typed out his response without contesting his manager's assertion.

Dr. Kramer:
Thank you for this opportunity.
— E.M.

Next, he moved into a shared view of his nemesis and new collaborator's calendar. Meetings and deep work blocks populated beside his own schedule, an overlapping clutter of dates and times that realistically should've safeguarded him from ever colliding with Erin by the coffee machine. That hadn't worked out.

They were both free in the midafternoon on Wednesdays and Thursdays, however. It was tempting to set a regular meeting from seven to nine o'clock on Saturday nights. He'd never run the risk of seeing her in the Wine Room again, or at Salt & Straw... although if Erin couldn't be at the bar or the creamery, neither could he. In making her life miserable, he'd also shoot himself in the foot. Still, he considered it. But eventually he scheduled a preliminary project period on Wednesday afternoons.

> Meeting (Recurring): *Quantum Gravity Work Block*
> Day/Time: *Wednesdays, 1:00 p.m.–3:45 p.m.*
> Location: *Sidewinder Conference Room*
> Required Attendees: *Dr. Ethan Meyer, Dr. Erin Monaghan*

Almost immediately, a message from SVLAC's internal communications channel zipped onto his monitor.

> **Dr. Erin Monaghan**
> I was scheduling a block.
>
> **Dr. Ethan Meyer**
> It's already done. Time management isn't your strength.

Her response was to decline his invitation and send a new one.

> Meeting (Recurring): *Quantum Gravity Work Block*
> Day/Time: *Wednesdays, 1:05 p.m.–3:50 p.m.*
> Location: *Sidewinder Conference Room*
> Required Attendees: *Dr. Erin Monaghan, Dr. Ethan Meyer*

That's how she wanted to play this?
Fine.

14

His week was... difficult.

Ethan had copied and pasted a paper—with its hundreds of theoretical and numerical footnotes—on lab-generated black hole models into a shared virtual document to assess its research potential for their project, and every time he opened it to make comments on the temperatures and methods required to cool atoms for use as quantum simulators, every time he drafted equations to calculate the necessary strength of an electromagnet to manipulate those experimental particles, Erin Monaghan's cursor was inline beside his.

It was *aggravating*.

But he couldn't deny that it was Erin who'd learned of the paper's existence prior to its publication in *Physical Review Research*. She'd leveraged her network of astrophysicists to connect with an astronomy associate at Sonnenborgh Observatory, who knew a researcher from the University of Amsterdam whose work was relevant to their own strain of proposed inquiry into the quantum gravity paradox. This was Dr. Liesbeth Tuinstra, whose studies centered on tuning the ease with which electrons hopped along one-dimensional chains of atoms, which caused certain physical properties to vanish and effectively created lab-generated models of a black hole's event horizon—including Stephen Hawking's theorized thermal radiation—by interfering with the wave-like nature of the electrons.

So, yes, he acknowledged her contributions to their work. She was always in his—*their*—document, however. Watching him think. Not that she wasn't analyzing how they might replicate aspects of Tuinstra's research by using ultracold atoms to facilitate greater experimental control over the black hole model and its matter, too.

But still.

He skipped his cursor down a line. Hers followed. As did his desk.

"Stop *doing* that."

He stepped back from his screen and rubbed a hand over his neck while his desk locked in its height. *Blink, blink* went Erin's cursor. He had to admit that she'd made impressive use of the resources at her disposal, galvanizing her network to identify crucial work on their topic before it was publicly available—but it was his own expertise with atomic manipulation that would put their ideas into practice.

Req. temperature of atoms: 0 degrees, he noted now in the document's margin.

Kelvin? came her question.

Standard International unit of thermodynamic temperature, he commented back.

Impossible to create conditions of absolute zero, she replied. *Particles stop moving. Anyhow, we need them to be mobile for manipulation.*

Laser cooling can chill atoms to 10 microkelvins, he answered. *Functionally 0 kelvins, but some mobility remains.*

An ellipsis dotted beneath his explanation, bubbling, stopping, and bubbling again. Then:

I hadn't considered using lasers to cool matter instead of heat it. That works?

Yes.

I'll stop researching cooling techniques and consult with Nadine about materials for optical lenses before she leaves. See? Time management.

Her cursor left the page before he could retort.

He frowned. But rather than leaving his office for a steadying cup of coffee, he reached for his sudoku calendar, inked his numbers, sketched a hurried constellation on a sticky note—a single dot of pigment caught under his thumbnail, but would anyone really notice such a tiny blemish?—then opened his manager's preferred report template to draft proposals for hardware and literature review libraries. He submitted the document well in advance of Dr. Kramer's deadline, even though its materials section was more theoretical than concrete: too busy transitioning into the power and bureaucracy of her deputy supervisory role for the Relativistic Mechanics group, or celebrating Fong's departure over Sprinkles cupcakes and a Cowgirl Creamery cheese platter, Erin hadn't contributed her recommendations by the earlier due date he'd set.

Dr. Kramer observed the materials shortcoming, of course.
"Well, Meyer?"
"Monaghan didn't provide—"
"Did Monaghan submit this proposal?"
"No… I did."
But during Wednesday's work block, when they'd debated laser angles from opposite ends of the conference table, exchanging more virtual comments than live ones, had he actually told her

of his intention to submit the plan early? He stood alone in Dr. Kramer's office now, late on Thursday afternoon and under a stream of cold air venting from the ceiling before his supervisor's immaculate, glass-topped desk.

Tap, went one of Dr. Kramer's fingers.

"I'll have a progress report by the end of next week," he promised before the finger could descend a second time.

A nod, anticipating his assurance. "You'll provide value, Meyer."

"Yes."

When he walked back past the bullpen to his own desk, Erin's cubicle was dark, but a message from her was waiting on his screen.

> **Dr. Erin Monaghan**
> I reviewed our optics needs with Nadine. She had some insights on materials, and I've finished drafting my recommendations. Let's discuss before submitting the charter tomorrow.

He cursed under his breath.

> **Dr. Ethan Meyer**
> I submitted it today.

Instantly, her profile icon went live.

> **Dr. Erin Monaghan**
> I said I was going to talk to Nadine about materials.

A screenshot of their earlier exchange zipped into the conversation. The data was irrefutable.

> **Dr. Ethan Meyer**
> Yes. I made an error.

> **Dr. Erin Monaghan**
> You did.

He could imagine her eye flashing in triumph—

> **Dr. Erin Monaghan**
> Which is unexpected and annoying. But gratifying. And it was just a first draft hypothesis for the project. Did Dr. Kramer have feedback?

The image faded from his brain, replaced by a pixelated buzz of confusion. Was that all she had to say?

> **Dr. Ethan Meyer**
> No feedback.

A check mark appeared beneath his reply.

> **Dr. Ethan Meyer**
> But we should review your materials analysis tomorrow before we meet with the MEC hutch engineers.

He sent an invitation for a work block the next afternoon at three o'clock, tapping on his phone while he elbowed through the Modern Physics doors, into a slap of heat, and out to his car. While he inspected his wheel wells for rattlesnakes dozing on the tires' hot rubber, Erin declined his time and sent a new invitation for five minutes after the hour.

He shook his head, and stepped into a lump of turkey feces.

Bunsen would be happy. He switched to his texts with Forster and shared the golden retriever's good news.

He watched his step better on Friday when he pulled into the parking lot—and he watched himself in the kitchenette when he retrieved his daily dose of caffeine, too, glancing over his shoulder, listening for Erin's steel-toed work boots. A fresh carton of oat milk was open in the refrigerator, but she wasn't using it. Since she wasn't in the bullpen, either, he bypassed his usual email routine and opened Thursday's messages.

> **Dr. Ethan Meyer**
> 3:05 p.m. for the materials analysis?
>
> **Dr. Erin Monaghan**
> Scheduled yesterday.

He rapped a pen against his sudoku grid.

> **Dr. Ethan Meyer**
> You're not at your desk.
>
> **Dr. Erin Monaghan**
> No. With Leah in the media room.
>
> **Dr. Ethan Meyer**
> Why?
>
> **Dr. Erin Monaghan**
> I'm printing out a MEC hutch blueprint. Since

we've gotten approval to use the space while it's waiting on upgrades to the laser enclosure, we should have a copy to diagram our cable and optics layout. And Leah was trying to replace the laminator cartridges.

She was right that a hard copy of the Matter in Extreme Conditions blueprint would be easier to mark up than a digital one, but he closed their messages without replying. She knew she'd made a smart decision. She didn't need him to tell her that.

What she did need, however, was, "…a material for the experimental optics that reflects well but won't get hot near the lasers." Seated across from him in the Sidewinder conference room with the sleeves of a taupe sweater pushed up over her wrists, Erin swiveled her blueprint on the table and poked a sticky note standing in for the proposed placement of their lasers in the hutch.

"Correct." He dragged the Mylar paper over to his side of the table, until she caught its corner under her elbow. "Glass isn't an option—"

"—since it insulates and retains too much heat."

"Plastic will melt under laser exposure. Most things will. Which means that using lasers to cool the atoms might not work for repeat experiments." He ripped off another sticky note from its pad with more force than necessary, then shuffled through a profusion of materials between them—reference texts, or drafted diagrams displaying clusters of cables, vacuum chamber layouts, and the placement of electromagnets and detectors for data readouts—while searching for Tuinstra's list of research components and his own prior materials analysis for Dr. Kramer.

"We'll have to use a… a different method…"

Erin blinked. Her elbow slipped off the contested blueprint. Her eyebrows edged above her glasses. "Did you just admit to needing to course-correct for your research plans? After you'd already confessed to making an error with the project charter?"

"What?" Heat rose into his ears. "And you never have to edit your ideas?"

"All the time. I just didn't think that you, that *Dr. Ethan Meyer*…" She pushed her lenses back up her nose, but sent them sliding down again almost immediately with a shake of her head. She pulled her lower lip between her teeth; if he'd meant to protest her emphatic use of his title, he didn't. "Never mind. What about using liquid helium to chill the particles?"

"Check the price before you commit. Helium needs to be cooled to four kelvins before it liquifies."

She rolled her eyes and released her lip—though the dents of her teeth remained. She moved her laptop into view, tabbing over from a forum site and closing out a JSTOR article to access their funding authorization from the Department of Energy. She highlighted a line of zeros. "I think we can afford it."

She was right.

He returned to a problem that she hadn't solved. "Dr. Tuinstra used crystalline optics, but noted the need for an improvement in reflectivity for future research iterations. We could try—"

"—an organic synthetic polymer?"

"Yes. How did you know what I was—"

"LIGO uses mirrors too. Anyhow," she extracted the analysis document that he'd been searching for in the chaos, "here's your rundown on using synthetic polymers for the holometer's lenses, before you ended up with glass. You identified the polymer as a better overall material—greater experimental flexibility, heat resistant, extremely reflective, easy to clean—except that you needed to build the device inexpensively. Off-the-shelf glass was cheaper. Right?"

He meant to reply with something insightful about synthetic composites. Instead, he heard himself say, "You agree with my analysis?"

"Is that a trick question?"

"*Uh*. No, I…"

"Obviously, I agree with your analysis. You're disturbingly good with data! *Your* data, at least. It's just your field's application that's wrong."

I agree with your analysis.

Did she?

Her gaze narrowed at his silence. *Suspicion*. So he uncapped a pen—*safe*—and wrote *organic synthetic polymer* on his sticky note. He cleared his throat. "Because cost—it's not a… not a barrier, now."

"Right, but what did you just…" She squinted at his note, her braid falling forward over her shoulder. "Oh. *Polymer*. You have medical-grade handwriting. Chicken scratch. Give me the pen."

His fingers clenched around it.

"Fine." She reached for a drafting pencil that he'd tucked behind his ear.

He shied back on instinct.

Not far enough.

Her nails brushed his neck instead of closing around the graphite, the freckled underside of her wrist skimming his jaw so that a haze of iris and juniper flooded the airless conference room, and static zagged across his skin as if her touch were a naked wire—

Blistering arousal surged through his groin.

"*Ah!*"

Erin dropped her hand. Eyes wide, their startled darkness ringed in gold, her gaze flickered to the marks she'd left on his neck. "Sorry, I didn't mean to…"

He didn't answer her apology. He didn't trust his voice not to crack. He didn't trust himself. Shoving a random sampling of notes and his laptop into his bag, he left her at the table with his pencil in her fist. He rushed out the door to the nearest supply closet, or server room—it didn't matter. Because: *what the fuck?*

Hunched over a sink in the bathroom a minute later with his sleeves rolled up to his elbows, he splashed water on his face, wetting his pounding ears and hot neck. It wasn't enough, though. He stared at the running faucet and tried to breathe. To master himself. His brain, his body. What was wrong with him? Erin had knocked into him with her backpack before, leaving him breathless in the control room. He knew the sharpness of her elbows from their scuffles by the coffee machine, too.

But she hadn't ever… touched him.

He hadn't wanted her hands on him. Why would he? Erin Monaghan, with her smart mouth, clever and annoying, posing her suggestion for liquid helium, and—

An adjacent faucet switched on with a spurt. He jerked upright.

"Dr. Meyer." Tomasz Szymanski squirted soap into his palms, lathered between his fingers, then assiduously rinsed his hands. Only then did he meet Ethan's gaze in the mirror. "You are… ill?"

"No."

Obviously, I agree with your analysis.

Her nails on his neck—

He doused his face again, shuddering.

"You do not have a fever? You are…" Szymanski tapped his own forehead. "Red."

"No."

"Dr. Kramer is with the technicians in the IT building, preparing a private network access to the servers for his SVLAC computer while he is at CERN." A damp hand touched his shoulder. "He is not here."

Dr. Kramer wasn't the issue.

"I'm fine." He stepped back from his colleague's concern, shifting his messenger bag over his belt. "But… thanks."

Szymanski nodded without making eye contact again, and left the bathroom. All researchers should be like that. He didn't need to be analyzed by a physicist. He needed…

Forster.

Now.

He pulled out his phone.

> **Ethan**
> I know we rescheduled our meetup for Saturday.
> But are you free tonight instead?

If he could finally meet her, talk with her about art and books and sudoku, if he could just see her and touch her, then Erin Monaghan's insane hold on him would loosen. Wouldn't it? He'd rewire his brain around her, because this mania had to be neural circuits crossing and misfiring—

Ping.

> **Forster**
> I'd like that. The Salt & Straw on University Avenue, right?

Ethan

Yes. 7 p.m.? We can discuss our progress in This Is How You Lose the Time War. And they have some interesting new flavors.

Forster

The goat cheese, marionberry, and habanero? I like my spice…

Forster

Or the boysenberry oat milk sherbet?

He adjusted his bag and his belt again, promised her one of each flavor with a chance to lick both spoons, and stepped back out into the hall. *Seven o'clock.* He could last that long. He just had to endure his proximity to Erin until five today, when they'd finish a preliminary engineering meeting about accommodating their new laser and optics needs in the MEC hutch.

A few more hours.

Willing himself to concentrate, he returned to the Sidewinder conference room. Erin was waiting. *But*, he reminded himself, *so was Forster*.

Working with her rival over the past week had been difficult.

Less difficult than she'd anticipated, however.

Yes, they had the disparate but complementary expertise to tackle one of the most herculean questions in physics—and to lead departmental research teams on the topic. Yes, they were both hungry for publication and recognition.

But when forcibly paired with Dr. Ethan Meyer, would she treat her opportunity like a punching bag? Compelled to cooperate with her, would Ethan cut off his nose to spite his face?

After that awful moment in his office during the Department of Energy's site visit, and its follow-up at the Wine Room?

The extant data screamed *catastrophe*.

She'd braced for a fight—

—and found herself in the midst of a decent research collaboration without quite knowing how it had happened. They'd even made progress on an experimental outline, in between snippy comments about the irrelevance of relativistic mechanics or the large-scale uselessness of quantum physics.

Maybe they recognized that despite their precedent of sabotaging each other's efforts, any mischief now would damage them both.

While predictive analytics was sometimes wrong, though, it frequently transpired that its outcomes were just delayed; she couldn't relax, despite Ethan's unexpected apology for submitting their project charter to Kramer without her materials review. She didn't want to forgive him. But she shouldn't have tried to borrow his pencil today. She'd offered an apology of her own… but then he'd reared back and slammed the conference room door on her.

Pushing away her laptop, she examined the hand she'd extended. Rosy eraser residue from the pencil he kept behind his ear had caught under her nails when she'd scratched down his neck. She scrubbed her thumb against her jeans. The pressure didn't eradicate the tingle in her fingertips from their brush against the razor-roughened skin of his throat, though, or from the unexpected softness she'd found behind his ear—

The door clicked open again.

She snatched up a journal from the table. *Advances in Physics* was upside down.

Checking his watch, all Ethan said was, "The West Experimental Hall. *Now*."

"Fine."

She didn't care that he'd ignored her journal's orientation, that he hadn't even looked at her—not when she had the anticipation of her updated meeting with Bannister to sustain her. She could wait a few more hours for her artist.

Couldn't she?

She tossed away the pencil and stuffed her computer and her notes into her backpack, snagging the zipper. She hitched a strap over her arm without pausing to straighten out its metal teeth and strode for the hall. Ethan blocked the door, as he'd once blocked her in the control room. But he stepped aside before her gaping, swinging bag could catch him in the chest, before she had to squeeze past him.

"Hurry."

"No—no harping on my time management?" She followed him to the exit, not quite jogging after his long strides.

He veered off toward the Modern Physics parking lot in silence.

"You better not have deflated my tires again. It'll be your fault if I'm late." She'd leave for Salt & Straw directly from the West Experimental Hall, so she forwent a scooter.

His hatchback unlocked with a chirp. The driver door closed. *Fine!*

Clipping on her helmet, she kicked her tires to test their pressure, then pushed off from the pavement with her left foot on its pedal, swinging her leg over the bicycle seat. She bulldozed through a stretch of native plant landscaping between the lot and Ring Road, flattening sprouts of fescue, California sagebrush, and a litter of turkey feces before gaining momentum as she swept by a scrapyard of discarded industrial equipment. She blew past a stop sign and pushed up an incline toward the experimental halls. Tires rumbled along the road behind her, then decelerated at the intersection. Of course, he was a law-abiding driver. She pushed harder, sweat prickling under her arms.

She could beat him to the control room.

His hatchback passed her in the wide parking lot outside the West Experimental Hall. She left her bicycle unlocked and badged through the entrance first. He caught the closing door with his utility boot and followed. But though he could've easily drawn level with her—was he a runner?—Ethan shadowed her to the experimental hutch, where Viktor Hasselblad, a hutch engineer, and the daytime operator were waiting. He didn't even attempt to scan his badge over the electronic reader for entry. He didn't try to push past her to open the door, either.

When her identification card released the lock, Erin stared at the green indicator light for a moment. Ethan waited. She readjusted her lanyard and rolled her sleeves back over her wrists, then stole a brief glance at him. Arms crossed, he was focused on the scanner with lowered eyes and a tight mouth, spots of color high on his cheeks from the July sun or his unspoken irritation.

Why not just tell her that he was annoyed?

He *always* told her.

And what had she done, anyhow? Scratching his neck had been an accident, the marks were already gone, and she'd apologized, but still—

The door blinked a warning as its lock prepared to re-engage.

Damn.

She yanked down on the handle, flicked back her helmet-flattened braid, and marched inside to greet the three engineers seated along the control room's wall of monitors. She'd do this consultation by herself if she had to. She didn't need assistance from—*newly, bizarrely*—standoffish Ethan Meyer. If he wasn't going to talk? She was completely capable.

"I'm here. Dr. Monaghan—"

"—and Dr. Meyer," with a click of hinges.

She gritted her teeth, refusing to turn. "Right."

"Quantum gravity," from Hasselblad, nodding.

"The government contract." The operator scanned his notes.

Not Martina.

"The project has experimental components and a hutch layout to review." She looked straight ahead while she fished for the documents in her backpack.

"Let's see."

Would it be better or worse if Martina had been their assigned operator today?

Keen-eyed Dr. Perez would've noticed the change between them.

Ethan's change.

As she struggled with her backpack, he passed over his own copy of their diagrams for modifying the layout of the machinery in the hutch to accommodate a quantum gravity laboratory setup of lasers, optics, electromagnets, and detectors. His fleece brushed her elbow. No static, but he twitched—and the tiny movement jittered through the whole right side of her body like the lone hot wire of a single-pole breaker, because:

Control room, fleece—

She bit her tongue to keep still.

"Making accommodations for a vacuum chamber is possible. Storing the liquid helium—also yes, if we move the laser enclosure." Happily ignorant of Erin's turmoil, the hutch engineer tapped her chin. "Our current data detectors can be repurposed. There's not much room for cables, though."

"Rack them along the wall adjoining the Coherent X-ray Imagining hutch," was Ethan's suggestion.

Eleven whole words.

Damn him.

"I disagree," she countered, maybe too loudly. "Placing them there will block the laser window into the vacuum chamber. Run them under the electromagnetic trap."

By changing their plans on the fly in front of the engineers and violating the truce of self-preservation, she'd left him with no choice but to engage.

"The trap will interfere with the cables' casing."

"It won't if the casing is made from pure rubber, which can't be magnetized."

"The diagrams are already set," frowning at the floor. "I designed the holometer's layout. I know what I'm—"

"But this hutch isn't empty like your loading dock. We have to accommodate the existing machinery—and you'd have us stringing cables over the laser window!"

"I—"

"*Um!* Quantum gravity." The beleaguered operator brandished Ethan's papers. "Priority research on a contract from the federal Office of Science. Important… stuff."

She stepped away from her rival. Because while she wasn't looking at him—and she wasn't, *she wasn't*—the engineers were watching her.

Watching them.

Popcorn.

Easy, Monaghan…

No.

"Yes, it's important." *Be calm. Rational. No emotion. No hallucinations about Dr. Ethan Meyer, about gripping an operator desk with her hips cocked back. Just real, tangible facts.* She went on, "Our aim is to replicate the University of Amsterdam's recent black hole model, but to enhance control over the experiment by using ultracold atoms. We'll study the behaviors of mass and matter as they move over the lab-made event horizon. Is that behavior consistent? Can we manipulate it? Ultimately, the project will assess whether space-time is fundamentally continuous or discrete."

"It's discrete," from Ethan.

"So, for your laser beam settings…"

"We know for certain that it's a wave, but yes, it's theoretically possible that it could also be—"

"I'm familiar with the ideas around quantum gravity, Dr. Monaghan and Dr. Meyer." The hutch engineer took the design document from her operator. "However, the question that's pertinent today is: what exact settings, placements, and removals do you require for the hutch equipment on hand? Lasers, detectors, cables you're intending to repurpose, that's what's relevant now. Any other experimental equipment you need brought in is yours to manage with Dr. Hasselblad."

"Well, the current optics can be removed. We'll provide organic synthetic polymer mirrors—"

"Will these new optics replicate the dimensions of MEC's current lenses?"

"They might not be an exact match, but—"

"The dimensions of off-the-shelf glass would match the current lens sizes to within a sixteenth of a—"

"Except that we've already decided that cost isn't an issue, so we don't need to use glass! We can use machine-customized polymers instead of—"

"Dr. Monaghan. Dr. Meyer," with a raised hand and a raised voice from the hutch engineer, cutting them off. "Do you, or do you not, have your specifications ready? These documents have one design setup and a list of experimental components. But there's obviously still disagreement on both your design and component needs."

"I was—"

"*I* was—"

The engineer set down their papers. "I'm not hearing an unqualified *yes*. Now, time in the experimental halls is tight. Due to some scheduled system maintenance, a personnel shift change and the setup for the next researcher using MEC's software both begin in thirty minutes. You have until then to present finalized specifications to us. Layouts. Sizes. Angles. Materials. If you can't, schedule another consultation."

An unspoken *"Don't waste my time"* was silent but clear.

"Don't waste my patience" was equally clear when the hutch engineer pointed them back into the hall.

They filed out. Disregarding an out-of-order sign—Closed for Repairs—posted at the entrance to the X-ray Correlation Spectroscopy control room, Erin badged inside the deserted vestibule for privacy. It took three tries to swipe her card for a green light; her exasperation rose with each rejection, and she rounded on Ethan as soon as the door swung shut behind them.

"We already decided to use a polymer. Why did you bring up glass?"

He remained by the threshold. "Off-the-shelf glass lenses will fit the standard dimensions of MEC's optics. A successful replication of Dr. Tuinstra's black hole model should be confirmed before resources are spent on an organic synthetic polymer."

"Cost resourcing isn't an issue!"

"Time, then." Again, he glanced at his watch.

Jerk.

"Just because you had to scrimp and build your holometer with commercial parts, since Dr. Kramer wouldn't give you the funding for anything else—"

"Our prefabricated elements have produced successful results."

"But for *our* project—"

They traded blame and research grandstanding for ten minutes. At least, Erin did. Ethan studied the frayed laces on his boots or continued marking time on his watch, mouth tightening and ears reddening at her caustic arguments but returning nothing beyond brief, factual replies. Ten minutes became fifteen. She argued against his silence through the staff shift change and over a series of muted announcements from the West Experimental Hall's address system.

"Are you planning to use a drug store thermometer to track any rises in temperature from the event horizon?"

"What?"

"Or maybe just the Scoville Scale, to *really* cut costs?"

"No," checking his watch for a fifth time. "The Scoville Scale is for peppers, not Hawking radiation—"

Thirty-five minutes.

Fifty.

They could've continued for hours. *She* could've. When her own watch read five forty-eight and his dogged focus still remained on anything in the control room except for her, however, she threw up her hands.

"This is pointless." It was—the Scoville Scale was nonsense—and it was late. She'd be with Bannister at Salt

& Straw in just over an hour. She pushed past Ethan to the door before he could edge away. "It's almost six o'clock. I have somewhere to be."

But when she tugged down on the handle, it didn't budge.

What?

She rattled the mechanism harder.

Nothing.

She put her full weight on the latch. It didn't release.

"*Damn!* The door's jammed."

"What?"

"I just said: *the door's jammed.* It won't open! Something must be wrong with the lock. The scanner, or…"

"Weren't the speakers reporting a test of the Personnel Protective System in the experimental halls?" SVLAC's Personnel Protective System was a lockdown protocol that remotely activated every failsafe deadbolt in the building. "Staff might've been instructed to go to the East Experimental Hall while the systems finished their checks."

Now he decided to talk?

"You knew this, but you didn't say anything?"

"I thought you'd heard it, too."

She swore. She tugged at the handle again.

"Maybe you're not doing it right."

Now he decided to snipe back at her?

"Harping on my spatial—*ugh!* But it doesn't matter, because it's remotely locked—"

"Move." Ethan reached for the latch. He cranked it, forearms tensing, tendons arching with effort—and his palms skidded off the metal bar. "*Fuck!*"

She agreed.

Not that she told him.

Massaging the marks on his hand, Ethan scowled at nothing while a new silence simmered between them. Erin paced and checked her phone. Her device couldn't get reception through the shielding insulation built into the foundation of SVLAC's experimental halls; it was strong enough to resist the electromagnetic pulses from an atomic explosion. The lab's valuable and volatile equipment would remain secure in the event of a nuclear disaster, and if some mechanical component in the hutches imploded from an experiment gone wrong, the fallout would also be contained. What chance did her budget cell service have of penetrating?

Fifty minutes became sixty-seven.

Eighty.

"Won't someone from MEC notify the system engineers that we're still here?"

"There was a shift change. The fresh crew won't know."

He was right.

Again.

"This can't be happening!" She hammered at the door. But there was no one in the West Experimental Hall to hear her. No one to come, no one to help. There was only Ethan, here in the control room. Obstinate Ethan, who was sabotaging her second meeting with Bannister, just like he'd ruined her night in the Wine Room.

Ethan fucking Meyer.

"*You.*" She swung around to where he'd retreated to the wall of blank monitors, his hair on end from raking his fingers through it. "You planned this, didn't you?"

"What? No. How could I?"

"I don't know! *Somehow*. You heard those announcements but didn't say anything, and I'm—"

Late.

She should've been out of the experimental halls with a quantum gravity experimental setup confirmed long before the Personnel Protective System test started. But no, Ethan had had to spur her into a fight by ignoring her.

"Now I'm going to be late, and I have plans!" She advanced on him. "I'm supposed to be—"

"*Don't.*" He backed away, up against an operator desk. His voice was gravelly. "Don't touch me."

"No? Or what? Don't order me around! My professors learned that the hard way, my brothers know not to interfere unless I call them, and I'd never let you—of all people!—tell me what to do, when I wouldn't even let Bannister—"

His hooded gaze flashed up. "*Bannister?*"

She cocked back her arm to prod his vest. "Don't interrupt me!"

"*Bannister.*"

He caught the syllables between his teeth—and then Ethan caught her wrist. But he didn't look at their hands, at the voltaic energy suddenly snapping between them. Instead, he looked at her. *Finally*: his eyes were nearly black, pupils eclipsing all light and color, yet somehow still glittering with that dangerous mica. And his grip—it wasn't violent. Didn't hurt. It shocked her, though: *almost gentle.* His lips moved, articulating the artist's name again.

Bannister.

…fuck.

"*Forster,*" he breathed—

—and then that breath was in Erin's lungs, and his mouth was on hers.

15

She could've screamed.

But the searing fusion of his mouth shocked her into silence, his touch a live wire and a nuclear explosion. His mouth, and—

Forster.

He knew. He knew that name. *Her* name.

How?

She could've wrenched away to slap him and demand an answer. She should've—but her free hand was fisted in the collar of his vest, hauling him nearer. Had she meant to strangle him? She couldn't remember, couldn't think, mindless, thoughtless, ravenous in his arms, an orbit collapsing, logic collapsing with it, desperate, fierce and angry, starving for his single-minded focus, for this break in his control—and she sank her hungry teeth into his lip.

"*Ah!*"

His gasp was electric. Erin swallowed it.

Pulling Ethan with her, she backed into an operator desk under the monitors. He must've released her wrist while exhaling his surprise, because her other hand was free now to drag through his hair as one ankle hooked around his calf, urging him closer, *closer*. She stole his balance as she stole his breath; he collapsed beside her onto the desk, a palm at the nape of her neck raking along her braid and the other clutching the base of her spine while she clawed her fingers under his fleece and his shirt.

He hissed at the scrape of her nails up his back. "Erin—"

"No—don't tell me to go easy, don't you *dare*—"

Click.

The door into the control room unlocked.

A system maintenance engineer in a safety vest stood in the hall outside, frozen with a key for the emergency deadbolt in her hand. "*Uh.*"

Fuck.

Fuck, fuck, fuck—

She pushed Ethan off the desk.

Off her.

"The… the XCS hutch is… *um*, closed for maintenance. The scanner's malfunctioning, so I had to manually reopen the room after the system check…" The engineer backed away, eyes wide and oscillating between them, hands raised. "But I can come back later."

The door closed again. Erin did the only thing *she* could do, and ran for the hall.

"Wait—" His voice was raw, rasping.

She didn't. Stomach churning, eyes blurred under the harsh lights in the corridor, she staggered past the gawking system maintenance engineer and the hutches for Macromolecular Femtosecond Crystallography and Coherent X-ray Imaging. His footsteps beat hard after her, but if she could just reach the parking lot outside, reach her bicycle, she'd be so much faster, could get away from him and herself—and her hallucination, her memory, *what the hell?*—so she smacked into the West Experimental Hall's exterior door—

"*Forster!*"

—and stopped.

Again, that name.

A gust of wind smelling of sunbaked metal whipped inside the vestibule and against her cheeks for a moment, before cutting off as the door ricocheted against its stopper and closed again. She didn't block it. She remained where she stood, facing an Exit sign and staring straight into a pocket dimension, down the sinkhole of some quantum tunnel, those syllables spoken in Ethan Meyer's voice echoing through her head…

"Forster." He was behind her now, breathless. "*Erin*."

Her names. Both of them.

"W-what?" She reached for the door a second time, but not to shove it open: to brace herself. Her palm squeaked and slid on the metal, and it turned her a hazardous inch away from her goal outside, toward him instead. Was the steel magnetized? Was she? "What… w-what did you say?"

"You're Forster. The writer." He took a step nearer. "*Aaron* Forster. It… it's a homophone. Isn't it?"

"*Uh*." She couldn't look away, couldn't breathe.

"Aaron." Darkness glittered in his gaze, and her stomach answered with vertigo when he repeated, "*Erin*."

"H-how…"

Data.

A few reddish hairs stuck to his jeans below the knees: affectionate canine detritus. Almost invisible, a speck of color under his left thumbnail was ink. The evidence answered her question.

"*Bannister*."

A jerk of his chin, a hitch of his inhale.

"…*oh*."

Just that, because *Forster, Bannister*—what more was there to say? What more *could* she say? What could she say besides everything, which was impossible, because this… *this* was impossible—so she just blinked back at him, one hand still on the door, the other contracting over and over into a fist, pulsing with the rapid rush of her heart, until—

Click.

Now it was the exterior door into the West Experimental Hall that opened as a badge swiped past the scanner. Arriving to run a data collection cycle for the Relativistic Mechanics group's binary pulsar study, it was Sandra O'Connor-Young and Leah Haddad who found them locked together this time, not on an operator desk but staring, immobile and silent and impossible, *impossible*—and really, which situation was worse?

"Dr. Monaghan? And... Dr. Meyer?"

Popcorn.

"I... I'm j-just leaving."

The muscles in her cheeks were too tense for a casual greeting and a smile. Leaving Ethan in the vestibule, she shouldered past her colleagues as they moved into the hall and groped for her bicycle, bumping its tires down a short flight of external stairs, the helmet dangling from her handlebars banging into the railing. She swung her leg over the seat. Her metal-capped boot slipped off its pedal, leaving her straddling the top tube bar, stupidly flat-footed.

"Erin," again. He'd followed her outside.

She singed her fingers on the sun-heated plastic of her chin clip. "What?"

"Are you..." His boots crunched into a film of industrial grit on the steps. Then, of all the things he could've asked: "Can you ride home safely?"

Thank God—because his doubt steadied her like nothing else. Rallied her.

"*Really?*" The hot, familiar prickle of her frustration was so much better than the shiver in her stomach under his unnerving focus—the focus she'd wanted from him, *demanded* from him, but now? "I've been making this ride for over three years. I've never had one collision, not even with an autonomous car—"

"I wasn't—"

"—or is this your clue that I should check my tire pressure again? I could ride through commute traffic into Palo Alto with a flat, and I'd still get there first!" She snapped her helmet clip.

"Get where first?" Somehow, his hands were on her handlebars.

"Salt & Straw. *Obviously.*" She glanced down to nudge his grip off the rubber sheathing, but the angle must've tilted her face into the lowering sun, because heat tingled over her cheeks again at the reminder that fleece-wearing Ethan Meyer had Bannister's ink under his nails, and—*fuck*. "If… if you let go before they run out of my habanero flavor."

"You're still going?"

She swallowed. "Well, it's… it's about ninety-five degrees out here, so—"

"Fahrenheit, Celsius, or kelvin?"

But again: *Thank God.*

"Take a wild guess." She wrestled her handlebars free. Maybe she could run over his foot like she'd done with a scooter outside the Science and Public Support building. Bunsen might appreciate the residual turkey feces that her tires would smear across his boot—

—because Bunsen was not only Bannister's dog, but Ethan Meyer's, too.

She pivoted her wheels toward the parking lot. She told him over her shoulder, "It's hot. I'm getting ice cream. That was my plan for tonight—and I'm not changing it just because of you."

He nodded.

"Don't say anything about me being tardy, either. We're both already late," and she pushed off from the pavement.

Friday's traffic along Sand Hill Road was heinous. Bumper to bumper between a Tesla and the wheezing sensors of an autonomous sedan at the Santa Cruz Avenue light, Ethan drummed his fingers on his steering wheel and eyed a pack of cyclists in branded athletic gear speeding past in their lane. Erin wasn't in the crowd, but she might've already coasted down the hill from SVLAC, breezing by him where he sat in a gridlocked crush of honking cars at the intersection.

She wouldn't wait for him.

Not that he'd expected her to.

She was Forster, but she was also Erin Monaghan.

God, she was *Forster*.

Standing there in the control room, arguing at him about materials and cables while he tried not look at her, tried not to answer her, tried not to breathe her in, because if he did for even a moment then she'd read the data in his body like she read her LIGO exports: *overheated skin, rapid pulse, pupils enlarged, messenger bag clutched over his jeans*—and she'd see how desperately he was still fighting the effect of her fingers brushing his throat—

Fuck. Fuck!

He shifted forward to crank up his air conditioning. Wincing, shifting his belt again like a teenager, he glanced into his rearview mirror.

Her nails on his neck. Her mouth under his.

Forster. Erin.

He'd kissed her.

...fuck.

He needed more time to make sense of that data than even Silicon Valley's traffic could loan him. Structuring an analysis from Dr. Kramer's error-riddled exports would be trivial by comparison. His supervisor's fury over another *Nature Physics* fiasco would be easier to manage than tonight's meeting at Salt & Straw, too. Not going, though? *Not an option.* Despite this certainty, however, his breathing began to accelerate—because it was Chase who was suave in these situations, Chase who'd know how to act and what to say, never him—but… Erin and Forster already knew about Bunsen. What if he drove to Redwood City first to fetch his retriever before he arrived at the creamery? He could swerve through another cyclist mob into Sand Hill's turn lane, then take Alpine Road onto the northbound Junipero Serra Freeway.

He could.

He *needed* Bunsen.

But when he inspected his mirrors and reached to flick on his signal, his blind spot didn't show empty pavement. No: *she* was there, speeding down the hill, a perfect proof of Bernoulli and Euler's conservation of angular momentum on her bicycle, her braid whipping behind her, just where he least expected her.

Blindsiding him again.

She didn't see him.

And he… he didn't turn. Fortunately, the traffic cleared by the time he reached Palm Drive. He didn't slow to flip a middle finger to the majestic, iconic view of Stanford's Oval and the Rodin sculptures fronting its Main Quad, but zipped across the El Camino Real overpass and into the City Hall parking garage, then threaded through the lively Friday crowds and musical buskers near the Wine Room on Ramona Street. A right turn onto University Avenue brought him to the line outside Salt & Straw.

Face to face with Erin again.

Well—*almost*.

Despite having already discussed their choices of ice cream, she was studying a sandwich board listing the creamery's seasonal flavors with such intense concentration that she didn't see his approach. She'd unraveled her braid and pulled her hair back into a regular ponytail, but now tiny kinks and waves fractured its usual straight length—something undone, something private exposed. Her cheeks were flushed under the twinkling evening lights embellishing the trunks of University Avenue's trees, either from the pace of her ride or with her determination not to notice his arrival. He was three feet from her board.

He pulled out his phone.

Ethan
I'm here.

Swish: the noise of an activating lightsaber. Erin's eyes darted away from the ingredient list for a vegan salted caramel and okara cupcake flavor. She didn't reach into her back pocket for her own phone, though.

Had she given him a custom text tone?

"*Um*... hi," she said, before he could crunch that data.

"You made it," seemed a safe answer.

"Yeah. And I got a good spot in line, too." She nodded at a queue behind her of chattering college students and parents wheeling strollers more expensive than Ethan's car, then stepped back from the menu and gestured for him to duck under a barrier belt separating Salt & Straw's patient hopefuls from line-jumpers. "Since I was waiting."

He stepped over the belt, crossed his arms, and studied the offerings. "Traffic."

"I know." She flicked her ponytail.

She *had* seen him stalled at the Santa Cruz Avenue intersection, then—and for some reason, laughter rippled over his tongue. So he coughed and asked her, "What are you ordering?"

"I already told you: goat cheese, marionberry, and habanero."

"That malted chocolate barley milk option didn't change your mind?"

"No. I'm loyal to my oat milk. When you leave any of it for other people."

"You're the one who admits to spiking your creamer with coffee—"

—but that wasn't something Erin had told him.

Forster had.

Did she realize that?

"*Uh.*" She edged forward through the creamery's glass double doors when a space cleared inside, very interested in the floor. Yes, she clearly did. "No, still habanero."

I like my spice…

Was that waft of juniper her perfume, or from a specialty ice cream?

"I'll get the… *um*, boysenberry oat milk sherbet."

"Why?" She shuffled along a snaking line toward the taster spoons, not looking at him.

"You just said you liked oat milk." And he'd promised Forster both the habanero and boysenberry flavors, with a chance to lick the spoons.

"Oh. Right."

They advanced to the counter in silence.

"Any taste tests of our seasonal options?" A server juggling a scooper from hand to hand in time to a bouncy pop track piping from the overhead speakers smiled at their approach; they declined tasting the malted chocolate barley milk, the salted caramel and okara cupcake, or the lemon curd and whey. "No? Then what can I get you two?"

"The goat cheese, marionberry, and habanero, please. In a cone."

"Boysenberry oat milk sherbet. Cup."

"Paying—"

"Separately," they said together.

"Sure." The server slung their orders onto the counter and tossed her used scooper into a bucket of hot water. "You can swipe your cards at the register. There's a stack of napkins if you need them. Next in line!"

Cup, cone, and napkins in hand, they weaved through an increasingly rowdy after-dinner crowd swarming the creamery, sliding onto a bench outside just as a giggling couple trading a few last licks of ice cream on their spoons vacated it. It was a very public spot. They wouldn't be whispering sweet nothings like the departing men, however, so it didn't matter—and if their conversation went according to form, they'd be shouting rather than whispering. Which was… safer. Or rather, their arguments *had* been safer, until today—

Ethan shoveled a heap of boysenberry sherbet into his mouth.

Erin mirrored him, plucking out a whole marionberry from her dessert. *Crunch*. Then, "*So*."

"*So*," he echoed.

"I'll start with the obvious question. How did this happen?" *This*.

Scramble its letters: *shit*.

He must've said that out loud, because she nodded. Eyes averted, she took another bite of ice cream. "You called me *Forster* in the experimental hall tonight. But did you already know?"

"What?" He froze mid-scoop. "No."

"No?"

"I play sudoku, not poker. I'm not a good liar. If I'd known before—I didn't. Not until you said that you had plans tonight and mentioned someone named *Bannister*... It could've been another person with that name, though."

"It wasn't."

"No."

"But you..." she frowned, digging one metal-capped toe into the pavement, "...you're good enough with data—well, not mine—that I thought maybe I'd told you too much about myself. Enough that you'd run the numbers and realized who Forster was. Who *I*... I was wondering during my ride if I'd been making a fool of myself with you at the lab."

"Only with your research."

"*With my*—excuse you?" She elbowed him, her chin snapping up in standard outrage.

Not standard: the small smear of marionberry juice dotting the corner of her mouth...

"*Ouch*," was his delayed retort. He plunged his spoon back into his sherbet instead of hammering home his point about relativistic mechanics.

She didn't apologize. But she didn't continue their usual arguments, either. Instead, after a beat, "So: you didn't know. I didn't know. But now we both know. What... what do we do with this information?"

"We've been rivals for years," he said. Just a fact.

"And we know what happened."

Bannister, Forster, the kiss. Rash, painful, glorious—

"We have data," she continued. "But the question is always: *why?*"

Right.

He breathed. Blood diverted back to his head. Because that was the root of all scientific inquiry: *why?* Facts were facts. It was the ability to explain them that brought publication and recognition, however.

And resolution.

"We have a fairly complete data set. Weeks of messages and years of rivalry." A quick glance showed her twisting her cone between her fingers, picking at its flaky edges. He added, "We could try to answer the question."

"Do you want to?"

"Don't you? Aren't you curious? Aren't you—" but a crumble of waffle broke off under her thumb while he spoke. Melting ice cream began to seep out, threatening her sweater and jeans.

"*Oops*—"

He didn't watch her swipe her tongue up the cone to catch the habanero drips. Instead, he cleared his throat, crossed his legs, recited the periodic table of elements, and stared at an advertisement for plant-based lamb kebabs at Oren's Hummus across the street, counting, counting, cold and precise and sweating under his collar and his belt—

"You forgot to say the ninety-ninth element. *Einsteinium.*" Erin flapped a napkin into his face a minute later.

Had he been working through the periodic table verbally?

Oh, God.

Maybe she took pity on him, because she left it at that. She wrapped the napkin around her damp cone and said, "Let's start at the beginning. I had a fairly major issue with the onboarding documents on my first day. After you shoulder-checked me by the bullpen."

"You sent my *Nature Physics* revise-and-resubmit form to the reviewers when I hadn't finished the edits to Dr. Kramer's paper," he collected himself to retort. "To *my* paper. You used my initials."

"They're also my initials," she replied reasonably, then licked her ice cream. Unreasonably. "Human Resources rushed me through the paperwork. I signed what they told me to sign. Your *Nature Physics* form got in the line-up somehow, so I submitted it, too. And since they took months to return my finalized documents, I only learned about the error after you'd already... But it was an accident."

He pressed the chilly sherbet cup into his lap. "Which I didn't know. Not until I'd switched the time zones on your calendar. When I read your introductory email after I got back from CERN, I thought you'd done reconnaissance on me. You'd submitted my paper to the journal with incomplete edits. That made me look like an idiot, and made Dr. Kramer—"

"Why would I have tried to sabotage you at that point? I didn't know you, and your shoulder-check wasn't *that* bad."

"*Um.*" He began to fiddle with his spoon, bending the plastic, testing its tensile strength. "You... you have competitive brothers, right?"

"Why does that matter?" She shook her head at his non-sequitur, then shrugged again and bit into her ice cream before it seeped through her napkin. "But I do. I didn't tell them anything about... *this*, though, because they *definitely* would've tried to sabotage you. I love them, but they can be insane about some things. Not about protecting me from losing at Monopoly or baseball, but everything else? When I mentioned that my doctoral advisor and research cohort—all men, by the way—had tried to scrub my name from a joint research paper before publication, they threatened to break skulls."

"You didn't tell your brothers about our rivalry, because they would've tried to help you."

"They would've made things worse. I can handle myself."

"I know you can." He dug his spoon deeper into the sherbet. "*Uh*, I… I also have a brother. But our rivalry isn't over Monopoly or fast pitches. It's not… fun. It's not… nice."

"Oh." She was quiet for a moment, eyebrows pinched over her nose, thinking. Then, with a slow nod, "Right. I guess it makes sense that with the data you had on hand and with physics being such a cutthroat field, it seemed plausible that I'd try something unethical. And, of course, I retaliated to your time zone switch by running a binary program on your data export, which *was* explicit sabotage—because it seemed like you'd come back from Switzerland and vandalized my calendar unprovoked, since Human Resources still hadn't told me about the *Nature Physics* signing error yet. Then you responded by… I don't even remember. But it was too late by then, anyhow. Neither of us was going to back down at that point, even once we knew… Though what *did* you do? Let the air out of my tires?"

"Yes. I thought about switching your brake configurations, too. I just never remembered to bring the tools. But that would've been actively dangerous—"

Her elbow tapped his arm. "You kept my practical mechanics skills fresh. Not just my relativistic ones. Should

I be thanking you for that? Next time my oldest brother's in town and his rust bucket of a Jeep blows a head gasket, I'll be primed to fix it."

He couldn't laugh with her, though. He could've hurt her. *Really* hurt her. He thrust away his cup, abruptly queasy. "I escalated things. With your bicycle. With everything I said about your research methods and data in that all-hands. I… I'm sorry."

"We both escalated."

"Still—"

"No." She knocked her boot into his. "Don't toss that sherbet. You promised that I could have the spoon, remember? Don't take my narrative from me, either. We each thought that the other person's actions were tantamount to declaring war, and I can see why we would."

"That's not an excuse for what I—"

"—what *we* did. I know. But based on the data and backgrounds we both brought to the situation, now we understand the *why*. Ethan…" She tugged at his sherbet and passed over her ice cream; his fingers automatically curled around the waffle cone, and when he raised his eyes in question, he found the berry-stained curve of her lips parted on an exhale, on his name, her gaze suddenly serious. "Ethan, I'm sorry, too. For my questions during the Department of Energy's visit, and for afterward. I was trying to even our score. But it wasn't right. And I… I didn't know. I only looked at the information I had on you. I didn't think about what I wasn't seeing. *Bannister*. I committed—"

"—the scientific cardinal sin?"

Her teeth clicked together, softness vanishing. But the dimple trembling in her cheek was evidence of a nascent, reluctant smile. "I wouldn't go that far!"

"Dr. Fong isn't here. Your secret's safe." He leaned back against their bench, breathing again.

"Maybe. But Forster's isn't. There's no putting Schrödinger's cat back in that box."

"Your odds are fifty-fifty."

"Generous, but no. Because now I'm in a situation where I know that *you* know. And since we both know, the cat's loose." She poked his spoon into the sherbet, shaking her head again. "Forster and Bannister—*God*. Tell me *those* odds, that we would've met this way."

"Very small. I might not even include their probability in a quantum analysis."

"Now, that's just insulting."

"I'm not wrong. It was unlikely that we would've met through *Galactica Magazine*. Even more unlikely that the editors would've paired our submissions together—"

"—and that our work would be complementary: black holes that—no. *Wait*." Gasping, Erin snatched back her cone. "You copied my research for your drawing. The movement of black holes and stars is *my* specialty!"

What?

He hadn't drawn inspiration from Dr. Erin Monaghan's research for Bannister's art.

Had he?

…*had* he?

"You—you don't have a monopoly on the topic. And," he stabilized himself with facts, "it's now the Department of Energy's topic. The behavior of matter and gravity that's proximal to black holes? It's ours."

Surprisingly, her indignant eyes dropped at that. "*Damn*."

"What? I didn't plagiarize your research."

"No, not that—it's… we're not just rivals anymore. We're not just Forster and Bannister, either. The odds don't matter. We're collaborators on a federal research contract."

They were.

"So, now what?"

Now what.

"We know the facts," he reminded them.

"'The Truth of Fact, the Truth of Feeling'."

"Ted Chiang."

"Yes."

"So?"

"So…" Gold-ringed and dusky, her gaze lifted again to meet his. She bit her lip, then posed the very critical, very non-rhetorical question: "What do we do? Because this… *this* shouldn't continue. *We* shouldn't continue."

Oat milk curdled in his stomach. "Right."

"I mean—we shouldn't, should we? We understand what we—*who* we… but we're still competitors for the Eischer-Langhoff grant."

"But we're *collaborators* on the quantum gravity project."

"Which is a federal research contract that could launch our careers if we succeed, and tank them if we fail! That means I can't afford distractions from my work. Can you?"

If you fuck up this opportunity for my department, you're done.

"No." The word hurt.

"Plus, we're both referencing research in our competing Eischer-Langhoff grant applications that we're using together in our literature review for the Department of Energy. That means we have a conflict of interest somewhere, don't we?"

"Probably. I'm not sure what. But… probably."

"Because I'm always right?"

"I didn't say that."

"Were you thinking it?" She dabbed her napkin over her cone, nails grazing its waffled texture.

"No." He swallowed hard. "I was thinking about... *uh*—about a hundred other reasons that this is a bad idea."

"Thousands. And—right. *I'm* right."

"Then what's our process plan?"

"Two key items, I think." Lobbing away her napkin, she ticked off the points on her fingers. "One: we'll keep things strictly professional."

"No more sabotage."

"Yes. And two:" *tick*, "no more communication as Bannister and Forster. Not until—"

"Until?"

"—until we execute the Department of Energy's quantum gravity deliverables."

Oh.

It was a reasonable plan to manage an impossible, untenable situation.

The rules of engagement were clear, the refreshed boundaries between their professional and personal lives neatly drawn. It was all very exact. Very sudoku-like. He usually relished neatness and exactness and sudoku...

"Agreed," he said, because what other viable answer was there?

"Good." Her thumb returned to scratch at the seam on her cone. "Otherwise, this is how we'll lose—"

"—the space-time war?"

A snort. "Yes—"

—and then a torrent of sludgy ice cream burst through its waffle container.

"*Argh!*"

Erin lunged down to suction her lips over the crack. But her eyes flickered sideways to him while she licked up the spill.

Was she laughing?

A disorienting flash of heat through his cold-numbed hands made him fumble his sherbet cup. Melted boysenberries seeped into his jeans.

Fuck.

16

Saturday. Sunday.

No new messages populated his phone's sparse personal conversations. (He sent the usual chastising call from the Meyers about missing family dinner to voicemail.) No typing notifications appeared beneath his latest message with Forster.

With Erin.

Not that he checked their thread. Much.

What would she have said? Anyhow, they'd agreed to keep all communication professional, so she would've used SVLAC's instant messaging system, not text, if she'd needed to contact him. There was no reason to monitor their discussion for a bubbling ellipsis—evidence that she was thinking of him like he was thinking of her. He tried *not* to think about her. He attempted to focus on sudoku, and when that didn't help, he ran himself to exhaustion with Bunsen along a lattice of exposed trails at the Baylands Nature Preserve. He created the framework for Dr. Kramer's status report on their quantum gravity work. He tried to distract himself, to redirect his brain into safe channels of productivity. He did. But—

The bold laughter in her eyes.
The flick of her tongue.
The taste of her mouth.
The weight of her silence.
Aaron Forster.

Erin Monaghan.
Her.

His fingers itched, but he didn't tap into the reply field beneath her texts. What would *he* have said? And his phone's lock screen read 11:28 p.m. So, he reached for a sketch pad; with a sigh, Bunsen dragged his bed beside Ethan's desk and settled down to wait. He drew past midnight. Galaxies spooled in coils across the paper and through the lines of a discarded sudoku grid. Flecks of pigment smeared his desk. No calm symmetry of ruled lines or perspective could secure guardrails around his inconvenient emotions. His memories. *Her.* He drew and drew until his pen ran dry, until its desiccated nib scratched through the drawing pad.

Her fingers on his throat, her nails on his spine—
Groaning, he scrubbed his hands over his face.

When his alarm blared at six fifteen the next morning, he was already alert and staring at his ceiling, mouth sandy, teeth gritty, skin damp, stomach knotted, and heartbeat loud in his skull. He'd hardly slept. He hadn't expected to.

He swung his legs out of bed and strapped on his watch. A monitor on its band immediately beeped a warning.

Heart rate exceeds safe limit! Slow down!

"We're going running again."

Mesh shorts, zip-up jacket, running shoes, Green Day, and he was out the door with Bunsen. He didn't treat himself to a warm-up jog but pushed straight into a sprint down the sidewalk toward Stulsaft Park. The retriever galloped across Farm Hill Boulevard and onto the trail beside him, occasionally halting their momentum when he braked to lift his leg or to ferret for something tasty under a barbecue grate. After twenty minutes of mindless exertion on the path, they returned to the condo for breakfast. *Seven o'clock.* He was behind schedule. But he shaved after his shower. He answered a few questions from Szymanski in SVLAC's messaging system. He set a timer for coffee, scrambled an egg, then brushed his teeth with attention to each molar. He flossed. He even took his temperature. He could call in sick and avoid the cause of his pounding heart and wet palms, couldn't he? But when had he ever missed work? His leave went unused, and expired each year. Was there a single day when he could've afforded to take it, though? With Dr. Kramer heading his department, with the never-ending race for peer-reviewed results and publication—races against expectation, against his competitors, against himself—and with Erin Monaghan in the bullpen?

7:49 a.m.

She was probably already at her desk. Dr. Kramer was likely in the office, too.

He didn't call in sick. He got into his car, into traffic, and eventually into the Modern Physics parking lot. Erin's bicycle was in its rack by the doors, with SVLAC's scooters. Instead of heading for his office and his inbox, his feet took him to the kitchenette. He needed more coffee. Or better yet, too much espresso. To anyone watching, the shots would explain the jitter in his hands. Though what if Erin was at the machine? What if she was standing there with a carton of oat milk, her expression unreadable behind glasses fogged by the frother, heat lifting the perfume off her wrists—

He tripped over an unsecured extension cord near the hallway copier: a direct violation of Human Resources' chartreuse flyers. An intern testing the spigots on the nearest water dispenser—he and Erin had switched those hot and cold outputs several times over the last three years, and senior employees must've warned the cohort to check the temperatures before filling plastic cups or metal bottles—saw him stumble through his late arrival. So did Szymanski, coming down the corridor with a coffee mug. However, his colleague was absorbed enough in his LED research or kind enough to say nothing except, "Thank you for your responses, Dr. Meyer," and to walk past.

But the intern?

The young woman had styled her sweater and jeans like Erin did, the knit fabric tucked into her waistband at the front and left loose at the back. She was wearing a ponytail and sneakers, too. Who knew what she'd heard about him? Or seen. Ears burning, he stepped past her into the kitchenette. Erin wasn't there. The room was empty, and smelled of nothing but coffee grounds and old fruit. Maybe he didn't need more caffeine after all. A glance at his watch showed that he didn't have time for it, either. Or for wondering where she was. But didn't he need to consult with Marco Rossi about something? Cosmic energy sources? That would suffice. The University of Amsterdam's black hole model simulated Hawking radiation—the thermal energy emitting from black holes—so it wasn't a stretch to have research questions for the physicist. The fact that Rossi sat near Erin in the Modern Physics bullpen was coincidental.

"Dr. Rossi."

"*Uh*—" Rossi startled, abandoning a *Scientific American* article on his desktop monitor and swinging around in his chair. He blinked over wire-rimmed glasses at Ethan standing outside his cubicle. A pause. Then he reached behind himself to replace the digital magazine with a spreadsheet, and offered an uncertain smile. "Dr. Meyer. How can I help you?"

"Energy sources," he said.

"Energy sources?"

He craned his neck past Rossi's cubicle divider instead of elaborating.

"Do you need batteries, or a… a charging port?"

"No, I have cables." He edged another step sideways. "Dr. Fong spoke about potential energy sources from pulsar radio waves at an all-hands earlier this year."

"Yes. The department theorizes that these regular radio waves could provide an unlimited and reliable power source for astronauts at the International Space Station, or even on interstellar missions."

"Long-lasting energy, like light-emitting diodes."

"Hypothetically. But our ideas are in a very early stage."

"Right." There was light in Erin's cubicle. "How… how does their power compare to the energy from LEDs?"

"The research hasn't progressed far enough to provide specifics." Rossi gave him an odd look; though Ethan registered it, he still craned farther over the bullpen's dividers. "Do you have a particular question about the waves? Or about the pulsars?"

"Questions?" Her light was the glow of a live monitor. He dropped back onto his heels.

"Yes. Do you have any?"

"Possibly. Or Dr. Szymanski might, since I don't study LEDs. But maybe something later about astrophysical thermal radiation." Then, leaving Rossi to his *Scientific American* article and his understandable confusion—there would be gossip in the kitchenette and the cafeteria later today, and he'd skip lunch to avoid it—he strode down the row of bullpen desks.

Dr. Erin Monaghan, read her nameplate. Her cubicle's walls gleamed blue from the photon output of a large desktop monitor, the pixelated illumination reflecting in her glasses. She was clicking around a series of data exports while typing annotations into the cells. With her headphones on, she was oblivious to his approach, even though he was now close enough to scan her notes: the quantum gravity project. She was analyzing reference material that both of them should be reviewing, together.

She was reviewing his own quantum unit data from the holometer.

She squinted at a data cell, nibbling her lip—and his stomach jolted. *Irritation.* That was the feeling, wasn't it? This lurch in his gut was familiar: vertigo, the rapid descent into an argument. The giddiness of watching her eyes flash and her cheeks flush, fighting back against his critiques, challenging him about the quantum field's theories—and in her very personal attacks, attributing those theories, those flaws, that work, that brilliance to him. Irritating, but also: *addictive, electrifying.* So he kept stoking the blaze of their conflict, eager for their clashes, for her acknowledgment, for her attention, for her blushes and bitten lips, for—

—for… *her.*

Oh.

If another extension cord had been nearby, he would've gone sprawling.

There wasn't, so he tripped into empty air.

…*oh.*

Focused on her monitor rather than his silent, blinding, gravity-defying epiphany—he might've fallen fast for Forster, but: *how long had he already been falling for Dr. Monaghan?*—Erin continued to click through his data, nodding along to her music. He could demand an explanation for why she was analyzing his work, call her out for her egregious breach of research etiquette—*like always.*

But instead… instead, *now*, he stepped into her cubicle and rested a hand on the back of her chair. To steady himself? An easy explanation. "*Um…* anything interesting?"

"*Ah!*"

Startled, she jerked away violently enough to wrench off her headphones and yank their cord from her computer. Indie pop switched to blare from her desktop speakers.

"*Damn!*" She jabbed at her keyboard, wincing.

"Sorry!" His voice was too loud; she'd muted the music.

"It's…" Maybe her ears were ringing from the noise. She just shook her head—then glanced down at his hand on her chair. Blotches of color suffused her cheeks. She pivoted around to her monitor again, addressing his data when she said, "It's fine. *Uh*—morning."

"Morning." Several curious heads popped up over cubicles around the office; he withdrew his fingers. But not far. "Did you… is there anything noteworthy in my exports?"

"Nothing so far." *Click*, went her mouse. "It's not that I don't trust your review—but I always do preemptive analyses on anything that might end up being collaborative reference material."

"Why?"

"It ensures that the findings of the later formal analysis have been objectively verified. Especially when the researchers involved are notoriously secretive about their data." Now her lips gave a tiny quirk.

"Fine." Office eavesdroppers or no, he couldn't stop himself from leaning back in, then, from leaning close to the bloom of iris and juniper behind her ear. "You'll have noticed that the standard deviation for the discrepancy in synchronization between the recombined laser beams is low. Outlier data points are minimal, and most are due to external stressors physically affecting the holometer's mirrors. Earthquakes or high wind events—"

"—neither of which impacts LIGO's data collection." She swung around in her chair, mouth widening into a smirk.

Their knees knocked.

Hard.

"*Argh!*"

Bent forward over Erin's desk, Ethan lost his balance and grabbed the back of her seat again. This time, dog hair on his vest brushed up against the zipper of her utility jacket draped over the chair. Static snapped. It leaped from the metal to his hand and Erin's arm, shocking them together. A hiss escaped her, and—

"*No.*"

Had he spoken, or had she?

Remembering that first flash of energy between them in the hall.

On Friday, too.

And today, *here*—now, when they both knew…

But it didn't matter, because Dr. Daan van Buskirk from the Optics group was walking past the bullpen toward a block of Modern Physics conference rooms, while paying more attention to their conversation than to his armload of papers—and Erin swiveled back to her desk with a squeal of wheels. She opened SVLAC's instant messaging system.

> **Dr. Erin Monaghan**
> We need to keep our distance.

He straightened, locked eyes with Van Buskirk, and pulled out his phone.

Dr. Ethan Meyer
Yes.

Dr. Erin Monaghan
We should limit interactions outside of our scheduled project hours. Messaging only?

Dr. Ethan Meyer
Agreed.

The physical effect of the static shock wore off quickly enough. The electricity of his nearness took a while longer to abate. The spark of his touch, the familiar heat in his ears and lips, when her mouth knew the taste of that warmth—

She stared at the latest news from STEMinist Online until she remembered how to inhale. But he'd shaved again this morning, and the amber musk of his aftershave lingered in her cubicle, in her hair, on her skin—and had the facilities team switched the building's air systems from cooling to heat in July? She tried to concentrate on her forum, to distract herself with the safety of outrage. After all, the post about the seedy physicist who'd appropriated his subordinates' work had continued to rack up fresh comments.

JustAKeysm@sh0K: *Is your old supervisor still at SVLAC?*

DataDominatrix: *Just checked the staff page. He is. Promoted to department head, too.*

JustAKeysm@sh0K: *Did you report him?*

DataDominatrix: *What good would that do? HR exists*

to protect the company, not the employees. He was—is—a valuable asset. I was new, so I left. Like the others.

This was new.

She shifted in her chair, jeans chafing her thighs. At least they'd agreed to keep their distance at the lab.

So she avoided Ethan for the rest of the day. Fortunately, it was now her responsibility to run the new fiscal year department meetings throughout Nadine's maternity leave and this swallowed up most of her morning. She'd never been so grateful for the mental load of bureaucracy. Following an hour spent debating inflation-based cost of living increases with Human Resources, the disdain of the poster from STEMinist Online for that personnel department made sense. Whenever she returned to her desk to prepare for her next administrative session, however, she knew whether his door was open or closed, whether he was in meetings or working in his office. Messages sent via SVLAC's official channel filled her desktop, laptop, and phone screens. None were from him.

He was busy.

She was busy.

But lunchtime found her desperate for distraction. After inhaling a salad at the cafeteria, she directed her scooter to an evergreen quadrangle between the Interdisciplinary and Classical Physics buildings, settling onto a bench in the comparative coolness of the redwoods' shade and extracting her notebook from her backpack.

Breathe.

She began to write.

> *There was no more Earth to shatter with earth-shattering changes. We had already left our planet and our home far*

behind. But the phrase—"earth-shattering" as critical, as fateful—still held true, though the change began as something quite small, so small that only in hindsight did we see. Or hear.

The change was a silence.

There was no crinkle from dehydrated ice cream packets after dinner that day.

The words weren't quite right. But then, her first drafts were always bad. She had to write a story before she could fix it. She'd said as much to—*no. Focus.* And couldn't she let herself have this particular mess? When the time came, she'd know how to resolve it. The characters would show her the way. She had to trust them to make sense of their narrative. Trust herself.

The trouble was that right now, she didn't trust herself at all. How could she?

How could she trust her narrative sense when all other senses had betrayed her? When she'd been so blind, deaf, and dumb as to mischaracterize all of her mental and physical data about Ethan Meyer?

She'd hungered for his notice on that first day at SVLAC—though after their collision in the corridor, how much of her zeal had sprung from his compelling, paradoxical research, and how much from her heated awareness of her own body in proximity to his?—and when he'd sabotaged her instead of offering respect and collaboration, she'd lashed out in frustration. In humiliation. She'd been determined to hate him then, because he obviously hated her. Proving that their animosity was mutual meant mean-spirited pranks that escalated from petty to dangerous, desperate to have the last word and show that she didn't care about his good opinion.

She'd wanted his attention, though.

Craved it.

Three years on, she'd been sure that *yes*, she did loathe him—and also deserved his undivided focus…

Any supervisor who didn't fire her for such a disastrous analysis of her own data—whether the Forster-and-Bannister bombshell was in the mix or not—was an idiot.

The data was her; *she* was the idiot.

"Everything's on you," she muttered to the astronauts under her pencil.

But she smiled—idiotically—while she wrote through her lunch hour, while her characters simmered in growing suspicion about why they had no dessert. She returned to her desk and the crew after her budget meetings (did closed office doors—no: *airlock doors*—feature too prominently in the story?) and then she holed up in her bedroom with her notebook that evening as Kai and Ashley commented their way through a documentary on the latest Silicon Valley titan to fall under the weight of turtleneck-wearing hubris, too much unicorn investment, and not enough regulation.

"She's such an interesting case study. Do you think any man would be getting this much negative press? Or would he just fail upward and into a new company?"

"The fraud was pretty egregious. Erin, what do you think?"

"Want to join us?" Kai raised a bowl of popcorn dusted with nutritional yeast. "We're watching a film on that FinTech startup founder who's on trial for fraud and criminal negligence."

"*Uh*—sorry, I have to work."

She didn't look at her LIGO exports, though, or read through the Kitt Peak National Observatory's multi-messenger astronomy review of the last batch of data that she'd sent over prior to her quantum gravity assignment. Instead, hunched up against her headboard, she scrawled nonsense onto the page until her pencil gave out—and she realized that she'd been scribbling in the dark. Writing about the chilly conditions of ice cream and space had failed to cool the heat still lancing over her skin, however. She tossed away her pencil, then eased out of her jeans with a grimace at the drag of damp denim down her thighs.

A little better.

Stripping down to a camisole, seeking elusive cool patches on her sheets and pillow, she splayed herself across her mattress and picked up her phone.

8:59 p.m.

Damn.

She'd missed Monday's call with her family. She tapped into the Monaghan thread to apologize and assuage their worries about her absence.

> **Erin**
> Sorry! I got caught up working on the Department of Energy's contract and lost track of time.

Not quite true, but better than a cross-examination from her brothers.

> **Dad**
> Good to hear from you, kiddo. But we kept it short today.

> **Mom**
> Adrian had to leave for the airport. You're not working too hard on your new project and those management responsibilities, sweetheart?
>
> **Adrian**
> When is she not working too hard? (Arrived and boarded. I should touch down in Austin around 4 a.m.)
>
> **Wes**
> Working too hard is a family trait.

A picture of his sandal-tanned feet hanging over a hammock strung between black mangroves on the Ecuadorian coast zipped into the chat. Adrian countered with a photo of his work laptop and a martini in business class. She left them to it, and switched over to her messages with Martina. Four unread texts were waiting for her.

> **Martina**
> I know we were both too busy for Pilates and brunch this past weekend (you're not the only one looking for government data right now—I might've found some financial dirt on one of the city council trustees and their investment in the development firm looking to bulldoze my park!)—but: what's new with you and Bannister? Did you get your date rescheduled?

Then, a few minutes later:

> **Martina**
> Wait… are you out with him right now?
> (Oh my God. If yes, call me once you're back!)

Bannister.

She squirmed. Friction from her sheets scratched her skin. Or was it guilt? She hadn't spilled the truth yet.

Yet, but should she?

Popcorn.

Easy, Monaghan.

Had Martina already suspected… well, not the reality about Bannister, Forster, Ethan, and Erin, but something else?

I wouldn't have clapped.

Her smugness would be unbearable. (She'd been smug enough when Erin had broken the news about her partnership with Ethan on the federal contract.) It might be even worse than her surprise.

If she *was* surprised.

> **Erin**
> No, I'm home tonight. Working on the quantum gravity project.

She should be. It wasn't even ten o'clock. She could grab her laptop and remotely double-check her calculations on their experimental laser angles. But… she had a question for her collaborator first. The obvious place to pose it was in SVLAC's messaging system; email would be too slow, and Ethan wouldn't thank her for stalling their research by burying an inquiry among the conference speaker requests, paper acceptances, and departmental bureaucracy overflowing his inbox.

What if he muted all work communications after hours, though?

(He didn't.)

(But what if he did?)

She needed her answer. Needed it *now*.

There was only one channel where she could be certain of reaching him.

She opened Bannister's messages.

> **Erin**
> I have a question about our hutch setup.

An instant typing bubble appeared beneath her text.

> **Bannister**
> Did you mean to ask me here?

> **Erin**
> It's urgent. I had to make sure you saw it.
> Anyhow, you're always saying that I need better time management. I'm trying.

> **Bannister**
> That's reasonable. Sorry for the delay. What's your question?

She snorted.

> **Erin**
> It took you—what? A full 10 seconds to respond? You call that a delay? No wonder you

think I'm always wasting time, since I'm not optimizing my life in 10-second increments!

Bannister
It's a quantum state of mind.

Erin
Very funny.

Bannister
Yes. Bunsen thought it was funny to raid my dryer for socks while I was cleaning the lint trap, too.

Erin
You've got to hand it to him, that's classic comedy.

Bannister
I'm not going to hand him anything. He was trying to bury a sock under a dead succulent on my patio. That's littering. It violates my building's regulations.

Erin
Wait—you have an in-unit dryer?

Bannister
Is that your urgent question?

She eyed her overflowing laundry hamper, and snorted again.

Erin
In the Bay Area? Yes.

Bannister
Fair.

Bannister
You also had a research question, though.

Erin
Right. I was considering whether we needed to adjust the hutch's lighting.

Bannister
Why?

Erin
MEC would usually be running a laser to create extreme temperatures and pressures in samples, so it should already be set up for dark-room experiments. But I'm not sure if we confirmed that. Did you talk with the engineers about lighting needs?

Bannister
No. We could check the hutch blueprint for wattage specifications.

Erin
I have it here. Let me look.

She retrieved an annotated hutch layout from her backpack. Returning to the circle of lamplight on her bed, she smoothed the Mylar paper across her sheets, tacked down its borders with her knees, and snapped a picture.

Erin
See?

Bannister
Is this a hard copy of the print you were referencing this morning?

Erin
Yes—before you interrupted me.

An ellipsis appeared in answer, then vanished... only to reappear again after a significant pause.

Bannister
Sorry.

A one-word reply. So what had taken him so long to type it? Curious, she enlarged the image she'd sent, and—*God*, she hadn't cropped her legs out of the blueprint picture. Articulated against the grid, her shadow on the laser-printed document made it clear that she'd stripped off her jeans, that she wasn't wearing much beyond her flimsy camisole and panties.

Fuck.

This was worse than her lingerie photo. But the tingle of heat suddenly dancing up her arms and gathering on her tongue... it wasn't embarrassment.

Swish.

Bannister
You don't have bruises from knocking our knees today, though. No damage from the static shock, either?

> **Erin**
> If I'd suffered a cardiac arrest, someone in the building probably would've noticed and called an ambulance.
>
> **Bannister**
> Only because all of Modern Physics was watching us in your cubicle.

Though what if they *hadn't* been surrounded by colleagues? The heat reversed course, slipping lower. Her pulse dropped farther still, down to a hum between her bare legs. What if they'd been alone?

> **Erin**
> Would you have resuscitated me yourself if our coworkers hadn't been there?
>
> **Bannister**
> There's a defibrillator by the kitchenette.
>
> **Erin**
> Too far away.
>
> **Bannister**
> Then I'd need to restart your heart manually.
>
> **Erin**
> Well, you're an artist. Get creative.

Before she could doubt herself or even think—*no time, heart rate stalled, emergency action required*—she pushed aside the blueprint and took another picture: legs extended across her bedspread, ankles crossed, the freckles around her navel peeking above her panties. Her fingertips rested against the lace over her hip. The edge of her thumb dipped beneath the mesh.

> **Erin**
> (And yes, I meant to send this to you.)

Then she waited, breathless, blood beating a fierce tattoo in her ears, until—
Swish.

> **Bannister**
> Erin, I know we agreed that messaging was fine, as long as we weren't communicating as Bannister and Forster. But...

His ellipsis lingered.

> **Erin**
> Do you want me to stop, Ethan?

Not *Bannister*.
Swish.

> **Bannister**
> No, I... but j-just give me a minute. I'm putting Bunsen out on the patio.

Ethan Meyer's precision with words was as exacting as his numerical analysis. He didn't message with a stylistic stammer. *Ever*. He must've switched from typing to audio transcription, which meant that his phone was detecting a break in his voice.

And he'd freed both hands, too.
Swish.

> **Bannister**
> (New Photo Message)

Illuminated in the beam from a lamp on a familiar industrial-style desk, he was sprawled across a couch with a pair of running shorts slung low on his hips, and... *oh*. Her thumb and index finger spread over the image. It expanded under her touch. *Closer, closer*, to a narrow trail of dark hair snaking down his stomach and under his waistband...

She hurriedly changed from typing to a voice-to-text input, too.

> **Erin**
> If... if we'd been alone and I'd collapsed on my desk, what would you have done?
>
> **Bannister**
> I'd need to get your heart rate up.
>
> **Erin**
> How?

She bit her lip while a tantalizing ellipsis appeared under her question. Each dot made a tiny point of imaginary pressure against her skin, and she quivered. The damp lace of her panties clung to her. She slipped another finger under it, to the centered beat of her heart.

Bannister
My first inclination would be to touch my pencil to your skin. Would… would that help?

Erin
M-maybe.

Bannister
I'd bend over you. Ease off your jeans. Slide them down over your hips. T-then I… I'd trace my graphite over your body. I'd map the divots beside your ankles. The curve of your calf.

Muscles tensed along her legs, reacting to the whirl of her imagination.

Bannister
I'd explore the back of your right knee. You have freckles there, don't you?

Her free hand stroked up her calf to shadow his touch.

Erin
I might… squirm.

Bannister
Good. But there'd be danger in sitting up too quickly. I'd put a hand on your thigh to keep you still.

Erin
I'll t-try to stay still.

Bannister

If you do, I'll trace up to your hip. How's your pulse?

Thundering.

Erin

Getting stronger. I—I think. Don't stop.

Bannister

I'll savor every scallop of the lace on your panties. First around your waist. Then… then between your legs. But I don't want to mark you. Not with my pencil. N-not yet. Stay still.

Erin

I'm trying—oh, G-God—

Licks of heat tightened and heightened along her inner thighs. Her hips bucked against the heel of one hand pressed over the exquisite, agonizing strain.

Bannister

Tell me what happens. Does your pulse stabilize? Or is it too erratic? Do I need to start over again from your ankle with my fingers?

Bannister

Do… do you want me to touch you?

Erin

Y-yes. Please. I n-n-need—

Bannister
What do you need?

She couldn't hear her words over the hammer of her heart against her ribs. Was she whispering, or shouting? She gripped her tongue in her teeth and sent a third picture: her finger and thumb dipping deeper under her panties, the lace cleaving to a nest of curls visible beneath the mesh, her heels braced on the footboard of her bed, knees raised, stomach taut.

Bannister
God, y-you're so flushed for me. So—so beautiful.

Swish, and she whimpered.

Bannister
I'd circle around your ankle. D-draw my knuckles up your calf. Still light pressure, but more than the pencil. Feel me.

She couldn't help herself, and gasped out, "I do."

Please God, let her roommates have abandoned their documentary for a bar.

Bannister
Over your knee. Up your thigh. H-higher.

Erin
Ahh…

Bannister
I'd cover your hand with mine, slipping under
the lace with you. I'd move our fingers together.
Touch you together. What pace should I set?

Erin
Please, just—f-faster.

Her palm ground down, circled. Her thumb sank to the knuckle.

Erin
Someone could be here soon, someone could…

Bannister
No one else is here. Just us.

God, his focus and precision and patience were relentless, and it was *so so so* good—

Bannister
While you're writhing under my fingers, I'll move
between your legs. Your panties are so wet,
aren't they?

Erin
Please—

Bannister
I want to taste you.

Erin
Y-yes.

Bannister

I kneel down by your desk. I lean close to breathe you in. Then I press the flat of my tongue to you, edging your panties aside, because I don't want their rough lace, I only want... w-want you—

F-f-f-fuck!

She couldn't breathe. Incandescent electricity was sizzling through her body, scorching strikes of pleasure building, *building*—but if she couldn't answer him in words?

A fourth photo: thighs spread, hips lifted, fingers blurred with movement.

Bannister

(New Audio Message)

"*Fuck*, I—*God*, Erin, you're—I can't—keep—I'm—"

She was burning, hot enough to ignite carbon fusion, combusting with the shockwaves of an exploding supernova, destruction and creation intertwined. A gasp, a groan, a cant of her hips, and she chased him into blazing oblivion, overwhelming her fingers and her panties in quaking, toe-curling, spine-arching currents of ecstasy, choking out his name.

"*Ethan...*" came her strangled whisper, sending in an audio message of her own.

And then, in the sweet, shivering, boneless silence that followed, her vision white with stars: again, "...*fuck*."

If she hadn't before, she definitely needed medical attention now. She'd driven them both insane. She must've. Because

17

He'd been right about the location of Modern Physics' defibrillator: mounted on the wall by the kitchenette in an attention-grabbing red case, its cover stamped with the jagged peaks of a heart rate.

But he'd been wrong to imagine that he could walk past it without thinking of—*her legs splayed for him across her desk, spine arched, tortoiseshell glasses misted over black, hazy eyes, throat convulsing as he worked his fingers past the lace between her thighs, as he bent close to inhale her, to taste the heat of her desire—*

He thrust a mug into the coffee machine's slot so hard that the ceramic rattled. *Breathe.* He didn't need a defibrillator. He didn't need caffeine. He needed a damn tranquilizer. At least a cold dose of oat milk. Or ice—that job assignment in Antarctica? Since Antarctica was out of reach for the moment, however, he yanked open the staff refrigerator to grab his creamer. When he swung the metal door closed again, Erin was entering the kitchenette.

The speed of traffic on Sand Hill Road had blown tangles into her hair; her ponytail was loose from its elastic, twisting over her shoulder and catching in the teeth of her utility jacket's zipper, half-closed over a burgundy sweater. Her lips glimmered where she'd run her tongue across the wind-chapped skin. A tiny fleck of grit dotted her nose.

"*Uh.*" His brain blanked. "You have a…"

she grinned through her body's aftershocks as she tapped back into her phone. She licked her lips while she changed Bannister's contact name.

Dr. Ethan Meyer

It wasn't how he'd meant to greet her. But was there any scenario in which their first conversation after… *after*… wouldn't have left him floundering?

One eyebrow lifted. "Something on my face?" She swiped at her chin.

"A little higher. Just…" He set aside his carton before he spilled it. He shoved his fists into his pockets. "On your nose."

"I got stuck behind a street sweeper on Oak Avenue." She swiped again. "There?"

"No."

"Great." When she rolled her eyes, dust glittered in her eyelashes. "But are you just going to… maybe not harass people at the coffee machine today, but watch me waste my time like this, when we have project deadlines to meet? …or are you going to help?"

He freed one hand to offer her a napkin.

She ignored it, stepping closer. A smirk scrunched up her nose, pink with the wind of her ride—and *God*, he wanted to touch her, to tap those tiny wrinkles and that speck of grit, to trace down her cheek to the corner of her lips, to swipe a finger across the chapped skin, savoring this evidence of her brash mastery of the road before slipping his thumb into her mouth, testing the sharpness of her teeth on his skin and the dexterous softness of her tongue—

"Really? No help?" When she snapped an elastic band around her hair again, its twang jerked through his groin, and her smirk widened with her nod at his brew cooling in the machine. "Then the least you can do is to brew me some coffee. Is that mine?"

Like she'd followed him into his own kitchen to retrieve a familiar mug from the dish drainer. He swallowed so hard that his ears popped. Heat flashed down his neck. "S-sure."

"Thanks."

"*Um*—milk?"

She turned with the mug cupped in her palms. She cocked her other eyebrow at him, cocked her hip against the counter, and slotted a second mug into place. "What do you think?"

I sometimes spike my creamer with coffee.

Hot and flustered, he hadn't meant to laugh.

"Menace." He upended the carton for her.

"A compliment from Dr. Ethan Meyer—for *me*?"

"Don't get greedy."

"I'm not greedy. I'm just..." she reached behind herself for his filling mug, eyes and lips bright, "...getting your coffee."

Space-time really *was* broken.

"Because you had a late night. Milk for you, too?"

"You don't have any hands free for the creamer carton," and before he could rationalize all his *why-nots*, he took both mugs from her. He set them away on the counter. His fingers were steady. *Almost.* "You can't send messages if you're holding these. Since we're only communicating by text outside of our project work blocks, you need your hands."

"Then this must be a work block, if we're talking at the lab. If my hands are free."

He nodded. "We never resolved your question about the hutch's lighting."

"A critical inquiry."

"*Critical*," and he swallowed too hard again when her thumb hooked into his pocket, drawing him into her breath and her smile.

"I'm very focused on getting an answer from you, Dr.—"

"Meyer!"

Dr. Kramer.

His department head strode into the kitchenette. Ethan stumbled back against the refrigerator. But though Dr. Kramer's glance identified their two mugs on the counter, his attention didn't continue on to Erin beside the coffee machine. Instead, he stepped past her and selected black coffee from the on-screen menu. How could he not notice her?

"Should I expect a delay on your weekly status report for the quantum gravity project?"

"*Uh*—no."

"Good. Preparations for my transition will occupy my time until I leave for CERN on Thursday. We'll review your work this afternoon." Dr. Kramer retrieved his coffee and left.

Silence.

Then:

"He wants our status update today?" Erin's smile had vanished with Dr. Kramer's appearance. Now, disbelief slackened her mouth. "*Today?* What does he think we'll have to report? We've only had two days—three, if you count today—at the lab since you submitted our project charter for review."

"Yes—but we… we've also had Saturday and Sunday." Ethan nodded at Tomasz Szymanski entering the kitchenette, requesting confirmation from his colleague, "Five days. That's a research week."

Szymanski returned his nod.

"By whose standards?"

Neither of them answered her.

"Fine. I was planning to meet with Human Resources to discuss an increase to our interns' summer stipend, but if the report needs to be finished today?" Coffee sloshed up her mug as she shrugged. "We don't have space booked for a work session, though."

Their hours in the Sidewinder conference room were scheduled for Wednesday.

"*Um.*" Ethan didn't look at Szymanski when he said, "My office at one o'clock?"

"Five after one."

He barricaded himself at his desk through the length of the morning and scrutinized row after row of reference data. Despite Erin's surprise over the timeline for their status report, they *had* been on their federal research assignment for over a week—if their time spent crafting its charter was included in the total; Dr. Kramer would expect results. Friday's consultation with the engineers in the West Experimental Hall had gotten… derailed… before they could finalize the structural updates needed in the Matter in Extreme Conditions hutch for their black hole model and before they could run even a preliminary atomic experiment, so that left them with Tuinstra's data, Ethan's holometer results, and Erin's LIGO outputs as pertinent reference material to include in the report. Tuinstra's data was a simple copy-and-paste from her paper. He knew his own numbers inside out, and Erin had reviewed them yesterday. But he hadn't gone spelunking into the interferometer's latest yields, yet.

His fingers inched toward his phone.

No.

He opened their SVLAC communications channel.

> **Dr. Ethan Meyer**
> Do you have your last six months of LIGO data available?
>
> **Dr. Erin Monaghan**
> Yes. I'll even share it with you, if you're sure you

> want to touch it. (Warning: it might contaminate your own data by proximity.)

> **Dr. Ethan Meyer**
> I apologized for that comment, remember? And yes, I do want it.

> **Dr. Erin Monaghan**
> Let the record show that I provided a hazard alert. Sending it now. Just give the file a minute to reach your inbox. It's enormous.

> **Dr. Ethan Meyer**
> Supermassive data.

He tilted back his headphones to catch her snicker from the bullpen.

> **Dr. Erin Monaghan**
> ...and supermassive fiscal meetings, too. See you at 1:05 p.m.

He replaced his headphones once he heard her move into a conference room with Rossi and Dr. O'Connor-Young. Then he sketched the Cassiopeia constellation and scarfed down an early sandwich from the cafeteria until her LIGO file came through. Opening its export spreadsheets, he enlarged them on his monitor, rolled his sleeves up over his forearms, and got to work—

—only to surface an hour later with his ears aching underneath the clamp of his headphones, his neck and wrists stiff with the intensity of his focus, still standing despite his lowered desk, and with his brain buzzing like Junipero Serra Freeway at rush hour.

"Because twenty-seven plus eighteen is forty-five. Not thirty-two," he confirmed out loud.

The math was easier than breathing.

And the relevant mass delineated in Erin's data was thirty-two suns. Not forty-five.

It should've been forty-five.

Unless…

The clock on his monitor read 1:00 p.m.

He couldn't wait, pushing past his empty chair hard enough to send it spinning into the wall he shared with another adjoining supply closet—a mop toppled audibly, followed by the clatter of dominoing chemical spray bottles—he rushed to the door, wrenching it open—to find her already there, a hand raised to knock.

"I know I'm early, but—"

"I found something."

"What?"

"You need to see this." Ignoring the heads popping up over cubicle walls in the bullpen, he seized her arm, towing her into his office and back to his desk. Not even her sweater riding up to reveal the jut of her hip bone and the freckles scattered across her stomach could distract him. He turned his monitor to show her the LIGO exports alongside his calculations. "*Look.* I saw it in your interferometer data. I don't know what this means for quantum gravity as a whole, since it's just one event and data point to reference—"

"You saw the principle of… addition?" She frowned.

"No, I—I'd planned to start Dr. Kramer's status report earlier, until—but this could be relevant to our event horizon model."

"What?" again. But this time, her frown was for the tiny numbers on his screen. Angling her glasses on her nose, tugging her sweater back into place, she dropped her backpack to the carpet and moved closer.

"It's possible that LIGO is detecting thermal radiation emitting from black holes," he said.

A breathless pause. She blinked. "*What?!*"

"SVLAC's Laser Interferometer Gravitational-Wave Observatory is—"

"—picking up naturally occurring Hawking radiation?"

"Yes. The holometer's construction and function is based on interferometer technology, so I'm familiar with how your instrument works." He highlighted the relevant mass differences, then dragged up a recent multi-messenger astronomy review from Kitt Peak beside LIGO's raw data; Arizona's observatory confirmed the merger of two black holes on the same date as the detector's output. "The mass of the black holes that merged during the interferometer's activation time was calculated as equivalent to about twenty-seven and eighteen suns, respectively. The merger should've resulted in a mass of forty-five suns. But it didn't."

"The combined mass is calculated at… at thirty-two suns, instead." She verified the documents' export dates. Her ponytail tilted over her shoulder to brush his arm across the desk. Its strands shivered with the acceleration of her breath. "Which isn't mathematically possible—"

"Unless some of that mass was lost."

"And the only way that it could've been lost…" Her eyes flickered up to his. Her pupils were cavernous, now: *excitement, incredulous wonder*.

"…is if that mass radiated off as gravitational waves."

"After the initial collision, a portion of the infalling waves would've been reflected away from the new black hole. Back to LIGO's detectors. These second waves would be weaker and slightly delayed when compared with the gravitational waves from the actual merger."

"They are."

"Which... which tells us that Hawking's theory about the emission of thermal radiation from black holes is observable in the wild, not just in a lab. We can measure it through LIGO's detection of gravitational waves. We might be able to eavesdrop on the behavior of mass and matter at the event horizons of black holes! Actual black holes!"

"There's your sole-author paper for *Nature Physics*."

"Yes!" But despite her hands clenching with visible adrenaline, she still somehow managed to exhale a breath of skepticism a moment later. "You'd really let me take the credit, though?"

"It's your research. Your data."

"That's true, so thank you. But..." she leaned forward over his desk on her knuckles, huffing and shaking her head, even while her cheeks flushed and her eyes shone, "...it's irritating that I'm only getting my second major paper—"

"—and your first one in a mainstream journal—"

"—because *you* found something in my data that I'd missed. By using multi-messenger astronomy, too! You're going to be insufferable about your genius in my field, aren't you? You probably want to be a co-author."

"No." He moved to meet her across his monitor and sudoku calendar. "The sole authorship's yours, Monaghan. I'd never pollute my reputation in the quantum world by voluntarily associating myself with relativistic mechanics."

She raised her chin. "Relativistic mechanics is half of our quantum gravity equation."

"I said *voluntarily*. Didn't we agree that none of this is voluntary?"

"Yes, because I can think of much better uses for my time than working on status reports and research bureaucracy with you. Like combing through *your* data to find something groundbreaking—"

"*Groundbreaking*?" He echoed the tilt of her head, which closed their distance by another inch. "More like, breaking space into discrete units."

"*I'm* the one who's good with words." Her gaze dropped to his mouth. "Don't get clever with me."

Clever. It was Chase Meyer Jr. who was clever with women, not him. But Erin Monaghan was here, perched over his desk, and she was… *Erin.* Not *women.*

So, "If you're so good with words, are you volunteering to type up our report?"

"Do I look like I'm sitting pretty behind your desk, ready to take dictation?"

"No. You're *on* my desk."

One finger lifted to trace along with the pencil he'd tucked behind his ear. "Do you *want* me on your desk, Ethan?"

Yes.

And: *fuck.*

Because he did—*he did*—and he might be clever with her, but Dr. Kramer expected a report on *his* desk by the end of the workday, which meant that his supervisor was waiting for research results, while he, Ethan, was…

"I… yes—but we agreed that we wouldn't. We need to focus, and this—"

"We're not violating our agreement. This isn't sabotage." Erin's hand slipped down his neck to fist in the collar of his vest, slightly too tight. But steadying, somehow—at least until she continued, "Thanks to Dr. Kramer, we're even in a project work block today. We need to write his status report. We will. But we also need to be strategic with our resources. *Time, focus*... and arousal is the opposite of focus. We'll work on the report once we've restored equilibrium."

"E-equilibrium?"

She nodded, tongue sweeping over her lips. Her eyes gleamed with danger and gold. With promises. "For science."

...was she right?

He wanted her to be right. He wanted *her*.

"For science," he whispered—

—and then finally—*finally*, Ethan let himself break. Not a moment of mindless impulse, like in the XCS control room. A choice. In a single efficient motion that manipulated angles and weight and gravity to his desire, he had her on his desk, her legs wrapped around his hips as he dragged the elastic from her ponytail to cradle her head, and he couldn't breathe for the fierce churn of anticipation and appetite, for his own wanting—*having*.

Their hungry lips collided. They toppled together back onto a stack of paperwork and sticky notes, almost crushing his laptop. One of Erin's hands wound into his hair while the other tugged open his vest to unbutton his shirt, and he gasped when her knees hitched tighter around his waist, a savage burst of kinetic energy flipping him over beneath her. Straddling him now, she raked her nails down his stomach and reached for his belt as he fumbled between them to loosen the maddening tightness of her jeans, then swiped his thumb under her waistband.

Lace.

"*Fuck—*"

She yanked his belt free. His zipper followed. Foil crinkled from her rear pocket when she shimmied her legs bare, kicking away her sneakers. She grinned—"That was a hypothetical activity for today, yes"—before ripping open the condom packet with her teeth and a wild shake of her hair.

He moaned and dug his fingers into the creases of muscle in her thighs, angling her over him again, coaxing her hips lower against his. "You have genius ideas."

"I know," with a scrape of lace against his boxers, her arms arching overhead to toss off her sweater and reveal a camisole clinging to the curves of her breasts and waist. "And I like to hear you say it."

"*Urgh—*" was all he could manage, however, because now her fingers sneaked down to curl around him. The cyclist's calluses on the heel of her hand jolted his skin with electrifying friction as she firmed her grip on his cock.

"Yes?"

"*U-uh!*" The pressure rolling down his length was a sheath of ribbed latex. Choking on another devout *fuck*, he thrust up against her fingers—and against her easy mastery of his body and brain, too, against those smiles and touches that knew the meaning of his every twitch and whimper. If he didn't take back an edge of control now, he never would, and he stood no chance if she remained poised over him like this, tantalizing and powerful, so—

"Higher," he told her.

"What?"

"Higher, Erin." He urged her hips away from his, coaxing her up over his body and his desk, to his mouth.

"*Oh.*"

For once, she complied. Eyes wide, lips parted, startled and so, *so* beautiful, she settled where he placed her with her knees splayed around his ears between his wobbling monitor and an equally unsteady desk lamp. He murmured at the apex of her thighs, "*Here*."

"...*oh!*" Her shudder rippled over his mouth. Erin lurched forward to brace her palms against the wall behind his desk.

Grinning now himself, he stroked up her thighs to trace the lace of her panties between her legs, where it whispered against his lips. He edged the fabric aside, exposing her to the cool air and the heat of his breath.

"Yes?"

"Y-yes. F... for science."

"*Mmm.*" He locked his fingers around her hips to hold her steady. Then he licked past the soft, wet curls to taste her. He set a slow pace, exploring with gentle nips, with firm suction and feather-light brushes, and she was almost motionless for a moment, just quivering in his hands and under his mouth, barely breathing. But when he slipped inside her, easing her closer, easing himself deeper, *deeper*, and flicked his tongue—her perilous balance on some internal precipice between pleasure and reflexive dominance shattered. Abandoning her brace against the wall, Erin's fingers knotted in his hair. She ground down against his mouth, gasping, urging him deeper still. He flicked his tongue again. Her hips bucked hard. *Again*—and now she was reckless, wild, canting to the motions of his lips and tongue and teeth. A pen hit the floor. So did his lamp. The desk creaked beneath them, activating its glitchy elevation sequence.

He didn't stop.

"*Fuck*, Ethan—" She was laughing as they rose, whimpering as he swirled his tongue, and it was *glorious*.

He only gripped her thighs harder for balance, his own hips jerking while he swallowed her wetness, groaning his satisfaction as he followed the currents of her desire and his, tongue coaxing, fingers digging, caressing, breathing nothing but her, drowning in her rough, tightening joy, her body coiling taut above him, her eyes fluttering, breath stuttering, until—

—*until*—

Erin buried her teeth in her forearm with a soundless scream. The noise vibrated into his mouth and his ribs, mute and potent. He caught her as she collapsed sideways. Cradling her to his chest, first in silence and then, once he could breathe a little, with wordless murmurs against her hair, he ran one slow palm along her thigh flung across his to soothe her through the aftershocks, gentling her back to herself… but also to prevent her overheated skin from sliding over his groin, because if she touched him right now, he'd embarrass himself like a teenager.

"Good?" he asked after a quiet minute, when her panting had steadied against his shoulder.

"Ethan…" Her lips quivered. She raised her head, eyes hazy and shining above the glasses perched low on her nose. "I *love* science."

I love—

The words scrambled in his brain, shifting configurations.

But he didn't say them. Instead, submitting to the simpler desires of his body and finally taking charge of his damn desk, he jabbed the descent button and said, starting to shoulder off his vest, "Yes. Experimental replication of results is key to our discipline, though."

"Right. So keep the fleece." Her thigh flexed with abrupt force, levering him up and over her while she twisted onto her back beneath him. One hand remained tangled in his hair and the other trailed down his chest, across his vest with naked satisfaction to curl around his latex-sheathed cock; obviously, he'd be leaving the fleece on. "But…"

"B-but?" Though he widened his stance on the carpet for leverage, for restraint, the rasp of her thumb still broke his voice.

"We should try some new data. Determine if we get the same results from this… input."

It was her smug smile that broke his control, however. A single snap of his hips buried him inside her. He groaned. "*Yes*. For science."

"Do you see my hair elastic anywhere?"

Having coerced her unsteady legs back into her jeans, bungled the buttons and zippers closed again, and retrieved her discarded sweater, Erin scanned the carpet while raking the disaster of her hair off her neck. Her glasses were smudged, and she squinted at scattered sudoku pages and minimalist ink sketches of fractal lines on notepaper. A copy of *This Is How You Lose the Time War* with a canine-chewed corner peeked out from Ethan's messenger bag behind the door. Dog hair on fleece—*that vest*—sudoku, ink sketches, sci-fi novels: *Bannister. God*, the truth was so obvious! Almost as obvious as the three years of data explaining her behavior around him, data that she'd so willfully mis-analyzed. If she'd walked one step farther into his office after his talk for the Department of Energy, she would've seen…

"Here." Ethan handed her a cleaning wipe.

She couldn't help laughing. "Not a hair tie."

He shrugged while he tucked his shirt back into his belt. "Sorry."

He wasn't, and neither was she.

"A comb?" She polished her lenses, then dragged her fingers along her snarled nape again.

"In my car. For Bunsen."

"Helpful."

He whisked up a stray strand framing her ear. "How about a rubber band?"

She scanned the floor a second time. Nothing. Martina would kill her for the damage she was about to inflict on her hair. Probably for other things, too. As soon as she finished screaming in—vindicated?—shock.

"It'll be better than nothing. I can't walk out of here like…" She gestured at herself with her free hand, accepting his rubber band and bundling the tangles into a ponytail. "Especially since we're meeting with Dr. Kramer. I wouldn't want to pollute your reputation this way, either."

He'd been grinning crookedly at her a moment before, watching her clean her glasses and tidy her hair while he straightened up the chaos on his desk, replacing a monitor on its stand, re-stacking sticky notes, aligning documents and blueprints, plugging the lamp back into its wall socket. Now, Dr. Ethan Meyer dropped an uncapped pen. The fingers that he'd stroked over her skin, across her lips, into her and through her pleasure, abruptly clenched so hard into his palms that his knuckles blanched. A dot of ink leaked onto the carpet.

"Ethan? What's…"

"The status report is due in one hour and forty-seven minutes."

His sentence was blank, inflectionless. Correct and sterile. His fists uncurled as quickly as they'd formed, populating meta-information into the header of a status report template on his laptop. But deep marks from his nails pitted his palms. His eyes darted to the time display on his monitor. 3:13 p.m. blinked to 3:14 p.m. His shoulders were high and taut. Was he even breathing?

She loudly unzipped her backpack and plonked her own laptop onto his desk. He didn't startle, just went on staring at his screen.

"I know we have our report due soon." Now she swiveled her computer into his line of sight. "You probably would've finished it last night, if you hadn't been busy."

No laughter, no smile.

She pushed on, "But we're not going to be late. I started drafting notes for it earlier, and while nothing's been completed in your template, we have a solid start. See?"

He looked at his clock again. 3:15 p.m.

"We can't perfect the report if we haven't written it." She retrieved his dropped pen, capped it and slid it behind his ear, then nudged his elbow aside to perch on the armrest of his chair. "Come on, critique my notes."

Maybe it was three years of habit that finally dragged his gaze to her screen. But as she talked through her transcription of their reference materials and research methods with ultracold atoms, electromagnets, and liquid helium, watching him rather than the lines of text and calculations, the tension eased fractionally from his forearms. Numbers and data were safe…

"Stop." He tapped her trackpad. "You've attributed the material analysis on organic synthetic polymers for the holometer's lenses to me."

"Didn't you run that study?"

"Under Dr. Kramer's direction." He replaced his name with his supervisor's.

"His department, his lab, his research?"

"Yes—and this reference to the paper on the electromagnetic manipulation of atoms?" He emphasized a paragraph that outlined aspects of the project's experimental methodologies and their proposed application.

"From your second publication in *Nature Physics*?"

"Dr. Kramer was the first author. His credit should come before mine. It was his idea to use ultracold atoms when manipulating their shape and motion to assess new quantum behaviors. I just executed his vision in the experimental halls." He jumped her cursor along the text. "Also, the design of the holometer wasn't my original idea."

"It's based on LIGO. Did Dr. Kramer design LIGO?"

"No."

"Right." She bumped his fingers off the keyboard. "Let's transfer everything into your template and litigate the rest of your critiques there. We don't want to be—"

"*Late*."

"It's just a status report on a couple days of work. An internal document—"

"—for Dr. Kramer. Due in—"

"Stop. Even if we submit it a few minutes after five o'clock, will that really matter?"

"Yes."

"To you, or to him?"

"Yes," again.

He turned back to the report template on his own screen, downloaded the work that she'd shared via email, and began to replicate her notes. *Click*. A citation of Greg Logan's quantum unit theories that had informed aspects of his work on the holometer, and consequently on their quantum gravity project, vanished. She watched his progress, frowning. But when he replaced the physicist's name with a generic credit for Fermilab, a distracting thread of memory tickled her brain: *Fermilab, supervisor, subordinates' research, quantum effects…*

"Your exponent value on Planck's constant is wrong."

"*Uh*—" She blinked. "You're right. Minus eleven instead of minus one?"

He fixed her notation. He synthesized the evidence for Hawking radiation that he'd located in her LIGO exports—it might be pertinent as project reference material, as well as her trajectory to publication as a first author in *Nature Physics*—and then scrolled down their document. "Action items?"

They debated their options for next steps and were hashing out a timeline for when they could expect a rush order of liquid helium to arrive at Innovation Drive, when Ethan's monitor clock flickered to 4:59 p.m.

"*Damn.*" He abandoned her mid-sentence to submit their report. No proofreading. "Hurry."

"Dr. Kramer's office is—"

"—fifteen seconds from mine." He jammed his laptop closed, shoved it into his bag, grabbed their blueprints, and was already at the door before she'd recovered her balance on his spinning chair. He repeated, "*Hurry.*"

"I'm coming—"

He left her behind, striding after their update email as if he could race it to Kramer's inbox. Even with her handicapped start from behind his desk, however, Erin outstripped him as he rounded the edge of the bullpen, heading toward a line of offices—larger than glorified janitorial closets, with windows overlooking SVLAC's evergreen quadrangle outside—reserved for the Modern Physics departmental leadership; his neck was rigid, his breathing was shallow, and his tread had shortened as they approached those doors. She slowed for him, scanning nameplates. Their earlier project meetings had taken place in conference rooms. She'd never had a reason to enter Kramer's space. She waited for Ethan to draw level with her again, conscious of the eyes on them from the central cubicles, and let him set their pace to a corner office at the end of the hall.

DR. JOHN KRAMER

The knuckles on both Ethan's thumbs cracked from the pressure of his fingers balling into fists again when he lifted a hand to knock.

"Are you…" She managed not to touch his shoulder, not to soothe the nape of his neck. She couldn't manage silence, though, not when he shook his head, not when it felt like a warning. "What—"

He didn't answer. He knocked.

"Yes?" *Kramer*.

They entered.

If she had spent any time considering John Kramer's office, or if she'd had to create a narrative backdrop for him, she would've designed a precise, minimalist space in grayscale, devoid of all personality except achievement: sleek, modern, every piece of ornamentation an award—physics or golf—and with the thermostat set several degrees below comfort. She would've been right.

What she hadn't been right about was its chaos.

When Ethan stepped past the door, he almost collided with two movers shouldering a Danish modern couch swaddled in protective bubble wrap out into the hall. A third mover knelt on a series of divots in the carpet that indicated the exodus of other heavy items, offloading the contents of several bookcases and checking the volumes off an itemized list. A fourth man removed plaques, certificates, and signed photographs from the walls, bringing them to archival boxes standing on a massive desk of metal and glass, where Kramer himself evaluated and allocated each item to its appropriate location—storage or shipping to Switzerland—from an Eames chair. The quantum gravity status report was open on his monitor.

"Meyer."

"Dr. Kramer."

Since Ethan didn't advance any farther into the room, she moved past him and stepped over a box of framed university degrees to address his supervisor. "As requested, we've submitted an early version of our weekly update on the Department of Energy's quantum gravity project. However, if this isn't a good time to review it—"

"I have several questions about your report, Meyer." Kramer clicked two fingers at the mover by his bookcases when the man lifted a mounted toroid from a shelf dedicated to prizes and sculptures. "Careful with that. It's an Eliasson."

A facsimile of a three million dollar check for the Breakthrough Prize—awarded twelve years previously to *Dr. John R. Kramer of Fermilab (Quantum Group) for Outstanding Contributions to the Field of Physics*—was among the honors ready to be sorted on his desk. No wonder he'd been able to afford an Eames chair.

"Yes." Still Ethan didn't move.

"Are you continuing to design the experimental hutch layout? I see a diagram, but no resultant data." Though Kramer tabbed back into their report, he watched the mover wrap up his

Breakthrough Prize and a nearby golf trophy in packing foam.

"*Um*. We met with the engineers to discuss storage space for the liquid helium, a placement of the electromagnet, sight lines for the laser window, and how to configure cables around the existing hutch machinery so that the vacuum chamber isn't contaminated and there's no interference with the angles of the lasers or with MEC's existing e-enclosure—" His voice cracked. The blueprints tucked under his arm crinkled.

"We have an experimental layout designed, yes." Erin willed Ethan to breathe.

They didn't have the engineers' signoff on their hutch specifications yet, but—*we have enough*.

She reminded him, "We also have extant reference data on gravitational waves that could prove pertinent for the project. As Dr. Meyer notes in our update, a recent LIGO readout provides preliminary evidence that the interferometer is detecting naturally occurring Hawking radiation. This might be—"

"Might be."

"It's a single data point, so yes. While I have ideas about what a reliable detection of thermal radiation from black holes could tell us about the behavior of mass and matter around event horizons—a central question in quantum gravity research, as you know—we haven't yet replicated—"

"Monaghan has *ideas*. Meyer, what is your output?"

"An—an analysis on optimal optical materials for the holometer's mirrors suggests that organic synthetic polymers are best suited for experiments involving the ambient temperature extremes that generate from liquid helium-cooled atoms and focused laser heat—"

"Your contribution to the project is proposing new practical applications of my earlier materials theory?"

"*Um*," again. Ethan stepped aside for the couch movers returning for Kramer's bookcases. His hands were still fisted, his knuckles and raised tendons white. "That's what I always…"

"It was Dr. Meyer who identified the Hawking radiation signals in my data." Erin tapped Kramer's desk to draw his focus. "I didn't observe them. The gravitational waves were so much weaker than those I usually look for in LIGO's interference fringes that my Fourier transform didn't catch them. But Dr. Meyer's attention to detail—"

"Double-wrap that photograph from the Shoreline Golf Links tournament. It's signed by the president of the Bay Area Golf Association. Well, Meyer?"

"I confirmed the thermal radiation with a multi-messenger astronomy review from Kitt Peak—"

"I have no interest in Monaghan's public data pool. Neither should you. What is your output?"

"I…" Another pause, long enough for the movers to shuffle one of the bookcases out the door. Then Ethan's head gave a small shake.

Nothing else.

As his tight silence lengthened, Erin's neck bristled. Award after award and framed abstract after abstract on time crystals, avian migration, quantum circuits, and quantum units went into Kramer's archival boxes, evidence of past genius— but the only brilliance that he demonstrated today was his identification of failures in process and progress, of supposed problems with other researchers' scientific inquiries. He *was* a genius at that. But he made no suggestions for resolving the issues he raised. So:

"What guidance would you offer to Dr. Meyer for his work on our project, Dr. Kramer?"

Kramer almost looked at her. "Monaghan poses a valid question. What contributions can you offer, Meyer? I'll be unavailable to supervise your work as closely while I'm at CERN. Will I be satisfied with your results? I expect you to provide value."

That hadn't been her question.

At all.

And Ethan remained at the door. He made no rebuttal, no defense of his project inputs. He'd been vocal enough in their data, materials, and process debates, competitive, collaborative, and often right, but here he was, standing quietly at the back of the room behind a barricade of boxes, taking Kramer's unrealistic expectations as fact and his supervisor's abuse as justified discipline, when she *knew* that his work was good.

When she knew that *their* work was good.

Preliminary, but good.

When she knew that he was brilliant.

Even in her earliest and most hostile tirades against Dr. Ethan Meyer to Martina, long before she'd been forced into partnership with him and learned to value his aggravating, effective research methods beside his results, she'd never denied his ingenuity.

But as the familiar heat of anger gathered on her tongue, she recognized that she wasn't angry with Ethan.

She was angry with Dr. John Kramer: decorated director of SVLAC's prestigious Quantum Mechanics group, Ethan's supervisor, *de facto* mentor—and complete asshole. He was more interested in the packing materials for his awards than in their quantum gravity report, and what he'd bothered to glean from their update was only criticism of their progress. They'd been tasked with researching one of the most fundamental and difficult unsolved questions in physics, and he was dissatisfied that they hadn't presented publishable findings in under two weeks? He denigrated Ethan's contributions and demanded that his subordinate provide more and better results, but gave no guidance as to how.

He ignored the merits of Erin's own work and field.

She hadn't expected anything else from a man like him.

The way Kramer treated Ethan, however?

For a supervisor to speak to an employee this way—casually dismissive, casually cruel, completely unhelpful, without any fear of repercussion—was wrong. Even a failing one. And Ethan wasn't failing.

But worse still: Ethan's rigidity wasn't surprise.

She knew his surprise, the zest and the spark of it.

No, he was rigid because he'd known to brace himself for this abuse.

Maybe he endured it for the sake of opportunities and funding, or because he thought he didn't have an option to protest his working conditions under such an esteemed name, not when a line of eager physicists would've clogged the freeway to San Francisco for a chance at his position, or because...

Is your old supervisor still at SVLAC?

He is. Promoted to department head, too, and *Fermilab, time crystals, quantum effects on avian migration, quantum circuits, first-author papers—*

Suddenly, everything slotted into place.

No dissertation awards from Kramer's alma mater were being packed into his archival boxes; his doctoral work clearly hadn't garnered him any particular notice. But once he'd networked his way into a leadership position at his first lab—failing upward into management at Fermilab?—and had access to a cohort of research fellows and to *their* work? A glance at his stack of abstracts confirmed that his first-author papers had begun to appear during the early aughts, in the same time period when, given the duration of his PhD, he'd likely taken on his first supervisory position: the use of quantum effects for navigation by migrating birds, the exotic construct known as a time crystal, quantum circuits, and Ethan's units. He'd actually framed those abstracts and hung them in his office like trophies! And they *were* trophies, tributes to his brilliance, because only a genius could specialize in so many diverse areas.

A genius, whose published research was very close to the expertise areas of his mentees: his subordinates and second authors, STEMinist Online's women. They had their credit—as collaborators. But his was the name associated with the discoveries. With the fame. If the women posting on the forum were right, his subordinates often left his department soon after their papers appeared. Some left the field entirely.

Why would they lie?

They had nothing to gain from venting their anonymous rage on the internet, from passing on their experiences and hard-won warnings. But she? She'd enjoyed the rush of righteous outrage—of *entertainment*—from their reports. The grueling, demoralizing experiences hadn't touched her, hadn't been her responsibility to confront, so she'd treated them like recreational reading.

She'd been part of the problem...

"Well?" Kramer's finger rapped his keyboard, a reprimand against Ethan's continuing silence.

"*Uh*, I—"

...but not anymore.

What contributions can you offer, Meyer?

She knew *exactly* what she could offer Kramer, Ethan, all the women from her forum—and herself.

Ethan might think he had to take Kramer's abuse.

But she didn't have to take this. Any of it.

She reached across Kramer's desk and closed their progress report. *Click.* Now *that* was surprise. She answered with a smile that showed more fury than teeth and said:

"What contributions are *you* offering to our quantum gravity research, Dr. Kramer? Nothing that I can see. I don't think we actually need your input. We don't need your status update sessions either, and… *oh.*" She snapped her own fingers, straightening. "This—*this* is how you've appropriated your subordinates' work! Demanding all this micromanaging meeting bureaucracy so you can identify interesting research concepts in their infancy, then resource and claim them as yours as you oversee their growth. Most physicists would be too grateful for your funding and attention to notice until it was too late, until the papers were written with your name as a first author. Maybe not even then. It's almost genius—"

Genius at spotting promising ideas.

And stealing them.

"—but not quite. Not now. So don't expect credit for our quantum gravity findings in SVLAC's report to the Office of Science. Instead, why don't you just enjoy the Swiss golf courses?"

Then she turned for the door. She took Ethan's arm and led him out of his supervisor's office before either man could respond.

"We're done here."

18

His mind was noisy, buzzing, neurons firing frenetic bits of static but generating no response to Dr. Kramer's inquiry about his relevance to the federal physics project.

What contributions can you offer?
I expect you to provide value.

And Erin, her fingers wrapped around his arm, exerting a pull of gravity to tow him from the office—

What contributions are you *offering to our quantum gravity research, Dr. Kramer?*

His pulse was frenetic, too. Too fast, irregular, a flicker pulsing in his skull and echoing her words: *We're done here.*

Insubordination.

His supervisor would retaliate. Dr. Kramer would retaliate against Erin Monaghan for her disrespect. That wasn't a hypothesis. It was a certainty.

He will retaliate.

But he couldn't warn her, his breath accelerating into pain now, his ears ringing, the throb behind his eyes overtaking his vision with a dark, threatening blur—and *fuck, not here*, because his own office was across the whole width of the watchful bullpen—

Erin hauled him to a recessed door at the end of the hall marked "Fire Exit."

No alarms wailed when she depressed the metal crash bar to access a flight of exterior stairs leading down to SVLAC's quadrangle. Summer air splashed his face, cooler than his skin.

"*Ah—*"

"Come on." She let the hinges slam behind them, careless of the noise, while she steered him beneath the redwoods, toward a set of shadowed benches in the fragrant conifer litter. Popular with the lab's more reclusive scientists at lunchtime, they were deserted now. She shooed a squirrel off the closest seat. "Sit."

He collapsed.

Breathe. In. Out. I-in—

He dug his fingers into the wooden slats to keep himself upright as he tried to count, dizzy, hyperventilating. Splinters wedged under his nails.

—o-o-out—

"How can I help?"

He couldn't answer her.

But maybe she understood that, because she perched beside him to narrow their distance. "How would Bunsen help you?"

She knew.

Shame careened through him in a hot, awful tide of self-loathing and humiliation, and *no—fuck—don't see me like this—please leave, please—*

"...s-stay," he said.

She nodded. Erin uncurled his left hand and slid their palms together, intertwining their fingers. The fierceness of the hold could've been her grip, or his. It didn't matter. He clung to it and to her as she extracted the crumpled hutch blueprints from under his arm, their edges limp with his sweat while she spread them over his knees, while she took the pen from behind his ear and uncapped it. She offered the nib to him.

"*One.*" She inhaled.

"*Two*," exhaling.

He fumbled for the pen. His balance was rickety without his grasp on the bench. She increased the pressure between their hands and said quietly,

"*Three.*"

A line of pigment straggled across the page.

"*Four.*"

He tried again, tried to trace the safe, orderly lines of the grid.

"*Five.*"

His breath was a hiss past his teeth.

"*Six.*"

He outlined one wobbly square.

"*Seven… Eight…*"

He traced a second square more slowly, while she counted.

"*Nine… Ten… Eleven… Twelve…*"

Pen and lines steadying slightly with his focus, the third square was acceptable. Not ruler-perfect, but the quadrants were clear.

"*Twenty-six…*"

He shifted her elbow aside by an inch to ink his next blocks. The warm weight of her hand remained in his. Nine squares down on the blueprint… and nine across. *Inhale, exhale… One hundred and thirty-seven*. The space between those squares became a sudoku grid. *One hundred and fifty*. He could design his own logic puzzle now, but he'd been sketching a constellation earlier today and hadn't gotten the angle of its rightmost star correct, so he marked the bright points of the northern sky, placing them within the neatness of his graph…

One hundred and eighty-eight…

"Cassiopeia?"

"Yes."

"The boastful queen. *Two hundred and four*," she exhaled. "I'm choosing to take that as a compliment."

"You're on *two hundred and three*." He drew the *W* line between Cassiopeia's stars.

"Thanks… and now, *two hundred and four*. Better?"

"*Two hundred and five*."

Better.

Was he?

In the dusky shelter of SVLAC's redwood grove, duff and shadow and a faint sough of sweet, earthy wind muffling the noise from Ring Road while Erin enumerated their inhales and exhales, while she held his hand, he was breathing.

He'd forgotten *not* to breathe.

He'd tasted her on his desk, had sheathed himself inside her and gasped out his release against her neck, but this… *this* was intimacy.

I love…

"Y-you could've set off the fire alarm."

"What?"

As always, it wasn't what he'd meant to say. He winced, then withdrew his hand to pick at his splinters. "*Uh*—when we left Modern Physics."

"I gambled on the alarm being broken. Most of our equipment is." She lifted one shoulder, massaging her fingers. "And it was an emergency. Wasn't it?"

"How did you know that I…"

No, that wasn't his question.

He swallowed. He abandoned his splinters, capped his pen. "*Why?*"

"*Why* what?"

Why did you stay with me?

"Why did you challenge Dr. Kramer?"

"Challenge him? Everything I said was true. All I did—"

"But he—"

"—was give that truth a voice. Besides, he'll be gone soon, and—look at me. No, not at your grid. *Look at me.*" The fingertips of one hand tilted up his chin, opening his throat before it could close again, easing the edge of his panic. She let the dimness breathe between them for a moment. She let him breathe. Then, speaking softly, firmly, "Dr. Ethan Meyer, your work—*our* work—is good. It's preliminary, yes. How would it not be? We presented a status report before anyone could reasonably have research information to share. But still: *our work is good*. Dr. Kramer's an idiot if he doesn't understand that. Or worse, if he won't acknowledge it. Which he won't, because he—he's a scientific parasite. I should've recognized that before, but I…"

She wasn't angry.

Or if she was, she wasn't angry with him.

"Is this what it's like, working in the Quantum group?"

And because she wasn't angry, he didn't trust himself to reply.

He didn't need to, however; when she went on through his pause, the softness in her voice simmered dangerously. "Then I'm sorry. And I'm sorry if you didn't know what he was doing. How he was—"

No.

Now, he had to speak.

"No—*no*, he's…" He had to make her understand *why*, because what if she was right? *Scientific parasite*. So he clung to the mantra he'd made for himself, since the alternative was to believe her, to believe that all his work had been—*no*. "Dr. Kramer's a brilliant scientist. And it's a privilege to contribute to his research, because his genius is—is…"

...identifying promising research concepts in their infancy, then resourcing and claiming them as yours. Most physicists would've been too grateful for your funding and attention to notice until it was too late.

He'd hypothesized the existence of quantum units at Berkeley.

Yes, he'd grown his ideas under Dr. Kramer's mentorship and resourcing.

But the initial concept that space might exist as minute, divisible chunks?

Mine.

My ideas, my research, my—

He couldn't deal with that right now, though. Just couldn't. Instead:

"He... he was right about my lack of progress on the quantum project. The only useful SVLAC data that we reported was your Hawking radiation signal."

"Maybe. But even if he isn't planning to weasel credit for our work—and that's still an open question—could he really expect anything else at this stage?" Erin tossed up her hands. "*How?* Research is a journey. We're just starting out. Co-pilots. Which means that we're both responsible for the route. The playlist. The snacks. The result. *The story*. There'll be side trips and backtracking, but we'll still be going somewhere, even if it's not a perfect line. *Perfect is the enemy of good.* So don't you dare take any of the blame or success away from me, or I'll make your life hell as a backseat driver."

Could she be right?

Again?

Maybe, but...

"Dr. Kramer will retaliate. For today. Because—"

"—I was insubordinate? Or because I spoke the truth?"

"Yes. Both."

"Ethan…" She laughed. She actually laughed. "I'm used to men trying to retaliate against me for being right when they're not. Or for even just executing my job well. It comes with the territory of being a woman in STEM. So, sure—let him try. Let him see what happens. My brothers never allowed me to win at family game nights or baseball. I could handle their bullshit, and I'll handle his."

Let him see what happens.

"You believe that."

Obviously, she did.

She didn't doubt herself, all confidence and determination, even after braving Dr. Kramer's wrath. After incurring it. *Demanding it?* And he didn't want to wonder, but—what would the past three years have been like if they hadn't been rivals? If they'd been neutral colleagues? If she'd even taken his part of an argument on occasion, collaborators instead of adversaries? If fierce, bright, relentless Erin had stood at his side, head high, eyes flashing, her hand in his, an ally, a friend, a lover—

—*no*.

He wanted her, yes—had wanted her for so long, longer than he'd known—and maybe she even wanted him, sitting in the twilight with dust motes scattering a prismatic glitter on her glasses, waiting for him to stabilize… waiting *with* him.

But the fact remained: Dr. Kramer would retaliate.

A second fact, almost worse: *this* was what happened when he surrendered discipline, when he let emotion guide him instead of logic.

A third fact: he needed to regain control. Of himself. Of the situation.

A fourth: if he stood any chance of mitigating her danger, he had work to do.

Today.

"*Uh*, I… it's late. I should…" Clearing duff and gravel from his throat now, he gestured toward the parking lot with a hand that was almost steady. "Thank you for… but Bunsen needs his run, and I…"

"Right, of course." She accepted his decision to be finished, to be alone. *So easy.* She brushed a layer of needles from her jeans and stood. "We both know what happens if you keep him waiting."

"Yes."

He dumped their research into his messenger bag, then inched and stalled his way home to Redwood City through the smoggy crawl of a Peninsula commute. After he'd taken Bunsen around Stulsaft Park and eaten something cold in a Tupperware over the sink, he sat down at his desk. But he didn't drag out his blueprints again. He didn't drop back into laser angles and cable layouts, into data analysis or hypothesizing about the behavior of electrons at the event horizon of a black hole. He didn't log into his SVLAC email. He didn't even begin writing an apology to his supervisor: accept responsibility, then offer up a new research proposal—something, *anything* to gain leniency. Or at least to avoid additional punishments. He *needed* to write that apology; the headache compressing his skull synchronized with his own mental pressure inside it. *Focus, focus!* When he opened his computer, though, he didn't start drafting excuses or *mea culpa*s. Instead, he clicked into a new browser window.

Dr. John R. Kramer + quantum units

Search results loaded.

He began to read.

Her tires whistled over the pavement, bumping across lane dividers, zipping between cars stalled in traffic. Thinking hard, Erin pushed her legs and her bicycle harder.

Dr. John Kramer.

Despite their adjacent work with optics and lasers—Ethan had admitted that the holometer was based on technology like LIGO—the laws of physics had isolated her department's research on general relativity from Kramer's quantum mechanics projects. *Until now.* Nadine's surprise that he'd deigned to revise and resubmit a rejected paper for publication had told her all she'd needed to know about him on her first day at SVLAC. While she hadn't gone out of her way to avoid him, she'd never sought his colleagueship, either. She just hadn't devoted any mental energy to the man. It wouldn't have been worth it.

Now, though?

Now, she saw the full narrative arc, and its data was clean, its meaning clear: *early aughts... supervisor at Fermilab... published subordinates' research on quantum effects in avian migration... changed research campuses... SVLAC... time crystals, quantum circuits... first-author papers... Is your old supervisor still at SVLAC?... Promoted to department head... I left, like the others.*

She'd spoken the truth in Kramer's office today.

Scientific parasite.

His appointment at CERN notwithstanding, he was clearly continuing to execute his strategy of appropriating credit for any major research achievements in his orbit: demolishing his subordinates' confidence in viable ideas, leaving them passionate about their data but so demoralized that they were grateful for him to champion and resource similar concepts, because at least he could see *some* use for their work. If she and Ethan could resolve the physics field's most obnoxious paradox by reconciling general relativity and quantum mechanics into a single theory of space-time, Kramer would want that glory, too.

More trophies for his walls, another Breakthrough Prize, or even a Nobel award.

He'd rob her of these potentialities without shame. He'd also take them from Ethan—Ethan, who was brilliant not because of, but despite, his supervisor's influence. It was so obvious! Kramer had discarded his earlier subordinates after he'd bled their genius dry: ground them down, burned them out, then shown them the door and let them walk through it on their own. But he hadn't been able to drive Ethan off. Dr. Ethan Meyer was too smart and too resilient to safely discard. And a man. So, Kramer kept him on, kept stealing his ideas, controlling him by doling out *just* enough recognition and resources to keep him hopeful. Maybe—*maybe*—Kramer did occasionally theorize brilliance of his own, but it was Ethan who executed his hypotheses, who made the data fit, who generated extraordinary results with slipshod components—

—who was insanely precise and insanely productive because he had to be.

That second part, a prominent scientist outsourcing experiments to his subordinates, withholding sufficient resources while demanding publishable returns, wasn't unheard of.

But the first?

The basis of Kramer's research technique was theft.

Let him commandeer even one more iota of Ethan's work on quantum units.

Try it.

She sped through a stop sign with her teeth gritted, then skidded to a halt in front of her apartment and wiped sweat from her eyes.

Just try it.

How had Kramer come by his lucrative, prestigious advisory opportunity with CERN's Director-General, anyhow? She hefted her bicycle over her shoulder and lugged it up the stairs, continuing to think. Ethan had been in Switzerland three years ago, determining that even the nearly seven tera electron volts of Switzerland's Large Hadron Collider weren't sufficiently powerful for his quantum unit research. He would've spent several months with the physicists there, awkwardly networking while attributing too much credit for his work to Kramer. Kramer, who *was* good at networking; it was both a prerequisite for his position, and a prerogative for his playbook.

Glad-handing and results—however they were acquired—bought funding and blind eyes.

Ethan's work had facilitated Kramer's opportunity.

Of course.

She kicked off her sneakers in the entry. They went flying into the living room.

"Erin? Is that you?" Ashley, perched on the kitchen counter with a glass of wine while her new man stirred risotto on the stove.

"Hi, yeah." She didn't stop, rushing after her shoes and into her bedroom.

It should be Ethan traveling to Switzerland next week.

She didn't doubt that, or anything else.

None of these insights excused his earlier sabotages, of course. *Deflated bicycle tires, missing oat milk, time zone switches.* But now... now she knew better why he'd acted as he had, what he'd had to do to survive.

Of course, he had panic attacks. In his position, who wouldn't?

Had she made everything worse for him, though? No, this was Kramer's fault. She could handle any fallout, of course—*try it, just try it*—but Ethan?

Vibrating with unspent fury, she yanked the rubber band from her hair and tapped into her messages with Martina.

Erin
Did you know about Dr. Kramer?

She didn't send the text, though. Her friend would want to know why she was asking. *What* she was asking. Then she'd have to explain... *no*.

Not yet.

Not until she'd dealt with this.

With everything.

Instead, she opened STEMinist Online's exposé post on the man who had to be Dr. John Kramer. Although the influx of new comments had slowed, the data was still rich. She'd get other data sets, too. A man with practices as slimy and depraved as his had almost certainly committed actionable scientific misconduct during the course of his career. It would be difficult to locate hard proof. He would've covered his tracks. He'd had plenty of practice. But she didn't mind getting her hands dirty in the filth of cyberspace to find gold. Then she'd take him down.

Watch me.

She was in a dangerous mood—itching for action, she almost wished she'd find turkeys planning world domination in the parking lot—when she pedaled up to SVLAC's security booth the next morning, so early that her breath fogged in the dawn air. A guard on the night shift even stepped out to question her.

"Dr. Monaghan?"

She raised her lanyard with its employee identification card in answer.

"You get a graveyard slot in the experimental halls again?"

"No. Just a busy day."

He flicked a Warriors bobblehead in the window of his booth, which nodded her past. "Good luck."

"Thanks."

She'd need it.

She selected espresso at the Modern Physics coffee machine and a sudoku grid at her desk. Despite her adrenaline, she needed both the clarity of the puzzle and the caffeine. She'd slept for no more than a few minutes at a time last night, tossing, turning, wondering: should she tell Ethan about her plans to investigate Kramer? Unlike with the inputs for her sudoku cells, she only had two choices.

Tell him.

Don't tell him.

(Not lie. Just... keep her mouth shut. For once. *Again*.)

If she told him, would he resist? Would he stonewall her efforts with habit and fear? He might. She wouldn't know until she spoke. But then again, when had a research project ever begun with a certain answer?

Everything started with a question.

Do I tell him?

No, that wasn't it.

Do I trust him?

Dr. Ethan Meyer, her academic crush and her adversary, her challenger, her colleague, her collaborator, her artist, her distraction, her grudging inspiration, her…

Yes.

So, after confirming her plans for a noontime call with Nadine Fong—new mother, perennial physicist—about their research budget, she ignored an email from the *Journal of Supermassive Astronomy and Astrophysics* prompting her to submit an author photo for inclusion with her paper in the journal's September issue, and pushed away her sudoku grid. She left her espresso and her overflowing inbox, pausing only to answer Leah Haddad's request for fifteen minutes to discuss a deviant data point in the binary pulsar study.

> **Leah Haddad**
> Thanks, Erin. I also wanted to ask you about mentorship opportunities at SVLAC. I know you're really busy, but do you ever take on interns?

She hadn't. But if she did? She could support Leah as she entered the STEM field. She could guide other young women interested in physics, too—and not just guidance on copier functions. She could offer feedback and maybe some protection from men like Kramer, could smash glass ceilings and shelter others from the debris, could replicate all that Nadine had done to facilitate her own autonomy and success at the lab, be a role model, a counselor, an advocate, an ally—everything that she'd needed and been lucky to have.

She wanted this. She really did… but it just wasn't a priority today.

It couldn't be.

Dr. Erin Monaghan
Let's talk next week.

She sent her answer with a few quick keystrokes, then moved just as quickly to the parking lot. She was waiting for Ethan by the Modern Physics bicycle racks when his hatchback pulled into its spot, striding to his passenger door before he'd cut the engine, rapping her knuckles against the window.

Morning, she mouthed, ignoring Marco Rossi exiting his sedan and almost tripping over a curb. Then, when Ethan rolled down the glass, "Can I come in?"

"What…" But he unlocked the door.

She didn't give either of them time for questions. She slid into the blast of air conditioning, Mumford & Sons, and dog hair on his seat, rolled up the hatchback's window, silenced his radio, and said, "I'm investigating Dr. Kramer for fraud."

Shhhhrreeeeeeeeeccchhh!

Tires squealed. The hatchback lurched up over its wheel stop when some reflex saw Ethan stamp hard on the accelerator pedal.

Rossi stumbled back.

He ignored their colleague. So did Erin, hurriedly grabbing the transmission lever to shift the car into *park*.

"You're investi—*what?*"

"Yes."

"No." In the sudden silence and a rising stink of rubber, he turned with tendons jumping in his neck, lips rigid. "Erin, don't."

"I've already started."

"*Please*."

"I'm sorry. I have to."

"No, you don't. You don't have to risk—"

She caught his hands fisting around his keys before the serrated metal broke skin. "Ethan—if it were just you, I'd respect your wishes. I'd leave him alone. Let him continue. I'd hate it. But I'd do it."

"I—"

"It's not just you, though. Not just us. It's all the others. The ones who came first. The ones he hurt first. There's a forum called STEMinist Online with so much data on what he's done, who he's sabotaged. Years and years of it! He's not going to stop, and I—I have a responsibility to those women…" *Ally*. "To the next ones. To myself, too. I hope you can understand."

"You don't know what he'll do."

"I won't involve you. Or implicate you. He won't know. If I fail, you'll still be safe. If that's what you want."

"*No*. No, that's *not* what I—*fuck!*" and he abruptly wrenched out of her grip, seizing his phone. He thrust the device at her. "Look."

"Ethan—"

"Stop talking and *look*."

Dr. John R. Kramer + quantum units

"…oh."

"I just wanted to know," and now, his voice was quiet. Terrifyingly quiet, as shocking in its low, taut intensity as his outburst. "What you said yesterday? You were right. His first conceptual articles about quantum units were published *after* I'd defended my doctoral dissertation at Berkeley. When he recruited me to the Quantum group, he claimed he'd conceived the idea several years earlier during the recession, and now there was finally funding available at SVLAC to pursue experimental research on it. But there wasn't. I had to write grants for every penny spent on the holometer. There was no money to study quantum units except for what I brought in. I was grateful that he believed in my ideas, but he… he lied to me."

"He lied to everyone."

"Which is why you're not going to stop."

"No."

"Then…" He studied his search results again for the length of a long, long exhale. But when he raised his head, his cheeks and eyes were fever-bright, burning with determination. Not tired, not despairing: *dangerous*. "You have your whisper network. But you'll need my data, too."

"You don't have to—"

"I do, because you won't stop. And maybe together, we have a chance."

19

"Coffee and sudoku. My office. Ten minutes." Ethan badged into the Modern Physics building ahead of her, speaking over his shoulder and almost running into loitering Marco Rossi for a second time. He adjusted a buckle sliding down the strap of his messenger bag and frowned at the Italian physicist. "Dr. Rossi. Do you have a question?"

"*Uh*—no?" Their colleague's glance between them was definitely a question.

Popcorn.

Again, Erin ignored it.

Screw our agreement.

"Ten minutes," she confirmed.

Back at her desk, she swallowed her dregs of cold espresso, accepted Leah's request for a data meeting on Thursday, and scanned her email for any emergencies that had occurred in the half-hour since she'd last scrolled through her inbox; nothing, but she really did need to provide a headshot for her paper. She disconnected her computer from the lab's highly secure, highly monitored internet service, then opened a hotspot on her phone and linked her device to that.

No point in taking unnecessary risks.

She typed her query into a search window.

Scientific misconduct

The first results were reports on the semiconductor Schön scandal—which had spawned a discussion in the research community about what responsibility the reviewers of scientific papers bore in detecting fraud, rather than simply finding errors or determining the relevancy and originality of an article—followed by Dr. Anna Ahimastos's misleading data on blood pressure drugs, the invented co-authors for Sir Cyril Burt's more questionable papers, and specious discoveries around elements 116 and 118 at Lawrence Berkeley National Laboratory. Then came a definition from the United States Department of Energy:

> *Scientific misconduct is the willful compromise of the integrity of scientific research, such as plagiarism or the falsification or fabrication of data.*

Despite a professional consensus that deliberate plagiarism, falsification, and data fabrication was rare in the field, how many researchers like Kramer had slipped by under the radar? How many others were operating just like him?

At best, the line between bad ethics and lawbreaking was a no man's land.

Bouncing in her seat with adrenaline and espresso, she toggled over to the post about Kramer on STEMinist Online's forum.

> SnarkyQuark64: *I work at SVLAC. I know this supervisor, and I have data on his current research activity.*

Then she closed her laptop and walked across the bullpen to Ethan's office. A clock above the water dispenser flipped to 8:10 a.m. as she knocked. When he opened the door, she told him, "Ten minutes."

"Coffee and sudoku." He handed her a sign made of flimsy copy paper: Do Not Disturb.

She slapped it over his nameplate and the door's "Supply Closet" designation beneath it. But, despite the jumble of action items zipping through her mind and her attempts to process them all simultaneously, her brain surfaced one very specific, very irrelevant thought: *we should've used this yesterday…* She braced herself against Ethan's desk—*not thinking about the twist of his tongue between her thighs*—with her legs tightly crossed.

"I located the Department of Energy's official definition of scientific misconduct and fraud. It's the willful plagiarism of another scientist's research, or data falsification-slash-fabrication."

"Did you—"

"I disconnected from SVLAC's internet before I ran the search."

"Good."

"Do you want to use my hotspot?"

"*Hot*…?" Eyes flicking to hers, did his ears flush? Then, "Right. Dr. Kramer will have VPN access to SVLAC's systems while he's at CERN, but not to this. What's your passcode?"

She offered her unlocked phone. "Don't change my settings."

"You're the one who ran a binary program on my data."

"True."

The clench of her thighs eased slightly when his focus redirected from her face to a critique of her screen wallpaper: a graphic of the Monaghan family in Ms. Frizzle's Magic School Bus, with their heads—expressions contorted in screams or laughter during a rollercoaster ride at Michigan's Adventure theme park in Muskegon—transposed into the yellow windows.

"It looks more like a submarine than a bus."

"You're a mechanical engineer, now? And a Beatles fan? What's *your* phone background?"

Plain black.

"For privacy. It looks like your family had fun, though. You have the same smiles."

"Adrian would be so offended by that. He's the only one who wears his retainer anymore. Last Christmas, he warned me that I was starting to look like an inverse chipmunk." She poked her tongue against the gap between her front teeth. "Again."

"What did you say?"

"I told him that I might be a renegade chipmunk, but he was a beaver. Since he's an architect."

"Nature's engineers." A half-smile deepened in Ethan's cheek. But then, sobering, flush fading from his ears, he took his chair and cracked his knuckles. "Not quantum, though. *So*. We could begin with a review of the papers I've co-authored with Dr. Kramer, and then—"

"No."

"No?"

She reached over to close the journal articles and spreadsheets he'd begun to open. "I don't want to include your data in our fraud set. Not unless we come up empty-handed for the rest of the search. Your papers with Dr. Kramer would be useful from a plagiarism angle. You said it yourself: he appropriated your hypothesis about the existence of quantum units and claimed it as his in publications. But if we submit your joint research for scrutiny, you'll be implicated in his fraud by association, even though you're the wronged party. People will identify your name with scientific misconduct—and you're still in the physics field, still publishing. The others he's stolen intellectual property from aren't. So, you're the expert on how he operates and you can spot his interference, but I don't want to use your work."

"Not unless we have to."

"We won't," she promised them both. "Let's start by scanning all the journals where he's been published. Not the *Journal of Supermassive Astronomy and Astrophysics*, of course—"

"No. But it'll be on his radar now."

"Because of me."

Ethan's chin jerked. He returned to his results. "This is a long list."

"Are there any papers without second authors?"

The search compressed. "Not many."

"Not since the very early aughts, either." She crammed behind his desk with him, her ponytail falling across his shoulder to tangle in the fibers of his vest as she leaned toward his screen.

He stiffened.

"Sorry—"

"We should—*um*. White noise." A stream of quiet, muffling static rose from his phone.

They should've used that yesterday, too…

"S-smart." Her voice didn't crack. *Much*. She swallowed and straightened, a spark of heat hitting her stomach. Hands shoved deep in her pockets—or as far as she could shove them into the useless denim pouches that taunted women who wore jeans—she stared at the pixels on his monitor until she could make sense of them through her brain's own static, until she could say, "The only pieces that he's published solo since he was promoted into management at Fermilab are speculative research. He doesn't have data—*original* data—to back up those claims. Let's see his earliest co-authored papers that went through peer review. Then we'll work our way up chronologically."

Ethan expanded Kramer's first paper, which examined the manipulability of weak bonds between atoms and their electrons in photovoltaic panels. "*Journal of Applied Physics*. The co-author is Dr. Marie Engel. Do you recognize her?"

"She could easily have an account on STEMinist Online, but her legal name isn't likely to be her user handle." Opening a bookmark to the Kramer post on her phone, she scrolled back into the comments. "No, nothing about solar cells in the thread. Let's try the next paper."

"Electron microscopes with Dr. Amélie Chloé Archambault."

"No, I don't think so. Next."

"Valence bond theory. Graduate student: Daiyu Lin."

"That could maybe be Bond_ValinceBond. I don't remember her commenting on Dr. Kramer's thread, though… no, the last time she posted, she was announcing a teaching position in Boston. Hopefully Harvard. Which is great. But not useful for us. Next one?"

He opened an abstract on atomic clocks for GPS systems. "Is Forster your handle?"

"Didn't you say that keeping art isolated from work was good hygiene? I agreed with you. So, not Forster. I'm SnarkyQuark64."

"Because quarks were discovered in nineteen sixty-four?"

"Obviously."

"Clever."

"Thanks. Who's Dr. Kramer's lackey for this GPS clock paper?"

They compared professional names with user handles for the GPS article, then for the next paper, the next, and on through a whole sequence of *next*s, but without success. The non-atomic, non-GPS clock on Ethan's monitor had ticked almost to lunchtime before a relevant abstract appeared.

"Number seventeen: the hardness of random quantum circuits, with second-author Dr. Lethabo Swanepoel, on how random circuit sampling could allow quantum processors to perform tasks that are impossible for classical computers. Anything?"

Erin's stomach rumbled. She ignored it. "Did Dr. Kramer publish this at Fermilab?"

"Yes."

"Someone commented about the hardness of random quantum circuits on his post. Let me find it…"

Comment Deleted

"But why would she… *damn*. That was an *almost*."

"Next?"

Quantum tunneling effects in negative differential resistance devices.

Superfluidity.

Orbital stability of electrons in atoms.

"No. Next."

"This one's with Dr. Laura-Jean Anders, about how a quantum computer created time crystals." Ethan pressed his thumbs into his temples, then moved to close the abstract. "No, that's just Ted Chiang's *Anxiety Is the Dizziness of Freedom* with citations. Next—"

"Wait." Her hand shot out over his. "Time crystals?"

He highlighted the words for emphasis.

Her fingers skidded across her own screen now. "Someone mentioned time crystals in the thread. Look!"

DataDominatrix: *Do you think he could've moved from Fermilab to SVLAC? I was doing preliminary research on time crystals in the Quantum group there about eight years ago. I had to take some unexpected medical leave, and by the time I got back, my supervisor had published a paper on the crystals and my job was eliminated. I was cited as a lab tech in the study, but that was it. All my research information was wiped from my computer. There wasn't anything I could do. I remembered a lot about my data, though, since I'd spent so much time cleaning it. Some of his claims about my numbers weren't conclusions I'd drawn—and I'm not actually sure that they were even my data sets in the paper. Not that I could prove anything.*

But maybe Dr. Erin Monaghan and Dr. Ethan Meyer could. "He didn't just plagiarize her work. He falsified data!" Almost giddy, she opened a private message with the user.

SnarkyQuark64: *Hi, DataDominatrix. You commented on a recent post about a Fermilab supervisor to say that you'd worked in SVLAC's Quantum group under the same man, that he'd published your research on time crystals without correct credit, and that he might've falsified your data. Can you verify that this person is Dr. John R. Kramer?*

Not that she doubted it. But she needed confirmation.

While waiting for DataDominatrix—for Dr. Laura-Jean Anders—to respond, she switched back to the mother-post and submitted a reply to her own earlier message, where she'd identified herself as an SVLAC employee with data on Kramer.

SnarkyQuark64: *If anyone is willing to make a formal claim of scientific misconduct against this man, please either respond here or message me privately.*

No ellipses bubbled beneath her comment in immediate, eager response.

She refreshed the page.

Nothing.

"It's the middle of the workday," Ethan reminded her.

"It's lunchtime!" She drummed her fingers against her phone, her impatience almost as loud as the rumbles from her stomach. "Come on…"

"It's a substantial request. Let them think about it."

"But—"

"*Lunch,*" he said. He switched his internet from their hotspot back to SVLAC's standard connection. "And afterward, if we're still waiting on responses: quantum gravity in the Sidewinder conference room."

"Fine. But I don't have time to eat." She tucked her phone into her pocket. "I have a call with Nadine."

"Didn't she start her maternity leave?"

"Yes. And I can count the days she's been gone on two hands—which includes her hospital stay, so she might've actually stopped to have her daughter on her last commute home—but she already wants to start planning for her return next quarter. Or maybe she's just craving a conversation about something other than babies. I don't know."

"Do you have noon calls tomorrow, too?"

"No. Why?"

"We… maybe we could go somewhere besides the cafeteria or Blue Bottle for lunch. *Um.*" He passed a palm over the back of his neck. "For research reasons. A place with an internet connection, so you wouldn't have to use data for a hotspot."

Oh.

"Good idea." *Was it?* She tightened her ponytail, businesslike or just busying her hands so she wouldn't retrace the path of his fingers over his neck with hers. "How about Stanford's CoHo? It's an easy distance and the internet's free."

"No."

"Why not? Their portobello mushroom panini is—"

He pulled up the leg of his jeans in answer, displaying a Berkeley bear on his sock.

She snorted. "Just leave those with Bunsen tomorrow."

"No," he repeated.

"Then what about the Moroccan cafe in the university's engineering quad? Some other grad students in my cohort took bachelor's degrees at Cal, but no one sniped them there."

Ethan's eyebrows rose while he rolled his jeans down again. The corner of his mouth twitched. "Seems like we'll be testing that academic tolerance tomorrow."

"Yes, we will."

Tomorrow.

So she stuck out her tongue at him instead of licking the aftershave from under his jaw or nibbling his smile, returning to the bullpen before she lost her battle with temptation. Fortunately, the floor's lunchtime exodus meant that no one saw her slip out of his office. She connected her headphones at her desk in the quiet, refreshed STEMinist Online just once before she reconnected to SVLAC's internet, and waited for Nadine to join their call.

She didn't watch Ethan's door to see him leave for a salad or a sandwich at the cafeteria. She *didn't*. She changed positions in her chair, tried to ease the prickle on her skin.

At least the call with Nadine occupied her through lunch: the requisite protests that her supervisor shouldn't be attending meetings right now—especially this early in her leave!—followed by congratulations to her and her wife Qadira, updates on the department's interns, budget check-ins, routine project status reports (she didn't mention LIGO's detection of Hawking radiation, knowing that the topic would launch their discussion into an hours-long thought experiment, and if she mentioned Kramer… but what was the point? Nadine had worked with him for years, so she knew what she knew), and an introduction to the newest member of the Jamil-Fong family, happily burping on Qadira's shoulder.

"Everything's running smoothly at the lab? No scheduling or personnel issues?"

"One of the interns is asking me to be her mentor."

"I assume you're going to take that on?" Nadine shifted to elevate her feet on her couch, pressing a hand over her still-swollen belly.

"Of course. We can discuss it later, though. You've only been gone for—"

"Yes, I know, but… *ugh*." Then, calling to Qadira, "Darling, can you help me up to the bathroom? I thought I'd be able to get a little work done, now that the baby's out, but no one tells you that your postnatal body is almost as hard to manage as the pregnancy."

"We'll talk once you're back." Waving and wincing in sympathy, Erin closed the call.

Her watch read six minutes before one o'clock.

As anticipated, no time for lunch.

Continuing to ignore her stomach, she gathered her federal resources—computer, blueprints, spreadsheets—and set up in the Sidewinder conference room, then refreshed STEMinist Online again. There was nothing new on Kramer's post, so she returned to her earlier review of the quantum gravity project's reference materials. A holometer export was the first spreadsheet to expand over her screen.

Ethan had found Hawking radiation in her data yesterday.

What if she could discover something advantageous in his?

He'd claimed earlier that the standard deviation in synchronization readings for the device's split laser beams was low. She ran the numbers herself, now: calculate the mean of the data, find the square of each point's distance to the mean, sum those values, and divide the sum by the data point total—millions of readings per second. As expected, the standard deviation for the results was minimal. She hadn't doubted his accuracy. He'd stated that the holometer's results were consistent. They were.

They were familiar, too.

She opened Liesbeth Tuinstra's paper beside the holometer data, scrolling past its abstract, introduction, and methods sections to the results. Tuinstra had hopped electrons along a one-dimensional chain of atoms, tuning their ease of movement and creating an event horizon, which produced a rise in temperature equivalent to Hawking's theorized black hole thermal radiation. That, she knew. Skipping the discussion portion, she hopped herself down to a list of references—and there it was: the measured distance of the electrons' jumps between atoms on the chain. Relegated to one footnote among hundreds, it wasn't of interest to the authors, and she'd overlooked its significance earlier in her focus on the paper's experimental processes. But:

$10^{-18} m.$

Preliminary readings from the holometer on the size of Ethan's units of space were almost perfectly aligned with the distance of the electrons' hops.

Oh my God.

Kramer was wrong about many things, not least his belief that he'd get credit for their quantum gravity project—but also his claim that his subordinate hadn't yet contributed data to it. Ethan had provided as much data as she'd done!

He just hadn't known it.

Pushing back her swivel chair, pulse spiking in her ears, too eager to wait for him to return from the cafeteria, she hurried to the door—

—where she almost collided with him. He was carrying his usual messenger bag and a... *pastry box?*

"I found—" he said.

"*I* found—" she said.

"Sorry," together. Then, together again, "What did you find?"

"...pastries. The Condensed Matter group is celebrating getting a paper into *Nature Nanotechnology*. There were leftovers in the kitchenette." He raised the lid: flaking cream cheese danishes, croissants, half a doughnut. "Everything's picked over and going stale, but there were no vegetarian options left at the cafeteria, and I'm assuming that you didn't eat after your call with Dr. Fong. What did *you* find?"

Yesterday, he'd made her coffee. Today, he'd brought her pastries. And tomorrow...

Focus.

"I was reviewing our reference materials again," she said. "You'd located the Hawking radiation signal in my exports, so I took another look at your holometer data because I wanted—well, you're right that the standard deviation around the recombined laser synchronization readings is low."

He nodded.

"The actual distance measured is microscopic."

"Colloquially."

"Yes. It's much smaller than anything we can see with a microscope lens. And the measurement itself is ten to the power of minus eighteen meters."

Another nod. He knew this, too.

"It's the same distance that an electron hops between atoms in Dr. Tuinstra's black hole model."

"What?"

He'd started to offer her a danish. Now, the pastry tumbled back into its box as his eyes widened, interest gleaming among the flecks of silver, his eyebrows lifting, his mouth tightening around an inhale.

His excitement and his almost-smile were for her.

"Show me?"

She dragged her laptop across the table, her screen split between the holometer data and the University of Amsterdam's paper. She leaned in to highlight the relevant footnote. Ethan bent forward with her—and then into a two-hour technical discussion that hardly left her with time to refresh STEMinist Online's exposé post on a hotspot for responses.

"If we can establish a definitive connection between the holometer and the electrons' measurements, or at least replicate the distance of Dr. Tuinstra's hops during our experiments—"

Two hours became three.

"—and if the data confirms that space-time is definitively discrete, with the electrons hopping over exactly one quantum unit between atoms, then string theory will be proven false, won't it?"

Five hours of data and a debate about what credit she'd receive on his first-author paper, while the pastries grew steadily staler.

Another refresh of the forum post.

Nothing.

Fortunately, the potential for the holometer's readings to dismantle string theory held her attention on their project, instead of on the burgeoning stubble shadowing Ethan's jaw, or the edge of his tongue poking over his lower lip with the depth of his interest and enthusiasm… or the continuing radio silence from STEMinist Online. They even finalized the layout of their cable network in the MEC hutch, and she focused on the electromagnetic placement of ultracold atoms, on the manipulable hop distances of electrons, on Hawking radiation, and on laser angles.

Mostly.

Seven o'clock, one last refresh of Kramer's thread, standing to stretch out the kinks in her spine.

Post Deleted

"What?" She scrolled down the page. "No, no…"

"What's wrong?"

"No, no, no, no—" Her clicking at warp speed through irrelevant comments on other postings returned nothing. "*Damn.* The original author who wrote about Dr. Kramer appropriating her research removed her post. It's gone, along with all the comments. One of our best data sources just got deleted!"

She had a new private message from DataDominatrix, though.

No.

Attached was an image of a redacted non-disclosure agreement.

"*Fuck—*"

But then: *ping*, from her SVLAC email.

"Wait, maybe…"

Journal of Supermassive Astronomy and Astrophysics: *Submission Update*

Dr. Erin Monaghan,

Our editors have received an allegation of fraudulent data present in "Investigating the Impact of Tidal Disruption Events on the Axis Rotation of Galaxies Proximal to Black Holes." Publication of your paper has been suspended at this time, pending committee review.

Regards,

Dr. Ronald Sams, Editor-in-Chief

She didn't swear, now.

She didn't say anything at all.

She just stared down at her email, unblinking. *Unbreathing?* Because if her sole-author paper was pulled from publication, its results that would've provided funding justifications for upcoming grants couldn't be cited, and she'd lost a critical opportunity to establish herself as a name in their field.

Or as a name that she wanted.

She wouldn't be linked to virtuosic analyses of black hole behaviors, Hawking radiation, or insights into the construction of space-time.

Dr. Erin Monaghan would be publicly associated with fraud.

"*Ah…*"

She swayed, her face white.

"Erin—" Ethan reached for her. Despite her colorless cheeks, her skin burned under his touch. Her pulse jittered as he guided her back into her chair. He pulled apart a danish into small bites and told her, "Eat this. Breathe."

"I..."

"I know." He did.

Dr. Ronald Sams was a name he'd seen as an attendee at various networking dinners for which Dr. Kramer had requested reimbursement through SVLAC's Finance department. He was also listed in the caption of Dr. Kramer's prized golfing photo.

His supervisor knew Ronald Sams.

Now Sams had blocked Erin's paper from publication.

Fraudulent data, just like Ethan himself had implied at their all-hands.

Fuck.

Not even twenty-four hours after she'd...

...and this—*this* was what he'd feared. This swift brutality, this retaliation for her defiance, her assertiveness, her challenge to Dr. Kramer's authority. For her clear-eyed insubordination. Her honesty.

What contributions are you *offering to our quantum gravity research, Dr. Kramer?*

Scientific parasite.

He'd agreed to help her find evidence of his manager's misconduct. Not in order to claim credit for his own past work, not even to ensure his attribution for the outcomes of their quantum gravity project. But to protect her. Because if they had documentation and Dr. Kramer knew it, then maybe he wouldn't act against Erin, wouldn't...

He'd failed.

He should've known that he had no time.

This is how you lose the time war.

Dr. Kramer didn't have to prove his claim about her scientific misconduct. Sams' review committee didn't need to uncover fraud in her paper, either. The damage to her professional standing was already done. A researcher's name was nearly as important as their data output for securing publication and funding; a notorious study conducted by social scientists Dr. Gabriel Bernard-Boucher, Dr. Jarred March, and Dr. Hannah Hedgehower, in which they'd submitted bogus papers to journals under their own credible names and been accepted for publication, was hard proof that reputation held greater weight than fact.

Dr. Erin Monaghan, fraud.

Whatever Dr. Kramer had told Sams over dinner or on a putting green yesterday had already impacted her career.

Maybe wrecked it completely.

He knew this, even while he was still stupidly offering his danish, even while she was clearly eyeing the pastry box not with hunger, but as a place to vomit.

She knew it, too.

"I'm..."

Not angry.

He knew her anger, knew its sizzle and flash: pyrotechnics, loud and vivid and short-lived as a lightning strike. But she was quiet and pale now, lips chapped with her thin breathing. Dilated eyes, bloodless hands.

Afraid.

She was afraid because she'd risked Dr. Kramer's wrath not just for the preservation of her credit on their quantum gravity project, or even for the sake of the women in her anonymous network. She'd risked it for Ethan.

She'd risked her career for him.

Bold, beautiful, lucky Erin had gambled and lost.

20

"I'm…" again, her breath shaking.

"Erin—"

"*Uh*… I n-need to…" Her backpack's zipper snagged under her fumbling fingers as she staggered into the corridor. "I—I… need… just need… *tomorrow*, I'll…"

She didn't answer when he asked if she could get home safely.

Fuck.

This was his fault. He followed her out, because imagining her on the road like this, pedaling among lanes of honking commuters shouting at their phones while driving on autopilot—and yes, she knew her streets, was master of her lanes and traffic lights, but she hadn't eaten lunch or touched the danish—

The building's exterior doors clicked behind her. He was alone in the dark, empty hall.

No: *almost.*

Dr. Kramer was also there.

Locking up his office prior to tomorrow's departure for CERN, carrying a final archival box with his briefcase under his arm, Ethan's supervisor hadn't seen him exit the Sidewinder conference room. He could backtrack inside. He could still dodge Dr. Kramer, could wave him off to Switzerland and its golf courses over email. He hadn't encountered his department head since yesterday's status report meeting, and although he'd originally hoped to make amends today if he could, that was before Erin had announced her investigation and he'd understood that pacifying his manager was impossible. So, he could avoid Dr. Kramer for almost an entire year, if he just edged back and closed the door.

But. He had this one chance to make things right for her—for brave, clever, resilient, frightened Erin. *Right now.*

A bright heat ignited in his chest. Not panic.

Fierce. Protective. And yes: *brave.*

He *would* do this for her.

This is how you win the space-time war.

Setting his jaw, crushing years of defensive habit that would've had him dodge confrontation, would've made him take Dr. Kramer's punishments and praises in equal indebted silence, he moved down the hall.

"Dr. Kramer," he said.

"Meyer?"

"Yes." He stepped closer, barreling ahead before he could think of anything but what he had to say. "You contacted Dr. Ronald Sams from the *Journal of Supermassive Astronomy and Astrophysics* with a claim that Dr. Monaghan's pending paper is fraudulent. That she's committed scientific misconduct. Retract your allegation."

Silence.

The demand had surprised his supervisor. *Any* demand would've been a surprise. But it was only a moment before the skin beside Dr. Kramer's mouth tightened. He didn't deny the charge. His briefcase gave an ominous creak. "*Or?* Careful, Meyer."

He didn't stop, didn't breathe, and pushed forward into the danger of his manager's pause. "Or I'll update every experimental holometer data set—*my* data analyses, from *my* instrument, from *my* hypotheses—that you've ever used in a paper. Change them.

Then I'll contact the journals. *Nature Physics*. The *International Journal of Quantum Information*. All of them. The Eischer-Langhoff grant reviewers, too. I'll give them the new numbers, and I'll lie. I'll claim that you manufactured the earlier data sets to support your theories. *Fraud*."

"I see." A vein ticked over Dr. Kramer's right eye. Then, "Who do you expect to believe you?"

"I have a paper trail from your revisions to the Eischer-Langhoff grant. You instructed me to change the data in Table 5 when it was already correct—and you might've been looking at an older set, but there's already evidence that you manipulated data on time crystals in an earlier paper, so we—" *Facts*. He continued, slower, "Your subordinate on the time crystal project might've had to sign a non-disclosure agreement, but we know that you stole and falsified her work. Just like you stole the idea of data fraud in Dr. Monaghan's research from me. Like you stole everything."

"You have no proof." Leather creaked again. "Which is irrelevant, however. Because the papers that you claim you'd report to the grants and journals list you as a second author. Remember that, Meyer."

How could he forget?

Erin had nailed the brutal truth months ago with her jeer in the kitchenette, that he was nothing but Dr. Kramer's lackey and second author.

Except—*no*. That wasn't right.

Dr. Ethan Meyer, your work is good, she'd also said.

The holometer was his.

The quantum unit concept was his.

Dr. Kramer's early exports hadn't been corrupted, had they? They'd been garbage from the start, generated only to simulate work. They'd never been real.

Nothing original.

All the data—and the evidence for sizing quantum units, preliminarily confirmed by the University of Amsterdam's black hole model—was his, Ethan's; Dr. Kramer would have no way to refute his lie by proving that any of the numbers had been retroactively falsified. Since he refused to share their raw exports with other scientists, and the exports themselves were overwritten every month by SVLAC's budget operational software, there was no one to support a challenge to Ethan's allegation of fraud by providing backup copies of the holometer data.

The work: *mine*.

But if all this was accurate, it also didn't matter. His name was linked with Dr. Kramer's on their articles. Damaging his supervisor's credibility would destroy his own. So his threat was a nuclear option. If Dr. Kramer refused to retract his allegations to Sams and if Ethan executed his pledge—committing scientific misconduct himself, knowingly and maliciously falsifying data—then no reputable journal would publish papers from either of them again.

No publication, no funding.

No funding, no research.

No research, no career.

They'd both be blacklisted.

Erin would be safe.

"I know," he answered his supervisor now. "Your name is on my research, and if you don't retract your claim, reporting fraud to the journals could cost me my career. But I won't lose my ideas—and when did you last publish anything significant that wasn't based on my work? If you don't retract the allegation, what will *you* lose?"

Then he walked away.

As he strode past the empty bullpen and the kitchenette, elation swelled through the adrenaline pulsing in his stomach. His parting shot had been the truth: his work was the backbone of Kramer's present achievements. *My research. My success.* Erin was right. *Again.* It was a truth he'd buried deep and tried to ignore, because there was nothing he could do except endure it and hope that, if he did everything Kramer asked, did everything right, then maybe someday his supervisor would recognize him, would recognize and honor his contributions… so he'd cached his knowledge, hidden it away from himself, but Erin had always gotten under his skin. She'd always found his weak points. Now, she'd found this courage, too.

This truth.

The Modern Physics doors slammed shut at his back.

He crossed the parking lot to his hatchback.

He might be walking away from everything he'd ever worked for.

Everything that gave him value.

He kept going.

He didn't regret his words or his ultimatum—*not at all*—and he was actually smiling, even if it was a shivery, unsteady smile with the muscles in his cheeks and jaw twitching—but he couldn't click his seat belt into its latch. He dropped his keys when he tried to slot them into the ignition. Safe now in his hot car, safe to crack and break, his breath began to hiss in a sickening, erratic whistle.

Fuck, fuck!

He gripped his thighs with both hands, digging his fingers in until his cold, sweating skin blanched under his jeans. He could feel the bruises forming, knew the precise pain that it took to raise them. He chose a fresh spot, and a third, a fourth, pressing and releasing, pressing and releasing, struggling to master himself, to just breathe—

The pen behind his ear clattered down into the hatchback's center console.

Thud.

…it wasn't a good pen, not one of his specialized sketching instruments. Just an ordinary ballpoint. He had no drawing paper either.

It didn't matter, though.

Because, really: what more could he risk today than he already had?

He pushed the cotton knit of his Henley up over his forearm. He pressed the pen against the damp crook of his elbow. Ragged lines began to jerk along his skin, down onto the heel of his hand. The feverish marks didn't produce the design of alien civilizations or track explorations along the final frontier, however. His precision was gone, vanished into the whorls of pigment twining between his fingers.

But shining in the heart of his palm: her face, barely recognizable, abstract, galaxies in her hair—a girl with kaleidoscope eyes.

And he breathed.

His arms were black with scrawls before he finally accelerated out of the Modern Physics parking lot, up Sand Hill Road to the freeway. His evening run with Bunsen in Stulsaft Park was a sprint. No music. His rhythm was the fast but steady beat of his heart.

He opened Erin's text thread a dozen times, saw her ellipsis a dozen times, and answered with his. No messages. Maybe they both understood:

Tomorrow.

Again, he breathed.

She was hyperventilating.

Crouched up against her headboard, arms locked around her knees, rocking, *rocking*, she couldn't feel the leaden weight in her stomach of the energy bar she'd managed to choke down, couldn't feel her fingers, couldn't feel her tongue. A typing ellipsis flickered back and forth in her text thread with Ethan; her thumbs were numb on the screen, her palms flashing hot and cold and wet, and she meant to assure him that she didn't regret what she'd done, because she didn't—she really didn't—*scientific parasite*—but *our editors have received an allegation of fraudulent data, publication of your paper has been suspended*—

Ping.

Not the *swish* of a lightsaber.

Martina
How'd Monday's spreadsheet analysis go?

She blinked.

Monday.

It was only Wednesday.

How?

Wednesday, just after eleven o'clock at night in Silicon Valley, and the Monaghans would be—*should be*—asleep in hammocks by the beach, in beds with soft, sagging mattresses where she'd bounced as a child on Christmas morning, or in... well, Adrian probably wasn't asleep. If Manhattan wasn't at rest, neither was he. But she couldn't call him. She was Dr. Erin Monaghan, and she couldn't have her brother stepping in to fight her battles and lose them—and he *would* lose, because he was powerless to help her now, no one could—

> **Martina**
> You're still typing. Are you writing your next story by text?

She'd been gripping her phone so hard that its screen registered the pressure of her thumb as a keysmash. A scream of letters, numbers, and symbols spewed under her hold. At least she hadn't hit *Send*.

> **Martina**
> What's going on?

Incoming Video Call: *Martina Perez*

She answered. What else could she do?

Martina filled the screen, her curly bob wrapped in a silk sleep scarf, her phone propped up on the Perezes' kitchen table and a notepad of dates, names, and numbers—likely the financial dirt she'd found on a city council trustee—receiving her focus instead of a plate of leftovers in plastic wrap by her elbow. But now, she pushed her notes and dinner aside to scrutinize Erin's face. "*Thank God*—you're breathing? You're safe?"

"Y-yes, but..."

"What's going on?"

This wasn't popcorn.

Not anymore.

"Ethan was right," she said.

Martina dropped her phone onto her enchiladas.

And then, it all came spilling out.

"Ethan was—he said—said that Dr. Kramer would retaliate, after *I* said he didn't have anything to contribute to our quantum gravity project, that he'd stolen his subordinates' research to publish under his name, that he wasn't a genius, just a parasite—and it was all true—*is* true—but then he warned me about what Dr. Kramer would do, and I—I laughed. *I laughed.* I thought I could handle it, because I can always handle it, always have to—but now my paper's being investigated for fraud, and I—I didn't falsify my numbers. I didn't. My name will still be linked with fake data in people's minds, though, and you know what the field is like. I'm… *me*. I'm not going to get a second chance at… at…" She choked to a stop, out of breath, her throat raw. Then, swallowing through her friend's wide-eyed, open-mouthed stare, "Like I said, Ethan was right."

"…*uh*."

"He's also Bannister."

"Bann—*what?!*"

"Yes."

"That… that's… you're… *really?* Right. *Right*. So, first: the situation with Dr. Kramer and your paper is horrible, and I'll do anything I can to help. *Obviously*." Recovering with impressive speed, Martina brandished her notebook of city council dirt, almost knocking her plate off the table before she dropped the pages and grabbed her phone close, mouthing her words to Erin on the screen. "But also—*Dr. Ethan Meyer and Bannister?*"

"I know."

"Did you?"

"Last Friday, but then everything just…"

"I knew before then." Martina began to pace her family's tiny kitchen, weaving between an asthmatic refrigerator and cluttered cabinets of spices. "Not about Bannister—though *Jesus*, it's really him?—but about you and Ethan. Because you don't have a poker face, and he… you were the only person he talked to in anything but monosyllables, if he wasn't discussing physics. I could tell that, even just from passing him in the office, which—this means that the pop psychology on those daytime talk shows is right! Opposites do attract!"

She'd expected to be flustered and embarrassed and defensive, almost ashamed of the truth, of her own bullheaded blindness.

Instead, despite everything, Erin found herself breathing, relaxing a fraction from her panicky hunch against her headboard when she said, "That's valid with particle charges, but people aren't just protons and electrons. There's only anecdotal evidence about romantic opposites attracting from song lyrics and films. From art."

"Like yours, and his."

"Yes."

"So?"

"When we were first assigned to the quantum gravity project, Nadine told us that there might be more common ground between our work than we thought. She was right. And I…" She fiddled with the edge of her pillowcase. "I think *we* might be more similar than we realized, too. Which sounds ridiculous, because we come at everything from very different angles, but—a coin has two sides. An atom has a positive and a negative charge. The universe is built from opposing and inseparable units. Maybe, just like our physics theories, those units aren't all irreconcilable…"

Dodging a swinging cabinet door, Martina began to laugh.

"Fine. You've convinced me. Because the only two hyper-competitive, workaholic, over-caffeinated, data-obsessed, wildly oblivious, oat-milk-swilling, beautiful people whom I can ever imagine applying universal laws to justify falling in love are Dr. Erin Monaghan and Dr. Ethan Meyer. And I want the full story of how you finally figured yourselves out, but," sobering, returning to her chair to flip open a fresh page in her notebook, "this isn't the time."

Love.

Did she love him?

That was the question.

But it shouldn't have been.

It wasn't a question at all.

Martina readied a pencil. "What's the exact wording of the email about your paper?"

Yes.

She cleared her throat. *Later*, she'd manage that later, after…

"I received it just after seven o'clock tonight. Four hours ago, and about twenty-two hours after I spoke to Dr. Kramer." She swiped her thumb over Martina's face to minimize their video window while she accessed her inbox, and revealed a push notification hidden by the call:

Journal of Supermassive Astronomy and Astrophysics:
Re: Submission Update

She frowned.

"What is it?"

"The… the journal sent another email."

"What does it say?"

Dr. Erin Monaghan,

"Investigating the Impact of Tidal Disruption Events on the Axis Rotation of Galaxies Proximal to Black Holes" has been cleared for publication.

Regards,

Dr. Ronald Sams, Editor-in-Chief

"*Uh.*" The short, stark sentence made no sense. There was also no way to misunderstand it. "The journal's going to print my paper in September."

"The reviewers didn't find your nonexistent fraud?"

"It doesn't say anything about reviewers, or my data, or scientific misconduct, just that I'm reinstated. Which is… clearly, I'm…" She floundered. *Happy? Relieved? Confused.* "Why, though? *How?*"

But that wasn't a question, either.

Ethan.

He must've done—*something*. Something brave and foolish, and if he'd torpedoed his career to get her paper published in this stupid journal—

"You know." *Tap*, went Martina's pencil. "Don't you?"

"I—I need to talk to him."

"What are you going to say? And no pressure, but if I didn't have this city council hearing at eight tomorrow morning—I swear, they keep planning for times when they hope the public can't attend—there's no possible experiment any physicist might run that could keep me in my control room when you two are—"

"*Popcorn.* I know."

"You could pack Oracle Park."

"Or just the Modern Physics parking lot." Shaking her head, she extracted her notebook from beneath a sudoku booklet and *This Is How You Lose the Time War* on her bedside table.

"Who would've thought that a slab of asphalt would be your final frontier? Go conquer it, Dr. Monaghan," and their call ended with a wink.

Was this her final frontier, though?

Either way, there was something good waiting for her tomorrow. She knew it. And she began to write. By one o'clock, she had what she needed. The single scribbled page required no revisions. It was messy and rambling and a little illogical, definitely over-dramatic—but right now, so was she. It was… *honest*. It was perfect. She trusted herself.

She clicked off her light and smiled.

Something good today.

She was in the parking lot again when Ethan pulled into his spot on Thursday morning: sneakers, helmet hair, pink graphic STEMinist t-shirt. She didn't wrench open his door, however, or throw herself into his passenger seat to take refuge behind the protections of tinted glass and sun visors. Despite the adrenaline thrumming in her stomach and up her spine, she clutched her backpack in full view of the Modern Physics main doors and waited for him on the curb.

"*Erin?*" Exhaling her name with hushed urgency, he was beside her in a breath.

She seized his vest, violently. "What the hell did you do?"

"What?"

"The journal reinstated my paper for publication last night—just hours after Dr. Sams pulled it from the lineup to investigate me for data fraud. *Hours!* Before anyone even knew about the accusation. No review committee works that fast. And don't claim that Dr. Kramer decided to forgive me for speaking truth to power, either, so that means you must've done—I don't know—*something*, and thank you, but if you've damaged your career so that I—"

He didn't deny it. Whatever *it* was. Instead, Ethan smiled into her tirade, softened into her grip.

"—s-so that I…" She faltered, caught off guard by his calm, and stopped.

"What did I do?" His fingers lifted to her cheek, tucked a loose strand of hair behind her ear, and lingered with the lightest pressure against her skin. "I gave Dr. Kramer an ultimatum: he'd retract his allegation about your paper, or I'd update all the holometer numbers used in our own publications, then contact the journals and claim that *he*'d committed scientific misconduct. He's never touched my data or analyses. He couldn't reconstruct them. He couldn't refute my claim without admitting that all the work on quantum units that he's published under his name is mine—that while he hasn't committed data fraud with me like he did with Dr. Anders, he plagiarized my research. My ideas. *All* of them."

"If he hadn't complied, you'd have—"

"Been implicated in his misconduct by association. I know. I wouldn't be forfeiting my theories, though. Or the results of any new research that I'll do. He would. He had more to lose than I did."

"But you…" She twisted her fingers tighter into his fleece. "You still risked your career when you didn't have to."

"No. I did have to." SVLAC's shuttle bus growled into the parking lot and he nodded toward it, at its disembarking interns with Leah Haddad in the lead, then turned back to her, so earnest when he continued, "They need someone like you. To help them work the copy machine, to open opportunities and advocate for them, to see their potential when they don't—or can't—see it themselves. So I had to make my gamble with Dr. Kramer. Not just for me. For you. For all the ways you'll keep challenging my research and my field. Challenging my thinking. Challenging *me*. And for this cohort. The next one, too. Because I… *I* needed someone like you. And…"

"…and?"

When Leah waved a greeting, she returned it without breaking their gaze. She ignored Sandra O'Connor-Young's curious eyebrows while her colleague walked toward their office building. *Let them have their popcorn.* Warmth and wanting stirred, building under his light touch, his pause, his breath, his serious smile.

"And what?"

He opened his left hand. "And I think I still do."

Oh.

Ink saturated his palm. Lines and curves and angles twined through his fingers, over his knuckles, down his wrist. Vanishing up his forearm under his sleeve were grids and graphs, binary pulsars and constellations—Canis Major galloping, leaving Bunsen-like paw prints in its wake, and in the cradle of his hand: Cassiopeia. The stars were her own freckles.

"Do you see?" Then risk-averse, cautious, bold, smiling Ethan said, "*This* was a gamble worth making. I just wish I'd understood that sooner, because I know we agreed to finish our quantum gravity research year first—you insisted that we couldn't afford distractions, and you were—*are*—right—but this future is worth waiting for. I want this, and more. I have for a long time. With you, I want to draw in color."

He wanted to draw in color?

Well, she wanted *everything*.

Answering his smile with a grin of her own that she knew *definitely* distracted him, she tugged him a step closer, and as Dr. Tomasz Szymanski opened the Modern Physics doors to hustle the gawking interns inside, she asked, "But what if we didn't wait?"

"You said—"

"*Ethan.* Didn't Ted Chiang's 'The Truth of Fact, the Truth of Feeling' teach us that perfect recall is inexcusable? But if you're really set on remembering every single thing I say for the rest of my life,"—she extracted a ragged sheet of paper from her pocket, though she looked at him rather than her illegible notes—"then remember this from Aaron Forster's 'The Lonely Lunacy of Lactose', too."

I took the Neapolitans. I confess it. I destroyed this last Earthly pleasure of ours. Why? Because I saw how we two measured our lives by what we had left behind, how we judged ourselves by servings of ice cream, how we suffocated beneath vanilla, chocolate, and strawberry flavors, beneath the flavor of our fear. Our fear of losing ourselves, and who we had been. I saw how we clung to that fear. But I saw also who we might become, if only we were not afraid. I saw who we might become if— instead of fear—we chose stardust. So rather than ice cream, I give you my hand now—now—looking not into dehydrated foil packets for our joy but outside, to the brilliant void. And I ask: will you brave the darkness to burn brightly with me?

He listened to her in patient silence through the hot sunlight beating down upon their shoulders, through the rumble of traffic and the slam of vehicle doors. But the instant she finished, Ethan said:

"Yes."

"Really?"

"Yes. Did you think I'd say no?"

"No, but... just *yes*? No questions, no challenges, no..."

The tip of his nose brushed hers when he shook his head. "Our rivalry has been beneficial. It's provided us with the opportunity to head SVLAC's quantum gravity research, and I've done good work to keep ahead of your funding numbers. But I didn't discover the synchronicity between my quantum unit measurements and Dr. Tuinstra's electron hop distances alone."

"I didn't discover LIGO's Hawking radiation signals in a vacuum, either."

"Technically space *is* a vacuum—"

"I appreciate that very valuable insight, Meyer."

"You're welcome, Monaghan." They traded crooked smirks for a moment. Then, "So even though we've received permanent head damage in paradoxical fields, does your electron hop distance revelation and my Hawking radiation discovery prove that we're better together than in opposition?"

She bumped her shoulder into his. "All extant data substantiates your theory, yes. And even if we occasionally get distracted from our research—"

"Essential work–life balance," he said.

"In this economy?"

"For science," Ethan reminded her, and then he finally closed the invisible distance between them to kiss her, one hand slipping around her waist, the other wreaking havoc with her ponytail while she stepped up onto his feet to draw him closer still...

Clap. Clap. Clap.

They raised their middle fingers in answer.

"Thank you, Dr. Monaghan and Dr. Meyer. This might be the first National Lab observational experiment that's ever ended both on budget and on schedule." Elias Schulz strolled past them into the Modern Physics building.

That broke them apart.

"Did we just flip off...?"

"...yes."

"Everyone at SVLAC—up to and including the director!—knew for *years*, except..."

"...us?"

"It's almost humiliating, being blindsided by data like this." Her indignation turned to laughter against his stubble. "But, *um*... that does mean I should probably notify you about one other historical data point, just so you know. Promise you won't mock me?"

"No."

"Fine." She would've shuffled her feet if she hadn't been standing on his sneakers. "You know that I didn't mean to sabotage your *Nature Physics* paper. What you don't know is that I did all that research on you for my introductory email because I was excited to collaborate with you. I admired your work so much, and had so many questions. I even wanted to ask you about quantum gravity."

Ethan drew back a full inch. "You just wanted to impress me?"

"There's no *just* about it. When we ran into each other on my first day, I was starstruck. And it's probably good for my ego that you went to CERN right afterward. You might've been unbearable about my... academic... crush."

"I want to say I would've, yes. But honestly? I probably would've avoided you. I wouldn't have thought that someone like you would be interested in me talking. Despite my—*uh*, genius at public debate."

So maybe they really had needed their three years, and everything from Pandora's box that had happened during them.

"Well, then for the sake of giving you something to talk about," she raised her eyes and her smile again, "I'm glad my initials ended up on your *Nature Physics* form. Look at the data: if I hadn't made that error and if you hadn't retaliated, if we hadn't clashed over funding, publications, and lab time so that we debated the merits of our research areas for the Secretary of Energy, and if we hadn't been forced to collaborate on SVLAC's quantum gravity project—just imagine the travesty for science! We never would've detected evidence of naturally occurring Hawking radiation."

"Or the synchronized scale of quantum units and electron hops in black hole models."

"Except that one of these discoveries is much more important—"

"Which one? There's solid evidence to support *my*—"

"*God*, yes." Erin grinned against the laughing outrage on Ethan's mouth. "Talk data to me."

SIX MONTHS LATER

Erin Monaghan

"You want rosemary for the potatoes, right?" Stretching onto her toes, a ratty sleep shirt riding up her bare thighs, Erin craned her neck over Grant's pot on the windowsill above the kitchen sink. She plucked a sprig and crushed it between her palms, inhaling the sharp, fresh fragrance while she swayed to the Beatles' "All You Need Is Love" playing on the radio. "He's much happier in this eastern light. He's putting out new shoots, even in the winter."

"Yes, please." Ethan tapped his spatula against a sizzling cast iron pan on the stovetop and pinched the rosemary from her palm to sprinkle over their egg-and-potato scramble.

She passed him their plates. "We could have Martina and Tomasz over for dinner to use up more of the harvest. Garlic artichokes or penne pasta in a lemon goat cheese sauce would both be good with rosemary. But we'd need to clear some space around the table. Find the other chairs, too."

"There's one in the bathroom." He dropped a nubbin of scramble into Bunsen's bowl as he stepped over a box of kitchen utensils, then threaded past the golden retriever and through a neat maze of packing material to a dining nook set between the kitchen and living room.

"Right. I was standing on it to hang the shower curtain." Nodding at a cluster of printed panels from PhD Comics, XKCD, and a sudoku sheet tacked on the refrigerator, she grabbed a carton of oat milk, snagged a takeout box of cream cheese danishes from the Palo Alto Cafe off the counter, and followed him to the table, where a pair of steaming mugs were waiting. "What about the other chair?"

"By the front door. There's mail on it. New address confirmations and coupons."

"Changing locations already generates so much waste. Adding flyers that no one wants to the mix is just rude." But she smiled while she propped up her feet on a crate of art supplies and took her first sip of milky coffee.

They'd moved into an older rental on Waverley Street in Palo Alto's Midtown neighborhood just last weekend. Its bathroom tiles clashed between 1950s Pepto Bismol pink and 1970s avocado green, the dishwasher didn't work, and the second bedroom had no closet. It was perfect.

They already had plans to convert the spare room into a studio and office, where she'd write and he'd alternately draw or fill orders from Bannister's website. They'd hang Erin's posters and her framed paper abstract (it *was* a trophy) beside Ethan's SVLAC beam tree, "Hunger," and his other original pieces— black and white, but also a few newer drawings inked in the blues, reds, and golds of their afternoons spent running along Crissy Field East Beach by the Golden Gate Bridge—over dents in the living room's drywall. They'd clean up the yard—maybe put Grant in the ground and build a bicycle shed—and she didn't mind flicking soapy water at Ethan while they did the dishes, even if it meant that they got distracted... very, *very* distracted... and left their plates to soak overnight...

"Ready?" Ethan plonked a bottle onto the table between their plates: Trader Joe's Habanero Hot Sauce. Right. They'd picked up the spiciest condiment available during their recent trip to the grocery store. Now it was time to test their metal against the Scoville Scale. And against each other, obviously.

Good: she was hungry.

"Yes." Licking her lips, she reduced the volume on the radio, then reached for the oat milk carton and stared him down while she poured out a tall glass for him. She added just a splash in her own glass. She nodded at the habanero sauce and their jigger, tucked her loose hair behind her ears, and picked up her fork. "Are *you*?"

He returned her stare, measuring sauce into the stainless steel cup and then dolloping equal portions onto their respective breakfast plates. She tried not to wince at the amount. He noticed her cringe, of course. His grin widened. "You can still—"

"No stalling." She set the stopwatch on her phone. Then she took a bite: eggs, potatoes, rosemary, and olive oil in a cocoon of warm, smoky flavor. She pushed aside her oat milk to plant her elbows on the table and continued to hold his gaze. The seconds ticked up on her screen. She bit into her danish before lifting her fork again, swallowing, smiling, confident—and the warmth exploded. No warning, no gradual escalation from glow to heat to inferno, just a pleasant tingle and then suddenly a combustion on a cosmic scale, numbing the roof of her mouth, burning her cheeks—

She dropped her fork. And hiccupped.

"*Ah!*" Ethan laughed. Or choked. Tears glazed his eyes as he gulped through his own pained mouthful. "It j-just—"

"—and all at—*hic*—once—"

"Milk?"

She exhaled another fiery wheeze, sweating and coughing but undeterred, laughing back at him. "Y-you first."

"No. I'm f—" But he couldn't finish his sentence.

"You were the—*hic*—one who mentioned—"

Groaning, he waved her off to brace his palms against the tabletop. Bunsen whined and nudged his arm. "*Ugh*, no—buddy, you don't want this—"

Her stopwatch showed that they'd been suffering for thirty-two seconds. Maybe if she lasted a whole minute without crying off, she could claim victory? She swallowed and swallowed, begging the time to tick faster while Bunsen continued to nose at Ethan's flannel pajama bottoms. When she'd counted forty-eight excruciating moments, however, a video call from Martina chimed onto her screen.

"*Thank God*." She flashed her phone at Ethan through her sweat and tears. "Incoming—"

"Marti—? Better—*hic*—answer her."

"T-truce?"

"—yes." He inhaled his oat milk with a grateful gasp.

Erin didn't protest when he filled up the splash in her glass to the brim. The heat dissipated from her scorched tongue, her hiccups subsiding by degrees while she drank. The relief was too sweet for principled defiance. This time, at least. She wiped her mouth and caught Martina's call on the last ring.

"Morning, Mar—"

"You're crying." Martina ignored her wave and greeting. She crossed her arms. "What did you do this time?"

"*Uh*." She dabbed at her cheeks with a napkin from their stash of takeout utensils, sniffing against the residual burn in her nose. "We had that new Trader Joe's hot sauce with breakfast. We were seeing who could tolerate it for the longest time, and things got a little—"

"—heated." Still red-faced, Ethan angled himself into the video frame with their evil habanero bottle, then shifted over to wrap a distracting forearm around Erin's waist, fingers tracing the freckles on her stomach and the scalloped hem of her starry bralette through her shirt. "Hi, Martina."

Martina rolled her eyes. "I was right about both of you all along. You really are two of the stupidest, stubbornest smart people I know."

"Wait—you know people who are more stupid, stubborn, and smart than we are?" Instantly refocused, Erin pivoted in her seat to trade affronted looks with Ethan. "We have competition!"

"Oh my *God*... Before this goes off the rails, I have a question for you."

"We weren't going to go off the—"

"You absolutely were. So: can we reschedule today's Pilates class and dress shopping to next weekend? I had a shift change in the hutch operator schedule, and there's also a Menlo Park city council meeting about a new dog park ordinance."

"Bunsen says yes, of course." She patted the golden retriever with her free hand; the other was creeping up Ethan's neck, twisting and tugging lightly at his overgrown hair. "I'll see if Kai and Ashley are free for coffee. Anyhow, there's plenty of time before Chase and Isabel's wedding."

"Next summer. Too soon," from Ethan.

"You'll be begging for the date when you see the piece I've picked out for her, though," Martina told him. "If your jaw isn't on the floor—if *everyone's* jaws aren't on the floor—"

"*Martina*. What are you—"

"It's gorgeous, and you can even make your entrance on a bicycle if you want to. So you'll love it. *Jaw, floor.*"

"*Hmm.*" Ethan leaned into Erin's paralyzed touch on his neck while she tried and failed to find a retort for Martina's sass. "You could wear this shirt you have on now, and you'd still have everyone staring. Because you'll be there with me. And… you're *you*."

Martina's next eyeroll was almost audible. She might as well have been mouthing *popcorn*. "Right. Anyway—Ethan, how's NASA Ames? If you can share any top-secret information."

"Different from SVLAC." He propped Erin's phone against the oat milk carton and handed his empty plate to her, which she stacked on hers and ferried to the sink, out of Bunsen's covetous reach. The retriever followed her into the kitchen and sat on her feet. "Most of my work involves quantum computing for the Hermes II project. The shuttles and probes are projected to reach the Moon, and eventually beyond Mars. They could even enter orbit around Jupiter in the next century. Of course, anything I do now will be prehistoric by that time and my department can't publish our research because the technicalities are classified, but I like it. The work is interesting, even if it's not quantum units and holometers. I might still go back to that field someday and I have ideas for improvements to the instrument and its integration with Erin's federal research, but for now, I just… it's good to take some distance from it. To recalibrate. To breathe. And I can do that at NASA. Like I said, the work is interesting—but more importantly, the people are good."

"There's that adage about leaving managers, not jobs, right? I'm glad it's going well—but only Dr. Ethan Meyer would consider NASA a sabbatical. Next question's for Erin, though: are any of these classified technicalities showing up in your latest story? Anonymized, of course."

"I might have sneaked a look at some calculations over his shoulder." Unrepentant, she squirted soap onto her sponge. "I have to take what I can get, since I can't barge into his office anymore for sabotage and secret-stealing. The commute to Moffett Federal Airfield is just too far."

"Isn't that in Mountain View?"

"Too far," she repeated with a sarcastic, rueful sigh. "He used to be just across the hall."

"Now you never see him."

"Tragic." She scattered a handful of suds toward Ethan, who popped a bubble out of the air. "Tell Martina about the time your new manager smuggled your team into the wind tunnel to fly kites."

"I can neither confirm nor deny that I flew Dr. Ndlovu's daughter's kite in the Unitary Plan Wind Tunnel. But if I had…"

Smiling while he recounted the story of what he might or might not have done in the NASA Ames tunnel, Erin reached for their cast iron pan and began to scrape out the egg residue. She missed working with him on the Department of Energy's quantum gravity project, but his relaxed sprawl in a dining chair among the boxes of the life they were building together was worth much more than her regret for the hiatus of their professional relationship and their scooter races to the cafeteria.

She would've given up anything for his laughter.

Easily.

Besides, she liked her replacement collaborator from the Quantum Mechanics group: a transfer from Jefferson Lab, brilliant in her field and eager to support SVLAC's summer program to broaden the participation of young women in STEM—where Leah Haddad had agreed to talk about her experience at the lab. The former intern shadowed their quantum gravity work in the West Experimental Hall every other week (they'd installed an electromagnet in the MEC hutch and their first attempt at recreating the University of Amsterdam's event horizon model with ultracold atoms was slated for next Wednesday), and she and Erin met for lunch at the Coupa Cafe outside Stanford's Green Library on Saturdays once a month. Sometimes Erin's new colleague, Sandra O'Connor-Young, or even Nadine—slowing down on her weekends now to sip a smoothie and to assess how the lab's women were *really* doing—joined them; the occasional social meal was just as important as time in the experimental halls.

A network of known allies invested in each other's success was so much more powerful than an anonymous collective. Only look at STEMinist Online! Once SnarkyQuark64 had formally identified herself as Dr. Erin Monaghan and laid out the details of Kramer's failure to sabotage her career—highlighting his weakness in being compelled to issue a retraction for his lies about her data, holding him accountable for possibly the first time—the floodgates had opened. Non-disclosure agreements were investigated and deemed fraudulent by legal advisors, since only National Labs could compel NDAs, not rogue supervisors, and the comments under her post had swelled with threads of relief and profanity—and proof. One call to *Scientific American*, and an exposé was in the works.

She hoped that Kramer wouldn't resign before the article went to press, before he could be recalled from CERN and fired from SVLAC. Blacklisted. *Squashed*, like a parasite. Soon, everyone would know *exactly* what he was. Because what good was a whisper network if no one acted on its information?

SVLAC's grapevine had been right about her and Ethan. The two of them had been wrong about the award results of the annual Eischer-Langhoff Grant in Physics, however. Neither had received funding; a cohort of physicists developing teleportation technology for the quantum internet at Fermilab had secured the award. So maybe it was for the best that they weren't collaborating professionally right now, because despite their mutual support for a new and better work–life balance, they would've inevitably spent several weeks griping to each other about the outcome in SVLAC's kitchenette, in their living room, in their studio… and in the shower, where, even more than on Ethan's desk, there were interesting applications of physics and leverage to explore—

Heat swooped through her stomach. She barely managed not to drop the pan.

But anyhow, there was a strong likelihood that she wouldn't be returning to the Hawking radiation signals in her LIGO data or requiring additional funds for the interferometer in the next year. Though she hadn't presented even preliminary quantum gravity findings for peer review yet, the Department of Energy's investment in the project and SVLAC's own high profile in the field meant that her inbox was already full of requests for interviews, partnerships, and a solicitation to speak at the International Conference on Physics in Kyoto…

"—the headwind in the tunnel broke the kite's cross spar, so we had to stop, but now Dr. Ndlovu has plans to swap in a new spar made of scrap material from the welding shop. It might be too heavy to fly, though."

"Not in a gravity-free zone," Martina reminded Ethan. "The crew could have the first—"

"—kite-flying spacewalk?" He rocked his chair back on two legs, sloshing his coffee, laughing again.

No, she didn't regret the Eischer-Langhoff loss. Wishing the Fermilab scientists well, Erin extracted herself out from under Bunsen's weight and returned to the call.

"You should see what happens to a frisbee next time you're hypothetically in the tunnel," she told Ethan, wrapping her damp arms around his shoulders and resting her chin on his head, inhaling the warm, familiar musk of his aftershave. "You could get clearance for Bunsen, now that he has his service vest and a registration with NASA's Human Resources department. Maybe Tomasz, too—but without the vest. Aren't you meeting him later today for a pick-up game?"

"*Damn.* I was supposed to confirm the time this morning." He fumbled for his phone.

"How can it be a pick-up game if they're planning it?" Martina asked Erin over the *thunk* of Ethan's chair settling back onto the floor.

"At least they've finally figured out that they're friends. It took me long enough to realize that I was the problem with Kai and Ashley—they were actually trying to include me in brunches and movie nights, but I always thought I had something more important to do. Besides," she carried her own phone and the oat milk carton back to the kitchen, "he'd better get used to it. Wes and Adrian have plans for him."

"Say hello to those gorgeous men for me."

"Gross—and always. See you next weekend."

While Ethan and Tomasz fixed a frisbee time, she ransacked one of the kitchen boxes for a drying rack—Ethan had labeled each carton with its contents—and finished their dishes, then snapped a picture of Bunsen with a dab of leftover egg balanced on his nose, which she sent to the Monaghan family thread.

> **Erin**
> Bunsen says hello to Cassie and wants her to know that he's a very good boy who sits nicely for his treats. (Though he does counter-surf.)

Lori Monaghan's ellipsis bubbled onto her screen.

Mom

Cassie is looking forward to meeting him at Christmas. I'll put the treat jar up. Tell Ethan that we all say hello too, sweetheart.

Erin

I will.

Wes's typing notification joined the chat.

Wes

How was your hot sauce competition?

Erin

Martina called, so we had to pause the clock before we summited the Scoville Scale. It's a draw.

Wes

That's the problem with a two-person competition. You need a third.

Erin

Not you. You got to the finals of that chili-eating contest in Beijing.

Adrian

Fine, I'll beat you both at Christmas. Someone has to. Wes gets to pick the sauce. Da Bomb Beyond Insanity Hot Sauce, maybe? Let's see if you can still keep up, Frizzy. Plus, trial by fire for your guy. (Also, we're racing the Dish next time I'm in California.)

Erin
I'll get both of you back for this!

She closed her messages and reduced her family—plus the addition of Ethan and Bunsen—to their grinning faces in Ms. Frizzle's school bus, then fished eggshells from the sink, knotted up a biodegradable bag of compost, and stepped over to the screen door leading from the kitchen to their backyard. As she kicked into a pair of scuffs and shrugged on Ethan's fleece vest, she warned him, "Wes and Adrian are planning a hot sauce competition for Christmas. They're floating the idea of something with a chemical component. We'd better build up our tolerance if we want to win. And survive."

"There's no stopping a Monaghan with a plan, is there?" He grabbed Bunsen's collar when the dog made a hopeful lunge for the bag.

"Never. I should let you know that if we're ever cornered into a duty dinner with your family, I have a *very* interesting plan."

"You do." It wasn't a question. He followed her out onto the porch, leaning against the doorframe while she lobbed their compost on top of a pile of brown, crackly leaves in a green waste bin. "Does your plan have anything to do with this hot sauce competition?"

"Maybe." She clomped back up the steps. "Plenty of hot sauces are red, and doesn't Karen Meyer pride herself on her authentic Italian tomato *salsa*? I'll run interference while you adjust your mother's seasoning."

"Erin, that's—*God*, you really are a menace." He pulled her in and kissed her smug smile. "*We're* a menace."

"And geniuses."

"Yes, and geniuses."

"But: I'm faster than you are," and she ducked away. "Do you have time for a run before frisbee?"

"I'm going to lap you around Hoover Park."

"You can try. Where are our running shoes?"

"*Bunsen!*" Ethan whistled to the golden retriever. Bunsen's tail began to thump in excitement. "Find my shoes."

No thanks to the dog, who devolved into a blur of ecstatic barks when he saw Ethan raking Erin's hair into a braid while she set her earbuds to Stars' "Hold On When You Get Love And Let Go When You Give It," they unearthed their sneakers in a box of miscellaneous hangers shoved under the dining room chair that was collecting mail by the door. Ethan clipped on Bunsen's leash, and she sorted through their latest collection of coupons and forwarded junk from a basket under the mail slot. There was a magazine in the mix today, too.

A familiar magazine.

She tilted its technicolor cover art toward Ethan while he wrestled his shoelaces away from Bunsen. "*Galactica* received our new address. Look, they're asking for artist–writer collaborations for the magazine's anniversary issue."

"Collaborations?" He straightened up.

"Which we're doing, right?"

"Yes—and whoever makes it to the park first chooses the subject. Good luck!" He took off along Waverley Street, whooping, Bunsen galloping beside him.

"That's not fair. I wasn't ready!"

But she couldn't help laughing through her own sprint down the sidewalk. Because whether or not she clinched this competition—and she was already gaining on him, would tackle him to the grass in the park in a minute, would straddle

him and steal the breathless happiness from his mouth with hers—she knew:
She'd already won.

Author's Note

Talk Data to Me is a work of fiction; however, I owe an immense research debt to the following real institutions, scientists, creators, and incidents:

- The SLAC National Accelerator Laboratory, on which the Silicon Valley Linear Accelerator National Laboratory is based.
- Craig Hogan's work with Fermilab's experimental holometer, from which Ethan Meyer's research on quantum units draws heavily.
- Lotte Mertens, Ali G. Moghaddam, Dmitry Chernyavsky, Corentin Morice, Jeroen van den Brink, and Jasper van Wezel, whose paper "Thermalization by a Synthetic Horizon," published in *Physical Review Research*, volume 4 (2022), forms the basis for Erin Monaghan and Ethan Meyer's quantum gravity research.
- Jorge Cham's "Methodology Section Translator" panel from PhD Comics (2012), which is quoted in Chapter 8.
- The "Grievance Studies" hoax (2017–2018), where Peter Boghossian, James A. Lindsay, and Helen Pluckrose submitted bogus papers rife with fashionable jargon to academic, peer-reviewed journals and were published with a decent rate of success, which is referenced in Chapter 19.

Acknowledgments

A debut novelist always has many people to thank for guiding her to the moment of sharing her writing with the world—and I'm no exception.

Firstly, thank you to my early readers: Lucy Haynes and C.P. Haynes. You've endured so many misplaced commas and dangling prepositions. Heroic. Thank you to my writing mentors—Jody Gehrman, Kate Gould, Adam Johnson, Beverley Spence, and Kirstin Valdez Quade—who taught me to approach first drafts with the tolerant forbearance that I'd extend to a potty-training puppy, and who patiently answered my bombardment of trade questions. Dominique White, thank you for sharing the tantalizing tidbits of your professional life that inspired this story, and for correcting my pronunciation of "interferometer" before I embarrassed myself in front of the brilliant, generous Cara Laasch, who made physics easy to understand and introduced me to a gamut of hilarious webcomics and genius sci-fi novels. (Cara, know that you did all you could to make a STEMinist of this feminist.) All scientific errors in the text are my own. Thank you to my agent nonpareil, Gaia Banks of Sheil Land Associates, a true partner in both creativity and industry, and without whom this book wouldn't exist. To Sarah Hodgson and the team at Corvus: *Talk Data to Me* couldn't have found a better publishing home. It's been an honor and a joy to work with you. Thank you also to all the friends and pen pals who've nurtured and/or endured my scribbling through the years, with special gratitude going to Elena Ayala-Hurtado, Emily Kohn, Christina Krawec, Ava Lindstrom, Danielle Ola, and Cai Redmond. And to N.H.H. Haynes—you know why you're on this list, darling.

Talk Data to Me wouldn't be here without you, any of you—including you, the reader!

So, finally, thank *you*.

Look out for Rose McGee's next sizzling romcom, coming soon.

SUCKER FOR YOU

H2O = hero + heroine + ... octopus?

A scheduling screw-up strands uptight marine biologist Isabel Wright and tattooed wildlife photographer Wes Monaghan at the same California beach house. She needs a U.S. visa—now. He needs a boat and a date to his family's holiday party.

What they get: a fake relationship that turns eight levels of complicated after they accidentally acquire joint custody of an octopus.

Can their agreement not to catch feelings survive sunset picnics, predatory gulls, bioluminescent skinny-dipping, and an investigation into a shady ocean research lab?

Or will their charming cephalopod and their own hearts sucker Wes and Isabel into diving straight into love?